Dedicated to my beloved wife Kim.

Redfish

Jim Haberkorn

A Black Opal Books Publication

Prologue

Rulon Hurt doesn't believe the earth is going to end from an asteroid strike, but his Swiss wife, Yohaba, disagrees. So does her grandfather, former CERN director Leonard Steenberg.

One-eighty-two Elsa is shaped like a potato—a potato 27 miles wide and pock-mocked with numerous craters, the remnants of impacts from other, smaller asteroids. Elsa originated several billion years ago, at the dawn of the solar system, a non-descript member of the main asteroid belt between Jupiter and Mars. At about the time Alexander the Great was conquering Persia, Elsa was side-swiped by a larger asteroid, lost some of its mass, but continued hurtling through the emptiness of space—this time on a different orbital path that will have it colliding with the earth just south of Geneva, Switzerland on April 13, 2029.

Its 27-mile-wide mass moving at 30,000 mph will plunge through the earth's 60-mile-thick atmosphere in just over a second. On impact it will release the energy-equivalent of 200 trillion tons of TNT. Even if it lands in the 6.86-mile-deep Mariana Trench it will still pierce the earth's crust. The resulting earthquake will topple every structure on the planet. All the oceans will boil. The earth's atmosphere will catch fire. Everything will die.

Shortly before his death, Albert Einstein predicted this would happen, even down to the exact date, but had time to confide his discovery and his proposed solution to only his three brilliant protégés. The youngest of them, Leonard Steenberg, still lives, and has dedicated his life to fulfilling Einstein's last and greatest mission.

Trouble is, mankind doesn't want to be saved.

Part 1

Chapter 1

Manufacturing vice president Andy Oderhardt sat in the lobby of IQ Technology's corporate headquarters in Santa Clara, California, consoling himself that no matter what happened today, it wasn't the end of the world. Just the end of a career. He tried to relax, to convince himself that it was just one more meeting in a career filled with meetings. Just one more time for him to go over the numbers in front of an audience thirsting for his blood. One more meeting where he didn't have to be brilliant, but rather just glib enough and quick thinking enough to avoid humiliation, to deflect blame, to survive. He closed his eyes and pinched the bridge of his nose. The numbers weren't good. Weren't good at all. In fact, they were bad enough to make a man do desperate things.

Andy stared at the reflection in the glass door in front of him. A silver haired, fifty-year-old man in a gray Brooks Brother suit stared back at him. In a few minutes the door would open, and he'd walk through it like a gladiator entering the arena. Andy grimaced at the image and took a deep breath. *Stay cool*, he told himself. *One way or another it will all be over in an hour.*

Just then the door to the executive chamber opened. Laughter spilled from the room and a thirty-something woman in a blue pants suit came out. She spotted Andy. "Sorry, Andy. We ran a little late."

"No problem, Gail," said Andy. He slid past her into the conference room, paused, and looked around. At the far end of the room, IQ CEO Connie Pratt stood at the head of a long, burled wood table, surrounded by five men in dark corporate suits, white shirts, and subdued ties, all as attentive as drones around a queen. Half a dozen other men and women sat around the table typing on their laptops or talking furtively among themselves. No one noticed Andy. He might as well have been one of the potted plants, or another plank of oak paneling, or one of the two de Koonings that were hanging on opposite walls.

Connie was tall and icicle thin. Her blond bob and stiletto-sharp side part announced to the world "take me very serious." Her face reflected an icy smoothness and her eyes glared off that frozen field as she made her points. She wore a light gray, two-piece Dolce and Gabbana business suit and a plain white Chanel blouse. Her only jewelry was a thin gold necklace and a gaudy diamond ring. Her shoes were dark gray Bruno Maglis. She had a closet full of them. So many, in fact, that her not always loyal staff referred to her as Imelda behind her back, or if she were really on a rampage, as Caligulette.

"Did you say something?" asked Gail. Andy shook his head. She touched his elbow and guided him to a chair at the opposite end of the table from Connie.

"I see you didn't bring your laptop," Gail said. "That's good. Connie says she's sick of being slide-whipped." She winked. "She likes to be the one doing the whipping." Andy completely understood.

He sat in one of the dark leather cushioned, high-back, wood chairs and passed the time observing Connie. After a few minutes, Connie nodded to her listeners, and everyone went back to their seats.

Once settled, Connie slowly brought the meeting to order while quietly chatting up the table, joking about lunch, fuming about the SEC, then telling a funny story about a meeting she once had with Schwarzenegger when he was governor, all the while twirling a pen in her hand and making piercing eye contact with everyone except Andy.

Andy watched the performance, mesmerized, and then, finally, the curtain opened on Act II, and there she sat twenty-five feet away, elbows on the table, chin in both hands, looking directly at him, judging him, taking his measure. She studied him for a full five seconds before she spoke.

"Welcome to the chamber, Andy or, as we like to call it, the quarterly chamber of horrors."

Everyone around the table laughed. Andy joined in. He felt the urge to wipe the sweat from his forehead, felt the urge to crawl under the conference table and escape via a trapdoor, felt the urge to leave a briefcase with a bomb under the table near Connie.

"You know who I am, Andy?" Connie asked. A few people around the table chuckled at the joke that was coming.

"What?" Andy asked, his eyes darting from face to face, not understanding the joke.

"I'm your worst nightmare," she said, and the twelve members of the Executive Committee all burst out laughing again. Things quieted down and she continued. "All kidding aside, nothing's changed since your last visit. You know the ground rules. This is the no-spin zone in here, Andy. In here we tell it like it is. We tell the truth, the whole truth, and nothing but the truth. Got it?"

"I do," Andy said, resisting the urge to raise his right hand.

"All we care about in here is accountability," said Connie. "Accountability is what made this company great. It's what makes any company great. Do you ever play *Risk*, Andy? You know, the board game?"

"Yes."

"Good. Then you'll understand this. It came to me the other day that *Risk* is the greatest game in the world. Do you know why?" Before Andy could open his mouth, Connie answered for him. "Because it's all about using your resources to crush the competition and expand your empire. It's about rolling the dice and dealing with whatever comes your way."

"Born to be wild, eh?" Andy said.

"Born to be what?" Connie asked with an expression like he'd just burped in her face.

"Born to be wild," said Andy. "You said, 'whatever comes your way.' That's a line from the old Steppenwolf song *Born to be Wild*. You know, firing all your guns at once. That sort…of…thing." His voice trailed off.

She glowered at him for a long second. "We were talking about a board game, not music and guns. Did you follow anything I said? *Risk* is about stacking the odds in your favor and wiping your competition off the board. It's the perfect metaphor for business. It's the furthest thing from being wild. Don't you get it?"

"Yes, I do," said Andy, now thoroughly on the back foot.

"I hope so. Now, let's get down to business. In the last four quarters you've managed to lose market share to every one of your major competitors. Are you asleep at the wheel, Andy?" Before he could answer, Connie looked down at the spreadsheet in front of her and continued, "In fact, Andy, looking at your losses over the last few quarters, I'd say you were more like a drunk driver coming home from an all-night binge." Everyone laughed, including Andy. "Well, what's the story?"

The moment of truth. Andy cleared his throat and reeled off his memorized speech. "You have cut R&D spending to the bone for years and now we are reaping what you sowed. Our products are old, out-of-date, and boring. We've been milking the profits out of them for years so you can keep getting your bonuses. The whole company is like a ship slowly taking on water. When it sinks, as it surely will, you're going to blame the debacle on the market forces beyond your control. But privately you'll blame the masses of employees who simply couldn't rise to the level of your magnificent vision. Then you and your cronies will jump off this ship like rats with your huge payouts, hopefully to get hired at another Fortune 100 company so you can pillage that one too."

There, he said it. Andy hoped he hadn't rushed it. He'd certainly practiced it enough back home in front of the mirror, but this was like kicking a thirty-yard field goal in the last seconds of the Super Bowl. The goal posts get mighty close together when the big game is on the line.

To say that the room was in numb, shocked, jaw-dropping, unblinking, time-stopping bewilderment would be an understatement. People who had been only half listening a few seconds ago were now staring at Andy as if he'd just spoken in tongues. Some actually didn't understand his words. Others paused in mid-movement, one foot on the gas, one on the brake, going into sensory overload. Andy sat there casually adjusting his tie and slowly flicking some lint off the sleeve of his suit; he had practiced that, too.

After the initial shock wore off, the entire table turned as one and looked at Connie. But she was also revving her engine in neutral at Andy's words and unable to speak.

Finally she stuttered, "What did you say?" Someone in the room laughed nervously.

Andy had been given explicit instructions to keep his mouth shut at that point until someone else spoke up. He'd been told he'd have an ally in the room, but he didn't know who. He looked around at all the faces. Forty-five-year-old Winston Klendenin III with jet black hair, nattily dressed as usual, the board's newest member and owner of the world's eighth largest private yacht, caught his eye for a moment then looked at Connie. "I think what Andy's trying to say is that this company has been mismanaged and needs a change of direction. Did I get that right, Andy?"

Ah, so Klendenin was the ally! Now Andy could deliver his next scripted line. "Yes, Connie has never been a straight shooter with her employees. The constant layoffs to cut expenses have shattered employee morale and now we're all walking around like zombies waiting to be shot in the head."

"Of all the impertinence," said Connie, recovering somewhat. "It's not your place to suggest anything. You're here to get reamed good and proper for not making your targets. And you're going to get reamed, and you're going to stay reamed, and you're going to like it." She pointed a long finger at Andy at the other end of the table. "Don't even think of deflecting blame away from yourself by attacking me." She smacked the table once for emphasis.

Julia Finch, the committee's longest serving member, chirped up, anxious to get her talons into Connie after years of being dismissed as a feather brain. "Maybe Andy's got a few good points. Maybe we should hear him out. Without new products we're doomed. Yes, there I said it. Doomed!"

"People are afraid to make major purchases because of all the controversy over the trade deals," Connie said, doing a little deflecting herself. "If they can turn things around in Washington, then we'll be back on track."

"There is shrinking demand for our products," said Winston. His eyes swept the table as he spoke. "That much is obvious. What have we got that's special? And don't recite for me the marketing nonsense. Let's have some reality in this room for a change." This time there were murmurs of agreement.

Connie continued on the offensive. "What we're doing is called 'returning value to the stockholders,' my friend. It's what great CEOs do. Wake up. Apple, Amazon, and Google are grabbing all the investment money these days. If we want to tear investors away from them, we need to have profits and revenues that are just as good. This is not rocket science. We can't afford to take our foot off the gas. Not for one second. We've got to hang on for a few more years and then we can start investing in R&D again. I don't need armchair quarterbacks second guessing my every move." She flamed the room with a glare. "Why is this so hard for you people to understand? I've finally gotten this company's expenses in line and now the guys in the division are screwing up my revenue numbers. If it's not one thing it's another. I can't keep fixing problems for you people."

"Yeah, you people!" said Andy, ad libbing as he got into the role. "You peons, you mean! In a couple of years this company won't exist and you'll be gone with a big payout. We've all seen how this story ends." And now he went back to the script. "You should step down for the good of the company. Everyone knows it and is just too afraid to say it out loud. When the fellow from CERN, that Steenberg guy with his asteroid project, offered us advanced nanotechnology we should have leaped at it, not bandied over who got the profits. It was exactly what we needed."

Connie stared at Andy, the pen twirling furiously. She scrutinized him with her trademark laser-beam glare and increased the strain by tapping her fingers loudly on the table. After an excruciating ten seconds she leaned back in her chair and made up her mind. "Gale, call security. Mr. Oderhardt is to be escorted from the premises. He is not to go back to his desk. We will have his personal effects delivered to his home."

"So, it's the death penalty," said Andy somberly, thinking this was the strangest line of all he'd been paid to say. "That's what I get for speaking my mind."

"Yes, Andy," said Connie. "The death penalty."

Winston immediately jumped to his feet. "Okay, everyone. Let's cool off. Let's everyone clear out except for Andy here, and me, and Connie. Let's see if we can't work this out."

"I'm not changing my mind," said Connie coldly. "He's toast. He's history."

Winston held up a hand to Connie as if to say *don't be hasty*. No one in the room moved. "Please, just give us a half hour to work this out. C'mon, please. Everyone, if you can just wait in the lobby. Thanks."

Once the room had emptied, Connie threw down her pen in disgust and walked over to the refreshment bar. While she was pouring herself a cup of coffee, Winston said nervously, "While you're up can you lock the door?" Connie made a face but twisted the lock on the door on her way back to her chair.

After she sat down, she sipped her coffee and started to relax. She looked at Andy with an expression of sadness and a slow shake of her head. "Andy, what the hell's gotten into you? I know it's tough out there. But you've been around long enough to know how the game is played. If you don't make your numbers, I chew you out. If I don't, I get chewed out by the board. I would have chewed you out and you would've kept your job. Why did you have to turn this into something bigger than it needed to be?"

Andy had done it because he'd been paid to do it by a very serious man representing himself as an emissary from the "director," who Andy assumed meant someone from the board of directors. He was told he was going to be fired at today's meeting and his severance would be under half a million. The man had then offered Andy $4.4 million to say what he did today. Half of that was already in his account. The rest would be there after Connie was dethroned. Now, at her conciliatory words, Andy, sitting two chairs away from her, felt like the world's biggest jerk. He didn't know what to say but could only shift uneasily in his chair, unable to look her in the eye.

Winston asked, "Does anyone mind if I smoke?"

"You don't smoke," Connie said. "But go ahead, knock yourself out. I won't report you. Hell, anybody got a bottle of scotch?" That got a small laugh out of Andy.

Winston took a small brown paper bag out of his computer bag but was shaking so badly he dropped the whole thing on the floor. He picked up the paper bag and shook out, onto the table, a pack of cigarettes and a cigarette lighter shaped like a pistol.

"Well, Andy?" asked a visibly tired Connie. "If you got any good reasons why I shouldn't fire you, now's the time."

In the chair to Connie's right, Winston began putting on two long, black rubber opera gloves, recently purchased from the House of Harlots online gift shop. He clumsily stretched the gloves over his hands and suit sleeves up to the elbow.

"Winston, what are you doing?" Connie asked. "Are you losing it?"

Winston took four deep breaths, fumbled to pick up the cigarette lighter then walked with it behind Connie. He said, "May I?" and grabbed her hand.

"What?" she laughed with a mixture of amusement and puzzlement.

"Please just bear with me," he said. Carefully he opened her fingers and placed the cigarette lighter in her hand. "Hold steady," he said as he pointed it towards Andy, who was paying more attention to his cup of coffee than to Winston and Connie a few feet away.

"Andy!" said Winston sharply. Andy turned to look, saw what looked like a gun, and started to laugh.

Winston pulled the trigger for Connie. Boom! Loud for such a small gun. A neat hole appeared in Andy's forehead a couple of inches off-center, and he fell forward on the table.

Winston stepped back. Connie shook and stammered out sounds—no intelligible words, just sounds. She stood up, her coffee spilled, and her chair fell over. She backed up over it and fell down herself. Winston dropped the gun next to her then screamed red-faced, "What have you done! Why did you shoot Andy! He's dead. You've killed him!" When he was finished, he looked into her eerily wide eyes and mouthed the words, "I'm sorry."

Then he threw up.

The police arrived fifteen minutes later. Connie tried to pin the murder on Winston, but everyone had heard her threaten to kill Andy in the meeting. The police took her to the station, where tests revealed gunpowder residue on her hands and face. As a formality, they tested Winston too, but as expected, found nothing. They apologized for the inconvenience. He understood. Just doing their job. Such a tragedy. It happened so quickly. He wished he could have stopped it. Connie was put on suicide watch.

Winston left the Santa Clara police station just before midnight in a daze and walked ten blocks to a sandwich shop on Stevens Creek Boulevard. Sitting in a booth at the back was his contact, Simon, dressed in his usual dark, pin-striped Armani suit. Hair to his shoulders. Big ears. Roman nose. Glaring at Winston from the adjacent booth were two silent men in Oakland Raiders jackets. Muscle. Winston slid into the booth opposite Simon. Per the prearranged rules neither of them spoke. A waitress came by but Simon waved her off. After she walked away Simon pushed a lined writing pad and a pen across the table. On the top line were the hand printed words, *Are we still cool?*

Winston took the pen and wrote on the next line in a shaky scrawl, *Yes. When will my family be released?* and pushed the pad back to Simon.

Simon wrote, *You do realize that Oderhardt is not dead?* He pushed the pad back to Winston.

"What!?" said Winston loudly when he read the message. "That's impossible."

Simon frowned and pointed at the pad. Winston slid it over.

Simon wrote, *Use the pad. Oderhardt's in a coma. But don't worry. The big boss said you're good. Mission accomplished.*

How long before I see my family?

As soon as I leave, I make the call. Simon looked at his watch then wrote, *Sixteen hours. The rest of the money is already in your account.*

I'm giving all the money to Andy Oderhardt's wife.

Simon wrote something and pushed the pad across the table. *Nice gesture. One more thing. Your daughter will continue to be an exchange student with a nice family until after the trial.*

Winston read it and groaned in agony.

Simon pulled back the pad and wrote, *Keep it down.*

Winston snatched back the pad. *Why is this happening to me?*

It's for a good cause.

Who's doing this to me?

Goodbye, Mr. Klendenin. Thank you.

Winston grabbed the note pad out of Simon's hand as he stood to leave, and scribbled, *How do I know he'll keep his promise?* He threw the pen on the table and held the pad up for Simon to read.

The words prompted a glimmer of compassion in Simon for the desperate, confused man. Bending close to Winston's ear, he whispered, "Don't worry. With the Director a deal's a deal." He grabbed the notepad, straightened up to leave, hesitated, then bent low again. "For what it's worth, he's done this before. It always turns out fine. Just do the deal."

It was two days after the shooting before all the details of the board meeting came out, including Andy's statements to the Executive Committee right before he was shot. When the full story hit the press, IQ Technology's stock price fell seventy percent in five hours. By the end of the trading day the company had a new majority stockholder, and Winston Klendenin had a good idea who "The Director" was. After a sleepless night arguing with his sobbing wife, he spent the next day locked in his study making phone calls to friends in the Pentagon he'd been hobnobbing with for years in his role as a defense contractor. *What's the point of having all this money*, he asked himself, *if you can't even protect your family?*

Chapter 2
Three months later

An icy wind slid down the eastern slope of the Sawtooth Mountains and slalomed through the tall pines at the base before blowing across Redfish Lake, disturbing the waters but not the two occupants of the canoe four hundred yards from shore. At the bite of the wind, the big man sitting in the front of the canoe merely cinched his black cowboy hat tighter on his head and continued patiently fishing. The woman in the back sat with a paddle across her legs, engrossed in a book, oblivious to the cold. Around the lake towered the serrated, snow-capped peaks of the aptly named mountains, once up for consideration as a national park, but now simply part of Idaho's Sawtooth National Recreation Area. Rugged but accessible, and mostly unpopulated except during summer months. That's why Rulon and Yohaba Hurt preferred coming in mid-spring when the weather was no longer subarctic, but there was still some ice on the lake, and it was still cold enough to keep away all but the local, hardcore nature lovers.

Redfish got its name from the sockeye salmon that once spawned there by the millions, so many that the surface of the lake looked red to the early trappers. Now only a few thousand Sockeye made it back every year, though the lake was well stocked with other fish. Hanging on a line over the side of the canoe was a string of three Kokanee, a land-locked version of Sockeye, and two Bull Trout. Not bad for late April when the water temperature was in the mid-40s and the fish were hardly feeding.

Bundled against the cold, parkas zipped snug, Rulon and Yohaba had paddled to the middle of the lake then drifted for two hours. Rulon was the fisherman in the family. Yohaba hated fishing, bored her to death, but these days they did everything together. An extra pair of eyes and an extra finger on an extra trigger were prudent precautions given their circumstances. Though Rulon was only thirty-five and Yohaba six years younger, they'd collected a long list of enemies.

As the canoe rocked in the swells, Rulon lowered his rod to gaze at clouds breaking over nearby Thompson Peak like a slow-motion wave. "If it were a few degrees colder, I do believe we'd be seeing snow before evening."

"Snow," repeated Yohaba, as if in a trance, without looking up from her book, a well-worn copy of *Moby Dick*. Rulon frowned.

"Wind's kicking up," he said solemnly.

"Yeah," she said from far away. "Wind will do that."

Rulon reeled in his line and stowed his pole under the bow seat. The fish hanging over the side got dropped slimy and dripping into a small red cooler wedged in the bow. He dipped his paddle in the water. "Let's go in."

Yohaba noted her page, closed the book, and looked up. "Probably a good idea," she said cheerfully. "Wind's picking up and it might even snow." She laughed merrily like the chuckling of the waves against the canoe's Kevlar side. The book went in her pocket, the paddle in her hand, and she pulled through the water with Rulon, smoothly and powerfully, a synchronization born of many hours together in a canoe.

After a minute of silent stroking, Rulon rested his paddle across the gunwales and peered closely at the other side of the lake. Yohaba also paused. "What's up?"

"You're not going to believe this," Rulon said. "But I think there's a grizzly over there." He pointed to a small cove formed on one side by a rocky, twenty-foot-tall promontory jutting thirty yards into the lake. Standing still in the water just a few feet from shore was a large bear with water up to its chest.

Yohaba squinted and said flatly, "It's a black bear. There are no grizzlies in Idaho."

"A grizzly killed a man in Idaho up near Montana last September. He wounded the bear then tracked it. He thought it was a black bear, too."

"That's terrible," Yohaba said. When Rulon showed no signs of picking up his paddle, she added, "It's a black bear. Look. It's black and it's a bear. It's a black bear. C'mon, let's go."

"His coat is wet and he's standing in a shadow. That's why it looks black. I can't really tell from here, but it looks like he's got a small hump. It's a grizz. A good sized one at that."

"Nope."

"Yep."

Yohaba dipped the edge of her paddle in the water and flicked a few drops at Rulon. "Nope," she said firmly.

"Wanna bet?" Rulon asked wiping his face with his sleeve.

Yohaba put down her paddle. "Cowboy. If we paddle all the way over there and find out it's just a black bear, we're both going to feel pretty stupid, not to mention tired. And if it turns out to be a grizzly, we're going to feel pretty stupid, not to mention dead. Nobody in their right mind heads towards a grizzly."

"If it is a grizzly, we need to check it out and tell the rangers. It's our civic responsibility."

"Ever heard of Lewis and Clarke?"

"Only one guy from the expedition died and it was from appendicitis," Rulon said. "I have no idea where you're going with this."

"They couldn't kill the things outright even with their fifty caliber rifles. They'd shoot them and shoot them, and the grizzlies would keep charging. They'd jump into a river to escape and the bears would jump off cliffs to get them. But what the heck, let's go over there and check it out! We've both got our peashooters. Why not?" She said this last part dripping with sarcasm which Rulon ignored.

"I agree, let's go. The more I think about it, it's probably only a black bear anyway." They both turned to where the bear had been, but it was gone, having drifted back into the trees. "Paddle hard," Rulon said. "He's getting away."

As Rulon's paddle hit the water, Yohaba blocked it with hers. "I will have no man in my boat who is not afraid of a whale."

"What on earth are you talking about now?" Rulon asked in exasperation.

Yohaba took out her book and waved it. "It's a line from *Moby Dick*. Just substitute the word 'grizzly' for 'whale' and you'll get my point."

"I *am* afraid of grizzlies, but I'm 90% sure that's a black bear," Rulon said. "C'mon."

"Any man dumb enough to track a grizzly is too dumb to track a grizzly."

"Please spare me your mumbo-jumbo logic."

"The only men qualified to track a grizzly are those too smart to do so."

"Your Jedi mind tricks will not work on me," Rulon said stoically. He resumed paddling vigorously, pulling with all his might, the canoe lurching forward with each thrust. "If it is a grizzly, and we don't report it, and it ends up killing someone, it's gonna be your fault. C'mon help." After a few strokes, Yohaba reluctantly joined in.

Fifteen minutes later the canoe ground against the inlet's rock sand bottom to within a few feet of shore. Rulon hopped into ankle deep water and pulled the canoe half up the gravel beach so Yohaba could step out dry.

Rulon was six foot and within spitting distance of three hundred pounds, a former collegiate hammer thrower and nationally ranked Greco-Roman wrestler—with the bone structure of a brontosaurus, Yohaba liked to say. Yohaba was almost as tall, slender but not skinny, with long, red-streaked auburn hair tucked under her bright blue Boise State knit cap. She had a gently rounded face with perfect, unblemished skin and brown eyes that tended towards Slavic. Beautiful from the tip of her toes to the top of her head, as Rulon always said, even in a worn parka.

Once on dry land, Rulon removed the .45 caliber Colt automatic from his shoulder holster and cocked it, sending a bullet into the chamber. "I'm sure you're right. Just a black bear. Heck, why would a grizzly come all the way down here unless there were lots of girl grizzlies running around." As he talked he ejected the magazine and added to it a loose bullet from his pocket, just to top it off. "It doesn't make any sense at all. Besides, there's rangers always patrolling. No way a grizz could come down all the way from Montana and not get seen." He now had nine bullets to work with. One in the chamber and eight in the magazine. He slammed the magazine back in and looked up at Yohaba. "For all their size, black bears are really quite timid. We'll be lucky if we even catch a glimpse." Meanwhile, Yohaba finished reinserting the mag into her SIG Sauer P239 and hit it with the heel of her hand as a finishing touch. The distinctive SIG click sounded like a dry twig breaking in the silence at the forest edge.

Yohaba noticed Rulon hadn't put his gun away so she didn't either. She asked, "How fast are grizzlies?"

"Faster than a horse for a short distance," Rulon answered with a smile. "But don't worry, honey. All you have to do is outrun me." He added a wink for good measure. Yohaba started to say something but Rulon cut her off. "Shhhh. We're going operational."

Behind them was the lake, ahead of them the forest, thick and deep with pine, fir, and Engelmann spruce. Overhead, wind rustled through the branches and an occasional mountain blue bird and meadowlark whistled. Otherwise it was quiet. The bear's footprints led into the trees in fuzzy steps pressed through the glaze of frost covering the hydrilla grass, and matted pine needles.

They advanced cautiously into the tree line and the shadowed forest, the pine needles crunching softly under their boots.

"What an adventure!" whispered Yohaba with feigned schoolgirl enthusiasm as she crept behind Rulon.

"*Last of the Mohicans*, Jodhi May as Alice Munro, 1992," Rulon whispered back. Then out of the side of his mouth he said with a heavy dose of irritation, "Why'd you bring that up? She died jumping off a cliff. Do you see any cliffs around here?"

They followed the bear's trail along an old deer run up a gradual slope. Soon the incline and the 6,500-foot altitude had them breathing hard, especially Rulon, and then the tracks veered to the left and the hill got steeper. Rulon pushed onward, breathing harder, Colt pointing forwards, one hand stretched behind, gripping Yohaba's to keep her from sliding back.

A ten-minute hike brought them to a flat section among the trees where a boulder and a fallen spruce blocked their way and the promontory jutted into the lake. The boulder offered a place for them to sit, so they did. After a minute, Rulon looked over his shoulder expecting to see the bear's trail pick up on the other side of the tree. To his surprise, it didn't. Curious, he left Yohaba and scouted around. Twenty yards away he found what he was looking for and waved her over. When she arrived he was squatting next to a picture perfect paw print pressed into a patch of muddy ground.

"Sometimes I get tired of being right," Rulon said.

"Good," said Yohaba. "It's a black bear then. That's a relief." She stuck the SIG in her belt.

"No, it's definitely a grizzly," said Rulon with conviction. "Yup. See the imprints of the claws? Black bears don't leave claw marks." He traced the imprint with his finger. "And look at the toe arc. See how close the toes are?"

"Okay, now we know," Yohaba said, pulling out her pistol again and looking around nervously. "Let's go back."

Rulon nodded, stood up to leave then paused to stare along the trail. The paw prints sauntered on a few yards further in a nicely defined pattern before getting lost in a jumble of prints where the bear had obviously paused. Rulon judged the bear had heard their voices and stopped to listen. Fifty yards away a meadowlark flew off, down slope in a rustle of wings and Rulon turned quickly, gun at the ready. He peered into the gloomy forest, every sense alert.

Yohaba tugged at his arm. "It's nothing. Let's go."

Rulon stared uphill and motioned for quiet. After a long, tense moment, he whispered, "Ah…it may be too late for that." His face was a stone hard mask of concentration. "This could get tricky."

Hand in hand they took a few steps backwards down the trail to the canoe, but then a faint rustling of leaves caused Yohaba to look up. Rulon instinctively followed her gaze. They both blinked at the incongruous sight. Eerily silent, tearing down the hill, came the bear, its mouth open, trampling over small trees, the whole forest in motion, clods of dirt and pine needles flying up behind him, now suddenly roaring like a nightmare vision of unstoppable death.

"RUN!" screamed Rulon. Yohaba took off through the rocks and trees along the promontory with Rulon right behind stealing backward glances as he ran. "FASTER!" he yelled. The bear was a hundred yards away and gaining fast. They came to the edge of the twenty-foot cliff at the edge of the lake and hesitated. Rulon said, "Oh look. A cliff," and pushed her off, into the water.

He turned to see the bear now only fifty yards away and leveled the Colt. When the bear was thirty yards away he opened up, aiming all nine shots at the depression between the eyes and the end of the nose. *Boom. Boom. Boom...* The crack of the pistol echoed against the mountain face and back over the lake. The bear flinched but didn't slow. In desperation, Rulon threw his gun at the bear and missed. He threw his hat—*why?* He had no idea—and hit the bear squarely in the face to no effect.

"Dang," he said then turned and jumped as far as he could over the water, hoping he wouldn't land on Yohaba. While he was still in mid-air the bear jumped too, following him over the edge, swiping at him with both paws as he fell. The two tumbled into the water ten feet apart. Rulon went in feet first, struck bottom and pushed off, knowing from the concussive force that the bear had hit the water close by. He bobbed to the surface just in time to see the bear emerge and look around with one good eye. When their eyes met, the bear's took on a wild, insane gleam and it started swimming straight for him.

Rulon, treading water, dropped a hand to the hilt of his knife, but quickly decided he wanted no part of this. Despite his boots and heavy clothes, he swam for all he was worth, the bear close behind and gaining. After ten seconds of furious effort, Rulon switched over to a backstroke so he could see what the bear was up to.

But the lake behind him was empty. He stopped and treaded water, still in a panic, looking in every direction. On a terrified hunch, he ducked his head in the water to see if the bear was coming up from beneath like Jaws. But the bear had sunk and was gone for good.

While he processed this unexpected turn of events, Yohaba glided up behind him in the canoe, dripping wet and shivering "Hold on," she said. "I'll tow you back."

"Where's the SIG?" asked Rulon breathing hard.

"Don't worry, I'm safe, my loving husband," said Yohaba sarcastically. "And yes, I managed to hang onto the SIG."

"My girl," said Rulon proudly, sloppy wet and with a big grin while clinging to the side of the canoe.

Yohaba said annoyed, "Just hang on for crying out loud."

"Not yet," Rulon said. "Be a good sport and paddle me back a bit, will ya?" When they reached what he judged to be the right spot, he worked his jacket, boots, and shoulder holster off and threw them in the canoe. "I'll be right back." He dove under and was gone for thirty seconds. When he came back up gasping with his knife in his hand, it was only to take a deep breath and dive again, and then again. Finally, he came up for good and threw the knife in the canoe.

"Okay, now," he said, exhausted, freezing, and too tired to answer Yohaba's questions. He hung on with one hand while Yohaba paddled. A minute later he was stretched out face down on the small sandy patch of ground where they'd originally beached the canoe.

Yohaba prodded him with her boot. "I'm cold here," she said. Rulon rolled over on his back.

"Did I mention that was a grizzly?" said Rulon.

"No. Did I mention I'm freezing to death?" said Yohaba to her beached husband, her teeth chattering through blue lips as she flapped her arms and stomped her feet to beat back the cold. "Sorry, but you can't rest. We've got to get back to the truck." Rulon slowly sat up and looked across the lake to the far shore where they'd parked a good mile away.

"We'll never make it like this," he said. "Hypothermia. We've got to get a fire going and eat something first. Wait here." He reached into his jacket pocket and threw her a soggy energy bar. "Eat this." He got up covered in wet sand, disappeared into the forest, and came back a few minutes later stumbling under a load of dead wood. Sinking to his knees, he could barely curl his frozen fingers around the branches to form them into a neat pile of cross-hatched pieces. When he was done, he turned an ashen face to Yohaba, and saw she was suffering.

"Keep moving, baby," he said, just as another gust of icy-fingered wind stabbed through their wet clothes.

"Don't you need kindling, Cowboy?" she spluttered, now almost blue with shivers racking up and down her body like an electric current. "I'm freezing to death. That wood looks wet. And the pieces are too big. You'll never get it lit. If you can't start a fire quick, I'm getting out of these wet clothes. Just lettin' ya know."

"If that was supposed to inspire me to work faster, you failed miserably," said Rulon. He smiled, got up, wobbled over to the canoe, and rummaged through their gear. In mid-rummage, he lifted his head. "Isn't Leonard supposed to be meeting with what's-his-name about now?"

Yohaba had to hold her hand still to read her watch. "He was supposed to land in Zurich two hours ago. Now focus. Focus. You're never going to get the wood lit."

Rulon came back with a road flare, struck it, watched it burst into a white-hot flame, then tossed it on the wood pile. "Wanna bet?" he said with a tired, lopsided grin.

Ten minutes later they were drying out next to a bonfire you could see from outer space.

Chapter 3

Leonard Steenberg thought he had made his last career move eight years earlier when he became one of the three directors of CERN, the huge European particle physics lab near Geneva, Switzerland. Now, as he sat on a bench at the corner of Poststrasse and Bahnhofstrasse across from Paradeplatz in Zurich, he was surprised how easily he had slipped into his new role as savior of the planet. He chuckled at the hubris of such a thought but couldn't deny the title did have some basis in fact.

It was one of those spring days when the pewter-colored clouds settled over the city in layers, the lower clouds moving in fast patches, the higher ones smooth and steady as a floating lake. The evening rush hour was over. The shops were closed. The crowds were gone and, like the last lingering drops after a storm, the dog walkers and the mothers with baby carriages were all that were left on the treelined Bahnhofstrasse. By tomorrow morning there would be another torrent of shoppers, on this, one of the world's most expensive shopping boulevards.

Steenberg knew he was being watched and didn't like the feeling. Paranoia and suspicion. Very corrosive, he decided. He watched the evening traffic go by, the trams, the innocent, unsuspecting people, and thought about all the lives at stake. He had his long, gray overcoat buttoned all the way up against the raw gusts whipping off Lake Zurich, his black fedora pulled all the way down over his white hair almost to his white eyebrows for the same reason. As he waited, he pulled from a small bag a glazed dark chocolate orange slice he'd bought at the Sprüngli chocolate shop catty corner to where he sat. Rulon Hurt, his granddaughter's husband, had gotten him hooked.

While he waited, his disciplined mind reviewed for the thousandth time his four most pressing current projects, looking for strategic holes and moves he hadn't anticipated from his long list of adversaries. When he was done, he felt at peace about his preparations.

Though he hadn't spotted any tails, he knew, surely, he had been followed ever since he left the Zurich airport's Radisson Blu Hotel on the train early that morning. His mind, always eager for an intellectual exercise, now wondered how he himself would conduct a moving surveillance on a wary subject. He closed his eyes and worked through the permutations. What might the target do? He might walk. He might hail a taxi. He might unexpectedly jump on or off a tram. He might break into a sprint and run away. Well, at his age, maybe not. He might go to a train station, buy a half dozen rail tickets to different destinations all leaving at about the same time, and then jump on one at the last second. The possibilities were endless!

The more he thought about it, the more he realized it would take dozens of people plus cars to successfully trail another person moving between cities. There would need to be strings of people ahead and behind lining the expected route, waiting in train cars, standing at bus stops, and riding up and down busy streets in trams, all constantly shifting position so as to avoid detection. Surely simply assassinating someone would be easier. He would have to remember that.

He looked around, curious, wondering where they were. Across the street two women hovered around a baby carriage in front of the Loro Piana shop. Maybe they were involved. Steenberg was half tempted to walk over just to see if the carriage indeed held a baby. To his right, a man in a brown leather jacket and a brown trilby walking a dachshund paused in front of a tram stop. Another woman behind him gazed in the window of the Blancpain watch store, but at such an angle as to see him in the reflection if she were so inclined. And then there were the cars. Two of them. A BMW and a Skoda, both with a hat on the dashboard and a turned down passenger visor, driving by from different directions every few minutes. Were they lost? And why the hat, why the lowered visor on a cloudy day? A signal to those on foot, perhaps? Or just the product of his overactive imagination?

Steenberg considered all the options and realized that the possibilities were endless on both sides. A person would have to be very wise in the ways of human nature and covert operations to play this game. He had much still to learn. Fortunately, as a precaution, he'd also brought along his own security. Money can't buy love. But it can buy protection.

A hand on his shoulder interrupted his thoughts. He turned his head to look up into the face of a man in his fifties, dressed like a banker, and staring down at him with unnaturally big eyes through the fishbowl effect of his thick black glasses.

"May I join you?" enquired the man courteously in German.

"No," Steenberg answered with a polite smile. This was not the man he wished to talk to. "And please remove your hand from my shoulder or I shall summon the police." The man did as requested. Only momentarily nonplussed, he stepped back out of earshot and murmured a few unintelligible words into what Steenberg presumed was a microphone hidden under his collar.

Thirty seconds later, Steenberg's head swiveled at the sound of a Mercedes with heavily tinted windows pulling to a stop at the curb. The man with the glasses stepped to the car and opened the rear passenger door inviting him in.

"Please," he said to Steenberg. "A trustworthy gentleman would like a word with you." Steenberg didn't move. The man looked around to see if he was observed, then discreetly pulled back his jacket to reveal a rather large pistol.

Steenberg controlled the urge to laugh. "Kill me if that is your plan," he said with a carefree wave of his hand. "Kill the golden goose if you're that stupid. But first look down." The man hesitated and Steenberg enunciated as if dealing with a particularly slow student, "At your chest."

The man looked and saw a dancing red light playing on his tie. He covered the tie with his hand and the light now danced on his knuckles. He raised his hand and the red dot followed—a sniper's way of saying *hello there*. He backtracked the beam's trajectory to a window fifty meters away in the steeple of the Fraumunster cathedral at the end of the street.

"Shall we try this again?" asked Steenberg.

The man dropped his hand, looked this way and that, looked down, shook his head and chuckled, finding a certain black humor in his predicament. "I was told you were only a professor. My apologies." He leaned into the open door of the Mercedes. Words were exchanged with an unseen occupant, there was a pause, and the man in the black glasses stepped aside. An old, mottled hand emerged first, then a leg, then a head, like a spider emerging from its den. Finally, a face of bloodless pale skin, with hawk-like features and dark eyes, like knots in a tree, behind wire-framed glasses. An impeccably dressed, very old man, a good six inches shorter than Steenberg's six feet, stepped out, and stood facing the old scientist.

"May I sit down, Doctor Steenberg?" he asked in Russian.

"Yes, be my guest," said Steenberg, in fluent Russian himself.

"Thank you," said the old man, and he sat down so close that their thighs touched. He signaled to his man to wait in the car. To Steenberg, he said, "There is no need for games."

"You have me at a disadvantage. Do I know you?" Steenberg asked.

"Oh, I think you do," said the thin man. He removed an expensive off-white envelope from his inside jacket pocket and showed it to Steenberg. "I'm the man you addressed this letter to. This is yours I presume?"

"It does look familiar," conceded Steenberg.

The old thin man studied Steenberg closely before speaking. "Since receiving your letter with its intriguing proposition, I have meticulously studied your file in the Central Archive of Scientific-Technical Documentation and even ordered certain internal departments at my disposal to make that file thicker. By now I feel I know you quite well, including your relationship to Einstein many years ago, your ex-Jesuit background, and your attachment to a beloved granddaughter in Idaho."

"Was that last reference a threat?" asked Steenberg.

"And if it was?" said the thin man. "What could you possibly do about it? I warn you, doctor, I've known many highly educated people in my life and found them to be generally useful tools but unresourceful adversaries."

"I think you will find that I am neither a tool nor an adversary," said Steenberg.

The thin man chuckled. "Oh, we shall see about that, doctor. We shall see. Before we leave this bench, we shall see. Whether you realize it or not, you have stepped through the looking glass. As soon as this letter was delivered, you stepped out of your world and stepped into mine. In my world neither your reputation, your money, nor your good cause will save you if I decide you need to exit—how do you Catholics say it?—ah yes…exit this vale of tears."

Steenberg considered the man and saw no malice in his expression, only a resolute will. He replied, "When and how I leave this world, it is God who decides. If it comes to that you will only be His instrument. To your own damnation."

"Yes," the thin man responded. "And I suppose the prospect would be terrifying if I believed in God."

Steenberg studied his adversary with a touch of sadness in his own equally resolute eyes. "A child ignorant of gravity will still die if he falls from a window. And just as surely there is a hell awaiting all who kill without cause."

"Must be a very crowded place then," replied the old man. "But at least you acknowledge room for extenuating circumstances."

While they talked, a phalanx of beefy hard-eyed guards had taken up positions around them but out of earshot, their eyes not watching the two old men but, rather, scanning in all directions, as vigilant as any presidential secret service team. The Mercedes engine purred while the one door remained open. The thin man's eyes bored into Steenberg's.

"I rarely have conversations these days," he said. "The people around me tend to have big ears and shriveled tongues from lack of use. I'm sensing with you that will not be the case."

The two men sat silently on the hard bench. "Let me tell you what you've been up to," said the old Russian finally, his eyes focused on the ground between his feet. "You've given advanced solar panel technology to the Chinese on condition they sell their first five years of production at cost to a criminal enterprise masquerading as a Russian energy company."

"True," said Steenberg.

"But strangely, the Russian company is financed by Italian criminals with money they've borrowed from China using Russian oil as collateral."

"You've done your homework," Steenberg said.

"The Russian company then marks the panels up a thousand percent and sells half of them to the Russian government in return for kickbacks to certain officials, and the other half to a global solar panel distributor owned by these same Italian criminals. These financial transactions were brokered by one of your associates."

"Again, true," said Steenberg.

"When this first came to my attention, I found it highly peculiar. The Chinese loan the money to the people who are ultimately buying their product with collateral put up by the company making the most profit. A rather circular arrangement. But my accountants have looked into it closely. Amazingly, it does work. All the parties make a profit though one sells below cost and another buys at higher than market value."

"Yes, it took some explaining but eventually all parties were satisfied with the arrangement," Steenberg said.

"And more amazingly still," said the old Russian, "all parties are sticking to their deals."

"Honor among thieves. Achievable with enough leverage," said Steenberg.

"Leverage on the Chinese? I find that hard to believe."

"So did they," replied Steenberg.

For a long minute neither man spoke. It was the old Russian who broke the silence. "And you are also amassing profits from both the interest on the Chinese loans as well as the consultancy fees and kickback profits from one of our more brutal oligarchs. And yet you are still alive? If I were religious, I would say it was a miracle."

"Somedays it surprises even me," Steenberg said.

"Your UBS account now contains just over three billion Swiss francs. You are perhaps the fastest self-made billionaire in history."

"Money. Simply a means to an end. Your information is old, but the number of zeroes is correct," replied Steenberg modestly. The old man remained silent and Steenberg added, "But it's going out rather quickly these days, I'm afraid."

"So I've heard," said the old Russian. "You've been busy." The two old men looked at each other and though they were of different worlds, their age, asceticism, intelligence, and iron wills forged links of mutual respect. Holding up the letter again, the spidery old man said, "And then this arrives on my desk one afternoon, a desk so deep in the Kremlin even Stalin's ghost couldn't find it."

"Yes, quite a challenge," replied Steenberg.

"Your messenger cooperated eventually. We were impressed at how long he resisted. Not that we learned much."

"Compartmentalization and a generous bonus," said Steenberg. "Human nature is not so very complicated."

Another long silence ensued. Finally, the thin man said, "Your file says you are a formidable chess player."

Steenberg shrugged, "It keeps the mind sharp."

"And teaches you much about your opponent," replied the old Russian. "Shall we?"

"Without a board?" asked Steenberg.

"Oh, don't be coy," said the old Russian. "I'll take white. Pawn to queen's 4."

After the game, after a short silence to compose himself following his loss, the old Russian said, "You do not fear me. Perhaps someday that will change, but for now I ask myself, is it his religious faith that gives him such confidence? Or is it his faith in his scheme? Ah, but what does it matter? You are neither religiously romantic nor materialistic and this makes you interesting. And you are reasonably ruthless. This makes you someone to keep an eye on." The Russian minister nodded ever so slightly in the face of Steenberg's implacable demeanor. "Perhaps we shall be doing business after all. I have only one question left, the one I've flown from Moscow personally to ask, the one I most need to know, and the one reason why I haven't already ordered your untimely exit."

He took off his glasses and rubbed the lenses with a small soft cloth he'd taken from his pocket. "Why?" he asked as he slowly rubbed away.

"Have you ever heard of 182 Elsa?" asked Steenberg.

Chapter 4

They paddled hard, the cold and thoughts of grizzly bears, $50,000 fines, and revoked gun licenses adding a strong sense of purpose to their strokes. Not to mention the beckoning heater in Rulon's '83 Chevy pickup. The wind barreled down the mountains, a frigid gale pushing them towards shore, and they had to fight hard to angle over to where the truck was. Rulon was in the back this time to help the canoe hydroplane, he joked, digging deep, putting all his weight into each stroke. The bonfire was by now a distant memory and they were freezing again.

"C'mon. Keep paddling," he said when he sensed Yohaba flagging. "One more story to tell our grandchildren."

"Yeah," said Yohaba through chattering teeth, "After the statute of limitations runs out."

"Yes, yes. C'mon, ten more minutes and we're there." Miserably aware of the damp and cold, they gritted their teeth and drove through the small waves to the opposite shore.

"Are we going to get in trouble for this?" asked Yohaba as they paddled.

"Nah, not a chance," said Rulon. "It was self-defense. Hey look, there's someone by the truck."

Yohaba looked up from her paddling. After a moment, she asked suspiciously, "Why's he staring off into the forest and not at us?" After another ten strokes, she said, "He should be staring at us."

"Maybe he's not a people person," Rulon said with equal suspicion. "Maybe he's a dendrologist." They both stopped now and rested their paddles across their laps.

"We're the only people on the lake," Yohaba said in a tone suggesting she was insulted. "You'd think he'd find us interesting. Heck, if I saw a couple get chased off a cliff by a grizzly, I'd be curious. Wouldn't you? How come he's not?"

"Maybe he didn't see us," Rulon said both serious and concerned. He looked behind him, checking the line of sight from the cliff to the visitor, and said, "Well, if he was there an hour ago, we would have been hard to miss with the gunfire and the roaring. Maybe he just got here. On the other hand, if he were dangerous, he'd be hiding, wouldn't you think?" Rulon grew edgy. "I can't see his hands. They're in his pockets. Must have forgotten his gloves."

"Yeah, or maybe happiness is a warm gun."

While they talked, Rulon moved his Colt from his shoulder holster to his jacket pocket. When he'd retrieved his hat and gun on the promontory, he'd immediately disassembled and inspected the pistol. It seemed okay, but just to be sure, after he'd reloaded with one of the spare clips he kept in the tackle box, he fired a test shot. Rulon didn't trust things he hadn't tested.

At the sight of Rulon moving the gun to a more convenient location, Yohaba's adrenaline kicked in along with a renewed sense of suspicion. "And what about the fire? Even if the cliff blocked his view, he should have seen the smoke. You'd think that alone would make him curious."

"Yeah, you'd think," said Rulon slowly. "Let's head over there just to be safe." He pointed with his paddle to a rocky, driftwood-strewn beach three hundred yards down from the truck. "We'll approach on foot."

Yohaba switched her paddle to the other side while Rulon used his as a rudder. Five minutes later, they beached the canoe and got out. Still, the man by their truck had never turned and never appeared to notice them. He wore a long black overcoat with a black scarf and a black cap pulled low over his brow.

"Dressed like he's waiting at a tram stop in Zurich," said Yohaba while Rulon stowed the paddles. "I say we throw him in the lake just on general principles."

From somewhere deeper in the forest that faced them twenty yards from the water's edge, a male voice said easily, "Good guess, Yohaba. He's from Switzerland. But you should be nice to him. He claims to be a man of the cloth and says he knows all about your grandfather. But you, Rulon, you're pathetic. How'd you ever live to be as old as you are? Your tradecraft sucks."

Annoyed, seriously annoyed, Rulon scanned the woods, searching for the source of the voice as it bounced among the trees.

"Dang it," he swore when he couldn't pin it down.

"Well, you're wrong about the tradecraft," Yohaba yelled. "He got a fire going with wet wood and in this wind."

"Ha, probably used a road flare," said the voice, a twangy, nasal sneer.

Yohaba whispered to Rulon, "Is he right? Was that cheating?"

Rulon angrily shook his head. In the shadows, movement on the right. Rulon leaned forward straining to see. Then a fleeting move on the left. Two branches cracked ten yards apart. Another movement to his right. A branch swayed—from the wind or was it brushed?

"Say Rulon," started up the voice again. "Yohaba wants to give you a merit badge. But you really haven't been a good Boy Scout today, have you? Okay, they're not on the endangered species list anymore, but geez, Cowboy, I don't see you lugging the meat home to eat. And that fire! Whoa! Not exactly a conservationist, are you?" A soft chuckle then with disgust, "You spotted the potential threat by the truck. That's good. But then you land at the obvious secondary ambush point. Predictable to the very end." Rulon could sense a head shaking sadly somewhere in the murky dimness.

A man of average height, mid-twenties, stepped out from behind a tree while Rulon was looking in a different direction. Long scraggly blond hair down to his shoulders, wispy blond beard, triathlete lean. Plain, dark blue ball cap, green camo pants, black Wellco jungle boots, a plain, threadbare, brown coat down to his knees, too thin for the weather. Pointed face, hawk nose, a predator's eyes that said hard miles, bad miles, eyes that said "I've done things," searching, ever searching. Walking towards them now easily, flowing, sticking to the shadows instinctively, a green and brown stealthy blending until he stepped onto the sand right in front of his two friends and said with an easy half smile, "Someday you're going to thank me for all the free training I'm giving you." As he walked, he angled his head back towards the woods and commanded sharply, "Tripod!"

No sound, no moving branches, but after a few seconds out of the shadows behind him came a mangy Belgium Malinois with a missing front left leg, moving silently despite the awkward hop. His left eye and part of his face were also missing, partially exposing a row of broken, jagged teeth in a perpetual grisly snarl. The dog quickly hopped up to the man and fell into a heel position at his left side.

As the pair approached, Rulon murmured a terse greeting while Yohaba clutched his arm and tried not to laugh. "My own dog," said Rulon with disgust, "and he doesn't come until the Prince of Blood calls."

"Stop calling him that," hissed Yohaba, and then merrily she said, "Howdy, Brother-in-law. Could have used you earlier with your Henry express," referring to the double-barreled .500 monster with a huge kick Brother-in-law brought back from Africa. At a nod from the man, the dog bounded towards Rulon and Yohaba for some affectionate ear rubbing.

"Would hardly be sporting unless it had tusks, Yohaba," Brother-in-law replied without breaking stride.

As he walked past Rulon, he poked him in the pocket where the gun was. "Not doing much good in there," he said. "Go say hi to your visitor. His name's Father Becker. I'll bring the canoe around." He reached the canoe and started to push off but paused. Turning back to Rulon with a piercing look, he shook his head and mouthed the word, "Rookie." He whistled softly and Tripod quickly left Rulon and jumped into the canoe without a backward glance.

The canoe's wake spread wider and wider as Brother-in-law put some distance between them. When Yohaba thought he was out of earshot, she said to Rulon, "He's the only guy who ever gets the better of you. Have you ever noticed that?"

"No," growled Rulon.

"Heard that," said Brother-in-law without having to yell, the sound carrying nicely over the water.

Rulon started to yell something after him but ended up just waving good riddance.

Rulon watched Brother-in-law paddle off. To Yohaba, he said, "Ray Suhaus called the other day." Ray was Rulon's former boss at OCD, Office Crimes Division, a CIA connected security subcontractor where Rulon used to work. "He says the SEALs want Brother-in-law back."

"Well, they can't have him," said Yohaba. "He's still not well."

"If you're waiting for him to become normal," said Rulon with a glance at the rapidly receding canoe, "don't hold your breath."

"Said the pot to the kettle," replied Yohaba amused. They began walking along the shore towards their visitor. She asked, "What else did Ray want? Did he want Tripod back, too?"

"Nah. He said we could keep him. Lucky us." Rulon thought back on the day when Ray had first driven into the yard with the ugliest, mangiest looking dog in the world sitting in the front seat of his pickup—a war dog injured in Afghanistan. He said they'd all be good for each other while they healed—Rulon from a head shot he'd recently taken from a neo-Nazi sniper, and Yohaba from the trauma of tracking down the responsible nest of vipers with Boris Zokolov, Rulon's Russian friend.

At the sight of the broken but unbowed dog, Rulon had held the dog's injured face in his two hands, touched the injured stump, looked into his one good eye, and said, "I dub thee Tripod. Hope that suits ya." The beat-up dog had answered to that name ever since.

Ray had also stayed to assess the security at the ranch. After four hours of walking the hills and checking fields of fire, he had declared the place a death trap. "My great grandmother could take you out here, and she's been dead for twenty years," he had said.

A week later Brother-in-law showed up on their doorstep in his beat-up VW with Missouri plates, and a duffle bag over his shoulder that contained all his worldly possessions. Which mainly consisted of an assortment of weapons, some of them legal. That was six months ago.

Now as they walked, Rulon and Yohaba reminisced about Ray's last words that day just as he drove off. He had warned them not to make eye contact with the morose visitor for at least the first two weeks—then he had laughed—joking, sort of.

The priest was close enough now they could see that his coat was shabby, and that he seemed to be studying the trees around him. After fifty more yards. Yohaba asked Rulon, "What were you diving after back at the lake? Were you making sure the bear was dead?"

"Nah. I knew he was dead," said Rulon, "but he'd be floating to the surface in a few days if I didn't open him up so the gases could escape. Make sense?"

Yohaba stopped and Rulon did too. She faced him and said, "I never would have thought of that."

"Gosh, darling. It's one of the first things they teach you in spy school." He laughed and they started jogging. Becker was a hundred yards away and still hadn't appeared to notice them.

Yohaba said through blue lips, "I never told you, but Leonard knew one day the Russians would show up here looking for him. Or the Chinese maybe."

"He's been gone for three weeks. When's he coming back?"

"After his meeting, he said he had a few things to take care of. But he should be back tomorrow."

"Did he say anything about a priest?"

"No, just the usual. *The whole world's coming to an end, Mal.* That sort of stuff."

"Okay but be careful with this guy. Priest or no priest, Brother-in-law's suspicious of something."

"Why do you say that?" Yohaba asked.

"Did you notice how he put it?" said Rulon. "'He *says* he knows your grandfather' and '*claims* to be a man of the cloth?'"

"Did he? I didn't notice."

"Yeah, well, that's what he said. He was telling us to be careful. So, don't give anything away. Okay? Let's just play along."

By now the priest had turned with a smile on his face and was watching them. Twenty yards away, they slowed to a walk and Rulon whispered, "Hey, looks like Charles Laughton."

As they drew closer, the old priest took off his scarf and black, knee-length coat revealing a plain black cassock underneath. He came forward and offered Yohaba the coat. "Here," he said.

"Thanks," said Yohaba without hesitation and quickly put the coat and scarf on. "I am so cold." She held out her hands and they shook.

"I'm Father Becker. I've come on urgent business in regards your grandfather." He held out his hand to Rulon. "And you must be Rulon, the hero of CERN."

"Right now I'm Rulon the wet and cold."

Yohaba asked, "Brother-in-law said you know my grandfather. What's this about?"

"He sent me to warn you," said Father Becker, now also shivering. He frowned as he spoke, his ample jowls sagging like two pillows under his neatly trimmed salt and pepper beard.

"Warn us? What about? Is the price of milk going down?" Rulon asked.

Father Becker rubbed his thick nose, blinked his heavy eyelids twice, and avoided the question. "He told me all about you two," he said. "He told me you like to make jokes." Behind him a branch cracked, and the priest swung sharply to the sound.

"You're spooked. Something's wrong," said Rulon flatly.

"Does this have anything to do with astronomy?" Yohaba asked.

Becker shrugged and smiled. "These are perilous times, and, yes, I know about Elsa." A hundred yards away a pickup truck rumbled down a dirt road past the parking lot. Becker stopped and watched. When the truck kept going, he relaxed and said, "It's better if we keep moving. We should leave. Now."

"What's the problem?" Rulon asked.

For a response, Becker looked around at the trees and said, "This forest is quite old and well preserved. I daresay that's an Engelmann spruce over there. What's the elevation here?"

"Around 6,500 feet," Rulon said.

"Ah, that explains it. They thrive in higher elevations."

While they were chatting, Father Becker had taken a pack of yellow post-it notes out of his pocket and was writing. He tore off the top one and handed it to Yohaba. It read, *Must keep moving.* When Yohaba looked puzzled, the priest pointed to the sky and wrote the word 'DRONES' on the next sheet.

Yohaba handed the note to Rulon. He read it and motioned for the pen and pack of notes from the priest. He wrote, *You are an idiot* and was giving it to Father Becker when Yohaba snatched it out of his hand. She read it, glared at Rulon and stuffed it in her pocket.

"What was that?" asked Father Becker.

"Nothing," said Yohaba. "Rulon likes to draw."

"Pardon me?" said the priest.

Then Rulon added to the awkwardness by saying, "Mind if I frisk you?" Yohaba groaned and the priest took a step back. Rulon shrugged. "Sorry. It's not you. It's me."

The priest sighed and held his hands above his head. "Leonard warned me there would be indignities."

Chapter 5

After the frisking, Yohaba shivered over to the truck with Becker while Rulon walked back through the dappled sunlight of the pine-needled forest to the lake. He arrived just in time to help Brother-in-law drag the canoe out of the water. Tripod had already jumped out and run off into the woods. "What did you mean by 'claims to be a priest?'" asked Rulon as they stowed the oars and rearranged the gear under the seats.

"I'm picking up a weird vibe," Brother-in-law said.

"What? Like he's not a priest?"

"No. More like I should be hearing his confession, not the other way around. But he could still be a priest. Wasn't Richelieu a cardinal?"

"Why did you bring him then?"

"Same reason you're riding back with him, curiosity." They hoisted the canoe to their shoulders and carried it to the truck.

⁊⊱⊰

Once inside the truck, Yohaba immediately turned on the engine and the heater. Father Becker climbed in next to her. After a minute, when the heater had kicked in and both of them had thawed slightly, she asked, "How long have you known my grandfather?"

"We have known each other for years. Ever since his days as a Jesuit scholastic."

"Funny. He never mentioned you."

"Yes," said the priest. "And I only found out about you two months ago. Strange, I know, but he's always been exceedingly private. Now it's even worse. Need to know and all that sort of James Bond nonsense. Independent cells with no knowledge of each other. No links. All inter-cell communication flowing through him. Code names for everything. A few months ago, he began severely limiting his use of email and phones. Too exposed, he said."

"He's never liked using cell phones, but I've seen no drop off in emails from him," said Yohaba.

"Are you sure they're from your grandfather?" asked the priest.

"Of course I'm sure. You don't think I could tell if someone was impersonating my grandfather? And they came from all over the place. He practically lives on an airplane."

"Yes, I've heard he has a private jet now," said the priest.

Rulon didn't have a trailer, so once he and Brother-in-law had reached the truck, they had to hoist the canoe into the truck bed and secure it over the cab. Before getting in, Rulon paused with one foot on the running board taking one last look at the black clouds rolling over the splintered Sawtooth peaks. *Storm's coming*, he thought to himself.

೧೭೮

On the drive up, the sun had been shining but now a thunderous black sky followed them home as they barreled down highway 75 in the direction of Sun Valley and Ketchum. Rulon drove with Yohaba sitting beside him and

Father Becker by the window. Brother-in-law hung back in his derelict '61 Beetle with Tripod in the passenger seat, letting them pull away and creating a tactical buffer in case anyone followed.

"So, Brother-in-law volunteered to drive you?" Yohaba asked suspiciously. "Sounds like a waste of time."

"He tried calling you first but couldn't get through," said the old priest. "The mountains."

"Anything to get out of work," Rulon said.

Father Becker stroked his ample double chin. "He seems like a rather competent young man, though not very talkative. When I pressed him, he told me he was a professional tap dancer. I suspect that's not quite true."

"He has a strange sense of humor. He's really a Navy SEAL," Yohaba said. "But don't listen to Rulon. The guy works darn hard."

"Yes. Military. That makes sense. Whose brother-in-law is he?"

Rulon and Yohaba smiled and Rulon said, "He's not related to either of us. It's his Hopi name."

"Ignore my husband," said Yohaba. "Funny. We don't even hear the words anymore. Brother-in law. It's just his name now."

"How strange," said the priest.

Yohaba explained, "Somebody in his SEAL unit said he looked like his brother-in-law and the name stuck. His real name's Orin Blackmon. He's from the Ozarks in Southern Missouri, if you know where that is?"

"*Winter's Bone* country," said Father Becker softly. "Yes, that fits." Rulon and Yohaba looked at each other— *ah...a fellow movie buff.* The priest continued, "You said 'is' a SEAL. Did you mean 'was?'"

"No, he's still on the books," Rulon said. "He's sort of on a leave of absence."

"He's recuperating," said Yohaba. "We should explain. He's a great guy, but you need to be careful around him. He's wound up tight. Don't ever approach him from behind unless he knows you're there. He spent three years in the Congo and…"

"GEEZ, YOHABA!" yelled Rulon. "Father, forget you heard that. America never had advisors in the Congo until recently. End of story."

"Of course," Father Becker said. "The Congo is a Denied Area. I understand."

"And don't mention the Lord's Resistance Army around him. Makes him crazy," said Yohaba, rushing to get the words out before Rulon could stop her. Rulon let out a long-irritated sigh, but took note that Becker knew the insider lingo for the situation.

"Don't worry," Father Becker said. "Catholic Charities has a strong presence in the region. There's not much that goes on there that we don't know about. Our workers there have a saying that in the Congo even the secrets are screamed." When he said that last part, his eyes lost focus.

"Is something wrong?" Yohaba asked when the silence continued.

Father Becker forced a smile and said, "Oh nothing. Just memories. But, please, I'm curious. He's such an interesting young man."

Yohaba looked at Rulon, and he nodded reluctantly.

"When we first met him," said Yohaba, "he'd just come back from three years in the Congo fighting the Lord's Resistance Army. He needed time to become human again."

"And you took him into your home?" said Father Becker. "Weren't you a little afraid he could be dangerous?"

"Dangerous?" considered Rulon thoughtfully. "Yeah, he was dangerous. Still is, but not to us. In fact, if anything, he's over-protective. When he first arrived, he would wake up at three a.m., put on camo paint, and skulk around the hills until breakfast with Tripod, a SIG Sauer, and a Mark three combat knife."

"Why did he do that?" asked Father Becker.

"When we first caught him at it, he said old habits die hard, much harder than people," said Rulon.

"We were never quite sure what he meant by that," said Yohaba.

"Oh, yes, we were," said Rulon annoyed. "He meant that I was a slacker who deserved to be garroted in his sleep for not running around with him. He was looking for snipers."

"I always got along with him just fine," said Yohaba.

"He likes her cooking," said Rulon.

Yohaba ignored him. "We were told he'd been through some rough stuff, but that he was a really great guy."

Changing the subject, Rulon asked, "Why didn't you just stay at the ranch and wait for us?"

"Your father said if the fish were biting you might never come back," said Father Becker. "That's why I couldn't wait. If it were up to me, I would have spared myself the long trip and simply called from Geneva, but your grandfather warned me not to use phones or the internet."

"And so it begins," Yohaba said ominously. "Just tell me, is my grandfather all right?"

"I'm not sure," he said. "He's quite paranoid and reclusive these days. This situation with 182 Elsa is confounding us all and that is why I am here. To warn you and ask for your help."

"How long have you known about Elsa?" Rulon asked.

"I knew about it from the beginning. And dismissed it along with every other expert, until Yohaba's extraordinary brother showed us the error of our ways. But I'm afraid

Leonard is feeling desperate these days, and that is not a state of mind you want someone of Leonard's abilities to be in."

"So you believe it then?" Rulon asked. "You don't think Elsa's orbit will change again? Shoot, for almost a year it kept changing."

"Rulon is skeptical," Yohaba explained. "It doesn't match his version of how the world's supposed to end."

"Mine either," said Becker. "But I still believe somehow, somewhere, somebody has to step up and stop it. It appears to me God has picked your grandfather." The old priest paused with his mouth open, tried to begin again, and met with no better success. "This is very complex," he said finally. "I hardly know where to begin. The situation is fluid and for the first time in all the years I've known him, your grandfather has not been transparent with me. Dark forces have been set in motion, and I'm worried your grandfather is at the center of them. I fear in his headlong rush to save the world he has aligned himself with evil, conspiring men." He said these last words with his eyes closed, as if stifling an inner pain.

"My grandfather would never be involved in anything sinister," said Yohaba firmly.

"My dear," said Father Becker, "when seven billion lives are at stake, the labels 'sinister' and 'evil' no longer have meaning. Perhaps neither does the word 'horror.' The only evil behavior is to not do everything you can to save the most people." When Yohaba looked skeptical, the priest continued, "With stakes this high, can you even contemplate an end that could not be justified? But let's not get ahead of ourselves. Before you judge, listen to the full story."

"Give him a chance," said Rulon.

"I have been your father's envoy to a secretive, malevolent, but sometimes useful Russian citizen, a man the popular press would categorize, probably accurately, as an 'oligarch.' A man with a black heart who lives outside the law, but is protected by his piles of money, and all the evil that money can buy. And in Russia these days that can buy a lot of evil."

Yohaba blurted, "I knew the Russians were involved somehow. Tell me, did you see a big, scary looking guy with this incredible bone structure with tattoos up the ying-yang?"

"My dear, you just described most of the Russians I've had to deal with."

"Never mind. Just tell us your story," Yohaba said. "Tell us straight."

"We've got a three hour drive ahead of us," Rulon said. "Plenty of time."

With a deep breath, the old priest began. "You need to first understand that Leonard is an idealist at heart. He's not naïve, and he doesn't have a utopian view of the world, but he is an optimist when it comes to the goodness of mankind. Or at least he was up until recently. What a shame. He managed to keep his faith in humanity alive for eighty-three years." Father Becker shook his head in dismay then continued. "He had a plan to marshal the world's scientific and financial might using the technology bequeathed in Einstein's trunk. His noble goal was to destroy the asteroid 182 Elsa before April 13, 2029.

"He pictured something momentous coming out of all this, another space race. Perhaps something that would capture the imagination of the entire world. The scientific spinoffs were going to be enormous. But just as importantly, the world's great powers would have to work together on a scale never before imagined. Perhaps one of the spinoffs would be a new era of human cooperation and peace. Leonard had huge and generous dreams all wrapped in an old man's magnificent aspiration to leave the world a better place."

"Even before Elsa, he was like that," said Yohaba. "A real visionary."

"Yes, but with Elsa it was a noble goal quickly crushed by the short-sighted lust for profits. Your grandfather toured Europe and the U.S. making his pitch to the CEOs and corporate boards specializing in the technologies necessary to destroy Elsa. Computers, batteries, rocket engines, GPS technology, solid state drives, metallurgy, energy, and plastics. He laid out the irrefutable science. He got all their heads nodding. Yes, something must be done, they all agreed. He offered them advanced technology from Einstein's trunk—for free. He saw their smiles widen at first…and then, just as quickly, freeze in place when he asked them to pledge their first five years' profits to fund the research required to destroy Elsa."

Rulon said, "I wish I could have been there to see their faces when he sprung that one on them."

"No, you don't," said Becker. "Uncloaked greed is never a pleasant sight. Suddenly the science wasn't convincing enough. How could he be so sure? Why wasn't this in the news? They had a counter proposal. Why couldn't he just sell them the technology? Or perhaps give it to them free for a small percentage of the profits? After all, what did an academic such as himself care about profits? Oh, they thought they were being quite persuasive, but little did they know whom they were dealing with. Steenberg roared at them dumbfounded. *The world is going to be destroyed!* He called them imbeciles and worse. They offered him stock options. That's what finally did it. They made the mistake of thinking he was as greedy as they. He went off and made other plans." Becker paused to consider what he'd just said. "Yes, indeed, other plans. What an understatement.

"Several times, lower-level corporate functionaries, disgusted with their leaders, came to him privately and confided that his plan never had a chance because spending R&D money now with no return for five years would kill everyone's quarterly bonuses and not do the stock price any favors either.

"In his eighty-three years, no one had ever called Steenberg naïve, but after four months of making his pitch to heads of state and CEOs in the U.S. and Western Europe he looked himself in the mirror one day and muttered, 'You old fool.' All this he confided to me in great anger and despair. I had never seen him so angry. It was an emotion so foreign to his being that he couldn't express it in words, only in actions.

"For six months he wasn't seen on the CERN campus at Meyrin. When he finally surfaced again he had a plan. His first call came to me, and with an eerie calmness demanded my contacts with the Russian oligarchs—the ones with links to the Russian mafia. How could I refuse him, my oldest friend?"

"How did you happen to know these men?" Rulon asked.

The priest looked a trifle embarrassed when he answered. "When the Russian Orthodox Cathedral of Christ the Savior in Moscow was rebuilt in 1995 after being destroyed by Stalin in 1931, the reconstruction was funded largely with money from the Russian mafia. Donated, of course, in return for political favors. Oddly, the Vatican was in possession of the original architectural drawings, and I was the emissary who negotiated their return. Leonard knew of my involvement. I'm telling you this in confidence and trusting that you both have a—" Becker searched for the right word. "—non-parochial view of the world."

"This does not sound like the grandfather I know," Yohaba said. "He would never involve himself with groups like that."

After a reflective silence, Father Becker replied, "I suppose he felt he had no choice. Besides, criminal enterprises were the only entities with enough capital and will to defer profits for long-term gain."

"Surely you're joking," Rulon said.

"I wish I were. Interestingly, the only legitimate companies that agreed outright to work with him were a few family-owned, non-public enterprises. They seemed to be the only ones able to take a long-term view, but in the end, Leonard judged them too small for what he needed to do. Leonard and I discussed this over many long evenings and many bottles of wine." The priest laughed. "Actually, as I remember I drank all the wine. Your grandfather has become quite the ascetic in his old age. But I digress. Our conclusion was that once the professional managers infiltrated a company, the company was doomed to short-term thinking."

Suddenly Becker sat up straighter. "I just had an epiphany," he exclaimed. "The criminal operations we were dealing with were, in a sense, all family-owned businesses." He paused to ponder, then shook his head as if to clear it. "Well, that's another impenetrable mystery I'll have to ponder over a glass of wine." He laughed and slapped his knee.

"It's why we like ranching," Rulon said. "Gives us time to contemplate the impenetrable mysteries. Keep going." A hundred yards ahead a white-tailed deer ran across the road and disappeared into the trees.

"Yes. Don't let me get distracted. Yes, the plan. The plan quite simply was to save the world whether it wanted to be saved or not. And to invite to the feast any who wished to come, even the spiritually blind, deaf, and lame.

In other words, any organization with the resources, money, or the will to work with him.

"Leonard had also approached several governments for help. Political infighting sabotaged the U.S.'s involvement—one party wouldn't fund without a reciprocal increase in the capital gains tax. The other party wouldn't fund for fear of giving the serving president a victory. Both parties had skeptics who denied the science. In Europe, the discussions continued with great eloquence but stalled when the French demanded control of the project."

"I'm sure his plan was amazing," said Yohaba. "He's the most brilliant person I've ever known."

"His plan was amazing, and I too have never met his intellectual equal." The old priest went on to describe the intricacies of Steenberg's plans, astonishing both Rulon and Yohaba.

"Milo Minderbinder's egg scheme," said Rulon when the old priest was done.

"Yes, yes. *Catch 22*. Exactly. Yes!" Father Becker slapped his knee again. And again, Rulon and Yohaba were impressed with the old priest's range of obscure knowledge.

"Okay. But in real life how does that work?" Yohaba asked.

"The Russian government had a contract with one of their energy companies to buy solar panels at three times the current market in return for kickbacks to senior government officials. Your grandfather even set up the bribes. Or rather his intermediary did." At that, Father Becker dropped his voice, causing both Rulon and Yohaba to silently wonder if Father Becker had been that intermediary.

"And how does any of this help Leonard?" Rulon asked.

"It enabled the Russians to garner huge profits which they were going to use to buy the nuclear technology they wanted from Einstein's trunk in the first place. But that wasn't Leonard's only source of money. He was working many angles. I've spent the last six weeks trying to uncover them. To say his schemes were labyrinthine would be an understatement."

"You're leading up to something," Yohaba said. "What is it?"

Father Becker cupped his hands over the heater and said, "Your grandfather has disappeared."

Yohaba gasped. "The Russians. I knew it. Cowboy, we're going there. We'll find him. Brother-in-law will help. Wait, they wouldn't let him in the country. Can he get a fake passport? Every minute counts. We need to plan this. Cowboy, say something!"

"He said 'disappeared,'" responded Rulon. "He didn't say 'kidnapped.' Let's get the rest of it. Which is it, Father? Disappeared or kidnapped?"

"It's hard to tell. Let me be clear. It's not the oligarch I referred to. It's the Russian government who has him. But I don't think kidnapped is the right word. Ultimately, he needs a government with a space program to make his plan work. I think this is part of his plan. But there are parts of the plan that are wickedly misguided, in my opinion. That's why I don't think Leonard is in control anymore."

Father Becker fell silent while he allowed Rulon and Yohaba to process the information. Thirty seconds ticked by before he said, "I know it's a lot to digest. But when you think of it, no plan to blast an asteroid apart would be simple."

Yohaba said, "True, but I still think I've been getting emails from him all along. As soon as we get home, I'm going to email him and get to the bottom of this."

"You should, but I really don't think it's been him answering you. He believed that agencies from a dozen countries had him under surveillance. Every communication with me was face-to-face or via email accounts where we had shared access. We'd write messages and leave them in the drafts folder for each other to read. I'll be honest. I think for at least two months, it's unlikely he was the one writing you. Up is down and down is up. Nothing is at it seems. We are surrounded by cunning, highly motivated people with unlimited resources."

"Okay," Rulon said. "If your story's true then Leonard has gone off the deep end. So why are you here?"

"I think I know where he is. He warned me to stay away. He can't face me, his old friend. Or won't. Or maybe he's trying to spare me further legal or spiritual entanglements. He's being held—let me rephrase that— he's living in a chalet in Stein am Rhein in Switzerland. He is guarded. I went to see him and got turned away."

"By who?" Rulon asked.

"Russians. Serious men who knew my name before I introduced myself. That's why I'm here. I think it would be very helpful if Yohaba came with me and we talked to him together."

"I'll go," Yohaba said.

"No one's going anywhere," Rulon said. "If he's working on a plan to save the world, I say leave him alone and let him do his job."

"There's more. You've read about the flooding in Thailand and how it's destroyed a third of the world's disk drive manufacturing capacity. Some of the dikes collapsed naturally but others nearer the disk drive facilities were deliberately weakened. Altogether they caused hundreds of deaths. I think the people Leonard is dealing with had something to do with it. In their own way they were returning value to the stockholders."

"But why?" asked Rulon in amazement. "This doesn't make sense."

"Oh, but it does," Yohaba said. "In a crazy way, it does. But it can't be true."

"What am I missing?" asked Rulon.

"Some of the science in Einstein's trunk had application to SSDs," said Yohaba, "you know, solid state drives, and something called memristors—an advanced storage technology. Leonard discussed it with me. A disk drive shortage would pump up demand for SSDs and perhaps increase funding for memristor development. It makes perfect business sense." Yohaba looked at Father Becker and he nodded agreement.

"It gets worse," said the priest. "Someone hired men to inflict further damage on the Fukushima Dai-ichi reactor ruined after the earthquake in Japan. The men who did this have since died from radioactive poisoning, but the damage to Japan and the nuclear industry worldwide is catastrophic.

"Already there is a growing movement to shut down reactors all over the world because of what happened. They are now viewed as too risky. And this means the world will look to other sources of renewable energy. Again, your grandfather benefits because of his investments in solar panels.

"Further, there are indications he was involved in the unrest in Libya trying to drive up the price of oil so the Russian collateral would rise in value. This is not acceptable and is also terribly confusing if you've known Leonard for over 50 years as I have. To say this is out of character doesn't even begin to explain it."

"Right," answered Rulon softly. Leonard was intelligent, grounded, and possessed of a solid moral core. Could he have collapsed like this so late in life?

While Father Becker calmly answered their follow-up questions, they continued down Highway 75 past the turn-off to Smiley Creek airport where the road ran straight for two miles until it turned into the narrow, curving, hairpin turns east of Alturas Lake.

While he listened, Rulon was surprised to see a black Chevy Suburban drive by, its windows highly tinted but not so tinted that Rulon couldn't see a set of big, serious faces staring back at him as it passed.

"Strange," said Rulon under his breath, assuming at first they were from some government agency. But what were they doing here? Father Becker and Yohaba were talking and hadn't noticed.

"What did you say?" Yohaba asked. By then the van was past.

"Nothing," said Rulon.

Father Becker cleared his throat and said, "Perhaps I should tell you. The Russian crime syndicate or the oligarch, I don't know which one, or maybe both or maybe they're the same thing... Anyway, they don't like your father being under the control of the Russian government. They're afraid he will reveal secrets."

"Sounds like a reasonable concern," Rulon said distractedly as he tilted the rearview mirror so he could keep the black Suburban in view. The van kept going, and he was starting to relax when suddenly its brake lights blinked on and its back end rose as it slammed to a stop. *Uh-oh.*

"They have what I think is referred to as a hit team searching for him," said Becker.

"Oh," said Rulon and Yohaba in unison.

"Former Spetsnaz. Very paranoid individuals," continued the priest as Rulon kept one eye on the road and one on the SUV. "Their trust in their fellow human beings, except for family, is non-existent. They kill, torture, and kidnap without conscience or fear of consequences. Normal people fear consequences. These men don't."

"Do what is wrong and let the consequences follow," murmured Rulon, intent on the Suburban behind him and only half listening.

"Yes, something like that," said Father Becker. "They drive around in big, black cars with tinted windows as if they were lords of the universe. With their thugs and psychotic family members. When they kill, they think they are doing it for their country. It's like they are at war, but their country is the Russian oligarch underground. They care only for profit. Utterly loyal, utterly ruthless, utterly callous to suffering, even their own. The best and worst of Russian qualities. Have you ever dealt with people like that, Rulon?"

At the question both Rulon and Yohaba looked at each other, their eyes alight with mutual memories of the race for their lives and the fight in the tunnels of CERN. Instead, Rulon said, "Well, over the years I've bought a lot of things from Amazon."

"Yes, he's dealt with people like that," said Yohaba. "He's a psycho magnet. They're drawn to him like flies to manure. No offense, darling."

"None taken, darling," Rulon said. Father Becker watched the interaction between them and knew there was a story in there somewhere but didn't pursue it. "So that's why you're here." said Rulon. "You're hoping Yohaba can talk some sense into him." He continued to watch the Suburban still stopped in the road, now half a mile back.

"Yes."

"Have they by any chance been following you?"

"I suspect so, but I doubt I could spot them unless they were amateurs. And they are definitely not amateurs. But there's another reason I am here. To warn you. They may show up at some point wanting to talk to Yohaba. She's the easiest way for them to get near him. They'll lie, cheat, kidnap, threaten family, kill, whatever it takes to get her cooperation."

In the rear-view mirror, Rulon saw the SUV do a 3-point U-turn and come rapidly in pursuit. There was almost no traffic on the road. Brother-in-law was nowhere in sight. It was just them and the Suburban, and it was moving well beyond the speed limit—and gaining.

"I think we've got company," he said.

Yohaba and Father Becker both turned to look.

"Oh dear," Father Becker said.

"It's them," said Yohaba. To Father Becker's surprise she pulled the SIG automatic out of her belt and expertly chambered a round.

Rulon entered a ten-mile section of winding mountain road and temporarily lost sight of his pursuer. He picked up speed, hit a sharp turn, and the tires squealed. He asked Yohaba to grab his cell phone out of the cup holder and hit the speed dial for Brother-in-law.

"Put it on speaker phone, will you, darling?" he asked as he took another turn way too fast. Yohaba complied and set the phone on the dashboard.

When Brother-in-law picked up, Rulon asked, "Where are you?"

"Just past Yellow Belly Lake," answered Brother-in-law. "What's up?"

"You're about five miles away. I've got trouble. Tinted windows."

"Crown Vic?"

"Suburban."

"Could be Virginia farm boys," said the SEAL. "Maybe you should just pull over."

"They couldn't talk to me at the ranch?" said Rulon. "I'm such an important person?" When Brother-in-law didn't respond, Rulon said, "I'm thinking they followed the priest here. I saw their faces. Could be Russian."

After a few seconds of silence, Brother-in-law said, "Make a plan."

"Maybe we should take our chances in the woods."

"You'd have to leave the priest," said Brother-in-law.

Rulon winked at Father Becker and said. "No, we'd take him with us for a human shield."

Brother-in-law chuckled. "How much of a lead have you got?"

"Maybe a minute."

"Think your old jalopy can outrun them?"

"Surely you're joking," answered Rulon loud enough to rise above the engine racket.

"Well, that sort of narrows down the options. Are they keeping you in sight?"

"Not always. Road's too windy," he said while skidding through a hairpin turn.

"Okay, so use your head for more than just keeping your ears apart. Make a plan."

"I'm getting to that," replied Rulon testily. "Hey, we've survived lots of stuff before you came along."

"He's only trying to help," said Yohaba to Rulon. She put a hand on Father Becker's arm. "They're really good friends. It's just that Brother-in-law's the only guy who ever gets the better of him."

"No, he doesn't," said Rulon, tight-lipped.

"Heard that," said Brother-in-law.

Rulon gripped the steering wheel. He took a deep breath. "Okay. Here's what we're gonna do. The next time we're out of their view, I'm gonna pull over and switch seats with Yohaba. Then she's going to make a U-turn and drive back towards them. She'll be wearing my cowboy hat pulled down low so they won't see her face clearly. Me and Father Becker will duck out of sight. Heck, half the cars on this road are beat up pickups. We'll be past them in a blink and with any luck they won't know it's us. You'll be waiting somewhere along the road. We'll pull over and if they come after us at least we'll be together."

"No hat," said Brother-in-law. "If they're foreigners, they won't know every bozo in the state wears one. They'll see it a mile away and focus on it. And tell Yohaba to change her hair style. Let her hair hang loose."

"Okay, no hat," Rulon said. He nodded to Yohaba and she quickly undid her ponytail and shook her hair to let it fall loose around her shoulders.

"I'm on my way. I'll meet you somewhere." Brother-in-law clicked off and stomped on the gas. His un-aerodynamic vehicle accelerated insanely, almost doing a wheelie, and he had to fight to keep the front tires on the road. It looked a heap, but the car was powered by a 2275cc JCS Turnkey engine with racing valves and MAHLE forged aluminum pistons. Once it settled down, he patted the dashboard and said, "Easy, big fella."

Chapter 6

S tay down," Yohaba ordered. She focused straight ahead as the black SUV barreled towards them and flashed past. Once again blank, flat faces stared through the windows.

From below the level of the dashboard, Rulon said, "With any luck, they didn't recognize us."

"With any luck they're on their way to a Transcendental Meditation meeting," Yohaba said.

"Benedictine monks are peaceful," said Father Becker from down near the floor. "As long as we're wishing, I'm wishing they're Benedictine monks."

The Suburban disappeared around a curve and Yohaba hit the gas hard. Rulon and Father Becker sat back up. Two minutes later they were out of the hairpin turns and onto the long flat stretch where Rulon had first spotted the SUV. Four hundred yards ahead in a turnout on the cliff side of the road, Brother-in-law stood in his blue cap and brown knee-length coat Tripod at his side, leaning up against his VW as if he hadn't a care in the world. What they couldn't see were the Heckler and Koch 416 with suppressor and ten-inch barrel and the Vietnam era M79 grenade launcher resting upright against the passenger side of the car.

Yohaba came tearing into the dirt turnout in a cloud of dust and skidding tires. As she roared in, Brother-in-law waved her to park behind his car. She turned to Rulon, and he answered her unspoken question. "He doesn't want you in his field of fire." She pulled around behind the VW and saw the two military grade weapons leaning against the door. Only Rulon knew the M79 for what it was.

As soon as they got out, Rulon immediately went to the toolbox in the truck bed and dug out two Turtleskin bullet-stab vests. He threw one to Yohaba and put the other one on under his coat. The temperature had continued to drop though the wind had died down. The pine trees that lined the road on the mountain side stood tall and straight. He looked up to the surrounding peaks and noticed new places where over the winter avalanches of snow and rock had gouged out sections of forest. Now most of the snow was gone and small, seasonal waterfalls had returned to cascade over the gray rock and fallen timbers. It was a hard but beautiful land.

Rulon walked over to Brother-in-law, who stared intently down the road while gently rubbing Tripod's ears. Rulon said, "I think we fooled them, but if they show up…ah…I'm expecting to talk. Just talk. These may even be our own guys. We're gonna be cool, right?"

Brother-in-law crouched down to look into Tripod's misshapen face and said, "What do you say, big fella. Do we play nice with these guys?" Tripod barked sharply twice and Brother-in-law stood up. "Sorry, Cowboy. If they're bad guys, no can do. Tripod says I gotta pump a couple of grenades into their sorry asses and roll them off the cliff."

Rulon chuckled nervously and started to say something but just then Yohaba and Father Becker walked up and he clamped down. They stood around together shooting the breeze while waiting for the Suburban to show. The sky darkened as the sun sank lower.

After fifteen minutes, a relieved Rulon looked at his watch, stood up straight, and said enthusiastically, "I'm hungry. What'd'ya say we head home and tie on the old feedbag."

He reached for the door handle, suddenly stopped, and said, "Or not," with a mixture of irritation and resignation.

Down the road the Suburban was edging slowly around the turn into view. It pulled off to the side and stopped on the narrow shoulder against the uphill, forested side of the road, big engine rumbling. They could plainly see the driver looking at them through the windshield, and next to him, a big man in a suit, head turned, talking to someone behind him.

"Damn," said Rulon.

"Better now than at the ranch," Brother-in-law said.

"What's your guess?" asked Yohaba.

"Bad guys," Rulon said.

"Yep," said Brother-in-law.

"I speak Russian," said Becker.

"So do I," said Yohaba.

After a minute of both sides measuring each other, the van eased off the shoulder and advanced.

Brother-in-law pushed off the truck and said, "You do all the talking. I'm just your average Ozark meth lab hillbilly." No one smiled at the strange joke.

Rulon asked, "What do you think's going on?"

"Don't know, don't care," said Brother-in-law in a slow, twangy drawl. "But if they're looking for trouble, they done treed the wrong possum."

Rulon stared. He'd never heard him speak in a backwoods idiom before.

"O Brother where art thou?" Rulon asked. "Are you channeling something creepy? 'Cause if you are, maybe I should just lock you in the toolbox."

"Don't get your knickers in a knot," said Brother-in-law in his normal voice. "Crazed hillbilly is a universal language that says 'don't make eye contact, back slowly away, then run'—even spooked the LRA when I used it on them."

The black SUV rolled slowly into the turnout crunching dirt with its heavy tires to stop twenty feet away. The driver was a thin-lipped man in a dark suit. He stared straight ahead, both hands in plain sight on the steering wheel. Next to him was another man, large and grim-faced. Muscle. Thug. Ex-military. Hands also visible. If he wasn't a Russian, he was doing a good imitation. There were figures in the back seat that Rulon couldn't make out. While he was assessing the threat level, the rear passenger window slid down halfway, and a hand popped out waving a lacy white handkerchief.

Rulon said quietly, "Might not be the toughest hombres I ever faced."

"If they're messing with ma friends, they're as low as a snake's belly in a wheel rut," replied Brother-in-law staying in character.

"Just stay cool, Mr. Tough Guy."

"This here rooster's so tough, them boys couldn't stick a fork in ma gravy."

"Please, don't embarrass me," Rulon said out of the corner of his mouth. "I graduated from college. I don't know people like you."

"That grizz leave you any bullets?" asked Brother-in-law in his own voice as he stroked his wispy blonde beard.

"Three full clips."

"If it comes to a shooting, remember, fast is fine but accuracy is final."

"Yes, and empty barrels make the most noise," said Rulon.

"Make the first shot count," retorted Brother-in-law.

"Make sure that first shot isn't in your foot," replied Rulon.

The white handkerchief withdrew into the car. From within the van, a young, male voice said in excellent but slightly accented English, "Don't do anything rash. I just want to talk. This is not what you think it is."

"He's Russian," said Yohaba from behind the truck when she heard the accent. "Be careful."

"You can trust me," said the voice. "I'm not a communist. I'm a businessman, a capitalist."

"Okay, now *I'm* scared," Brother-in-law whispered.

Rulon cleared his throat. "Who are you?"

"My father does business with Leonard Steenberg," said the Russian, careful not to show himself. "Please relax. I know this must seem strange, but please hear what I have to say. I'm coming out. Okay?"

Rulon resettled his hat and scratched at the dirt with the toe of his boot. "Okay," he said, "but keep your hands where we can see them."

"I'm sending one of my men out first. Okay?"

"Okay. Same goes for him."

The muscle in the front passenger seat came out on the far side of the SUV and walked around the big van. Casually, Brother-in-law shifted his position over about five feet, so the bodyguard always remained exactly between him and the SUV. The bodyguard kept walking and Brother-in-law kept shifting to keep the big Russian between him and anyone with a weapon in the Suburban's dark backseat. The bodyguard smiled, knowing what this little dance was all about. His shoes were too thick and heavy to be considered dress shoes, and he had a stout, heavy duty watch. Despite the cold, he wore only a suit jacket. Not even a hat over his blond, closely cropped hair.

The bodyguard saw the Missouri plates and checked Brother-in-law out from the top of his scraggly-haired head to the tip of his scuffed-up jungle boots. In an amused tone he said in reasonably good English, "Did you get lost? You're far from home."

"Not as far as you, Comrade," drawled Brother-in-law while standing relaxed and expressionless with his hands hanging loose at this side.

The bodyguard smirked, shifted his gaze to Rulon, and studied him just as closely. But Rulon was a known quantity to anyone with contacts in Russian security agencies. There was nothing secret about the danger he posed. He next scrutinized Yohaba and Father Becker. There had been stories about the woman. She needed to be watched as well. The priest drew a derisive nod as an acknowledgment.

The Russian said, "I'm going to walk around your vehicles. Don't get nervous." He came over, hands visible and walked behind the truck and VW and immediately saw Brother-in-law's heavy armament. He stopped, put his hands on his hips, glared in the direction of his boss in the car, and shook his head, as if to say *I told you*. He continued on, peering inside each vehicle then walking along the length of the cliff, looking down over the edge to see if anyone was hiding. All the while Rulon watched the Suburban and Brother-in-law never took his eyes off the Russian.

The big Russian completed his security assessment, walked back to the Suburban, and leaned into the open passenger window. There was a brief discussion and what appeared to be a difference of opinion, but a curt word from inside silenced the bodyguard. The door opened and a young man stepped out. From the passenger door on the opposite side stepped out a short, elegantly dressed man in a thick coat who looked to be in his mid-seventies.

The youth looked as young as his voice suggested, maybe sixteen, five foot eight, thin, pale cheeks. Once out of the car he buttoned his thick coat, started to put his hands in his pockets, but stopped at a curt word from the old man. He smiled at Rulon and then held his hands up to show they were empty. He wore a traditional Russian fur hat with the flaps pulled down over his ears. He beat his arms across his narrow chest and said in a loud, exuberant voice, "Idaho! I love this place! Reminds me of Mother Russia. The forests, the wild rivers. And weather with a real bite to it." At the word "bite" he clenched his teeth in a wild grin. "Yes. Yes. I can see why you like it here."

"Aren't you a little young for this?" asked Rulon.

"Alexander the Great was only eighteen when he led the left wing at the Battle of Chaeronea, and I'm much more experienced than I look," replied the young Russian. "But don't worry," he said gesturing to the old man who was now coming around the car to stand at his side. "My grandfather is here to keep an eye on me. His name is Vladimir. He won't show it, but he's very excited to be here. For both of us, this is our first time in America, and there is so much to see. Have you ever been to Disneyland?"

"Yes, many times. Okay. Pleased to meet you both," said Rulon. "What can I do for you?"

"I'm here on behalf of my father," said the young man. As he talked, his eyes swept back and forth as if expecting an ambush. His grandfather stood next to him with the bodyguard a few feet behind on his left.

"Nervous?" Rulon asked.

The bodyguard answered for his young boss. "You're the ones who should be nervous. Don't make any sudden moves. Keep your hands where I can see them."

"Enough, Yevgeny," said the teenager. "To answer your question. Yes. I'm a little nervous. Is it that obvious? Yevgeny here doesn't like me being in the same time zone with you. You see, we know you. You're not exactly a Russian's best friend. We trust you about as much as you trust us. But my father always says that if trust were essential, no business would get done. We can at least talk."

Rulon studied his eyes. Young but maybe a hidden strength. Maybe not. Intelligent brown eyes over an engaging half smile. Excellent English. A slightly Americanized accent. Still youthfully naïve. Or maybe not. The grandfather stood next to him silent and glowering. Neither youthful, nor naive.

"Seriously, aren't you a little young for this?" Rulon asked.

Without a trace of embarrassment, the young man replied, "For everything there is a first time. My father said it would be good experience."

"And maybe someone younger would be less threatening?" offered Rulon.

"Threatening is my department," interjected Yevgeny.

The young man smiled. "Ignore him. But, yes, my youth may have also been a factor. I'm supposed to handle everything. My grandfather's English isn't very good."

"You've come a long way. Talk then," Rulon said.

"He gets right to the point. They told me you would do that. But where is Yohaba? I have looked forward to meeting her. Oh, there she is. As beautiful as her picture." He waved and smiled at Yohaba behind the truck. Then he saw Father Becker and his face darkened. "And there's the priest. The humble servant of God." He said something to his grandfather in Russian and the man grunted. "Yes," the young man continued. "The man who would rather spill over a waterfall tied to a cross than hurt the meanest of God's creatures. Look, Yevgeny," he said to his hulking friend, "they are all together. Makes you believe in astrology, doesn't it? All the planets aligning. All the asteroids, too, except for Elsa. How are you, Father Becker, my father's former friend?"

"Still alive, Vadim. Surprisingly."

"Come now. Don't tell me your feelings are hurt. Did you really think after the cathedral negotiations that my father would forgive and forget?"

"Or that I forget," added the grandfather with a look that would have skewered a wild pig. The grandfather said something to Yevgeny, and the big bodyguard waved at Father Becker and smiled.

"Forgiveness from you people? A fool's hope," said the priest.

Rulon broke in. "Maybe you should start with why you flew all the way over here and why we are meeting on a mountain road."

"To save the world for socialism," said the young Russian. When he didn't get a reaction, he laughed and said, "Actually, we flew here in my father's private jet. We're the very embodiment of capitalism. We're hoping we'll have you and your wife's company when we go back. There is something important we need to do together. This thing with Elsa, do you believe it's real?"

"Why are we meeting here? On this road?" Rulon asked again.

The Russian didn't immediately answer, instead turning to his grandfather and Yevgeny to exchange words in Russian. Again there was a discussion and an apparent disagreement, loud enough for Yohaba to hear as she was only ten feet away.

Yohaba spoke up. "They're arguing over how much to tell you."

Vadim looked up at Yohaba's words and said to Rulon, "Ah! She speaks Russian. I wish the agencies we bribe would update their files." He jerked his head towards Yevgeny. "All my father's people are obsessed with secrecy. Me, I'm more transparent. My father says that's the beauty of capitalism in a democracy. If you get enough votes anything can be made legal, and there's no need for hiding. My father told me to tell you we're honest crooks. When we are bribed, we stay bribed. Haha!

"My name is Vadim Polykov. You can look me up on Google under *Russian oligarch's playboy son trashes London hotel room.* I may even be in Wikipedia. Haha! Yes, we've been following the priest. So what? It's not like he didn't know we were following him. Somewhere in his devious little mind, we are probably all pawns on his chessboard as we delude ourselves that he is on ours. As usual when we Russians are involved, there are many chess games going on at once, but that should surprise no one." The young Russian paused for a few seconds to gauge the reaction to his words. When no one moved or spoke, he said, "This road would not have been my preferred meeting spot, but my father said time was of the essence."

Before Rulon could respond, Yevgeny asked, "Who is he?" indicating Brother-in-law. He'd been staring at Brother-in-law since he got out of the Suburban. Brother-in-law tended to have that effect on people.

"I'm the comic sidekick," said Brother-in-law, as he slowly uncoiled from leaning on the truck.

"He's a friend," said Rulon. "What's the matter?"

"Is he well? He looks like something the dog dragged in."

"Ah'm in ma prime," said Brother-in-law, standing loose and easy.

"Yevgeny!" Vadim said. "Stay out of it! No insulting the Americans. You were to follow my orders. Remember?"

"For crying out loud," Rulon half-shouted, his exasperation fueled by worry over how Brother-in-law might react. "Why the bejeebers are you here? Can we get to it?"

Vadim said, "I have a story to tell you. After which you will help us. You don't think so now. But you will. Forget the lies the priest has told you. Even the extraordinarily difficult Father Becker will help us eventually. I promise you. Can we go somewhere to talk? It looks like it's going to rain." He looked up at the sky. "Or maybe snow."

Rulon consulted with Yohaba and Brother-in-law for a short minute then said to Vadim, "If you want, you can drive back with us in the truck. Just you, me, and Yohaba. That suit ya?"

"That suits me right fine," said Vadim with a big grin and a wink at Yohaba, proud to be showing off his proper use of the vernacular. "But I need to consult with my entourage. They're very protective." Vadim stepped away and talked or, rather, argued with Yevgeny while his grandfather listened in. Again Yevgeny was overruled, but the grandfather said nothing. The young Russian walked over to Rulon's truck and stood defiantly by the door.

Yevgeny fuming at the disrespect, looked around for an outlet, and fixed his stare on Rulon. He said, "For many Russians, dealing with you would be patriotic act."

"Well, they would still have to take a number like everyone else," said Rulon.

"Knock it off, Yevgeny," ordered Vadim. He asked Rulon, "Can we please go now?"

Yevgeny, looking disgusted, reached for the SUV's handle, but suddenly Brother-in-law's twangy voice, surly and hostile, froze him in his tracks.

"Hey, Comrade," he crooned.

The big Russian paused, his hand six inches from the handle. He slowly turned and in a deep, confident voice said, "Are you talking to me?"

"Yep. Ah could'a been pract'ly home by now if ah didn't have to pussyfoot around here with you polecats."

"What?" said the big Russian, not understanding the reference but sensing it was an insult.

"So, you owe me five bucks for ma time." This Yevgeny understood perfectly well.

The Russian stopped and said to Rulon in his heavily accented English, "I suggest you put a leash on him before he gets hurt."

Rulon spoke calmly and low to Brother-in-law. "Don't do this. Be nice."

"He gives me five bucks," Brother-in-law said. "Then I'll be nice." With that, he gave a command, and Tripod instantly transformed into a raging devil, something Rulon had never seen him do. The dog strained as if against an invisible leash to reach Yevgeny, the hair on his arched back charged and rippling, beside himself with rage, snarling and barking, saliva dripping, his single evil eye fixed on the big Russian but seemingly unable to lift his feet, as if they were stuck in cement. Brother-in-law said with a laugh, "You can pet him. He don't bite."

"Anybody got five bucks?" Rulon shouted over the din.

Behind him Yohaba checked her wallet. "Just a couple of twenties. Sorry."

"Vow of poverty," said Father Becker.

Brother-in-law deadpanned, "It has to come from a comrade." The big Russian's face went hard. He casually pulled back his jacket so Brother-in-law could see the MP445 Varjag .40 automatic in his waistband.

In response, Brother-in-law reached behind his back with his left hand and pulled his jacket away to reveal a faded, threadbare t-shirt with the words *Fortunate Son* across the front and a 1972 Browning Medalist .22 revolver in a holster on his hip. He stood there, one hand behind him gripping his coat to keep it from interfering with his draw, the other hand hanging free and easy with the butt of the pistol sitting halfway between his wrist and elbow.

"Geez," Rulon yelled. "What's gotten into you? Have you gone crazy? Everybody back." As he spoke, he herded Yohaba away from Brother-in-law. Tripod was still going at it.

"What's Brother-in-law up to?" asked Yohaba, but all she got from Rulon was a look that told her she'd said something wrong. By now Vadim was standing next to her.

"Don't push," said the big Russian to Brother-in-law, his face rock hard.

Vadim ordered, "Yevgeny! Get in the van. No games." The grandfather, looking amused, had his hands in the pockets of his black, knee-length overcoat and said nothing.

"I wouldn't touch that car if I were you," Brother-in-law said.

Vadim started to move forward, but Yohaba stopped him with a hand on his arm. "We need to stay out of it," she whispered. "Let the Alpha males work things out."

"No," said Vadim. "Yevgeny is a hot head. This is not good." Then turning to Yevgeny he yelled in Russian, "Do what I tell you! He's not going to shoot you. Just get in the van."

Yevgeny maintained a cool smile. "Sorry, no cash," he said and turned away.

"Ah'll take a credit card," said a relaxed Brother-in-law.

Yevgeny stopped and turned back to Brother-in-law again, fury whipped by pride etched plainly on his face. He was a flicker away from grabbing his gun, until Vadim barked at him again. Instead, exercising massive self-control, he again reached for the door handle. Brother-in-law gave another command and Tripod went deadly quiet and stared at Yevgeny, saliva still dripping down his misshapen teeth and over his disfigured lips to the ground.

Yevgeny paused and looked Brother-in-law in the eye, saw a crazy light in there pulsing away, and suddenly was afraid. He swallowed and said, "You're crazy."

"I don't rightly know. Am I?" Brother-in-law asked, sounding genuinely curious. Yevgeny didn't move. Didn't blink. Didn't breathe. Somebody in the car rolled down the window and said something, but Yevgeny didn't acknowledge. Brother-in-law pulled his jacket a little further back to give his gun hand more room. "In the whole wide world, you got two choices. You know what they are. Even if no one else does." He laughed. "Hey, maybe I am crazy."

Suddenly eternity seemed pretty close and everyone stood frozen watching each other, not knowing how this was going to turn out. There were more armed men behind the tinted windows of the SUV. That was a lot of fire power just a few feet away. A recipe for a bloodbath. Surely the crazy hillbilly knew that. You would think.

The grandfather waved Vadim over, took out his wallet, and handed Vadim a credit card. Vadim walked over to Brother-in-law, swore an oath, and threw the credit card on the ground at his feet. "Animal," he said furiously. "We came here in peace. You're a maniac."

"Ah'm just a simple country boy, son," said Brother-in-law. Without taking his eyes off the big bodyguard, Brother-in-law crouched down and picked up the credit card. He turned it over as if inspecting it. "Gold card. Cool. You must be rich. Ah'm so poor ah couldn't buy hay for a nightmare." He turned it over in his hand a few times and said, "Fix yer peepers on this," then flipped the card up and away like a Frisbee. Every eye followed the spinning, sailing card as if mesmerized. Just before it hit the ground eight yards away, Brother-in-law drew and fired in a blur of speed, like the snap of a mousetrap, so quickly, so unexpectedly, that everyone except Tripod and

Rulon, who had a good guess what was coming, jumped at the crack. Dirt kicked up and the card shot off in a different direction to be caught in some cheat grass near the cliff edge.

Brother-in-law twirled the pistol in his hand with a flourish and returned it to his holster.

At the sound of the shot, three men in suits scrambled out of the car with guns drawn. Rulon and Yohaba whipped out their pistols in response. Becker hid behind the truck. Brother-in-law held up one hand while still gripping the butt of his holstered .22 with the other.

"*Stoyte*! Halt!" he said in a voice of command. And halt they all did, in their tracks, frozen and looking at each other, wondering why they were obeying this skinny, ragtag nobody. *All under Brother-in-law's spell*, thought Rulon observing the scene.

Vadim quickly stepped in to defuse the situation. "Everyone in the car! Back in the car! Everything is fine," he shouted. They looked to Yevgeny for confirmation, but he was staring at Brother-in-law. No one moved.

"I was just funning," Brother-in-law said with a hint of a smile. "That's all. You can all get back in your rented vehic-le." At that the tension deflated. "Go on now," he gently prodded and the bodyguards did as they were told.

Along with everyone else, Yevgeny got into the van, pausing with one foot in just long enough to cast a murderous look back at Brother-in-law. Once inside, he looked down at his feet, fuming at the humiliation. In the quiet of the van, one of the three men in the back said in Russian, "That skinny guy is scary good with a gun, don't you think?"

"Shut up," Yevgeny said.

The same guy asked, "The big guy. Is that Rulon Hurt?" Yevgeny didn't answer but another man grumbled an affirmative. The man with the big mouth continued. "He doesn't look so tough. I'd like a piece of him."

At that, everyone in the car burst out laughing, including Yevgeny. Somebody slapped the man alongside the head. "Hey, what's so funny?" he asked.

Yevgeny exhaled deeply and said, "You're so tough, make yourself useful, find out who the skinny guy is. The woman called him Brother-in-law. Her maiden name was Meleksen. See if they're related. Track that down. Marines, SEALs, Rangers. He's got to be ex-military."

Meanwhile, Rulon had wandered over and picked up the abused credit card. He whistled, peered through a neat hole and held it up for all to see. "Hey, whadya know? Missed the magnetic strip. No harm done." He walked over to the grandfather and handed it back.

"I'll talk to him," Rulon said in a near whisper as the old man put the card back in his wallet. "He's protective. Gets these funny ideas sometimes. Takes things personally. But your guy did the mature thing. Tell him for me he has my respect."

Vladimir stared at Rulon without expression, but Vadim seethed, "We come here. All this way to discuss something serious. There was no reason for this. No reason. This was totally unprofessional."

"This is like to deal with Chechnyans," said the grandfather in fractured but understandable English. He spat on the ground.

"I couldn't agree more," Rulon said. "I'll talk to him so it doesn't happen again." Rulon noticed Vadim staring hard at Brother-in-law and said in a panicked tone, "No, no. Don't look at him. Don't make eye contact." Vadim quickly looked away, and Rulon, struggling hard not to laugh, continued talking to the grandfather. "C'mon. Let's forget it. You wanted to talk to us. You came all this way. Don't let something like this ruin it. Don't give him the satisfaction. Let Junior here drive back with us like we planned. He'll be safe. You have my word." To add emphasis, Rulon glared mightily at Brother-in-law, who waved at him dismissively while he chatted with Yohaba.

The old man grunted and said, "Ask the boy."

"Yes, absolutely. I'm coming," said an unnerved Vadim, still struggling to control his temper. "But you tell him and make sure he understands. We may be bad guys but we're not the enemy. Not this time. And you tell him we can play rough too if we have to."

Rulon glanced at Brother-in-law, who was now absently stroking Tripod's head and grinning at something Yohaba was saying. "I'll tell him," said Rulon, "but I really don't think he cares."

Chapter 7

Yohaba and Rulon stood together waiting for Vadim, who was over by the Suburban explaining to Yevgeny and the other men what was happening. When Vadim came over to the truck, Rulon asked him to stand still so he could search him. The boy protested, but Rulon said, "Simmer down, Junior. You're not getting in the same truck with my wife unless I search you. Now raise your arms."

Vadim reluctantly complied and after a quick but expert pat down, he climbed into the old Chevy between Rulon and Yohaba. They drove out of the turnout, tires crunching gravel, followed by the Suburban. Brother-in-law brought up the rear in his supersonic VW with Becker sitting next to him. Tripod was relegated to the small back seat and not liking it.

In the truck, no one spoke for a mile until Rulon jerked his head up with a start as if suddenly waking up. "Wow," he said, "that was a weird dream."

Vadim looked at him anxiously then said to Yohaba. "Maybe you should drive."

Yohaba reached behind Vadim and slapped Rulon on the back of the head. "No, my husband's just pulling your leg. That's what passes for a sense of humor here in Idaho."

"You remind me of my kid brother," said a smiling Rulon.

"In case you're wondering, that was an insult," said Yohaba.

"No, it wasn't," Rulon said. "But let's drop it."

"Yes, it was," said Yohaba in a stage whisper.

"Your friend is strange," Vadim said, referring to Brother-in-law. "Is there something wrong with him?"

"Yes," said Rulon at the same time as Yohaba said, "No."

Yohaba said, "Why don't you start out by telling us who you are?"

Vadim tapped his fingers on the thick coat folded neatly on his lap. He looked around nervously. Rulon couldn't tell if he was nervous because he was fearful for his safety or because he was afraid of getting his Brioni suit dirty.

"How'd your family get all its money?" Rulon asked, trying to lubricate the conversation with an easy question. As he spoke, he adjusted the rearview mirror so he could see Vadim's face. "What are you guys anyway?"

Vadim nervously played with a gaudy ring on his left thumb. "My father is in the oil and natural gas business. Don't judge. Russia is not America. We will not apologize or explain ourselves to anyone. But we need your help for something and you need ours. I told you before, you may not realize it, but we are going to be allies before this is over, and you are going to have to make a choice about whom to trust."

"Okay, let's start with the basics," said Yohaba. "Is your father part of the Russian mafia?"

"I don't know what you mean. There has been no mafia in Russia for fifteen years," said Vadim proudly.

"C'mon," said Rulon. "Are you trying to tell me there's nobody in Russia anymore who kills, kidnaps, and blackmails for power and money?"

"Of course there is. But those are the government agencies, not the mafia."

Rulon and Yohaba gave each other a look. Rulon asked, "Okay then, which government agency does your father belong to?"

"Go easy on the kid," said Yohaba.

"He is Gazprom, not an agency," said Vadim, not taking offense. "He's got the whole Yamal peninsula. But aren't we getting off track?"

"Yes, we are a bit," said Yohaba, "but I just have one more question. How does that work in real life? If you don't pay your protection money on time, who comes to threaten you?"

"That would be the police," said Vadim. "It's very well organized."

Yohaba paused for a beat to consider his answer then said, "So your father really is an oligarch then. You have a private jet. Do you also have a thug army?"

Vadim smiled. "Yes, definitely. It's part of the cost of doing business in Russia. But I prefer to think of my father as a—"

Yohaba cut him off. "Robber baron?" she suggested.

"Blood sucking capitalist?" offered Rulon.

"No, no. These are supposed to be insults, right? But no, I was going to say 'business tycoon.'"

"That works," said Yohaba. "Okay, we've got a three-hour drive ahead of us and a broken radio. Just do us one favor."

"What's that?" Vadim asked.

"We most likely won't believe you no matter what you say but make it a good story anyway. Okay?"

Vadim laughed. "You have no idea. The world as we know it is going to end in two weeks. How's that for a beginning?"

"No, Elsa's not going to hit until April 13th, 2029," said Yohaba. "If you don't know that much, you don't know my grandfather."

"I know your grandfather very well," Vadim said. "Or at least my father does. But no, it's not Elsa you should be worried about. Your grandfather is bringing down the temple. He's arranged for something of his own creation to happen in two weeks, something catastrophic."

Rulon flexed his fingers on the steering wheel. "Okay. Good beginning." Ever since they'd stalked the bear, the day had had a surreal quality. The bear charging silently down the hill. Them jumping in the lake. The slow motion plunging into the icy depths. Brother-in-law. The priest. Then the Russians showing up. Brother-in-law in his hillbilly alter ego. Tripod acting like a hound from hell. Now the world's imminent demise. A weird symmetry. "I'll bite. How is the world supposed to end in two weeks?"

"Steenberg's got his hands on a nuclear weapon and he's planning to use it," said Vadim slowly and dramatically. "The world's not really going to end. I just said that for dramatic effect. But it's going to be turned upside-down. That's his goal." When neither Rulon nor Yohaba reacted, a bewildered Vadim said, "Doesn't that bother you!?"

"It would if I believed you," Yohaba said. "But I don't believe you. Now Rulon here, he's more trusting than me. He believes you but he's probably wrestling over whether nuclear weapons are protected by the second amendment."

"Oh, they're definitely protected," interjected Rulon with conviction, "though in Leonard's case I'd insist on a three-day waiting period."

"My husband," said Yohaba beaming. "A voice of reason in an age of insanity."

"Neither of you believes me, do you?" Vadim said.

"Nope," they answered in unison.

"If you want to convince Rulon," said Yohaba, "you're going to have to do better than that."

"I'm telling the truth!" Vadim said. "We don't have all the details but the thing is a monster. It started out small, but he's got it rigged to blow sixty times bigger than it should." At the mention of sixty, Yohaba and Rulon caught each other's eye over Vadim's head. Sixty was the yield increase Steenberg had calculated from Einstein's equation.

"Ask yourself," pleaded Vadim. "What's a private citizen doing with a nuclear weapon? Why does he want one in the first place? And who's he been hanging around with? Could *you* just wake up one day and get your hands on a nuclear weapon?"

Rulon listened to Vadim and thought, *Maybe he's telling the truth.* Leonard could be very secretive sometimes. He noticed Yohaba wasn't leaning away from Vadim like she had with Father Becker. It was wise of the Russians to send someone so young.

"Your grandfather has a finger in many pies these days," Vadim said. "I don't care what the priest has told you. That so-called man of God cannot be trusted. Did he tell you about Steenberg and the Chinese?"

"A little," Rulon said. "But why don't you tell us your version?"

"This is not a version. This is the way it is," Vadim said.

♥♥♥

Several hours later they pulled into the Hurt family ranch in the flatlands along some hills about thirty miles northeast of Twin Falls. Rulon let out a big breath and turned off the engine. To the east the last of the sunlight was disappearing from the bare, purple hills. Yohaba jumped out to greet Major, their lab mix, who came barking and bounding off the porch. Vadim and Rulon stayed in the truck. The lights were on in the kitchen.

Rulon said, "Looks like Dad's cooking dinner."

While Yohaba played with Major, Rulon pondered the possibilities. Was Leonard still trying to save the world or had the temptation of all the sudden money and power been too much for him? Rulon didn't want to believe Vadim, but Leonard had always been ultra-secretive. And it was hard to get to the bottom of anything with him. If you disagreed with him on any subject, you had to be wrong. He knew it, and you knew it. Maddening.

Vadim started to get out, but Rulon grabbed his arm and said, "Wait a sec."

Rulon tended to categorize situations in moral terms. From his perspective, most of the world's woes were the result of sin. And most of the good things were the result of repentance and obedience to good principles. It was a simple way of looking at people and events, but in Rulon's thirty-five years of observing human behavior it seemed to work as well as any of the other more complex constructs claiming to explain human nature. If Steenberg had gone over to the dark side after years of being good, well, it was a sad story but one that had been repeated many times before throughout history. Again, he thought maybe Vadim was telling the truth. *But a nuclear bomb?*

Still sitting in the truck, Rulon said to Vadim, "If we lead your people to Leonard, they'll kill him."

Vadim hesitated before he answered. "We think we know where he is. If my father wanted him dead, he'd be dead already. You of all people should know this. My father told me you were no pilgrim." Vadim gave a little laugh, again pleased with himself for his mastery of the cowboy lingo.

"Maybe," Rulon chuckled. Then he continued seriously, "But that doesn't give me a reason to believe you."

"Then how about this? Money. We make money if he is alive, no money if he's dead. It's that simple. Now if it turns out he's double-crossing us then, yes, my father will have a major problem with him, but I don't think that's going to be the case. I've never met him, but my father doesn't think he would ever double-cross anyone. Which is strange for my father because he normally is not trustful."

"We feel the same way about Leonard, and that's why none of this is adding up," Rulon said.

"That's exactly why my father sent me. This isn't making sense. You have heard of dogs who are fear biters? My father told me to tell you that people can be like that too, and right now Steenberg is making a lot of violent people, people with resources, very fearful. Not just my father. I didn't want to say this in front of Yohaba—" Vadim looked quickly at Rulon to see if he'd object to him using her first name. He didn't. "—but we're giving you a fair and honest chance to save Steenberg's life and time is running out."

"And Becker. What about him?"

"He betrayed us once, but he's a priest. He's off limits."

"Still working on Rulon, I see," said Yohaba, having come back and stuck her head in the truck window. "We're not getting in your fancy plane no matter what, so you can just forget it."

"Why not? It's a Gulfstream 550. We flew non-stop all the way from Moscow. Better than first class." When he saw Yohaba was not impressed, he added enticingly, "Gold-plated seatbelt fittings." Yohaba laughed.

Vadim pressed. "If your grandfather won't see you, you can stop in and see your grandmother and brother. Come with us to Switzerland. We think your grandfather is staying in a massive chalet near Stein am Rhein. Very bucolic. Green hills and lots of cows. Very Swiss." Rulon and Yohaba both noted that Father Becker and Vadim agreed that Steenberg was at Stein am Rhein.

Vadim reached under his coat and handed Yohaba a plain white envelope. She opened it to find half a dozen photographs, each with a brief description on the back. One said 'Flood waters in Thailand.' Another said 'Wrecked nuclear reactor,' and another 'Burned German windmill factory.' There were more. There was also a folded, hand-written letter.

"It's from my father," said Vadim. "Go ahead. Read it out loud."

She did.

"Leonard, my friend,

We have come so far together. Why have you abandoned us now? Was the money not good enough? If so, we can solve that. In truth, we have made even more than we anticipated. What are you up to? You are making us nervous. We have heard things. We need to talk. Meet with us. We wish you no harm."

Underneath were a phone number and an illegible signature.

"We would like you to give this to him. That's all," said Vadim.

"Why not mail it to him?" asked Rulon.

"We cannot use surface mail, phones, or email," replied Vadim. "Nothing is safe."

"That's baloney," Rulon said. "You just have to know what you're doing. We'll think about it. In the meantime, do you want to stay for dinner?"

"Sure!" said Vadim. He and Rulon got out of the truck and went over to the Suburban where Vadim's men were milling around and smoking. The grandfather was also there.

Rulon said to him, "Your boys are invited for dinner, but they can't smoke inside, and I don't want to see any butts on the ground."

The grandfather nodded sternly at Vadim, and the young man gave the orders to the men. Yevgeny and his men put out and field stripped their cigarettes and put the filters in their pocket. *Ex-military*, noted Rulon. Everyone followed him and Yohaba into the house.

In the kitchen, an old man in well-worn bib overalls with a bushy white beard hunched over the stove. There was a faint tang of manure in the air.

"Listen up, everyone," said Rulon from the doorway. "This is…well, why don't all of you just call him Mr. Hurt." Then louder, he said, "Hey, Dad. We have company."

"Yohaba already told me," said the old man without looking up.

"This is my father," announced Rulon to the small crowd now pushing into the kitchen. "The unflappable Mr. Hurt."

At Rulon's comment, his father shot him a frown. "How many this time?"

"Seven extra, but your little buddy"—referring to Brother-in-law—"hasn't shown up yet. I have no idea what he's up to." Mr. Hurt walked over to the refrigerator and started to pull out a cooked turkey sitting in a pan. "One more thing," said Rulon. His father paused with his hands on the turkey. "They're Russians."

Without a word, Mr. Hurt reversed direction, slid the turkey back in the refrigerator, walked over to the pantry, and grabbed half a dozen cans of beans. From a hook on the wall, he took down a bigger pot, opened one of the cans, and dumped it in. He said, "They'll like beans just fine."

Yohaba pushed past him and pulled out the turkey. "Dad, c'mon," she said. "Remember Boris. He was Russian, and he was a good guy. He kept his promise to you, don't forget."

"He ate like a horse," grumbled Mr. Hurt.

Chapter 8

It was 2 a.m. at the Moscow politsiya headquarters on Okhotnoy Ryad, and Boris Zokolov sat behind the desk looking bored while he waited for the next question. Across from him sat soon-to-be-retired plainclothes detective Amare Brokhin and a square-faced agent from ODON, the feared Independent Division of Operational Purpose. Detective Brokhin scribbled Boris's previous answer in his little notepad with a worn-down pencil. The ODON agent next to him had a hand under the table out of sight, gripping a MP-433 Grach automatic on his lap.

Detective Brokhin looked up. "So then, let's start from the beginning. What is your full name?"

"Illya Kuryakin," said Boris.

"Yes, a little humor, Mr. Zokolov. Thank you," said Brokhin. "Is that Kuryakin spelt Z-o-k-o-l-o-v?

Boris nodded.

"So, you were at a…what did you call it?…a cage match, when Lieutenant Shevernenko fell down the stairs in his apartment, broke his hip, shattered his jaw, suffered four broken ribs, and a serious concussion."

"Yes."

"And you have witnesses who can attest to your whereabouts?"

"Yes. Hundreds. Even more."

Brokhim smiled at the answer then went on patiently. "And six months before that when Lieutenant Aksentyev was found unconscious just before he was to board his flight to—"

Boris interrupted. "How's he doing?"

Detective Brokhin stopped writing. "He's walking now." Boris nodded, satisfied, and the detective continued. "Did you know him?"

"I bumped into him once."

"And when Lieutenant Ivankov got out of the hospital and abruptly quit his commission, you had nothing to do with that whole ugly episode either?"

"I've answered that question every six months since his accident."

"Please answer it again."

"I am sorry for his misfortunes, but I do not know the man, and he does not know me."

"Yes, he swears with sweat running down his face and his eyes darting back and forth like a caged rat that he never met you, never saw you, never heard of you, never knew anyone who knew you, or could even imagine a person such as you in his wildest dreams." The detective paused and laid the pencil on the desk. "Well, what's the point in going on?"

"Yes, very true. I guess that's all then," Boris said, "until some other clumsy oaf has an accident." He leaned forward in his chair as a prelude to standing up. Beneath the tabletop, the agent from ODON flipped off the safety of his pistol, just in case Boris decided to leap across the table at them. Boris heard the click and smiled.

Detective Brokhin closed his notepad and stuck the pencil behind his ear. He slouched in his rumpled blue suit and tapped his finger on the desk.

"Why?" he asked.

"Why what?" asked Boris with an exasperated sigh. He settled back down.

"Why are you systematically beating these people half to death just before they are to go to America?"

"If someone is spreading lies about me, I'd like to know who they are."

"Yes, and, no doubt, their addresses as well," said Brokhin drily.

"Moscow is a dangerous place with the Bratva running loose and their ongoing bitch wars," Boris said. "Some men fell down some stairs in Moscow. So what? I'm sure somewhere in this city someone is jaywalking too."

Brokhin was only half listening. He'd become distracted by the ornate tattoos spilling out from under Boris's collar and shirt sleeves. He said, "They say you can tell a man's rank in the Vorovski Mir by his tattoos, but I never learned the code."

"Google it," said Boris. "Seriously, it's on Google. Just like everybody's address. Even yours."

"I understand that you no longer work for the SVR," Brokhin said, ignoring the implied threat. "Why is that?"

Boris shrugged.

When he made no reply, Brokhin said, "You disappoint me, Mr. Zokolov. I had hoped for more candor."

"You want candor. Here is candor," Boris said. "I have vindictive friends with long memories."

Brokhin chuckled. "And yet you are here." In response, Boris got up and walked out.

After Boris left, the inspector turned to the agent from ODON and asked, "What did you think?"

As the square-faced man put his gun back in his shoulder holster, he said, "Why didn't you tell me you were questioning Boris Zokolov? Are you crazy? Next time go by yourself."

❦

Once on the street, Boris waited for a few seconds while a black Mercedes half a block away pulled out of its parking place and pulled up in front of the politsiya station. Boris got in and the car drove off.

Once inside, Boris looked at his watch and did a quick time zone calculation. Ten hours ahead of Idaho. Should be about right. He pulled out his cell phone and texted a message. *How is she? Did you get any pictures?*

Back in Rulon's kitchen Vadim took out his cell phone, saw the message, and snapped a few quick pictures of Yohaba as she worked over the stove. "For posterity," he said when she caught him at it. "Smile," he said, and she did.

❦

After dinner, everyone wandered outside except Mr. Hurt and one of the bodyguards, who stayed behind doing the dishes under the old man's watchful eye. Yevgeny, the driver, and the other two bodyguards wandered over to the corral for a cigarette and to watch the horses. Rulon and Yohaba relaxed on the porch with Vladimir and Vadim. Brother-in-law and Becker still hadn't shown up. The air was still and the night was cool but about twenty degrees warmer than the mountains. At one point, Mr. Hurt stuck his head out the door and announced he was going to bed because someone had to get up early and milk the cows, and it sure would be nice if the Rooskie watching TV would remember to keep the sound down. And no watching MTV.

While they sat there, Brother-in-law drove up with his headlights off and parked close to the barn. A thin trail of black smoke rose from the rear engine compartment. Brother-in-law and Becker got out. Becker came over to sit on the porch with everyone else.

"We had car trouble," he said. Everyone watched as Brother-in-law opened the rear engine lid and peered inside.

Rulon walked over and the two men huddled together for ten minutes before determining it was the carburetor's electric choke. Brother-in-law closed the lid, got in the car and steered it into the barn while Rulon pushed. Brother-in-law came out a few minutes later in running shoes with his large duffle bag on his back and carrying an HK MP5. He jogged off without a word or a backward glance with Tripod loping along silently beside him. A minute later Rulon came out of the barn and returned to the porch.

"Where's he going?" asked Vadim.

"Checking the hills for snipers, I imagine," said Rulon.

"Here," laughed Vadim. "This is the middle of nowhere. Wow! I thought my father was paranoid. Haha! Has he ever found any? Haha!"

"Not so many lately," said Rulon as he absently touched the spot on his head where he'd once taken a sniper's bullet from those very hills.

"Oh," said Vadim.

"I think word's gotten out," added Yohaba.

Rulon looked around. "I'm bored," he said. "Anyone want to play Rummikubs?"

೧⊙೧

The eyes of the Russians leaning on the corral fence followed Brother-in-law as he disappeared into the night. Yevgeny's especially bored after him with a mixture of hate and puzzlement. "He's ex-military," said Yevgeny.

"Definitely ex-military. He was playing me with that hillbilly nonsense."

After a few minutes of silence, Mikhael, the driver, said, "This place is weird. It's like Marlboro man meets…meets that American sitcom from the sixties? The one with the perfect family and the little kid who kept getting in trouble. The one I was telling you about."

"You mean *Leave it to Beaver*," said Ivan, one of the bodyguards.

"Yeah, that's it," said Mikhael. "This is like Marlboro Man meets *Leave it to Beaver*."

"I was thinking the same thing only different," said Tomas, another bodyguard, as he fumbled with his lighter and another cigarette.

"Where do you think he's going?" asked Ivan.

"Not squirrel hunting," replied Yevgeny. "Have you found anything out yet?"

"Ah, give me some peace, man," Ivan pleaded. "I've got people working on it, top people. But you have to give them at least a day. So far all they've got is that Hurt had a twin sister who died when he was three so no brother-in-law's there. And there are no brother-in-law's on the woman's side. She's got one retarded brother and no sisters. The fact that he's someone's brother-in-law is not a lot to go on."

"Who's working on it?" asked Yevgeny. Ivan gave him two names and Yevgeny grunted approval.

A couple of cigarettes later, Ivan said, "The kid's driving me crazy. Do you see the way he hangs around the Cowboy's woman? I swear he's got a crush on her."

"Not like the rest of us, huh?" said Tomas with a laugh.

Ivan kept at it. "What was his old man thinking, putting a kid in charge?"

"Better him than you," said Yevgeny, who had been staring into the dark lost in thought. "The old man knows what he's doing. We're inside the ranch, right? The plan's more or less working, right? It's the priest you should be thinking about. If he doesn't at least plant the bugs, this whole trip has been a waste."

Just then a flare went off in the distant sky in the direction Brother-in-law was last seen. Everyone watched it drift slowly to the ground. "Give me a break," said Mikhael. "What's he up to out there?"

"Can this place get any weirder?" said Tomas.

After another silent minute while everyone smoked, Ivan said in disgust, "And that dog! Man, that dog is like some kind of extraterrestrial mutant." Subdued laughter.

"Makes the Chechnyan mutts look like show dogs," added Tomas.

"Yeah, and did you catch those teeth?" said Mikhael. "What do you think happened to him?"

"Afghanistan, I'm guessing," said Yevgeny, only half listening. "A retired hair missile."

"Right," said Mikhael slowly as he considered the implications of Yevgeny's answer. "Haha! When you add everything up, maybe it's us who are walking into a trap." A short, reflexive laugh from everyone followed by a long, pensive silence.

After a while, Ivan said, "The guy ran like a cockroach with that bag on his back and that thing hanging around his neck. What was that anyway?"

"Night vision goggles," said Tomas. "Four tubes. Really expensive. That's what they used in *Zero Dark Thirty*. I wonder how he got his hands on them."

"There's a clue for you," said Yevgeny to Ivan after a drag on his cigarette and a long exhale. "Find out which service branch uses them. Start with the SEALs."

Before Ivan could respond, a burst of laughter erupted from the porch, Vladimir's hearty laugh booming over everyone else's. The men at the corral all turned to look. The Rummikub game was in full swing.

"Can this place get any weirder?" asked Tomas again.

ꙮꙮꙮ

Up in the hills on the opposite side of the ranch from where the flare had gone off, Brother-in-law sat on his haunches in the dark sipping a water bottle and nibbling an energy bar. Tripod rested his head heavily on the man's shoulder, striving now and then to steal a bite. Below them, the partially obscured moon cast its light across the dark valley, the corrals, and the lit-up ranch. Occasionally, the wind carried the sound of voices and laughter, reminding Brother-in-law of the sound of African villages—which were usually happy places until they weren't.

His thoughts drifted to Haut-Uele in the Congo, a district where he'd fought the LRA during his second tour. "Stop me if you've heard this one before," he said, and then told Tripod the story about the village he'd come across where all the women had had their ears and lips cut off and all the children kidnapped and how he and his team had tracked them for sixty hours on five hours sleep and finally caught them just as they were crossing the Uele river. "I've done things," said Brother-in-law. "Yes, indeedy."

Tripod listened intently, his good ear just inches from Brother-in-law's mouth. When he was done, Brother-in-law gave him the rest of the energy bar and tucked the wrapper, the bottle, and the flare's remote detonator back into the duffle bag. He stood up and slipped on the four-tube night vision goggles. Tripod looked eager.

"Well, old buddy," Brother-in-law said. We've got another long night ahead of us. Let's get to it." Together they melted off into the bush.

☙❧

The Rummikub tournament went on for an hour and ended just before 9 p.m. Yohaba and Vadim had beaten Rulon and Father Becker while Vadim's grandfather looked on and gave unsolicited advice. Rulon, Yohaba, and the grandfather were now on good terms. Not only did they have a mutual interest in firearms, but during the course of the evening they discovered they had two mutual acquaintances in Boris Zokolov, a former Russian foreign service graduating class valedictorian, now gone over to the dark side, and Dmitry Pligin, who had worked for the SVR out of Zurich for years.

Yohaba glanced at her watch as the losing team collected the pieces and put away the game. She caught Rulon's attention and posed a question to him with her eyes. He nodded as he stacked the pieces, and she said to the grandfather, "It's getting late. Vadim says he's never ridden a horse before. If he wants to, you and he can stay the night and we can take him riding in the morning." To Father Becker she said, "You know you've got a room, if you want."

The priest quickly accepted the offer but Vladimir, back to his taciturn self, said, "Boy goes nowhere without guards."

"I understand," said Rulon. "but I'm afraid we've only got room for one of the guards. Unless the rest want to sleep in the barn."

Vadim conferred with his grandfather, and they agreed that Yevgeny would stay, the rest would drive back to Twin

Falls and return in the morning. The two Russians went inside to tell their men, who were watching TV. Father Becker asked where his suitcase was, said goodnight, and went to his room. Rulon and Yohaba were left by themselves on the porch.

Rulon moved over to the porch swing and Yohaba came over and sat next to him. She took off his hat and rubbed his ears with her hands. Rulon rolled his eyes and lolled his head. "This is like rubbing a crocodile's stomach only more so," said Yohaba. "You are in my power. You will do anything I say."

"Let's test that theory," said Rulon, suddenly perking up. "Order me to carry you off to bed." After a long kiss, Rulon said, "I hope you know what you are doing, Mrs. Hurt."

"Keep your enemies close," said Yohaba. "That's what you taught me."

"I never said that," protested Rulon. "Keeping your enemies close seems like a pretty stupid thing to do if you ask me. I say keep your enemies a thousand miles away on the other side of an ocean and nuke 'em if they try to cross."

"So why did you go along with it then?"

"I was hoping you knew what you were doing. Do you?"

"I want to give Becker time to plant all the bugs Brother-in-law found in his suitcase. He said to tell you they were a something B21."

"Did he say Edic-mini Tiny B21?"

"Yeah, that was it," said Yohaba.

"They're Russian made. What about a gun? Did he find a gun?"

"No, no gun."

"That means Becker came by commercial jet. Maybe, they're not all in cahoots after all."

"Or maybe they're just playing it smart."

"Which reminds me," said Rulon, "I found your panicked reaction to hearing your grandfather was kidnapped very convincing."

"As long as Becker was convinced," said Yohaba. "Do you think he was?"

"Maybe," said Rulon. "But now tell me why you invited Junior to stay?"

"He's never ridden a horse. Can you believe it?"

"He follows you around like a calf. Have you noticed?"

Yohaba smiled. "I think it's kind of cute. Maybe we can turn him away from the dark side."

"We'll baffle him with kindness," said Rulon.

Satisfied, Yohaba settled in closer and asked, "Why did you give me a look this afternoon when I asked you what Brother-in-law was up to?"

"You used his name," said Rulon. "And they heard it."

"That's not his name."

"In the circles these guys run around in, that's his name. Better if they don't know who they're dealing with."

"Okay, but after that fancy shooting, I think they know all they need to know about him. By the way, what was he trying to prove back there?"

"Friendship, I think."

"Friendship? I don't think so. I think they all want to kill him now."

"No, not friends with them. Did you notice he didn't speak up until that Yevgeny guy threatened me? He was trying to take the heat off of me. Make himself the target. Maybe make them so mad they wouldn't think straight. I don't know for sure, but it's something like that. Does that make sense?"

"In a weird sort of macho, parallel universe sort of way, yeah, I guess it does. But what would've happened if Yevgeny had gone for his gun?"

"There would have been a shootout. That's why it worked. And that's why Yevgeny didn't go for his gun. Yevgeny could sense that as stupid and pointless as it was, our boy was ready to go all the way."

"But all he had was a .22 and Yevgeny had a cannon," said Yohaba.

"Hmm…yeah, but I think that got Yevgeny thinking too. With only a .22, he knew Brother-in-law would have to go for a head shot. It was another way of saying he was playing for keeps. There was a lot of communicating going on back there. A lot more than just the words."

Yohaba thought about the ramifications of what Rulon said. After a few moments, she said, "He's not wired like the rest of us, is he?"

"No. You talk to him more than I do. Did he ever tell you he had two wives? That didn't faze him either."

"No way. He's too young."

"No, no. I mean he had two wives *at the same time*. They were from a tribe in the Congo called the Lubas. Polygamy's cool there. He really loved them, too. Had three kids and everything. I've seen the pictures."

"The military never would have gone for that," said Yohaba. "You're pulling my leg."

Rulon's face darkened. "You think so? The wives and one of the kids were killed by the LRA. He doesn't talk about it, but the other two kids were kidnapped. That's why he kept re-upping. Explains a lot, doesn't it? He had his SEAL team and a couple dozen husbands like him who had lost their families. He trained them. Led them. His team cleaned out entire districts and almost single-handedly backed the LRA into the Garamba National Park. The LRA had a bounty out on him. Even kidnapped witch doctors for extra protection from him. He'd still be there if another SEAL team hadn't tracked him down and convinced him to come back in. Ray told me about it." Rulon kept his voice low and told her the whole story.

By the time he was done, Yohaba's head was down, her shoulders were shaking, and her hair hung limp around her face. Rulon put his arm around her and let her softly cry herself out. Finally she sat up straight and wiped away her tears. "When did you find out? Why are you telling me this just now? Gosh, my heart is breaking for the guy. That is terrible beyond words. He's never talks about it. That's not good."

"I'm just glad he's on our side," said Rulon. "He'd make a really, really bad enemy."

"Can we try that again from a glass half-full perspective?" said a sniffling Yohaba.

"Okay. He makes a really, really good friend."

"Much better," said Yohaba, "but he should talk about stuff more."

"Why?" asked Rulon. "The fewer words the better, I say. 'Rulon tired. Bed. Us. Now.' See how clear that was? And only five words."

Chapter 9

Yohaba and Rulon lay in the dark with the windows open. Rulon was on his back with his hands behind his head and Yohaba was on her side talking and occasionally kissing him on his head and face.

"Did you get a hold of your grandfather?" asked Rulon.

"No," said Yohaba, "but I'm not surprised. If everything went according to plan, he's in his jet over the Atlantic now heading back to Idaho. "But we're agreed. Right?" she said after gently kissing Rulon's brow. "They're all lying."

"Agreed," said Rulon. "A little lower next time, darling. Would you mind?"

"What about Vadim?" asked Yohaba after a kiss to the tip of his nose. "Him, too?"

"Afraid so," said Rulon. "Though I think the crush he has on you is real."

Ignoring his comment, Yohaba said, "And we think Becker and the Russians are in cahoots. Right?"

"Agreed again," said Rulon. "Can we hurry this along?"

"Omigosh!" exclaimed Yohaba. "The bugs! Did you sweep this room?"

"Relax, darling," said Rulon. He reached over, felt around on the side table, and came up with a device shaped like an iPod with a blinking green light. "My Acme bug jammer is on the job. Good thing too. The guy must be some kind of voyeur. He's put more bugs in here than in the living room and kitchen combined."

"My hero," she said, and kissed him on the lips. After the kiss, she said, "Being married to you is just like that old frog in the boiling pot story. If I had just met you and had to worry about bugs, assassins, renegade priests, and Russian oligarchs, I would have gone screaming into the night."

"Don't forget grizzly bears."

"And grizzly bears," said Yohaba. "But now, I don't know, it just seems so…so normal."

"Part of the rich tapestry of life, darlin'," said Rulon. He put the bug jammer back on the side table and said, "Can we start focusing on something else now?"

"First, tell me why I love you so much," Yohaba said.

"It's simple," said Rulon. "I'm a wife whisperer. I have this power over women. It's a gift even I don't completely understand."

"That's totally insulting."

"I should be traveling around the country giving advice to husbands with difficult wives," said Rulon. "Here. I'll prove it." He leaned over and whispered something in her ear. Yohaba laughed and laughed.

∽∾∽∾

Winston Klendenin III, chairman of the board of IQ Storage, desperate father, blackmail victim, and now shooter of unarmed men, couldn't remember the last time he dared look himself in the mirror. Behind him, out of sight under the lip of the hill he was standing on, were three black Humvees. Around him were the mercenaries he'd assembled to make the snatch. The night was cold, and the wind was picking up. He looked up at the sky.

Thin clouds raced by, backlit by a silver moon. A couple of hills over a pack of coyotes yelped and crooned.

Leonard Steenberg had kidnapped his daughter. Well, he would kidnap Steenberg's granddaughter and see who blinked. Nothing personal about the girl, but Klendenin had already shot an innocent person and framed another one for attempted murder just to save the rest of his family. Now, kidnapping an innocent bystander hardly registered on his conscience. A self-made multi-billionaire, firmly entrenched in the military-industrial-energy complex, for the first time in his life he felt he was spending his money on something both personal and useful. He now had his own eleven-man team made up of former SEALs, Special Forces, and Marine Recon veterans. Below him was the Hurt ranch.

It had been forty-five minutes since Winston and his lethal team had all looked across the valley, stunned to see a military-grade parachute flare drifting slowly to the ground. Even from six hundred yards away it had turned the night into day. When nothing else happened, Winston assumed it was just a bunch of crazy Idaho cowboys having a good time on a Wednesday night. But the rest of the men were wary.

Winston was rich and for most of his career had been fawned over by the sycophants that surrounded him. Consequently, he had an inflated sense of himself as a leader of men, when really he was only a giver of gifts. Perhaps he had the potential to be more, but the men around him now judged their leaders according to a different standard. Deluded, but unable to shake the self-image that he was a man of action, he now decided it was time to take charge and settle the men down. He spoke up authoritatively.

"Let's go over the plan again, men." Everyone turned to look as if he'd just sprayed them with rotten fish oil.

Retired Special Forces Colonel William "Wild Will" Jefferson was the real leader of the team. He was fifty years old and still as fit as a bull, with short salt-and-pepper hair and a broad, flat face. He and his men all wore the latest Crye Combat uniforms. So did Klendenin, though it looked ridiculous on him. Long sleeves and cargo pants with ten pockets stuffed with all sorts of useful stuff. Winston was paying them well and had outfitted them with the best. But that didn't mean the men had to like him.

Wild Will knew the mood of the men and asked Winston to walk with him away from the group. Once they were out of earshot, Wild Will said in his flat Nebraska accent, "Mr. Klendenin. I would appreciate it—we would all appreciate it—if you would not talk to any of the men. I'm not happy you're here. We've discussed it. This is your show. I was overruled. So be it. But now we're going operational and I'm going to have to ask you to not say another word or you might get hurt. To the men here, you're just a royal pain in the ass. Do you understand what I'm saying?"

"Stop right there, Colonel," ordered Klendenin. "Who do you think you are talking to? I'm paying the bills."

"Yes, Mr. Klendenin, you are. And that meant an awful lot until we got here. Now, it's not about the money with these men. It's about getting the job done, and the way they see it, you're getting in the way. You're not part of the Brotherhood. I don't know how else to say it. So for right now, with all due respect, just shut up. Sir. We'll handle it. We're going to incapacitate everyone in the house and snatch the girl. It's not as easy as it sounds. These people are ranchers. There's still six males there now, three more than we expected. There's bound to be guns in the house. There's two dogs around. The one old man appears to have insomnia and gets up at all hours of the night. We're a little high-strung right now. So just keep quiet and let us do our job."

"What's the problem?" asked Winston. Truth was, Winston knew Wild Will was right, knew he was getting on the men's nerves, but didn't really understand why. "What have I done?"

Wild Will took off his black ski cap and twisted it in his hands. "Okay," he said, "it's like this. We're going to do the job, but the men aren't liking it. We'd rather be going after the kidnappers, if you know what I mean. But we understand what you are trying to do. So let's just not talk about it for now. Okay. Just remember, not another word, please, and we'll get through this."

Wild Will walked back to his men, leaving Winston on his own. One of the ex-Marines, a rangy, athletic-looking man sporting a trim, red goatee, said loud enough for Klendenin to hear. "If he says another word, I'm going to chew his face off."

Wild Will said, "Shut up, Murphy. I've had speaks with him. He got the message." He looked at his watch and said, "Listen up, everyone. It's on. We'll be hitting them at oh-three-thirty. In the meantime, we've got some time to kill. Let's go over the plan." The men gathered around and Winston sauntered over, too, but stayed on the periphery. Wild Will walked them step by step through the plan, drilling each of them on their responsibilities.

In the midst of answering a question, he suddenly held up his hand for quiet and pressed his throat mike. "Say again," he ordered. "Where? Are you sure? Damn! Can you cut him off? Damn!" Around him his men tensed. Wild Will broke off conversation with his sentry and yelled, "We've got trouble. There's a guy—" He stopped to point to a prominent outcropping on the next hill. "—over there, and he's got a listening device."

One hundred yards away as the crow flies, on the next hill, on a straight line of sight from Wild Will and the knot of men, Brother-in-law said to himself, *Time to go*. He took off his headphones and folded up the 20-inch parabolic dish. Tripod was on patrol somewhere in the bush. Once everything was back in its carrying case, Brother-in-law gave a low whistle in the song of a grasshopper sparrow and stealthily made his way down the opposite side of the hill from Wild Will's snatch team. After fifty yards, Tripod caught up, and they walked together for another fifty yards until they'd gone behind a stack of boulders and were out of view. Then the two of them changed direction and broke into an easy trot.

One hill over, Wild Will picked up Brother-in-law in the eerie green of his night vision goggles and saw him walk nonchalantly with Tripod down the hill and out of sight. He barked orders to the nearby men and the three sentries positioned in the surrounding hills to converge on the point where he thought Brother-in-law would emerge. For thirty minutes he listened in on their intra-team communications, sharing in the excitement of their false sightings and the frustration of their dashed hopes as they scattered through the hills with their own NVGs looking for Brother-in-law. At last, huffing and puffing from running up and down the rugged hills, they all returned with their reports, angry, baffled, and unsuccessful.

While his team cooled off around him, Wild Will compulsively checked his watch again and gave his field of view one more sweep with the goggles. The long-haired intruder with the injured dog was long gone. "Expect the unexpected," he said out loud to the heavily breathing men.

"A hippie with a sophisticated listening device and a three-legged dog. Yes, that was definitely unexpected," said Russo, a short man in full camo, face paint like

Rambo, and carrying the same type of four-barrel night-vision goggles that Brother-in-law had.

"By the way, Russo," said Wild Will. "You did a good job spotting him."

Russo acknowledged the compliment. "Just doing my job, Colonel."

Wild Will asked, "What do you think? Did he hear anything?"

"No question. He started folding up as soon as I alerted you."

"He knows the plan then, the timing, everything."

"That I don't know. I spotted him only a minute before I called it in. He might have just gotten set up. I don't know."

"So there is a chance he didn't hear much?"

"A chance," said Russo. "Another thing. When we couldn't find him, we ran to the ranch to cut him off, but he never came down that way. He must have gone in a different direction. It's possible he's got nothing to do with the ranch."

"If so, that's good news," said Wild Will. "What do you make of him?"

Russo ran a hand through his sweaty black hair before he answered. "At first I thought he was some kind of hippie pot farmer out checking his crop. But then when I saw the gear he had, I knew he was trouble. And the easy way he moved through the brush. Well, it was just plain eerie."

"And the flare," added Wild Will.

"And the flare," admitted Russo. "And I swear, it was a little hard to tell through the goggles, but I think he was wearing face paint and camo."

"Geez," said Wild Will. "What the hell is going on?"

"I don't know, Captain. This is Idaho. Doesn't necessarily mean what you think it means. He looked awfully scraggly. Could still be a goofy, high-tech pot farmer who spends all day playing paint ball and *Soldiers of Anarchy*."

"So you don't think we should call it off," asked Wild Will. "I'm worried we missed something."

"He's one guy."

"Yeah, one guy with a parabolic listening device and face paint. This isn't feeling right. We missed something." While they talked, the other men moved in closer.

Benny, the ex-Special Forces sniper, said, "What's the problem? We've got enough tranquilizer darts to drop a herd of elephants." All of them were armed with small automatic pistols, mainly to shoot in the air while they beat a retreat if things went sour, but also Cap-Chur 1300C mid-range tranquilizer pistols. As the sniper, Benny also carried the team's only Cap-Chur 1000c long-range rifle.

"Do you see any elephants around?" scoffed Murphy.

"No, all I see is a big, ugly—"

"Shut up," snapped Wild Will. "Both of you."

"What's the plan, Colonel?" asked Russo. He had served under Wild Will in Iraq and Afghanistan.

"We're sticking with the plan," said Wild Will after a moment's reflection. "We're going to assume this guy will pop up again. But this is still a snatch job against a bunch of civilians. If he was listening, he thinks we're going to hit them at oh-three-thirty. We're going to hit them at oh-one-thirty instead. Same plan, different time."

"What if they try to run for it?" asked a tall, thin ex-SEAL.

"Frank and Earl will shoot their tires out if the tire spikes don't stop them," said Wild Will, referring to the men he had watching the main dirt road that ran from the ranch six miles to the main highway.

"If the hippie's from the ranch, they'll call the police now," said Benny. "What do we do then?"

"Russo. Speak to Frank. Make sure the phone lines are down. And try your cell phone. Make sure the jammer's working properly." To Benny he said, "If the police show up, we abort. If they're coming, they'll be here long before oh-one-thirty." Wild Will looked at his watch again. "We'll shove off in an hour."

The team drifted apart to check weapons and get ready. Winston Klendenin stood there by himself looking foolish. Wild Will wanted him out of the way.

"Tell you what," he said to Klendenin. "You want to do something useful? Go find the men watching the road. You saw where we dropped them. Their names are Frank and Earl. If you don't want to get darted, use the password. *Flintstone*. Got it? Tell them there's been a change of plans. Tell them the fireworks will start at oh-one-thirty. Tell them to keep their eyes open and not let anybody through. Can you do that?"

"Sure," said billionaire Winston Klendenin III, trying not to sound too eager. "Don't worry, I can handle it, I used to—"

Wild Will held up a hand to cut him off. "That's okay. Just do me one big favor. Don't say another word until we've got the girl and we're in the air. Go straight down the hill and stick to the road. If a car comes, hide in the bushes. You can do that, right?" Winston nodded. Wild Will turned away and Winston started to follow. Wild Will stopped and said, "I am going to my office now. Don't follow me. Just go." Wild Will strolled over to a nearby flat rock and sat down. He pulled a cigar out of his pocket and bit off the end. "We've missed something," he said to himself for the third time.

Yes indeedy, thought Brother-in-law from two hundred yards away. *You have.* Instead of going to the ranch after he was spotted, Brother-in-law had circled around the hills to approach their camp from a different direction, set up the DetectionEar again, and continue his eavesdropping. He now packed up for the second time and was about to head back to the ranch when he had an idea. With his night-vision goggles, he watched Klendenin stumble down the hill to the road.

"Are you thinking what I'm thinking, dawg?" whispered Brother-in-law to Tripod. The former war dog didn't growl and didn't otherwise make a sound but his nose was working furiously in Klendenin's direction. Brother-in-law could feel the fur rippling on Tripod's back. "Great minds think alike," whispered Brother-in-law.

ℰↃℰↃ

Yohaba had drifted off to sleep, but Rulon lay awake worrying. Overall he felt he had things under control, but he knew from past experience that situations like this could burst at any seam. Too many people with guns and murderous intentions in too small an area. The problem was that people were unsteady and made many miscalculations when under stress or when forced to think quickly, which made them inherently unpredictable. He pondered all the things that had happened over the last twelve hours, starting with the bear, and marveled at their luck.

As he lay there, a voice just outside the open window said, "Knock, knock." It was Brother-in-law.

Rulon sat up and nudged Yohaba. "C'mon in," he said. He heard Brother-in-law give Tripod the curt command *patrol* and then watched his friend step gracefully through the window. His face was painted camo, and he was wearing his bulletproof vest. Yohaba, in a t-shirt, popped her head up over Rulon's shoulder, immediately wide awake.

Brother-in-law came over and sat in a chair in the corner of the room without saying anything. When the silence threatened to continue indefinitely, Rulon said, "Nice night, isn't it?"

"Yeah. Visibility's good. No slope fog," replied Brother-in-law. "Getting colder, though."

"Running around with a bulletproof vest will keep you warm, though," said Rulon.

Brother-in-law chuckled at Rulon's oblique but pointed reference and said, "If you don't get dressed, you're going to miss all the fun."

"Does this fun involve Russians?" asked Yohaba.

"Surprisingly, no," said Brother-in-law. "The Russians got ambushed a couple of miles down the road. They said they were on the way to town. Was that true?"

"Yes," said Yohaba. "Vadim, Vladimir, and your good buddy are staying overnight. The rest were heading to a motel."

"So, they were telling the truth? I feel bad now."

"Should we be calling for an ambulance?" asked Rulon. "Is that what this is about?"

"No, not if they were half-way competent. I made them inject themselves with the Sufentanil they'd brought to use on us."

"How'd you get them to do that?" asked Yohaba wide-eyed.

"When I explained the alternatives, they suggested it themselves," said Brother-in-law. They couldn't see his expression in the dark but sensed him smiling. Rulon didn't respond and when Yohaba started to say something, he squeezed her thigh under the covers to say *stop*. Brother-in-law stayed quiet too.

After a full minute of silence, Rulon said heatedly, "I'm not falling for your Yoda Jedi master baloney. You're in my bedroom just after midnight wearing a bulletproof vest.

It is your responsibility to explain yourself. I shouldn't have to play twenty questions with you to figure out what's going on."

"Yohaba's lying next to you," said Brother-in-law. "I should think you'd be more curious, at least for her sake. Why aren't you?"

"Aaarrrghhhh," said Rulon through clenched teeth. "All right! All right! What the heck is the fun I'm going to be missing if I don't get up right now in the middle of the night and traipse around the hills shooting off flares and watching my dog take orders from you?"

"Finally, you're asking the right question," said Brother-in-law, and again they sensed him smiling to himself. "There's ten armed men and a moron out there. Guess who they're after."

"What nationality?"

"American."

Rulon thought for a moment. "Yohaba."

"Bingo. Walk me through how you figured it out."

"You spotted them," Rulon said seriously. "Which means they're an oblivious over-confident lot. Which means they don't know about me or you or the local branch of the Russian mafia. They must therefore be after someone they think is a total civilian, and if they're American then I doubt they'd be after the old man. Ergo, Yohaba."

"Not bad, grasshopper," said Brother-in-law.

"So why are they after me?" asked Yohaba. "You sure there were no German accents?"

"Sure," Brother-in-law said. "The man who hired them is Winston Klendenin III, and he assured me that none of this is personal. He thinks Steenberg kidnapped his daughter, and he wants you for leverage." He saw the puzzled look on Yohaba's face. "I bumped into him in the dark. Don't worry, he's alive under a bush somewhere.

Here's his clothes. See, no blood." Brother-in-law threw her a bundle of clothes wrapped by a belt.

"He'll freeze to death out there," said Yohaba.

"Not for three or four hours," said Brother-in-law. "But the clock is ticking."

"So we're going to dial 911 and wait for the police," said Yohaba. "Right?"

"Not a good idea, darling," said Rulon. "You wouldn't want that on your conscience. Too many people with guns. Too much military thinking. Local police would be outgunned, outnumbered, and tactically unprepared."

"It's their job to protect us," said Yohaba.

"Darling, close your eyes and picture Vernon. Now picture Vernon facing ten highly paid mercenaries."

"Okay, point taken," said Yohaba after a moment's thought.

"It's a moot point anyway," said Brother-in-law. "Phone lines are down, and our cell phones are jammed. There's money behind these guys. Apparently, Winston Klendenin III is rich."

"Okay," said Yohaba. "So let's all just get Dad, jump in a car and drive off then. Let's not make this more complicated than it has to be."

"They've got tire spikes and a two-man blocking team ready to shoot out our tires if we try," said Brother-in-law. "If they managed to stop us, we'd be on foot with an old man. Not a good situation. Of course, we could take care of this pretty easily. They'll be coming down Go-Right-and-Lose-Your-Job," he said, referring to the furthest of the two hills that ran east to west along the north side of the ranch. He pulled another one of his remote-control devices from a leg pocket of his camo pants and mimicked pressing a button.

"No," said Rulon emphatically.

"What's that for?" asked Yohaba.

"All that time you thought he was working in the fields, he was really gallivanting around the hills planting Claymore mines," said Rulon. He looked sharply at Brother-in-law. "Thought I didn't know, didn't you?"

"What's a Claymore mine?" asked Yohaba.

"It's a pound and a half of C4 packed into a plastic case along with 700 ball bearings," said Rulon.

"Brother-in-law!" exclaimed Yohaba. "You do realize this is Idaho, not the Congo, don't you?"

"Said the lady with the ten armed men wanting to kidnap her," said Brother-in-law.

"Hmmm…good point," said Yohaba. "Okay. What's the plan?"

"But no Claymores," said Rulon.

It took Brother-in-law fifteen minutes to explain what Wild Will and his crew had planned and to answer all of their questions. When he was done, he stood up and said, "Start getting everyone together. I'll be back in a few minutes. I need to go talk to my Russian buddy," referring to Yevgeny. "Which room is he in?"

Brother-in-law stood outside Yevgeny's bedroom door with his hand on the doorknob and activated his cloaking device. Rulon had tried many times explaining it to Yohaba—that ability some men had to shut down their predator aura, those primordial vibes that most prey can sense on a subconscious level when they are in the presence of a predator—a talent that Brother-in-law knew Rulon also had to a remarkable degree.

He turned the doorknob and walked in as quiet as a shadow. He searched the room, moving in a strangely syncopated rhythm calculated not to alarm Yevgeny's sleeping but subconsciously aware brain. Something he learned from his father-in-law, an old Lubas village elder in the Congo. Last he checked under Yevgeny's pillow and carefully found and slipped out the Varjag automatic.

Brother-in-law backed into the far corner of the room and sat down on the edge of a small wooden desk and de-cloaked. Yevgeny stirred and in a flash of movement reached under his pillow then spun empty-handed to face the danger.

"Relax," Brother-in-law said softly. "Didn't want you hurting yourself." He threw Yevgeny his gun.

Yevgeny caught the Varjag with one hand and slowly sat up. He checked the load and placed the pistol on the nightstand. "Are you here for some unfinished business?" he asked.

"I need you to do me a favor," said Brother-in-law.

"Screw you," said Yevgeny.

Brother-in-law smiled. "Get dressed or you're going to miss all the fun."

It took Brother-in-law five minutes to bring Yevgeny up to speed with an abbreviated version of their predicament, both what he'd overheard and what he'd managed to coax out of Klendenin. He lied and told Yevgeny the snatch team was after Vadim and convinced him that stopping the threat in the hills was safer for Vadim and Vladimir than fighting off the attack from the house. Yevgeny's first instinct was to call his men, and after Brother-in-law told him what he'd done to them, his second instinct was to kill Brother-in-law. The two almost drew on each other until Brother-in-law defused the situation by drawling, "Hey, honest mistake, comrade," and got Yevgeny to crack a smile.

Now the two of them were leaning together over the bed perusing a map of the ranch and the surrounding hills. "They're going to be coming down here and here," said Brother-in-law as he traced the routes with his finger. "I need you to park yourself here between Morsel and Go-

Right-and-Lose-Your-Job"—He touched an open spot in a valley between the two hills about three hundred yards away.—"and wait. I'll be driving them to you."

"How?"

"My problem. But keep your head down."

"Then what?"

"Disarm them if you think you can do it, otherwise wait for me. They won't be getting there all at once, but they're armed and trained. If you don't screw up, we'll feed you breakfast."

"I can't leave the kid."

"Take him with you then. I don't care. Or leave him with the Hurts." When Yevgeny hesitated, Brother-in-law said, "You know the Hurts, right? You heard the stories, right? The Hönggerberg forest? CERN? Einsiedeln?"

"Yes." Yevgeny didn't bring it up again.

Brother-in-law took Yevgeny down the hall to the metal gun cabinet in the study. He unlocked the cabinet and told Yevgeny he could choose any weapon except the M224 mortar and the handheld LAW—Light Anti-tank Weapon. Yevgeny ignored the Parker Hale PDW, the various H&K models, the Swiss TSI Vector, and the Steyr TMP, but lingered for a few seconds over the Thompson. Finally he settled on the PP-19 Bizon submachine gun and five extra clips.

"Just gave yourself away," said Brother-in-law. "How long were you Spetsnaz?"

"*Chetyre goda*—four years," said Yevgeny, momentarily slipping into Russian as he stroked the Bizon like it was a favorite pet. In English he asked, "Is all this legal to own in your country?"

"In my country, yes," said Brother-in-law.

Yevgeny mimicked mowing down a line of men with the Bizon. Brother-in-law said, "If you're half the man I think you are, you won't have to use this except to maybe fire it over their heads. They're armed but want to pull this off with tranquilizer guns. Their boss told them that if anyone gets shot, none of them gets paid. This does not call for lethal force. If you kill anyone unnecessarily, you'll answer to me. Da?"

"Then why give me the Bizon?" asked Yevgeny.

"Is it da or nyet?" asked Brother-in-law.

Yevgeny hesitated but eventually repeated, "Da." Brother-in-law rummaged in the gun cabinet and tossed Yevgeny a loaded magazine. "Use this," he said. "It ain't much good without bullets." Brother-in-law also gave him one of Rulon's Turtleskin bullet-stab vests just in case. It was big on him but would do the job.

"Why am I trusting you?" asked Yevgeny.

"Why am I giving you a submachine gun?" said Brother-in-law in reply.

They walked out on the porch and stood together for a minute while Brother-in-law oriented Yevgeny with the hills and the perspective of the map. While they talked, Brother-in-law looked around, wondering where Tripod was. Yevgeny stepped off the porch. Brother-in-law said, "Remember, screw up and no breakfast." Yevgeny raised the Bizon over his head in acknowledgment but didn't turn around. Brother-in-law watched as he moved among the shadows in the direction of Go-Right-and-Lose-Your-Job.

After he lost sight of Yevgeny, Brother-in-law waited on the porch for Tripod. In the house, the lights were still out, but he could hear Rulon and Yohaba making noise, getting everyone up to move some equipment into the main bedroom, where behind the wallboard and in the reinforced ceiling and floor there was enough sand, old manhole covers, cement blocks, and steel plating to stop anything short of a .50 caliber bullet.

As Brother-in-law waited, he saw Tripod lurch into the lamplight by the west corrals and then disappear again into the dark. Then reappear ten seconds later, closer now, in the yellow circle of light in front of the barn and out again. Then up onto the porch, where he immediately keeled over at Brother-in-law's feet. Brother-in-law dropped down and felt his heart. Still beating. He ran his hands over the dog's body looking for a wound and was relieved when he found only a tranquilizer dart stuck in his rump. He took it out, touched his finger to the tip, and gingerly tasted. *Midazolam. That did it*, he thought angrily.

Fuming, Brother-in-law put on his night-vision goggles. At that moment, if anything had stirred in his field of vision, he would have shot. But all was quiet and still, and he calmed down. He carried Tripod into the house and laid him on the couch, knowing he'd catch hell later from Yohaba for bringing the dog inside. He went outside again and cautiously walked along the porch and around the house to the duffle bag he'd left outside Rulon's bedroom window. One more look around, then he grabbed the heavy bag by the straps and hopped with it onto the porch railing. He swung the duffle bag back and forth until he finally had enough momentum to fling it onto the porch roof. Nimbly he followed, retrieved the bag, and climbed to the next level of the roof and the protection of the brick chimney.

In deep shadows, with his back against the chimney, he could hear Rulon's voice coming up through the fireplace.

Somewhere in those hills were ten men armed with tranquilizer guns wanting to kidnap Yohaba. And one moron. But the moron was lying in the bushes, wrapped in duct tape, in his underwear in the growing chill, after having spilled his guts to Brother-in-law about why Yohaba was a target. Though Brother-in-law now knew the team was composed of brother SEALs and other professionals, he felt no emotional link with them. They had moved against his friends and darted his dog.

From the duffle bag, Brother-in-law removed the M79 grenade launcher, two bandoliers of grenades, a half-dozen remote control devices the size of cigarette boxes, and a plastic map that showed the location of all sixteen Claymore mines he had planted over the past half year around the property and in the hills.

"Old men and their hobbies," said Rulon with a nervous laugh when he flung open the door to one of the spare bedrooms. Father Becker, Vladimir, and Vadim stared at the stacked and assembled computer equipment. Before the questions could start, Rulon got everyone involved in moving the equipment to the fortified protection of the main bedroom. In between loading everyone down with laptops and document binders, he looked over his shoulder at Yohaba. Shaking his head, he mouthed the words, *We're blown.* As soon as he had a chance, he excused himself to go to the bathroom and arm himself with the easily concealable Colt Mustang .380 that was taped to the underside of the toilet tank lid.

In fifteen minutes, they moved eleven laptops, an HP 3PAR disk array, and four HP Proliant DL360P G8 servers into the bunker that was their bedroom. The spare room had been so filled with computer equipment that there wasn't even room for a bed. And despite the cool outside temperature, there was an air conditioner running.

"Be careful with that stuff," hissed Yohaba to Rulon and Vadim as they wheeled a rack filled with servers down the hallway. "Pretend the fate of the world is in your hands." Rulon rolled his eyes.

"Shouldn't you first power down the servers or something before you move them?" asked Vadim while he and Rulon struggled to get the three-hundred pound rack around a corner.

"Normally, yes," said Rulon, after a mighty heave. "But this is an emergency, and all the information is synchronously remote copied to another location. It's safe to move. They'll resynch again once they're up and running."

"I didn't expect to see this on a ranch," said Vadim. "This is heavy duty stuff."

"No one understands what the small American rancher has to do to survive nowadays," said Yohaba, who was supervising. "These days you need a Ph.D. just to milk a cow. C'mon, move it."

The house was dark except for flashlights. Rulon's father had wandered off and was nowhere to be seen. Father Becker and Vladimir stood in a corner whispering conspiratorially to each other, which struck Rulon as suspicious, since officially they were supposed to be enemies holding to an uneasy truce.

"I think that's the last of it," Rulon said as he passed them.

When the final rack was in the room, Rulon and Yohaba turned to see their three guests, now clearly all back on speaking terms, staring at them with their backs against the fireplace. In Vladimir's hand was a nasty looking Glock 17.

"Where is Leonard Steenberg?" demanded Vladimir. "Tell us and we'll be gone within minutes. But no tricks or the consequences will be severe. We have no intention of hurting him…or you…unless you give us cause. We just want to talk. We know he must be here in Idaho somewhere close. Tell us where."

"Wow!" said Yohaba. "Your English has really improved since this afternoon. I've always said you have to live with a family and sit around the kitchen table with them to really learn a language."

"She really does say that," said Rulon as he moved ever so slightly to shield Yohaba and also to bump against her so she could feel the Colt Mustang against his back under his vest. "But tell me the truth. What gave us away? Was it the data center in the spare room? Be honest."

"I'm sick of your stupid jokes," snarled Becker. "I've had it up to here—" He held a hand a foot over his head. "—with your idiotic sense of humor. Nobody ever laughs. Haven't you noticed!?" Becker fought to calm himself. "Our men are just down the road. One phone call is all it would take. We can do this the easy way or I can call them, and in two minutes we can do it the hard way. What's it going to be?"

Rulon asked, "Was the hard way going to start two minutes from the time you called or two minutes from the time they got here?"

"Give me the gun," said Father Becker. He tried grabbing the gun, but Vladimir slapped his hand away.

"I suggest for your sakes you don't make this any more difficult than it has to be," said Vadim with a surprising degree of animosity and conviction. "You have no idea what we are capable of."

"Where is Steenberg?" repeated Vladimir ominously. "I'm not going to ask again."

Vladimir raised the pistol menacingly but stopped when from behind him a silent-as-a-cat Brother-in-law stuck the barrel of his .22 in his ear and said, "The Glock. I'm not going to ask again." The old man's face clenched like a fist and Brother-in-law reached around and grabbed the gun out of his hand. He then used the Glock to club the old man alongside the head, not to knock him out, but only to let him know he'd been bad. Vladimir grunted and staggered but didn't fall.

Brother-in-law glared at Rulon and said, "I really don't have time for this. I should be on the roof." He took a step towards Becker, who was backing away with his hands up to ward off what was coming.

"You wouldn't hit a man of the cloth," said Father Becker with a mixture of pompousness and hope. "Even the mafia wouldn't stoop that low."

"Put your hands down," said Brother-in-law. Becker slowly complied and Brother-in-law clubbed him too, right behind the ear. Becker grabbed his head and howled like a banshee. "Shut up or I'll really give you something to holler about," said Brother-in-law. Becker went immediately quiet but continued rubbing his head vigorously. "No pointing guns at my friends," said the SEAL. "Are we clear?"

Next, Brother-in-law scrutinized a cringing Vadim. "Did he touch the gun?" asked Brother-in-law of Yohaba.

"No. I don't think so."

"Leave him to us," said Rulon. Brother-in-law frowned and tossed Yohaba the automatic.

"Where's Yevgeny?" she asked.

"He's gainfully employed. Don't worry about him," said Brother-in-law. "Think you can handle things?" He left through the window without waiting for a reply.

With his hands on his hips, Rulon surveyed the motley crew in front of him. "It was the cooking, wasn't it?" he asked. Becker paused from rubbing his head to shoot Rulon a glare. Vladimir said nothing. Vadim mumbled something about none of this being his idea.

Rulon gave a curt laugh and ordered the three of them to raise their hands high. He cleaned out their pockets, wanting especially to get their cell phones. Vladimir and Becker he told to go lie on the bed. To Vadim he said, "There's a half-dozen rolls of duct tape in the kitchen cabinet just below the silverware. Go get them." The young Russian scurried out of the room and Rulon sat down in a rocking chair.

"So much for baffling them with kindness," said Rulon while he scrolled through the call logs on Vadim's phone.

"Anything interesting?" asked Yohaba.

"Junior was sending pictures to your buddy Boris of you cooking dinner. Wow! There are some things a husband doesn't want to know."

"Give me that," said Yohaba. She snatched the phone out of his hand and saw the pictures. "I look terrible." She handed Rulon back the phone just as Vadim returned with the tape. Rulon made him get into the bed with the others.

Rulon announced. "I am now going to duct tape you like you've never been duct taped before. The only thing missing will be the pyramid and embalming fluid." Becker started to sit up to say something, but Rulon roughly pushed him back down. "Looks like we have a volunteer to go first," he said.

"I'll get the camera," said Yohaba.

A few minutes later, he was finished with the two old men and had only a few more passes left to go on Vadim when he stopped and said to Yohaba, "Hey, it just occurred to me. Where did my father run off to? As soon as there was real work to do, it seems to me he disappeared mighty quickly."

"He's eighty years old. Give him a break," said Yohaba. She then yelled, "Dad! You can come out now."

"No need to yell," said Mr. Hurt from the doorway in his bib overalls, nonchalantly stroking his beard. Again, there was that faint smell of manure. "How did I do?"

"You were fantastic," said Rulon. "That touch with the beans was great."

"Really," said Mr. Hurt, quite pleased. "I thought so too."

Chapter 10

Mr. Hurt walked to the bed and stood over Becker for a few seconds. They locked eyes, and Mr. Hurt said, "Hiding behind religion." He shook his head in disgust.

Rulon asked Vladimir. "Should we still trust you and your clan?" Vladimir nodded ever so slightly.

Yohaba said, "I don't think Leonard knows anything about those guys in the hills. Do you think there's a connection between them and Vladimir?"

"Brother-in-law thinks not," Rulon said.

"But the men in the hills surely have a connection to Leonard's work. He'll want to speak with them when he gets here. If there's a misunderstanding, he'll want to clear it up."

"What if there wasn't a misunderstanding?" asked Rulon.

"Don't go there," said Yohaba. "Anyway, I've asked Brother-in-law to try and arrange something."

"Oh, he thinks he can do anything," said Rulon gruffly. "If you asked him to build a time machine, he'd ask you what color."

"He said something about rounding them up," said Yohaba. Just then there was an odd sound from the roof—a sound like two hollow plastic pipes struck together. Rulon recognized the sound and grimaced. Yohaba simply looked puzzled. Then came the distant explosion.

"I need to get up on the roof," said Rulon. He tossed Yohaba the roll of tape.

"What was that?" asked Yohaba, but Rulon was already gone. With Mr. Hurt's help she finished duct taping Vadim and added a few more loops to the others for good measure. While they were wrapping, they continued to hear that funny popping sound from the roof, each time followed by a far-off explosion. When done, Yohaba stepped back to admire her work. They were trussed up like mummies, their expressions unreadable except for Vadim's pleading eyes. Boris, Yohaba's Russian admirer, had taught her well.

During the time it took Rulon to find a ladder, Brother-in-law had fired off three more M79 rounds and two Claymores. The mines went off with a flash and thunder like the end of the world.

Once on the roof, Rulon frog-walked to where his friend was crouched on one knee behind the chimney wearing night vision goggles and squinting down the tall sight of the M79. Before he could say anything, Brother-in-law, without turning his head, said, "Don't worry. I'm just herding them." *Pop!* He fired off another round. Brother-in-law watched for a moment then averted his eyes from the flash. Another fiery explosion in the distant hills. He looked to inspect his work, then turned to Rulon with a wild, happy expression. "They're running around so crazy they're bumping into each other." While he was talking, he opened up the M79's breech and slipped in another high-explosive round.

"They teach you this in SEAL school?" asked Rulon. "How to herd guys with M79s and Claymores?"

"Yep. First day," said Brother-in-law without taking his eyes off what was happening in the hills. He laughed proudly. "There is now zero unit-cohesion out there." He poked his head above the chimney to get a better view and fired off another round. "I hope you're paying attention. This isn't as easy as it looks," he said. "The M79 is lethal within five meters and almost guaranteed to wound within twenty. You need to lay these babies in there nice and easy, close enough to get'em moving but not too close."

"Should I be in a lotus position?" asked Rulon drolly.

Brother-in-law looked down to check a small hand-drawn map he'd duct taped to the roof. He traced his finger down a line on the map and said, "Number 5B should turn them nicely." He grabbed a remote control from where it was wedged between the roof and the chimney, clicked through a few numbers on a dial, and pushed a button. Up in the hills another mine flashed and boomed. Even from three hundred yards away they could feel the concussion.

Brother-in-law laid down the M79 and put on the throat mike and earphone he'd taken from Klendenin. He smiled as he listened. "SEAL team eight meets Keystone cops," he said with barely concealed glee. "Here, listen." He handed Rulon the earpiece while he fired off a few more rounds. Soon Rulon was laughing too.

"Fall back! Fall back!" yelled Wild Will into his throat mike. Trying to keep his cool, he fought to reassure himself. *This is nothing. I've been through worse.* He threw himself to the ground just as another M79 round landed seventy feet away. "Run now!" he yelled to his team after the dirt clods stopped raining down. He looked up from the dirt patch where he lay halfway up Go-Right-And-Lose-Your-Job just as a member of his team ran past. "Burke, Burke," he yelled but wasn't heard. A few seconds later another team member ran past, but in the opposite direction. He called to him too, but the man kept running. Another M79 round went off fifty meters to his right.

"They're walking them up the hill," screamed Russo, pressed flat to the ground, his face just inches from Wild Will's. "They've got us pegged. We gotta move!" More dirt rained down. He'd been screaming his words for the past five minutes, ever since the first Claymore blew out his hearing. "We're surrounded. It's a trap. We have to abort, Colonel."

"I've been trying to abort," said Wild Will angrily through gritted teeth. Into his mike, he yelled, "Fall back to niner, alpha, two seven! Do you copy? Anyone. Do you copy?" A cacophony of incoherent voices answered back, men gasping out words as they ran and fell and ran some more. Half the team was stumbling in the dark with impaired vision after getting flashed while wearing night vision goggles.

"Burke's down," cried one man.

"How bad?" asked Wild Will, tasting the bile from the stress eating into his stomach. He'd lost men in Iraq and Afghanistan in some pretty hairy stuff just like this. Nighttime. An unseen enemy. Unable to pinpoint the source of the attack. He started to flashback then shook his head to clear it. *This is Idaho. This is Idaho.*

❧❧❧

Yohaba sat with Rulon and Brother-in-law on the roof keeping up a constant chatter. When she was nervous, she liked to talk. Rulon split his time between watching the kidnappers in the hills through the NVG and keeping an eye on two small fires caused by Brother-in-law's grenades, willing them to burn themselves out. Brother-in-law sat quietly, listening to them natter, making an occasional small comment but mostly focused on unloading and reloading his Browning .22 over and over again, thinking.

"Fires are dying down," said Rulon finally, much relieved. "And the explosions hardly spooked the animals."

"They've gotten used to it over the years, darling," said Yohaba.

"Yeah, I guess you're right," said Rulon seriously. Then sadly, he added, "But it still affects their milk production."

"True," said Yohaba. She could see Rulon was worried about the milk. Wanting to get his mind off the subject, she pointed to the M79 propped up against the chimney and said, "Are there no gentlemen left in the world? Which one of you is going to show me how to shoot that thing?"

"You'd be good at it," said Brother-in-law. "I'll show you. Do you want to blow up a Humvee?"

"Sure!" said Yohaba.

"There's three of them," said Brother-in-law. "We can each do one."

"Forget it. We're not turning the ranch into a junk yard," said Rulon firmly.

"War zone okay. Junk yard not okay," said Yohaba. "We have very strict family rules." She playfully kicked Brother-in-law's foot. "C'mon. Teach me." He looked at Rulon, and Rulon nodded okay.

Brother-in-law finished loading the Browning, slid it back into his holster, and attached the hammer thong. He made Yohaba hold the M79 and walked her through the parts and how they worked.

Rulon stayed focused on the men in the hills. After a few minutes, he said, "Except for the two guys still watching the road, they're all together now and staying put. I think you should call them now."

Brother-in-law told Yohaba to continue practicing loading and unloading the various types of ammunition from the bandoliers. In addition to the high explosive rounds he'd been firing at the men in the hills, he had an assortment of smoke and illumination rounds, three very nasty shotgun rounds for close-up work, and a few varieties of non-lethal rubber bullets and tear gas rounds.

He turned to Rulon. "Pop quiz. I'm me, you're the bad guys. I walk up the hill to parley. I'm alone. What do you do?"

"Hold it," said Rulon. "If you're going up there, I'm going with you."

"Tactically stupid," said Brother-in-law. "You can't leave Yohaba and your father alone. What if one of the Russians gets loose?"

"You would be walking into a trap," said Yohaba.

"As long as I've got a gun, I'm the trap," said Brother-in-law.

"Oh brother," said Rulon scornfully. "Do all SEALs talk like you? I swear, I don't care how many miles you run or pushups you can do, it's not gonna stop a bullet."

"And how was *your* combat training at OCD?" snapped Brother-in-law. "Bet it was the toughest weekend of your life."

"Girls, girls," interrupted Yohaba. "You're both ninja death gods in your own unique way."

"I'm coming with you," said Rulon.

"Okay," said Brother-in-law, "then you have to off our three buddies downstairs. We can't risk them getting loose with just your father and Yohaba here. You got the stomach for that then you can come. And then you have to say goodbye to Yohaba, because if you come with me, I promise you, those guys up there will get her, and she'll be gone when you get back."

Rulon glared at Brother-in-law, angry because he was making sense. After Rulon simmered down, Brother-in-law said again, "Pop quiz. I walk up the hill by myself to parley. You're the bad guys. What do you do?"

Rulon let out an aggravated sigh but this time played along. "As soon as you tell me where Klendenin is, I dart you and come down and kidnap Yohaba."

"What happens if the two of us walk up the hill together?"

"Well, if I'm there," said Rulon, "they throw down their weapons in terror."

"Yeah, yeah, but after they beg for mercy, what happens?"

Rulon said seriously, "If it's both of us, half their team circles around to kidnap Yohaba while we're coming up. Then we get darted as soon as we show. Later, after we wake up, they threaten Yohaba, and we tell them where the moron is."

"Yep. Either way, they win," said Brother-in-law. "So here are our choices. Option one. Right now, if I fire off Claymores 3C and 6A, they'll sweep right over their position. Then all we'd have to deal with are the two guys by the road. We could end this pretty easily. We'd have to get the backhoe and dig a hole big enough to bury them and the three Humvees. It'd be a pain but doable. That's our best option."

"I think you're joking," said Yohaba. "But just to be clear, no one's killing anybody. These are Americans. They're only doing this because they think Leonard had something to do with kidnapping that guy's daughter. They're being lied to and used. We can talk them out of this if everyone will just settle down and be reasonable."

"These guys are not philosophers," said Brother-in-law. "They won't see it that way. They're hardwired to finish the mission and talk afterwards. The word 'quit' or even 'detour' is not in their vocabulary. We're making plans. Believe me, right now they're making plans, too. They're hoping we're just dumb enough to come up and want to talk."

"What if the three of us went up there together?" asked Yohaba. "What would be the dynamic then?"

Brother-in-law fiddled with his wispy beard as he worked out the possibilities. Finally, he said, "That would probably give us the best chance of ending this peaceably. They'd see you and hear your voice and then you'd be a real person to them and not just a target. They'd see you with your husband and that would make it even more personal. It might work."

"Well, that's it then," said Yohaba happily. "There's our answer."

Brother-in-law knew without even looking that Rulon was shaking his head. He said, "Listen to your husband."

"No can do, baby," said Rulon. "He said it *might* work. But if it doesn't, we'd be in the worst possible situation, and this could easily escalate into a full-blown shootout, and it wouldn't be with tranquilizer darts. You'd be right there. A successful mission staring them in the face. Eight of them with all sorts of weapons, including Yevgeny's Varjag, and they'd be—"

Brother-in-law cut him off. "I forgot to tell you. I gave Yevgeny the Bizon."

Rulon stared at Brother-in-law for a few seconds then slowly dragged his hand over his face in disbelief. Exercising massive self-control, he said, "Let me rephrase that. There would be eight of them with tranquilizer guns, regular guns, and a Bizon sub-machine gun as a present from us. And they would be up against only two males. They would like those odds. It would be hard for them not to try and take us and still kidnap you. At the very least there'd be a heck of a fight. I promise you that."

"It could go either way," admitted Brother-in-law. "But if it makes you feel any better, the Bizon is loaded with blanks."

"I don't want anyone getting hurt on account of me," said Yohaba. "Especially you guys."

"That's wonderful, darling," said Rulon, who found it laughable that Yohaba would think he wouldn't risk everything he had, including his life, to protect her. To Brother-in-law he asked, "What are you thinking?"

"I figure their pride's pushing them on, but their heart's not in it. They hate this Klendenin guy because he's paid them to go against their own code and they're ashamed of themselves."

"What's their code?" asked Yohaba.

"The code is you don't run ops against non-principals. Someone's daughter gets kidnapped then you go rescue the girl and kill the kidnappers. You kill the principals. But you don't kidnap someone else's daughter who's not even involved. It's chicken, and they know it."

The three of them sat quietly on the roof thinking. Rulon put on the night vision goggles again. "They're still there. I don't know how much longer they're going to wait."

Brother-in-law cleared his throat, pressed his throat mike and said, "Anybody home?"

"Who is this?" growled Wild Will into Brother-in-law's ear. "Who am I speaking to?"

"I hope you realize," said Brother-in-law with a wink at Yohaba," you'd all be dead right now, if the woman you wanted to kidnap hadn't begged for your lives." While Wild Will fumbled for words, he added, "If you try to move from where you are, the fireworks will start again. I've got two Claymores angled to roll right over you."

"So, what do you want?" asked Wild Will.

"I'm coming up to talk," said Brother-in-law. "Stay where you are."

"I have your Russian," said Wild Will.

"I have your moron," said Brother-in-law. Laughter in the background told him the rest of the team was listening in.

"Are you the hippie we saw?" asked Wild Will. "How many others are you?"

"We're an entire army of deranged hillbillies," said Brother-in-law. "Just wait where you are. Don't be an idiot. You don't even know what you got yourselves into or whose side you're on. Just wait there. I'm coming up."

"Will you be coming alone?"

"Maybe, maybe not," said Brother-in-law, "but all the same you better just wait there or you're going to be dodging Claymores and M79 rounds all the way back to your booby-trapped Humvees."

Brother-in-law took off the earpiece and mike and handed them to Rulon. "Hang onto this. I'm not really going up there. I'm just buying us some time."

Rulon stared at Brother-in-law. Brother-in-law stared back. "Okay," said Rulon. What's the second option?"

"I've changed my mind. We've only got one option. We should run. Just all get in the truck and take off. Then all we have to do is watch out for the tire spikes and deal with the two guys guarding the road."

"I like that idea!" said Yohaba.

Brother-in-law said, "Once we've got cell phone reception, we call the police and ask them to come with lights and sirens blazing. Our visitors will know they're blown and leave."

"So how do we knock out the two guys guarding the road?" asked Yohaba.

"There's lots of ways," said Brother-in-law. "But a .22 round in the head would be the preferred method."

Yohaba leaned close to Rulon and stage whispered, "He's being funny again, right?"

"Of course," said Rulon but with a worried look at Brother-in-law.

"If you say so," said Brother-in-law to Yohaba, and she felt a chill run up her spine. While he talked, he rummaged in his duffle bag until he found a square, flat metal box. He unlatched the lid and took out a flexible white plastic pouch holding twelve small hypodermics. He used a penlight from a leg pocket to read the labels and select the one he wanted. Rulon and Yohaba looked on in horror.

"Ah…we don't do that here," said Rulon.

Brother-in-law smiled as he flicked the needle with his finger to get rid of the air bubbles. "This is Flumazenil. It's a benzodiazepine antagonist drug that neutralizes Midazolam—the stuff they darted Tripod with. If we get darted, this will keep us on our feet." He rolled up his sleeve and injected himself. While he did, Rulon and Yohaba rolled up their sleeves too. Brother-in-law selected two more hypodermics, but before he could inject Rulon and Yohaba, Rulon grabbed his wrist and checked that the labels on all three needles were the same.

"You don't trust me," said Brother-in-law, amused.

"I trust you like my own brother," said Rulon honestly.

Brother-in-law injected them and they all sat still for a few minutes, breathing deeply and feeling their muscles relax.

Brother-in-law ran two hands through his long, stringy blonde hair and said, "I know how they think. I'd like to end this without having to shoot it out, but maybe that's the way it's got to be. But it'd be a waste. Everyone knows I've been trying to keep the body count down. I could've taken them all out with a single Claymore, the way they were coming down out of the hills all bunched up. But I didn't, because I understand where their heads are at. They don't want to use lethal force. The guy's just sick about his daughter and thinks Steenberg is the puppet master that's got her. So, I was cuttin' them some slack. But now both sides are backed into a corner, and the situation is sitting on a knife edge.

"Anyway, they're going to point guns at me if I go up there, and I'm not going to like that, and I may have to shoot a few of them. But, hey, when you go to kidnap someone sometimes you get shot. That's how life is. That's not the way—" Suddenly Brother-in-law caught himself and laughed out loud. "Wow, I think the stuff is working. That was fast!"

"That's the longest single string of words I've ever heard come out of your mouth," said Rulon. "But something's wrong. I'm not feeling a thing."

"You're so big, you'd need a fifty-five-gallon drum of the stuff," said Brother-in-law.

"But why are you talking like this?" asked Rulon. "We're driving out of here. Remember?"

"Yeah. I'm just saying, it could get messy if we tried to confront them. That's all. And besides, those guys at the roadblock also have dart guns."

Rulon was picking up strange vibes from Brother-in-law, but before he could ask another question Yohaba interrupted. "Funny," she said. "That thing you said about what happens when you go to kidnap someone. When I was in Zurich, the Russian you've heard us talk about, you know, Boris, the big guy, he said almost the same thing. He accidentally killed a guy who was chasing after me and he said, '*When you chase a girl into an alley with a knife, sometimes you're the one who gets killed.*' The way he said it, it sounded like some kind of commando proverb." Brother-in-law found that very funny and Rulon and Yohaba couldn't help laughing too.

"If they try to outflank us to get Yohaba, I'm going to be really angry," said Rulon, back to being serious. "I wasn't angry until now, because I knew it wasn't personal, but if they keep trying, I'm going to take it personal."

"They're not done trying," said Brother-in-law. "Just as sure as we're sitting here, they're not done trying. That's why we should leave. But it's not personal."

As soon as Brother-in-law clicked off, Wild Will gathered his battered and bewildered team together.

The team had certain expectations when they accepted Klendenin's offer but walking onto Omaha beach with grenade bursts and Claymore ball bearings whizzing over their heads wasn't even close to being on the list. Three of them were just getting their eyesight back after being flash blinded through their night vision goggles. Burke had a badly sprained ankle that he hoped wasn't broken. And Yevgeny had roughed up four of them pretty hard before he got overpowered. Russo and one other guy had busted ear drums, and none of the rest were hearing well either.

"The hippie's coming up to talk," said Wild Will with gusto. "This is our first break."

"Yeah, yeah, we got them right where we want them," said Murphy in an uncannily accurate impression of Wild Will. "Yeah, yeah. Let's turn this thing around on the bad guys. Hey, wait. We are the bad guys." There was laughter and a few murmurs of assent among the team.

"Shut-up, Murphy," said Wild Will. Just then, off to the side under a large mesquite bush, Yevgeny groaned and rolled over on his back. Wild Will signaled to the mostly deaf Russo to go check.

Russo went over to Yevgeny and shone a penlight in his eyes. "I told you we gave him too much," said Russo overly loud, referring to the sodium amytal to make him talk. He rolled Yevgeny onto his side, back into a recovery position.

"He held out. That's what happens when you hold out," said Wild Will to the men around him. "But now we know that all we're dealing with is a crazy hippie and a fat rancher."

"Yeah, a crazy hippie who's hell-on-wheels with a pirate gun," said Murphy. "Makes you wonder what the fat rancher can do."

Wild Will gritted his teeth but refused to rise to the bait. "We know what we're up against," he said calmly. "If the guy comes up here by himself or with fat boy, makes no difference. We all know the drill. Either way we get the girl. Mission completed. We will turn this situation around."

Murphy's mocking voice rang out again. "Screw the situation. I say we turn the Hummers around. Yeah, I say we declare victory and get the hell out of Idaho."

Softly, Wild Will said, "Shut up, Murphy."

"Man, I'm never stepping foot in Idaho again," said Murphy without missing a beat. "Never. In case no one noticed, those were Claymores. What kind of redneck, inbred loon buckets plant Claymores on their ranch? Huh? Huh? Answer me that one, will ya?"

"Shut up, Murphy," said Wild Will a little louder.

Murphy said, "Yeah, so simple. So well planned. Just a simple snatch job. So, what's a little grenade dodging and a few psycho ranchers on the side? Hey! Bring on the midget tag team wrestlers, I say."

Wild Will took off his black knit cap, threw it to the ground, and charged. Murphy readied himself, but cooler heads grabbed Wild Will and held him back before they could tangle. After a few seconds, Wild Will stopped struggling, shook off the hands that held him and walked to the opposite side of the circle of men away from Murphy. The team fell into an awkward silence.

After he cooled off, Wild Will walked up to Murphy and said, "I apologize for my loss of control, but geez, man, you keep pushing and pushing." He sighed. "Can we just get through this mission?"

"I apologize that I'm a lot funnier than you," said Murphy. "Mother always said my big mouth would get me in trouble someday. That's why I joined the Marines, because I am a free spirit." Everyone chuckled, even Wild Will, grateful to Murphy for easing the tension.

With the team's morale relatively back on track, Wild Will said, "We came here to kidnap a girl. Not to hurt her or anyone she was living with. Just hold her for a few days until Klendenin got his daughter back. Sounded like the easiest thing in the world. And all for a good cause. Whether we like the guy or not, there's no backing out now. We took his money, and we've got a job to do. And we're going to do that job, even if it means we have to kick up our game a few notches and play rough. Okay, round one goes to the hippie and the fat rancher. Now, it's round two. New ballgame." He looked down and said softly, "This isn't the military. Any of you can quit anytime." Silence. "Okay, then. Let's get ready. Who wants the submachine gun?" Benny held up his hand and Wild Will tossed him the Bizon. "Think you can handle it?" he asked.

"If it's got bullets and a trigger, I can handle it," said Benny.

Someone asked, "What about Klendenin?"

"No one's forgetting Klendenin," said Wild Will.

Standing together in a small circle just out of earshot of the rest of the team, the two team members who were ex-SEALs looked at each other. One of them had a flat nose, a swollen right eye, and hair spilling out from under his knit cap. The other was a head taller and unmarked. The one with the flat nose pulled his headphones off and said, "It can't be him. Last I heard, he was killed in the Congo."

"Yeah, I heard he was killed lots of times," said the second, taller SEAL.

Chapter 11

Brother-in-law, hypodermic in hand, stood over Vladimir, Becker, and Vadim, all restless and bound with layers of duct tape on Rulon and Yohaba's king size bed. "I'm going to peel the duct tape off your mouth," he said to Vladimir. "If you yell or otherwise get abusive, the duct tape goes back on."

He ripped away and Vladimir exploded, "You're dead! You're all dead! The fat man's dead! The woman is dead! Steenberg is dea—" Brother-in-law replaced the duct tape, stuck his knee firmly on Vladimir's chest, and wrapped his mouth with a few more layers of tape from a leftover roll.

He next turned to Becker. "I'm going to peel the duct tape off your mouth," he said. "If you yell or otherwise get abusive, well, I think you can fill in the rest." He yanked.

"You're a gentleman and a scholar," said Becker with his first breath. He wriggled the stiffness out of his jaw.

Brother-in-law held up the needle and said, "I'm going to give you guys something that'll put you out for a few hours. You'll be a lot more comfortable that way and less likely to hurt yourself or others. If you cooperate, we'll cut the tape off once you're out cold."

"Thank you," said Becker.

Brother-in-law walked around the bed to sit next to Vadim and asked, "What's it going to be?" Vadim nodded furious agreement, so Brother-in-law simply yanked the tape off.

"Where's Yevgeny?" asked Vadim calmly once he got his jaw working. "You realize, of course, my father will kill him for allowing this to happen."

"Your man's a hero," said Brother-in-law. "There's eleven guys out there wanting to torture you and your grandfather for your father's secrets. He went after them, and now he's probably dead."

"Then let us go," pleaded Vadim.

From the doorway, Yohaba, with Mr. Hurt at her side, said, "Yeah, and have you shoot us in the back. Let's see, what was that you said? Oh yeah. *You have no idea what we're capable of.*"

"It's just an old Russian expression," said Vadim sheepishly.

"Rooskies," murmured Mr. Hurt disparagingly.

"My nurse will administer the drug and cut the rest of the tape off," said Brother-in-law. "I've got somebody more important to take care of." He handed Yohaba the hypodermic and his Mercworx fixed-blade knife and left.

Standing over Vadim with the needle in her hand, Yohaba said, "Don't worry. I've done this lots of times on rats and gerbils."

When Yohaba was done, and her patients were asleep, she and Rulon's father walked through the dark, creaky house to the front door. They stopped in the hallway when movement in the living room caught their attention. Brother-in-law was sitting on the couch in the dark with Tripod's head resting on his lap.

"They darted him," said Brother-in-law.

Yohaba suggested to Mr. Hurt that he go help Rulon with the truck. After he left, she walked into the room and sat down beside Brother-in-law. She gave him back his knife, and asked, "How is he?"

"He's okay. He must have run a couple a' hundred yards with the dart stuck in him just to warn me. The dosage would have been set for a full-grown man. I don't know how he did it."

"He loves you," said Yohaba. "Most of the time, I don't even notice he's around. He's like your shadow."

"He's all banged up," said Brother-in-law, "but it doesn't slow him down. Nope, not old Tripod. Not one bit. That dog's one tough muchacho. But he's got scars under his fur. I can feel them. Man, the wounds he's got. Here, feel this one." He took Yohaba's hand and made her feel a thick scar that ran from Tripod's left shoulder all the way to the last rib. "And he's so ugly, the ugliest dog west of the Helmand, but he just carries on like there's nothing wrong, three legs and all. What a spirit, huh?"

"He's a strange animal," said Yohaba. "You make him feel useful with all your patrolling in the middle of the night." She punched him playfully in the arm. "You're a strange animal yourself."

"We gotta go," said Brother-in-law.

As he started to rise, Yohaba laid a hand on his arm and said, "I want to ask you something."

Brother-in-law settled back down and said, "Okay, but I won't kill Rulon for you."

Yohaba exploded off the couch. "You are the flat-out weirdest person I have ever met," she half-yelled, half-whispered, bending over Brother-in-law and jabbing a finger in his face. "How does that pea-brain of yours work to even say such a thing? No wonder you don't have a social life. You're a sorry, sorry…" Brother-in-law laughed quietly. Yohaba sat back down. "You love pushing people's buttons, don't you?" she said.

"What did you want to ask?" said Brother-in-law. "I've got some bad guys waiting."

Yohaba took a deep breath and started again. "Is it true you had two wives and your family was killed by the LRA? Rulon told me."

"You must think you know me pretty well to ask that question," said Brother-in-law.

"Yeah, I think I do. You have to talk to somebody about it," Yohaba said.

"Some SEAL shrink talked to me about it once. He said I'd feel better if I hunted down all the LRA and killed as many as I could. I kinda went with that."

"Stop it. No shrink would ever say that." She groaned in frustration. "You're impossible to talk to! I thought Rulon was bad but compared to you he's Oprah Winfrey."

"If it bothers you, we don't have to talk about it." Brother-in-law started to get up. Yohaba touched his arm again.

"I'm not through," she said. "How do you manage to always do that? You should talk about this with someone. This is not normal."

"Sure it is," he said. "This is normal for a man who's had almost his whole family killed and couldn't save them, because he was off saving others. Can you beat that? Other people's families, other people's children, but he couldn't save his own. Couldn't do anything but bury them. I didn't even have a shovel. I had to carve out their graves on my knees with a flat rock. Put what was left of them..." He stopped abruptly. "Shall I go on?"

Yohaba was silent. After a minute, without looking up, she said softly, "You said 'almost your whole family.' What did you mean?"

"My two sons might have been kidnapped. At least I didn't find the bodies with the others. Actually, I'm pretty sure they're still alive. I've been hunting for them. That's why I have to go back."

Yohaba couldn't find the words. After a minute, she said in the dark, "You know we love you." Tears rolled down her cheeks. "There are some things a person shouldn't have to endure alone. I love you. Rulon loves you. Don't interrupt. I just want you to know that this is your home forever as long as you want to stay. We'll always be your friends. My grandfather thinks of you like a beloved grandson. He's always taking you on trips with him. And who is the only person Rulon ever loans his favorite sniper rifle to? Our favorite assassin. You, that's who. Grandfather wouldn't risk his life with anyone else. Rulon and I feel the same way."

They sat together silently for a full five minutes until Brother-in-law said, "Well, it's been nice talking with you." They got up and went outside leaving Tripod asleep on the couch.

While Yohaba was inside with Brother-in-law, Rulon was outside pushing the truck around in the yard with his father steering until it was poised on the edge of the driveway's downward slope. He knew from experience that the truck could roll for a mile from the barn almost all the way to the crossroads that led to the Titus ranch five miles away. He didn't dare turn on the engine or the headlights for fear of attracting attention.

Yohaba and Brother-in-law came out of the house together and walked over to where Rulon was sitting on the truck's tailgate breathing hard. Yohaba saw in the truck bed all the weapons Rulon had brought.

"If the police stop us, we'll be arrested as terrorists," she said, having wiped away her earlier tears and regained her composure.

"Not in Idaho," said Rulon. "Let's roll." When no one laughed at his joke, he said, "Roll. Get it? Let's roll. The engine will be off, so we'll be *rolling* downhill." He made a little gliding motion with his hand. Still, no one laughed. "Oh, forget it," he said in disgust.

The plan was for Rulon to be in the cab alone while his father, Yohaba, and Brother-in-law lay low in the truck bed with the weapons. Mr. Hurt climbed in and Yohaba and Brother-in-law pushed to get the truck going. Rulon saw them having trouble and jumped out to help. With Rulon pushing, the truck quickly picked up speed and everyone scrambled back in.

The truck came around the west corrals, sweeping past the long line of birch trees and the dark silhouettes of the cows in the field. It picked up speed then slowed a little, then as the road steepened, got back up to twenty and stayed there.

"Yeehaa," said Rulon quietly.

Brother-in-law spoke through the cab's open rear window. "They done bought themselves a whole heap a' trouble this time."

"Oh no. Winter's Bone is back," said Rulon. "Darling, close your ears."

In his normal voice, Brother-in-law said, "The tire spikes are coming up. Stop at least thirty yards back so they won't be tempted to inspect the truck right away. And turn your lights on so you ruin their night vision." Rulon always joked his old truck could drive this road by itself. Turns out he wasn't half wrong. Some clouds had returned and the moon was covered again. Visibility was bad but the truck stayed on the road. He came around the last hill and turned on the high beams.

Twenty seconds later, Rulon said, "I think I see them."

"Remember," said Brother-in-law, "you're a dumb rancher. You've never seen tire spikes before."

Rulon slowed the truck to a cautious stop and sat there for a few seconds. Slowly he got out and looked around.

He ambled cautiously towards the chain of tire spikes blocking the road. Yohaba lifted her head ever so slightly to watch through the back window and windshield. Brother-in-law joined her. Brother-in-law had his pistol out and there was a gleam in his eye.

They watched as Rulon picked up the chain in both hands and eyed it curiously in the glare of the headlights. He looked up, stood there acting puzzled, then glanced around. Suddenly there was a sound as a small tree branch snapping. Rulon immediately grabbed at the back of his neck, pulled out the dart, and stared at it. He swayed and took a step.

"Watch," whispered Yohaba. "We saw *King Kong* the other day." Rulon stumbled then fell to one knee. He swayed for a few seconds, then the other knee came down. A few more seconds, and he fell forward on his hands. "Now he's going to crawl forward for a few steps, then reach out for Naomi Watts. She won't be able to help, and he'll collapse to the ground as the gas takes effect. Look at him. There he goes. Crawling, crawling. Yes, yes. Now, one last gasp. Perfect." Out on the dirt road, Rulon lay stretched out collapsed and perfectly still. "Give that gorilla an Oscar," whispered Yohaba.

Five minutes later, Rulon was still lying on the road and all was quiet. "What are they waiting for?" breathed Yohaba softly.

"Just being smart," whispered Brother-in-law.

Three minutes later two men, armed, dressed in black, and wearing ski masks, emerged from the bushes on the left side of the road. They looked around warily and moved slowly towards Rulon, one circling left and the other right, each with a hefty tranquilizer gun in his hand.

One of the men prodded Rulon with his foot. Rulon didn't move. "You got a great husband," whispered Brother-in-law sincerely. "Wait for it. Wait for it," he whispered. They both watched as the second man dropped to one knee to check Rulon's neck for a pulse. The first man put his hand to his own throat, presumably to activate his throat mike and report back to his team what happened. "Good, let him make his report," said Brother-in-law, talking more to himself than to Yohaba. "Anytime now would be fine."

Yohaba held her breath. "What is he waiting for? Do it, Cowboy." The two armed men now noticeably relaxed. Their murmuring voices reached the truck.

Without warning, Rulon struck. Yohaba and Brother-in-law watched in jaw-dropping admiration as Rulon grabbed the kneeling man by his dangling hand and jerked him to the ground while at the same time kicking the legs out from under the other one. "Ouch," said Brother-in-law as the man hit the dirt flat on his back. In a flash, Rulon, the ex-hammer thrower and Greco-Roman wrestler, quick as a cat, was on his feet and rolling both frantically struggling men into a human sandwich. Brother-in-law had seen Rulon in action before, but his quickness was always a surprise. "Dang, he's fast! Dang, that big boy can move!"

"Uh-oh!" said Yohaba. "Here it comes!" She closed her eyes.

"Yeow!" yelled Brother-in-law. "They bounce!"

"Tell me when it's over," said Mr. Hurt from his prone position in the truck bed.

Yohaba opened her eyes. "It's over," she said.

Brother-in-law leaped out of the truck with the Browning in his hand. By now Rulon was rolling the unconscious men onto their sides to keep their windpipes clear. Brother-in-law picked up the two dropped tranquilizer pistols and looked them over.

"Cap-Chur. These are for animals," he said. "I wonder if this is what the agencies are using these days." He fired a dart into each man's leg.

"Let's get them off the road so they don't get run over," said Rulon. Together he and Brother-in-law carried one of the men twenty-five yards into the bush. When they came back for the second one, Yohaba was there.

Brother-in-law said, "Can you two handle this? I need to ask Rulon's dad something." He trotted off into the looming darkness between them and the truck.

Rulon grabbed the unconscious man under the armpits and began dragging him off the road. Yohaba grabbed his feet, and they carried him over to his buddy.

As they stumbled along in the dark, Yohaba said, "Have you noticed how much more talkative Brother-in-law is with that stuff in him? I talked to him about his family."

"That was a mistake," Rulon said.

"Yeah, well. I told him we both loved him." Yohaba replayed the conversation.

"He normally keeps things bottled up," said Rulon. "That's why I like him."

"Not like you, huh, Mr. Sensitive?" The man they were carrying groaned. Yohaba said, "You know, you hurt these guys pretty badly. I think in football, it's called unnecessary roughness. Did you have to pile drive them into the ground?"

"I was celebrating a touchdown. Besides, they resisted," said Rulon.

"They didn't," said Yohaba. "From the moment you grabbed them, they were trying to get away."

"Yes. So they could continue their quest to kidnap my wife," said Rulon. They reached the spot where they'd dropped the first man. "One, two three," said Rulon. On three, they tossed their man onto his buddy. Rulon next moved both men into a recovery position and checked to make sure they could freely breathe.

On the way back, Rulon finished his thought. "They needed to learn a lesson," he said.

"And I'm sure they'll thank you for it once they get out of the hospital," said Yohaba. "What was the lesson, Obi-wan?"

"You can choose your actions, but you can't choose your consequences."

"You know what's funny?" said Yohaba.

"What?"

"I'm the only person in the world who knows you're actually serious when you say stuff like that. You really believe you were doing them a valuable service, and if they would only reflect on life's little lessons brought to them courtesy of G. Rulon Hurt, they would repent and lead happier, more productive lives."

"I wouldn't put it quite that strongly," said Rulon. "But I'd be a liar if I said the hope wasn't there." By now they were back at the road where Rulon's dad was dragging the tire spikes to the side.

"Good design," said Mr. Hurt looking curiously at the spikes in his hand. He dropped the last section of chain into the side ditch, saw Rulon, and said, "Is everything all right?"

Rulon said, "Yes. Let's not get rid of the spikes. You never know when they'll come in handy." Rulon retrieved the spikes from the ditch and put them in the truck. When he got back to the truck, Yohaba gave him a disapproving look. Rulon said, "Hey, spoils of war. It's an honored military tradition."

"Where's Orin?" asked Mr. Hurt, looking around.

"I thought he was with you," said Rulon.

Rulon let out a big sigh and walked around to the back of the truck to see what Brother-in-law had taken. The M60 machine gun and ammo boxes were still there as well as the case with Rulon's Remington 700 AcuSport VTR 308 sniper rifle with the Leupold Mark 4 8-25 power scope. Those were the most valuable items. But, surprisingly, the M79 grenade launcher with its ammo bandoliers and the four SIG Sauer 556 assault rifles were also there.

"He'll be back," said Yohaba.

"I don't think so," said Rulon. He sat down on the tailgate to think. "What's the one thing all night he never brought up?" he asked.

"Well, I don't know, Cowboy," said Yohaba. "Would you prefer I started with the A's or work backwards from the Z's?"

"I'm being serious," said Rulon. "There was one thing he never talked about, and he should've."

"What's happened to the big Russian?" asked Mr. Hurt.

"Precisely," said Rulon. "Why do you think he never brought up Yevgeny?"

"Shoot," said Yohaba. "I'm so stupid. He left Tripod back at the house. He would never do that. This whole thing was a setup to get us out of the way so he could go back for Yevgeny by himself. What a sneak! Geez, and I thought Tripod was hopelessly loyal. What are we going to do?"

"Oh, he's a crafty one, all right," said Rulon, highly irked. "He's gotten me a mile away from the action, and he thinks I won't leave you and Dad. Dang! Dang! And he knows that even with these new tires my truck's too old and beat up to go four-wheeling."

"He's the only guy who ever gets the better of you," said Yohaba unhelpfully.

Rulon glared at Yohaba, kicked a tire, and fumed. He kicked the tire again and fumed some more. Then he came to a decision. "Well, not this time. Everyone back in the truck," he ordered.

Chapter 12

The latest procession of clouds still lingered, but for the moment there was a break, and a full moon shone down, adding the cold, pale shadows of trees, rocks, and bushes to the landscape. Brother-in-law walked into the clearing where Wild Will and the other seven members of his team were waiting and stood quietly. The oval clearing was forty meters at its widest point—one of the few places on Go-Right-And-Lose-Your-Job that was free of brush, having been burned out by a lightning strike the previous fall. Wild Will and his men were spread out in a half-circle in the middle of the clearing. Sitting on the ground off to the side was Yevgeny, looking groggy even in the dark, but seemingly in one piece.

It took a few seconds before a couple of the men noticed Brother-in-law. When they did, they nudged each other and pointed. Wild Will noticed the stirring just before someone said, "We've got company." Wild Will jumped up from the rock where he was sitting as soon as he saw Brother-in-law. He sized him up and down as well as he could in the moonlight. He noticed the bulletproof vest and the .22 on his hip, and that otherwise he was unarmed. He also saw he had a bundle in his hand. For a horrible split second, he thought it was Klendenin's head.

Russo came down from the rock perch where he'd been keeping lookout with the night vision goggles, and said, "Sorry, boss. Don't know how he got past me."

"Which one of you is the bull goose?" asked Brother-in-law once he had everyone's attention.

Wild Will stepped forward. "I am. We've got night vision too. We know you're alone and your fat rancher friend is lying face down on the road. You wanted to talk. So talk."

Brother-in-law walked over to Yevgeny. The big Russian looked up. Brother-in-law could see he'd been worked over good and proper. He looked into his eyes. Possible concussion. Definitely drugged. "No breakfast," said Brother-in-law gently.

"First, we trade," said Brother-in-law, nodding down at Yevgeny. "Klendenin for him." Yevgeny gave a weary, crooked smile. Brother-in-law was close enough to the other men to see marks and swelling on several of their faces. Yevgeny had gone down fighting.

From out of the darkness, Murphy said, "You can have the Russian if you keep Klendenin. That's our final offer."

"Shut up, Murphy," snapped Wild Will. Speaking to Brother-in-law, he said, "Where's Klendenin?"

"He's somewhere wishing he'd worn thermal underwear. Here's his clothes." Brother-in-law threw him the bundle. "For his sake, I hope you're a fast negotiator. Temperature's dropping."

"My new best friend!" exulted Murphy from somewhere in the dark.

"We need to settle this," said Brother-in-law. "Klendenin told me all about you sorry pack of losers. Marine Recon, Special Forces, and SEALs." He shook his head sadly. "And you're all too chicken or too dumb to save Klendenin's girl, so you go after a non-principal. A gal who never did no harm to you or your kin." At

Brother-in-law's words, the team's confidence took a big hit, each convicted by his own conscience.

Wild Will tried to explain. "Klendenin called the shots and paid us to do a job. No one was going to get hurt, and nothing would have happened to the Hurt woman even if Klendenin didn't get his daughter back. We all agreed to that."

"Well, thanky kindly for clearing that up. Ah will mail you your medals," drawled Brother-in-law. Wild Will started to protest but Brother-in-law ignored him and helped Yevgeny to his feet. "Get on back to the ranch," he told him. Yevgeny took a few wobbly steps and fell to all fours. Brother-in-law helped him into a sitting position, and said to the mercenaries, "One of you men go bring around one of the Humvees and take him home."

The man next to Wild Will started to obey but Wild Will grabbed his arm and stopped him. "Where are you going?" he asked angrily. Then to Brother-in-law he barked, "Who are you to be giving orders? Your Russian buddy's not going anywhere."

"Let your man go," said Brother-in-law. "You'll need the Hummer for Klendenin anyway."

Wild Will released his arm, and the man started to walk away then stopped. "Should I be worried about booby traps?" he asked Brother-in-law.

"Fair question, but no," answered Brother-in-law. The man disappeared off into the dark.

"Who darted the dog?" asked Brother-in-law.

Benny stepped forward and sneered. "That would be me. So what?"

"So, when this is over, you and I will be having a private conversation."

"Can't wait," said Benny.

"My money's on the hippie," said Murphy.

"Shut up, Murphy," said Benny. "After I'm done with him, you're next."

"Listen, Buckwheat," said Murphy. "I'm not afraid of a man who abuses crippled animals. If you had a fork, no puppy would be safe."

"Shut up!" yelled Benny. "For the love of life, just shut up for once!"

"That did it," said Murphy jumping to his feet. "If there's gonna be a fight, I'm on the hippie's side. I mean it."

Listening to the exchange, Wild Will was momentarily confused. He looked over his men. Burke was lying prone with a bad sprain, but all the rest were standing. Except for Benny, who looked eager for a fight, their body language was vague and indecisive. He was losing command.

"Where's the girl?" asked Wild Will. "This isn't over. You coming up here just handed us another hostage."

"I wouldn't be so sure," said Brother-in-law, slipping into his backwoods persona. "This here possum ain't so easy to tree. I'm walkin' off this hill with ma friend. And that is not negotiable." At Brother-in-law's words, Yevgeny looked up at him and staggered to his feet. He swayed and Brother-in-law caught him. With Yevgeny's arm draped around his neck, Brother-in-law spread his legs for balance, flexed the fingers of his gun hand, and undid the Browning's trigger thong. "Starting now, I'm playing for keeps."

"Look around. It's over for you," said Wild Will, sensing the danger in Brother-in-law, but still not believing he was ready to take them all on. *For crying out loud, who the heck is this guy?* he thought to himself. Out loud he said, "There's eight of us here and only one of you."

"Make that seven and two," said Murphy. "I told you. I'm on the hippie's side. Let 'em go."

"The girl's long gone," said Brother-in-law. "A dollar to a nickel says your two guys guarding the road are not pickin' up."

"Russo, try them," ordered Wild Will. Russo walked off to the side and spoke into his mike. He repeated himself over and over. Finally, he looked at Wild Will and shook his head.

"What do you want?" asked Wild Will. The Humvee could be heard approaching.

"I want you to knock off this nonsense, and you and Klendenin come down to the ranch house with me. There's someone you need to talk to. This thing is bigger than you think, and the bad guys are not who you think they are. You're all out here making fools of yourselves."

Just then, the Humvee drove up with the high beams on, heavy tires crunching over bushes. Everyone squinted and shielded their eyes, surprised to see their man back so soon. Someone yelled to turn it down. The vehicle pulled to a stop and the driver got out, leaving the engine running and the lights on. Something was wrong. It wasn't the same guy who'd gone. This man was big, way big. Then Rulon put on his cowboy hat and was instantly recognizable. He came out of the headlight's glare and his silhouette snapped sharply into focus. Slung behind his back out of sight from everyone except Brother-in-law was the M79 grenade launcher. His Colt automatic was tucked away in the small of his back.

"Say hello to the fat rancher," said Brother-in-law. As Rulon walked past, Brother-in-law discreetly mouthed, *Keep it short.*

Go home, mouthed Rulon in reply. He continued striding into the clearing until he was twenty feet away from Wild Will and the men around him. He looked them over and sighed.

"What you are doing is ethically and morally wrong on so many levels," said Rulon. He paused. His audience stared back at him with expressions of intense puzzlement. Rulon tried to gauge their reaction and was himself puzzled. Brother-in-law growled something unintelligible. Rulon cleared his throat and continued. "You're on my land to kidnap my wife. In the United States of America. In Idaho. Let's think this through and ask ourselves if that sounds like something a normal person would be doing."

When no one responded, Rulon decided to ratchet up the pressure by completely leapfrogging the four steps of repentance and going directly to consequences. "If you kidnap a stranger in America, no matter how valid you think your reason is, you will immediately go on the FBI's most wanted list and when they catch you, which they surely will, you will go to prison for twenty years. That's twenty years without getting to shoot guns or blow stuff up, without having Christmas with your families, and without being able to swap stories with your commando buddies about how macho you are. You will come out of prison a broken, twisted shell of your former self with the only things to show for it a tattooed body and good dental care. And all this for kidnapping someone who is a really nice person. Now, does this sound like a choice that a mature, responsible adult would make?"

Rulon paused again. Just as he was beginning to think he had gotten through to them, everyone burst out laughing except Brother-in-law, who simply looked down at the ground shaking his head.

Someone said, "Excellent. Now we have three hostages." All the men except Wild Will, Murphy, and Burke, who was hurting, drew their tranquilizer guns.

Someone else said, "Maybe if we wait here long enough, the girl will show up." More manly laughter.

Rulon sighed again. Wild Will gave a curt order and someone fired a tranquilizer dart into Rulon's leg. Rulon pulled it out and flicked it away. The prospects of this ending peaceably seemed increasingly remote. Another tranquilizer dart hit him in the arm. He pulled that one out too and dropped it. Thanks to the Flumazenil, there was no effect.

"You know, you're acting like a bunch of jerks," said Rulon. "Is that what you want your legacy to be—died being a jerk? Great legacy to leave your parents. Hey, how did your son die? 'Oh, after a distinguished military career he died on a hill in Idaho while trying to kidnap some poor girl he'd never met before. We're so proud.'" Another tranquilizer dart struck Rulon in his bullet/stab vest. As everyone waited for him to drop, Rulon reached behind him for the heretofore unseen short, stocky, and murderously lethal M79 grenade launcher. While his hands were moving slow and careful, he kept talking. "Whether you want to believe me or not, this thing is gonna end here, right now, on this hill. If you don't back off, people are gonna start bleeding. I don't think I can make it much plainer than that."

Wild Will said, "We never meant for this to get that rough, but if that's what you want, don't forget, you can bleed too."

"Yeah," said Rulon still puzzling everyone as to why he wasn't lying face down on the ground. "Well, I guess it's possible for both of us to be right. Ain't that a shame?" The way he said it and the look on his face had the hair on the back of everyone's neck standing up, including Brother-in-law's. Rulon added a final exclamation mark by whipping out and leveling the M79, completing his message with the finality of a coffin lid slamming shut.

At the sight of the grenade launcher, everyone jumped, dropping their tranquilizer guns, and going for the real thing stuck in belts and small-of-back holsters. But something in Rulon's voice and demeanor told them quite correctly not to draw or the bloodbath would begin. The men stood or crouched, frozen, hands on the butts of their weapons. Wild Will jumped between Rulon and his men and shouted for everyone to "Stand down, stand down!"

Taking control, Wild Will said to Rulon, "The grenades in that thing have to travel thirty meters before they arm. You're less than ten meters away. Nice try, son."

Rulon snorted and replied, "Yeah, and that would be a problem if this pirate gun was loaded with a 40mm HE round and not an M576 E2 buckshot round." He slapped his palm a few times with the barrel of the M79. Nobody dared move. "I need to be extra close because this thing's got twenty-seven of these really nasty twenty-four-gram slugs, and they spread way too fast. Some folks consider it a design flaw, but I don't."

"Oops," said Murphy. No one dared move. Murphy said nice and loud, "Fat Rancher. If you let us live, we'll pick your potatoes for you." This time no one laughed, and no one told him to shut up. There was a moment or two of continued silence while both sides ran the calculations. A single twitch away from a firefight, the tension like a humming electric wire. Men, wanting room to maneuver, edged imperceptibly apart.

No one spoke, and the tension continued to build until it was an angry swarm of bees. Brother-in-law laid Yevgeny down and came over to stand next to Rulon. He held up the remote detonating device. "I will sweep your position clean. I promise."

Benny started to raise the Bizon then thought better of it and stopped. Rulon lowered the M79 ever so slightly. Murphy's voice boomed over the clearing. "Fat Rancher. How can you still be standing? Answer that and I'll die a contented man." A few snickers, leading to a few chuckles, leading to Murphy's hearty Irish laugh and suddenly the tension broke.

The SEAL with the flat nose put his hand on Wild Will's shoulder and said friendly and consoling, "What'd'ya say we pick Klendenin up and call it a day. First beer's on me."

Wild Will started to say something and stopped. "Oh, forget it," he said in disgust and stormed away. With that everyone started breathing again, then the jokes started in earnest, everyone relieved that this ridiculous, ill-advised fiasco had mercifully come to an end.

In the Humvee's headlights, Rulon saw the tired, dejected men for what they were. "If you boys are hungry," he said, "I suppose I could get my wife to rustle up something."

"Hey, I'm not your servant!" yelled Yohaba, from inside the Humvee. An M60 machine gun with its dangling ammo belt poked out of the Humvee's sunroof followed immediately by Yohaba's lovely head and torso.

"I'll talk to her," said Rulon.

✑✑✑

It took some persuading, but Rulon the wife whisperer finally managed to convince Yohaba to cook breakfast for her would-be kidnappers. It helped that one by one all the mercenaries except Wild Will and Burke, who couldn't walk, came up to her and apologized. Even Benny. By now the man originally sent after the Humvee had returned and taken Yevgeny back to the ranch.

Standing off by themselves, Yohaba, Rulon and Brother-in-law watched the men collecting their gear and loading it into the rest of the Humvees. She said, "I'm proud of my two boys. A little stick, a little carrot, and the casualties were minimal. And none on our side, if you don't count Yevgeny."

Brother-in-law said. "We need to get our stories straight. Yevgeny knows now that they were really after you and not Vadim." He added with a chuckle, "If he finds out the Bizon was loaded with blanks, and I deliberately sent him up there to take a beating for you, he might not take it too kindly."

"What about Yevgeny's team?" asked Rulon. "They're gonna want your scalp no matter who was the target."

"I'm working on that," said Brother-in-law.

While they were talking, the two former SEALs walked up obviously wanting to talk to Brother-in-law. "I think I saw you once," said the taller of the two, a thin man well over six feet with a long, droopy mustache. "It was at Rumangabo camp near Rutshuru."

"Never heard of it," said Brother-in-law.

"Never been to the Congo then?"

"Nope."

"You came in just for a meal and ammo. You and your team. Left again right away. We were all told to stay away from you."

"Sounds like good advice," said Brother-in-law, and he walked away.

The shorter SEAL with the flat nose called after him, "Hold on a minute." Brother-in-law let out an irritated sigh and turned slowly to face them. "Look," said Flat Nose. "We screwed up with this gig. We know it. But it's hard making a living in this economy. Once we got out, we were all broke in six months. This was a job we knew how to do. It wasn't personal."

"You ran an op against my friends," said Brother-in-law. "You made it personal for me."

"This hasn't exactly been our proudest moment," said Flat Nose. When Brother-in-law didn't respond, he said,

"The only easy day was yesterday," hoping a reference to the SEAL motto would draw Brother-in-law out. He held out his hand, which Brother-in-law ignored. "Guys call me Dilly."

"We wanted to ask you something," said the tall SEAL. "They told humdingers at Little Creek about a guy named 'Brother-in-law' who had a team in the Congo they used to call the 'Spooky Pandemoniums.' Ever heard of him?"

"No," said Brother-in-law.

By now, Rulon and Yohaba had caught up and were listening. Rulon put his arm around Brother-in-law and interrupted. "My friend here is afraid you'll find out his Hopi name and steal his spirit. Isn't that right, Brother-in-law?" Rulon laughed a booming laugh, and he and Yohaba went to go talk to Wild Will.

After they left, there was a moment of silence. Finally, Brother-in-law exhaled deeply and said in mild disgust, "Rumangabo camp is closer to Kiwanja than Rutshuru. Did you even know what continent you were on?"

"Not really," said Dilly with a smile. "I just knew it wasn't Kansas anymore. I used to get lost in camp. But everyone thinks my partner here must be part Indian the way he can track and find his way around."

"They call me Stringbean," said the tall man. He held out his hand and Brother-in-law took it."

While they were talking, Brother-in-law caught Murphy's eye and waved him over. Murphy nodded back and began wrapping up a heated conversation with Benny.

"He's a Marine," said Dilly nodding towards Murphy. "Makes a lot of jokes, but he's okay. Got through their Infantry Officer Course. Heard that was pretty tough."

"Well, we've got something in common," said Brother-in-law. "Before BUD/S, I was also a Marine."

Murphy broke away from Benny with a disgusted wave and came over. He started talking to Brother-in-law when still fifteen feet away. "You're not one of those regular hippies. I can tell. You're one of those backwoods, hillbilly hippies that kilt him a bar when he was only three. You've read every Louie Lamour book ever written and think *Gunsmoke* is the greatest series in TV history. You once gave serious thought to changing your name to Matt Dillon. I'm an infallible judge of human nature. Some people think I'm psychic. I could have made a fortune as a palm reader, but I chose to serve my country instead. In fact, I'm getting vibes that you are an ex-Jarhead. Don't try denying it." By now, Murphy was standing in front of Brother-in-law, looking slightly down from his six-foot two-inch height. He held out his hand and they shook. "So, am I right or am I right?"

Brother-in-law said, "They canceled *Gunsmoke* after only twenty seasons. Go figure."

"The world is upside down," said Murphy.

"There were 635 episodes, and I've seen them all," said Stringbean.

"I hate the show," said Dilly. "Because of *Gunsmoke*, they cancelled *Gilligan's Island*."

"I fight so no one will have to live in a world without *Nick-at-Nite*," said Murphy.

Brother-in-law looked over the three men in front of him and made a decision. He said, "I got something to do. If you don't come with me, you'll miss all the fun."

Rulon and Yohaba found Wild Will sitting off by himself and strolled over. "Nice night," said Yohaba. As she walked up, the moon broke through the clouds and made her hair and eyes shine.

Wild Will looked up from stuffing a map in the flap of a small rucksack. "Not really," he said gruffly. "Are you going to press charges?"

"Only, if you don't come down for breakfast," said Yohaba. "You and your boss need to meet my grandfather. He should be showing up in a few hours."

"If you don't mind, lady, I'm calling it a day," he said wearily.

"Let me make it simple for you," said Rulon. "If you don't come, I'm pressing charges, and you and your men can all go to jail. Or you can come down to the ranch and try to sort this out. Your call."

"Darling," said Yohaba gently. "Ask nice." With a wisp of a smile, and a hand on Wild Will's arm, she charmed him in an instant into a different frame of mind. "C'mon," she said with a gentle pull and a voice like falling into feathers. "We make far better friends than enemies."

Wild Will, the grizzled veteran, looked up into the sky and laughed, knowing he was being charmed but unable to resist. "Why not?" he asked the moon. He picked up his rucksack and walked off with Yohaba, leaving Rulon to lag behind for a few steps.

Rulon watched them from behind and marveled not for the first time at the power Yohaba had over him and every other red-blooded man she met. Boris the Russian, Brother-in-law the SEAL, all the cowboys at the Rockin' Rooster where she and Rulon sang on Karaoke Wednesday. There was Yohaba, always the unspoken, overwhelming presence in every room she entered. Beautiful but approachable, comfortable in jeans, boots, and a cowboy hat riding in a beat-up pick-up truck, or strolling down Zurich's Bahnhofstrasse decked out in Gucci and a two-thousand franc handbag. He remembered their first day together, that fateful day in Zurich, when he and his hammer saved her from some Russians looking for Einstein's trunk and then later from another Russian waiting in her apartment. It was right after that he experienced how adept she was at whatever that thing was called that she was so adept at.

Rulon burst out laughing at the winding track his thoughts had taken, and Yohaba turned around quickly at the sound. "C'mon, slow poke," she said with a smile.

Chapter 13

Breakfast around the heavy wood kitchen table was a subdued affair. The men were tired and hungry and ate steadily of the cheese omelets and the mountain of waffles that Yohaba and Rulon rustled up. Most of Wild Will's men were nursing wounds of one kind or another. Two had picked up a few superficial punctures from half-spent shrapnel. There were several busted ear drums, Burke's sprained ankle which was packed with ice but swelling badly, and Frank and Earl, the two men who had tangled with Rulon, both had broken collar bones, broken fingers, and probable concussions. No hard feelings, though. Hard men, hard lives. Sometimes you dish it out, sometimes you take it. The ones who needed to would get to the hospital eventually.

Surprisingly, Winston Klendenin III had survived the night in relatively good shape. True, Brother-in-law had taken his clothes, but he'd left him in a hollow out of the wind, and after a hot shower and some food he'd made his entrance at breakfast, a sadder, wiser, and more humble billionaire, but still resolutely determined to rescue his daughter. It turned out Winston might not be the bumbling fool Wild Will and his team thought he was.

Vladimir was walking around with a bag of frozen vegetables on his head, a peace offering from Rulon. The gnarly, old Russian seemed to hold no ill will. Vadim, however, stared sadly at Yohaba like a puppy who'd been spanked unjustly. With Vladimir's hearty approval, Rulon made Vadim come with him when he went to milk the cows, figuring that hard work was the antidote to most personality problems. It turned out that old Father Becker really wasn't a priest after all, but rather an unscrupulous retired actor hired by the Italian mafia family that Steenberg was doing business with to ferret out Steenberg's whereabouts. Or so he said. However, while his identity was fake, his old age was real, and he was in bed, exhausted and with a migraine. Or so he said.

ↄ৩ↄ৩

Halfway through breakfast, the Suburban crept into the yard with Murphy behind the wheel and his head out the window shouting cadence. Walking behind was Brother-in-law with Dilly and Stringbean and the four Russians he'd had sedate themselves hours earlier, and who had to be assumed were holding a murderous grudge towards Brother-in-law. Weapons were out and the groggy Russians were clearly under guard as they stumbled along. Once in front of the ranch house they milled around and smoked under the watchful eye of Murphy and the SEALs while Brother-in-law went into the house. Yevgeny came out a minute later, took his team over to the barn out of earshot, and brought them up to speed on the situation. When he was finished, they were angry.

"Okay, we don't kill the hippie now," said Ivan. "I understand that. But later we come back and kill him. Right?"

"No," said Yevgeny. "Use your head."

Ivan slapped his forehead. "Right, right. We torture him first. What was I thinking?"

"Look at my face," said Yevgeny. "Does it look like I'm joking? He's off limits."

"Boss, I am looking at your face, and it's uglier than usual," said Tomas. "You've been worked over, we've been drugged, and he's still strutting around like a commissar."

Just then Brother-in-law came out of the house lugging his duffle bag with Tripod leaping joyfully beside him. He disappeared into the barn.

For a long moment, no one spoke. The silence continued as Rulon strode out of the barn with Vadim behind him lugging two slopping pails of milk. Rulon growled at Vadim to watch the spilling and Vadim immediately straightened up to trail awkwardly after him with short, mincing steps. The Russians stared as the two walked across the yard and up the porch steps into the house.

Once they were inside Mikhael asked, "Did I just see what I thought I saw—the kid doing work?"

"He must have drugged him too," said Tomas.

While they talked, Tripod bounded out of the barn followed by Brother-in-law, who was carrying a heavy, half-full potato sack over his shoulder. The SEAL nodded a friendly greeting to the Russians but never broke stride as he headed off towards the hills. A few seconds later, Murphy, Dilly, and Stringbean came tearing out of the house after him.

When they were out of earshot, Ivan asked, "What do you think he's up to?"

"Replanting the Claymores he fired off last night, I think," said Yevgeny.

Mikhael asked angrily, "Why are you protecting him?"

Yevgeny put his hand on Mikhael's shoulder. "Really? You think it's him I'm protecting. Really?" Yevgeny gave his team a moment to process his words then said, "No wonder Americans are so fat. You should see the breakfasts they make. Come. Let's go inside."

ᑌᏱᏱᏱ

Everyone was waiting for Steenberg. Yohaba had spoken to him on the phone. He was on his way.

After breakfast Klendenin and Wild Will went for a walk by themselves. When they came back, they paused by the long, pole fence that connected to the barn. Rulon was there in the enclosed south meadow, happily grinning through the mud covering his face, with an equally muddied, rowdy, and happily exhausted group of Russians and Americans. Somehow Rulon had cajoled the restless and mutually suspicious men into forming teams and flip-racing the length of the meadow with the big five-hundred-pound Michelin tractor tires he sometimes used for working out.

Klendenin and Wild Will stayed to watch. Brother-in-law, Murphy, Dilly, and Stringbean returned too late to see the best out-of-five finals.

Chapter 14

After everyone was cleaned up, dried off and had lunch, Vladimir and Klendenin sat around the kitchen table talking about the world economy and the latest elections in Russia. The rest of the men were outside except for Ivan and Mikhael who were in the living room watching TV. Rulon, Vadim, and Yevgeny were off somewhere fixing a fence. Yohaba and Mr. Hurt were in the kitchen puttering around, listening to the conversation.

Vladimir just finished making a point when Russo poked his head in the kitchen and said, "You don't want to miss this. The hippie and Benny are going at it." Immediately, wood scraped wood as chairs slid back and Klendenin rushed out with Vladimir hobbling gamely after him faster than Yohaba would have thought him capable.

After they left, Mr. Hurt put down the plate he was drying and said to Yohaba, "Who cares about two grown men making fools of themselves?"

"Yeah. So immature," said Yohaba as she leaned over the sink trying to get a better look through the kitchen window. "Maybe I should go too and make sure this doesn't get out of hand."

Mr. Hurt said with a sarcasm that was lost on his daughter-in-law, "Sure, I don't mind finishing up by myself." Yohaba flew out of the kitchen so fast she almost knocked over a chair.

Mr. Hurt, now alone, finished drying the plate he had started. Outside men were yelling. *So immature*, he thought to himself. Finally, not able to contain himself any longer, he too rushed outside.

Brother-in-law and Benny stood in the center of the yard a few feet apart. They were both hatless, wore black camo, and had a Cap-Chur tranquilizer pistol in their hand. Rulon wasn't back yet with the others, but everyone else was there, including Tripod, who was at Brother-in-law's side, growling low now and again as the two men talked.

"This is pretty stupid," said Benny. "What kind of a dog is that? Is that a German Shepherd?"

"He's a Belgium Malinois."

"That's still a dog. You're gonna get yourself darted over a dumb dog."

Tripod growled at the sound of Benny's voice and Brother-in-law crouched down to speak in his ear. "Yes, indeedy, old boy. This here's the pole cat that stung ya. Smell him good up and down. You shouldn't have to work your nose too hard." Murphy and the two SEALS let out a laugh.

Benny threw up his hands and turned to everyone lined up against the barn and sitting on the porch steps. "Geez, he's talking to dogs. The man talks to dogs."

From his place on the steps, Murphy yelled out, "He wants to have an intelligent conversation." This time everyone burst out laughing.

"Murphy," said Benny. "How 'bout when I'm done with Dueling Banjoes here, you and I go a few rounds, huh?"

"No problemo," said Murphy.

Brother-in-law stood up and said, "Even in the dark he knew who got him. Man, this dog is smarter than ten of you."

Except for Murphy, Yevgeny and the SEALs, everyone else was on Benny's side urging him on. The yard resounded with calls of *You can take this guy, Benny. He won't even clear his holster. He's yours. Kick the hippy's butt. Nighty-night, Hillbilly.* But the Russians, though hoping to see Brother-in-law flat on his face, weren't so optimistic, having seen him handle a gun on the road coming back from Redfish.

By now Mr. Hurt was on the porch and Yohaba had snuck through the knot of men to sit next to Murphy. "Is your guy fast?" she asked.

"I hate to admit it, ma'am," said Murphy, "but he's greased lightning."

"Rulon is going to be so mad he missed this," she whispered.

In the yard, Benny said, "So, what now? Do we stand back-to-back and walk off ten paces? Is this like a duel or something?" He turned to his admirers and guffawed. More hoots of encouragement.

Brother-in-law said, "You and me twenty-five feet apart. Then we see how you like it when sumpin's shooting back."

"Makes no difference to me," Benny said. "What do we do? One two three, go?" As he spoke, Benny casually sighted off to the side down the barrel of his pistol.

"No rules. You just draw when it suits ya. I'll be ready. No sneak shots though."

Benny snorted derisively at the suggestion of a cheap shot. "I don't need any tricks to outdraw you. But you do realize both of us are going to get darted. These drugs take a few seconds to work."

"But you won't shoot me," said Brother-in-law.

"Yes, I will," said Benny.

"No, you won't," said Brother-in-law.

"I don't know what you've been smoking, Festus, but yes I will," said Benny. "Watch me. No matter what happens, you're getting darted. You can shoot me in the eyeball, and I'm still going to dart you. *Capisce*?"

Brother-in-law held up a hypodermic and said, "Winner gets the antidote, and I've only got one. Chew on that." He let Benny get a good look at it and tossed it to Murphy.

Brother-in-law gave a low command and Tripod hopped over to join Yohaba. Benny stuck the gun in his belt, shrugged, and walked off about ten feet. Brother-in-law holstered his Cap-Chur and walked off in the opposite direction till they were about the right distance apart. He turned and ran a hand through his long hair. The sun was bright but the shadows were getting long. Everyone fell quiet, even the cows and horses in the field. Just the rusty creak of the weathervane atop the barn.

"Anytime," said Brother-in-law, eyes half-closed and so relaxed you'd think he was about to nod off.

Benny reached for his gun so fast it was a blur. But as fast as he grabbed, Brother-in-law was faster, so fast in fact that he seemed almost to hesitate in mid-draw, pausing just for a nanosecond to let Benny's weapon clear his belt. As soon as the gun was clear, Brother-in-law fired and darted Benny in the hand, causing the ex-sniper to yell, jerk his hand, and drop the pistol. A groan erupted from Benny's supporters.

Brother-in-law returned his own pistol to his holster with a twirling flourish. After that, he didn't move. Didn't flinch. Just waited for the inevitable with a faint smile on his face. Benny pulled the dart out of his hand in disgust, looked at it, then glared at Brother-in-law. He angrily spiked the dart in the dirt and stooped to retrieve the pistol with his good hand.

Benny stood back up, steady, still seconds away from the drug taking effect. "Well, you won. And now you're gonna get darted. I hope you're happy. Luckily, I'm just as good with my left hand. Smile."

Brother-in-law said, "There's only one antidote. If you shoot me, I guess I'll be the one getting it. I won."

Benny pointed the pistol at Brother-in-law and held his aim. His eyes narrowed, and his jaw firmed. His fingered tightened slightly on the trigger.

Brother-in-law said, "Enjoy your long nap. I hope you'll maintain bladder and bowel control while in your unconscious state."

The hippie in his sights. Benny savoring the moment. Brother-in-law calm, making no move to even turn sideways to make a smaller target. Benny steady as a rock, everyone tense, anticipating the shot. But suddenly and strangely, Benny returned the weapon to his belt.

"You cunning, devious, son-of-a…" At a loss for words, he ripped off a string of obscenities that had Murphy making a move to cover Yohaba's ears. When done, Benny took two unsteady steps towards the house, stopped, and slowly keeled over. Brother-in-law rushed forward and caught him before he hit the ground.

A ranch yard in Idaho about thirty miles outside of Twin Falls. Hardened mercenaries stood around together for half an hour talking about what they'd just seen and drinking the beer that was in one of the Humvees. Brother-in-law used the antidote on Benny and soon had him walking. Some of the men kidded Benny that it was really the next day, and he'd been knocked out for twenty-four hours. Brother-in-law told them to quit their jawing. And they did.

❧❦❧

When Rulon and the others came back an hour later and heard the story, already taking on mythic qualities, they could have kicked themselves for not being there. Sitting on the porch, Murphy was waxing poetic about the showdown, when in mid-sentence, he stopped. The sound of a low-flying helicopter caused all eyes to turn to the south. The sound came closer and then a small helicopter appeared over the hills. It flew directly towards the ranch, slowed and began a controlled, spiraling descent into the ranch yard. It landed and a white-haired man in his early eighties, sporting a short white beard, black Armani sports jacket, black turtleneck, and matching trousers, emerged. He stood tall and straight, belying his age. The helicopter took off again in a swirl of dust and noise.

The man brushed himself off and looked around. By now everyone was either on the porch or in the yard watching. Yohaba ran to his side, and they kissed each other three times on alternating cheeks, Swiss style. With his arm around Yohaba's shoulder, the man turned to the assembled group and said, "I am Leonard Steenberg. I understand someone has been spreading unsavory rumors about me."

"That would be an understatement," said Yohaba.

"This can be easily straightened out," said Steenberg. "Who is first?" Klendenin and Vladimir stepped off the porch and approached. "Kidnapped daughter trumps sinking profits," said Steenberg. "Sorry, Vladimir, my old friend. Mr. Klendenin. Come. Let us go for a walk. I'll show you the fence I helped build." Klendenin stepped forward, shook Steenberg's hand, and started to say something about his daughter's kidnapping. Steenberg cut him off. "I listen better when I'm walking," he said with a benign smile. "Come."

Once past the barn, Klendenin blurted, "Did you kidnap my daughter?"

Steenberg stopped and looked straight into his eyes. "No, I did not. And, yes, I am insulted by your question."

Steenberg started walking again and Klendenin caught up with him. "Do you know who did?"

"No but tell me. Why did you think it was me in the first place? Does this have something to do with IQ Technology?"

"Yes, and because whoever did kidnap my daughter calls himself the Director. And you're a director at CERN."

"Former director," corrected Steenberg.

"And there were other factors. There are reports my daughter is being kept in Switzerland, and you are Swiss. And when you presented to the board you were dying to get your hands on IQ's intellectual property."

"Interesting, certainly, Mr. Klendenin, but hardly conclusive," said Steenberg, annoyed. "For your information, I have since sold all my IQ shares to a Russian solar energy consortium. They made me an offer I could not refuse. Were you aware of that?"

"No," said Klendenin surprised. "But Russians, you say. The kidnappers send me a video of her every week. I sometimes hear Russian accents in the background. But I don't see the connection."

Steenberg looked pensive. "What did the kidnappers say to you? What was their demand?"

Klendenin could not answer those questions honestly without admitting he had shot Oderhardt and framed Connie. He said, "They haven't asked for anything yet."

"Mr. Klendenin," said Steenberg. "Please. First you tell me that it has something to do with IQ Technology, and then you tell me they haven't made any demands. Do you take me for a fool? What is it you are not telling me?"

Klendenin evaded both Steenberg's eyes and the questions. "If it's not you, it must be the Russians," he said.

"Is this linked to the shooting that day?" asked Steenberg.

"Possibly," said Klendenin.

"I'll take that as a 'yes,'" said Steenberg. "Who took that woman's place as CEO? I would start there."

"But why not just kill *her* then? I don't get it."

"Check her compensation package," said Steenberg. "Was there a clause in case of murder or workplace violence? There has to be a reason."

"I'll check," said Klendenin.

"I will also do some checking," said Steenberg. "I have a very powerful contact in the Russian government. If Russians are behind it, he could find out, perhaps, even secure your daughter's release."

"I would be forever in your debt," said Klendenin deeply.

"Yes, you would," said Steenberg. "And not only for that. I'm still debating whether to press charges over your misguided little adventure here. You put my granddaughter's life and liberty at risk."

"I told you. You became the majority stockholder after I shot Oderhardt. I was convinced it was you. I was desperate."

"A flimsy excuse, Mr. Klendenin," said Steenberg. "Wouldn't you agree?"

"Yes, and I'm very, very sorry."

"Actions speak louder than words, Mr. Klendenin," said Steenberg. "You were there when I explained Elsa to the board. If I should ever need you, can Yohaba and I count on you?"

"Yes, absolutely," said Klendenin.

"Good. I may have something for you then," said Steenberg. He waved away Klendenin's obvious next question. "Not now. Let's get back. Vladimir is not known for his patience." When they got back to the house, Vladimir was waiting on the porch swing. Klendenin went inside. The old Russian and Steenberg strolled off together having much to discuss.

❧❧❧

An hour later, after he returned from his conversation with Vladimir, Steenberg found Yohaba on her laptop in the living room. She looked up when he entered. "Your turn," he said. She accepted his extended hand and rose from the couch.

Once outside, they walked past the barn and the corrals. Most of the men were lined along the railings watching Rulon give horseback riding lessons to Yevgeny and Vadim. Rulon saw Yohaba and Steenberg and waved. Yohaba waved back.

Once they were out of earshot, she asked, "How was Zurich? Did everything go all right?"

"Very well," said Steenberg. "Our friend in the Kremlin is on board. He knew all about our little operation. A little too much, actually. I believe he and Polykov have been conspiring. In any case, I have to rush back to Zurich. We played a game of chess, and he is requesting a rematch." Steenberg chuckled. "Actually, there is still much to discuss. Will you come with me this time? You and Rulon. Our new ally would like to meet the two of you."

"You know I will," said Yohaba. "And Rulon will too."

"I'm asking Orin as well," said Steenberg.

Yohaba swallowed hard. "You're expecting trouble, aren't you?" she said.

"With these particular Russians, that's always a possibility," said Steenberg. "They want the whole pie and couldn't care less about Elsa."

"You always said they'd be trouble."

"Yes. It's best we bring Orin." As they walked, he filled her in on all the details of the meeting. When they reached the spot where the tire spikes had stretched across the road, they turned around. Yohaba then told her grandfather the story of how Rulon had taken out Frank and Earl. He listened patiently to Rulon's exploits wondering all the time what exactly his brilliant granddaughter saw in him.

On the way back, Yohaba asked, "What's the story with Becker? Was he with the Russians?"

"Yes, it appears so, but I sense they are not convinced of his fidelity. And frankly, neither am I. He's worked for the Italian mafia in the past. I've made a few inquiries, but no one is taking ownership for him."

"Would you?"

"Fair point," chuckled Steenberg. "As a precaution, I had Brother-in-law sedate him again."

"I hoped you used something strong," said Yohaba.

Steenberg shook his head. "You mean like Etorphine. He's too old for that. It might have killed him. I used Midazolam."

She laughed. "He's probably built up an immunity by now."

"It seemed to be working," said Steenberg, taking her concern seriously.

"Sooo…what else is up?" asked Yohaba.

"The Chinese," said Steenberg. "They're interfering."

"You always said they'd be trouble, too."

"Yes. I'm feeling quite clairvoyant these days. They need to be distracted." He filled her in on his conversation with Klendenin and Vladimir, including Klendenin's story about being blackmailed after somebody kidnaped his family in St. Petersburg. Yohaba asked about the man who was shot and the daughter.

"Amazingly, the man survived and is expected to fully recover after extensive therapy," said Steenberg. "The daughter is twenty-two and studied agriculture at U.C. Davis. Klendenin tells me she has a flair for rhythmic gymnastics. That's why the family was in Russia. She was training at the Zhemchujina gymnastics center in St. Petersburg, which is quite hard to get into, I've heard."

Yohaba said sadly, "Klendenin. Klendenin. I googled him. All the money in the world, and all it's done is made him and his family a target. What's he going to do now? He must be shattered."

"Strangely, no," said Steenberg. "This quest to save his daughter has held him together. But yes, a tragic story. Oh, thank the saints there is a merciful God in heaven for all us frail creatures and our awful tests. But I believe I've convinced him to assume a new role, one more befitting his talents." Steenberg told her his plan to use Klendenin against the Chinese. As she listened, her admiration—no, her awe—at her grandfather's amazingly versatile and creative mind swelled her heart with pride. "Do action" was ever his motto, taken from Theodore Roosevelt.

"I never would have thought of that," she said when he was done, "but how does a man work on anything when his child's been kidnapped?"

"He can't unless he has confidence in his child's positive outcome."

"Short of his daughter being rescued, I can't imagine what he'd consider a positive outcome."

"Me neither," said Steenberg somewhat ominously.

Yohaba looked at her grandfather trying to read his expression. "Is this going to involve Rulon?" she asked finally.

"No. I think not."

"Brother-in-law then?" Steenberg nodded. She asked, "Have you spoken to the critter? What if he says no?"

For an answer, Steenberg reached inside his jacket, pulled out a photograph, and handed it to Yohaba. The picture was of a lovely young black woman in jeans and a t-shirt standing in a garden under a purple blue canopy of interwoven Jacaranda branches.

"Who is this?" asked Yohaba.

"Batu Maitha Klendenin. Klendenin's twenty-two-year-old rhythmic gymnast daughter."

"You're joking. Klendenin's wife is black?"

"No. She's white. This is their adopted daughter. They've had her since she was four weeks old. Her parents were killed by the Lord's Resistance Army while they were working for one of Klendenin's Congo mining operations. Can you see where this is leading?"

"So you know about Brother-in-law's family then," said Yohaba. "I just found out."

"I would like to believe fate has fashioned him for this moment. When I saw the girl's picture, I knew immediately what I had to do. She even looks like his youngest wife. He couldn't save his own family. He will see Klendenin's daughter as a form of redemption." Steenberg's jaw clenched slightly. "Human nature is in the end not so difficult to predict."

"Wow, I just got a chill," said Yohaba. "Heaven help the kidnappers if you're turning Brother-in-law loose on them."

"I'm counting on that. I promised Mr. Klendenin we would move heaven and earth to rescue his daughter."

"Diplomacy by other means," said Yohaba.

"Precisely. And don't ever forget the lesson." He tapped her on the forehead for good measure.

While she admired the plan, Yohaba had to ask, "Don't you feel a little guilty manipulating him like this?"

"No," Steenberg said without hesitation. "And not for Klendenin either. The world is at stake. We serve the greater good. No one's life, not my life, not Rulon's life, and my child, hear me well, not even your life is too high a price to pay. Never forget that. If anything happens to me, you must continue the plan and be strong. And don't ever, ever underestimate yourself." Yohaba nodded.

For a moment, Steenberg stared at her closely, gauging her resolution. "Remember the story of King David in the Bible. Before his fall. When he was still strong. A young man in hopes of a reward, told David that he had personally killed King Saul, David's bitter enemy. Instead of rewarding him, David ordered his death, thus convincing the twelve tribes that he was an upholder of the law and fit to lead them. Heed this lesson well. Above all else, be strong."

"But wasn't that man lying?" asked Yohaba. "I thought Saul killed himself."

"Yes, that's true," said Steenberg. "And there's a lesson there as well about currying favor with the powerful."

Convinced he had made his point, Steenberg's gaze softened and he said, "Now this Klendenin, he's a complex one, isn't he? What did Lincoln say? *Show me a man without vice, and I'll show you a man without virtue.* I'm not sure I agree with that, but I suppose it depends on how you define vice and virtue. In Klendenin's case, he has much to answer for, but he is deeply remorseful for shooting that poor man and framing someone else for it—quite ingeniously, I might add."

"The whole thing sounds contemptible to me," said Yohaba. "How could you possibly call it ingenious?"

"Because it was," said Steenberg. By now they were back at the corrals. No one was around, but there was whooping and hollering coming from inside the barn.

"Sounds like they have a winner," Steenberg said drolly. "What is it this time?

"Hay bales probably," said Yohaba. Steenberg shook his head.

They reached the porch stairs and Steenberg said, "I'll be out in a minute. Can you get everyone together? I have something to announce."

❧❧

Steenberg, now showered and shaved, stood on the porch above the steps in the sinking, late afternoon sun with Vladimir, Yevgeny, and Vadim on one side and Klendenin and Wild Will on the other. He waited for the men gathering in the yard to settle down. Brother-in-law leaned against the porch railing on Steenberg's right. Yohaba and Rulon were furthest away sitting on the corral fence. Except for Becker, who was still sleeping soundly, everyone was there. The sun shone through a blue sky of patchy clouds.

Steenberg waited until everyone had quieted but just as he opened his mouth to speak, Murphy shouted, "Are we gonna vote now to see who stays on the show?"

"Shut up, Murphy," said Wild Will, in what was now a running joke.

Steenberg smiled patiently. "Something like that," he said. The laughter died down, and he began again. "By now you know who I am. Let me make it perfectly clear. I am most certainly not the man who kidnapped Mr. Klendenin's daughter." He paused, waited a few beats then cleared his throat as a prod to Vadim. The young man jumped into action, translating what Steenberg had just said into Russian. When he was done, Steenberg continued, pausing for the translation after every sentence.

"That unfortunate misunderstanding has now been cleared up."

At his side, Klendenin nodded agreement and Steenberg continued. "I also have not reneged in any way on my agreement with Mr. Polykov and Gazprom." Vladimir interrupted to say something to his men in Russian. Steenberg waited then said, "I think after all you have been through, you deserve something, so I am going to tell you a story. It will clear up some of your questions, but certainly will provoke many more that must remain unanswered. Not because I wish to be secretive, but because there are yet no answers.

"But, in any case, when I am finished, you will know something that only a very few people in the world know. I'm going to dispense with the dramatics. On April 13th, 2029, an asteroid called 182 Elsa is going to strike the earth. Within a few months after that date, a thousand-year winter will set in and civilization as we know it will end. This was predicted by Albert Einstein, my long deceased mentor, who also, most thankfully, provided mankind the means to preserve itself. You have all unwittingly stepped into and almost thwarted a global conspiracy for good to prevent that unimaginable catastrophe from happening. Rejoice in your failure."

It was a measure of Steenberg's charisma and presence that no one laughed or otherwise interrupted, not even Murphy. Vadim finished translating. The wind blew across the yard. From somewhere beyond the barn a cow mooed. Otherwise, all of nature was quiet.

Steenberg gave Vadim a get-ready nod and continued. "I am telling you this because you are human beings with cherished families and friends. What I am telling you here today will be yours to use as you wish. I hold you to no bonds of secrecy. If you choose to tell others and this starts a world-wide panic, maybe that will be a good thing. I don't know. Maybe rioting citizens will provoke a response from their governments that I was unable to stir. But I don't think that will happen—neither widespread riots nor effective action.

"In my experience, very few men are ruled by reason or by evidence. Most make up their minds based on the feelings of their spirit and then only afterwards search for facts to support their conclusions. No one profits from a narrative that the world is going to end in their lifetime. For that reason, no one will believe you, maybe not even your own families, as perhaps you are not believing me now.

"The powers that be in this world will not lift a finger to save it until Elsa is bright in the sky, the world crumbling around them, and they have been left free to maximize profits till the last possible instant. Until then, they want everything to continue as it is. They want stability. Because stability means predictable profits. And that is why I don't think anything you say or don't say will change the inevitable. One-eighty-two Elsa hurtles silently towards earth as I speak. The greedy are counting on the less greedy to come to the world's rescue while denying them the power and resources to do so. Such is the age we live in."

By now Rulon had come down off the fence where Yohaba was sitting and inveigled himself in front of her between her knees with her chin resting on his shoulder. Turning his head slightly, he said quietly, "Why's he's spilling his guts?"

"He's always looking for converts," whispered Yohaba.

"By the way," whispered Rulon, "Vadim said that while I was busy you and Steenberg went off together talking mighty serious."

"So? Was the little tyke jealous?"

"Probably. But that's not why I brought it up."

"So now I can't even talk to my own grandfather?"

"You took an oath of minionship in regards to your grandfather. Remember? We agreed you could be a minion. No more," said Rulon. When Yohaba didn't respond, he asked firmly, "Are you or are you not still just a minion?

"You'll be proud to know I was promoted a few months ago," said Yohaba quietly in his ear. "I was going to tell you. If we save the world, I get the movie rights." Rulon seethed in silence. Steenberg continued talking.

"The man's a Svengali," said Rulon angrily after a minute while Steenberg continued to speak. "Are you one hundred percent sure Becker and Vadim weren't telling the truth about him?"

"Decrepit minds think alike," she answered. When Rulon didn't crack a smile, Yohaba said patiently, "Darling, this is a chess game and everyone's a pawn."

"Pawns get sacrificed," said Rulon.

"Shush," said Yohaba. "Just listen to what he's saying." Rulon turned his head to glare off into the distance. After a few moments, he turned back to focus again on Steenberg.

Steenberg was explaining to his audience what caused the misunderstanding between Klendenin, Vladimir, and him in the first place. The kidnapping of Klendenin's daughter wasn't the only issue. There were the disk drive factories in Vietnam, the reactors in Japan, China heavily investing in Iraqi oil fields to pry oil away from the west, and other examples that didn't make the news, such as the black market in Chernobyl-contaminated car parts to fund solar power research in Russia. Someone with tentacles was interfering, trying to accelerate the move to solar power regardless of consequences.

"But there is hope," Steenberg said in conclusion. "Sometimes the crucible of adversity and honest disagreements can forge new bonds of trust." He motioned to Vladimir and the old Russian stepped forward to endorse Steenberg's perspective.

Rulon squeezed Yohaba's hand and whispered, "The man has this wonderful delusion that every world disaster is part of a master plan to make him happy. What's the opposite of paranoia?"

"That would be pronoia," said Yohaba. "So what's wrong with rolling with the bad karma?"

"Karmic jujitsu. Why didn't I think of that? And all this time I thought he was simply manipulating us to do his bidding. And now these poor suckers, too."

"What? Now you got something against saving the world?"

"Not usually," said Rulon under his breath. "But that's my point. Becker was right. When the end of the world's at stake, any end can be justified. This is out of control, and I don't like it. I can sense it down to my boot heels. People are going to start dying by the bushel before this is over."

"As opposed to people dying by the billions if he doesn't do anything."

"You just made my point," growled Rulon. "There is no end he can't justify."

Vladimir spoke gruffly in Russian while Vadim translated into English, reassuring his people that he'd seen the astronomical proof and that Steenberg had his full support. Next Klendenin spoke and said basically the same thing. After they finished, both men gave Steenberg center stage again on the weather-worn porch. It was a strange podium from which to announce a plan to save the world. A porch in Idaho on a brisk spring day in front of a group of men from different countries who a few hours before would have sworn they were enemies and perhaps wouldn't take much to become so again.

"The plan is simple," said Steenberg. "The world must work together and build missiles with warheads powerful enough to destroy an asteroid traveling at 56,000 miles per hour. This is not as simple as it might sound."

While Steenberg's voice droned on about his plan to save mankind from utter annihilation, Rulon's mind wandered off to more mundane matters. If it didn't rain soon there wouldn't be enough hay this year to get the cows through winter. Which reminded him, his Idaho Cattle Association dues were due. Did they take credit cards, he wondered? And Juanita, their big black-and-white Holstein, was only weeks away from giving birth. Also, two of the horses needed shoeing. And the weathervane atop the barn needed oiling again. Hmm…and the truck was overdue for an oil change. And he promised Brother-in-law he'd help him fix his Beetle.

Rulon loved ranch life. No matter what you thought about it, you couldn't say it wasn't real. Animals and people and weather and good old earth under your feet. Sometimes he'd hop down off the tractor in the middle of plowing a section and hold a handful of rich, chewed up topsoil to his nose. Ground up vegetation and wet earth mixed with a little volcanic ash still there from the 1980 Mt. St. Helens blow. There was no other smell like it. It must have been how the world smelled when it was new. The Bible said God made man from the dust of the earth, and even now every living thing on earth depended on six inches of good topsoil. Precious life from the earth. It made sense if you were a farmer. Sometimes he'd crumble the dirt between his fingers and watch it blow off like smoke…or ashes.

A dark cloud overshadowed Rulon's thoughts and one by one the faces of the men he'd killed took shape before his eyes. Their images came together like an Etch A Sketch in reverse, little specks of dust drawn together into a soulless face. Ashes from faces. For the first time in years, he thought about Freya, the old faithful Wilton Demolition four-pound hammer he had wrapped in plastic and leather and buried in the barn after they got back from CERN four years ago. He had buried the hammer mainly to convince Yohaba he was leaving his old life behind. Through no fault of his own that ended up not to be true. He pondered all this while Steenberg talked away, hatching his ingenious schemes that seemed so foolproof while the pixie dust was falling—but Rulon wasn't buying it. Steenberg's plans were going to cost men their lives. Rulon could see that plain as a full moon over Redfish.

Did Steenberg, as smart as he was, even have a clue? Sometimes his detachment annoyed Rulon no end. But still he plowed on, oblivious, patient, careful, and meticulous, thinking all was under control. Well, ranch life had taught Rulon that control was an illusion. It rained too much. Then it didn't rain enough. And when it rained just right, the cows would get sick or the hay would go moldy. There was always something that you couldn't account for.

But Steenberg didn't see life that way. In his world, people and events lined up like numbers. But the reality was, he was determined to save a world that was kicking and screaming to be left alone. He thought people could be manipulated as easily as his beloved numbers. He thought people were 20-year-old mares who became docile if you fed them enough carrots. But here he was matching wits with greedy CEOs, corrupt officials, crime families, and government functionaries with ruthless resources at their command. Did he really think they would play by the rules?

By now Yohaba had hopped off the fence and was standing by his side. He looked at her listening, mesmerized by her grandfather's words. She sensed his attention on her, elbowed him, and said, "Pay attention. This is history in the making." Inwardly Rulon groaned, and then it hit him. It was time to unbury Freya. He didn't know why. Just knew he had to do it. He pondered the feeling, and it felt good, felt right. His heart skipped a few beats at the thought of once more feeling Freya's heft in his burly hands. Man, he'd wreaked some havoc with that thing in his time, he thought a bit too proudly, and he mentally dialed down the emotion a few clicks. Then he thought, *No, this whole thing is stupid.* He heard his name and looked up just as Steenberg stopped speaking.

"What did the puppet master just say?" asked Rulon.

"Earth to Rulon," said Yohaba. "Weren't you listening? And stop calling him that!"

"Tell me," Rulon said. Yohaba gave him the short version. Klendenin had agreed to help and Wild Will and Russo were going to stay on as his bodyguards. Rulon grunted.

"But here's the neat part," she said. "Leonard's taking us to Zurich with him for a meeting! Isn't that great? We haven't been back in over a year. Honald's bakery! Sprüngli chocolates! The Desperado restaurant! We can even maybe swing by Bergün and see granny and Alex. It'll be like a vacation!"

"The catch please," said Rulon.

"There's no catch, just a little meeting to attend."

"The catch please."

"There's no catch. It's just that after all these years, we finally get to meet the thin man. He specifically asked Leonard to bring us along. Don't give me that look. What happened to Rulon Hurt, the so-called great peacemaker? You'll meet him. He'll meet you. You'll see the humanity in each other's eyes. Isn't that your favorite expression? And then you can work out your mutual problems. I thought you'd jump at this."

Rulon couldn't believe what he'd just heard. He looked around to make sure no one was paying attention to them.

"Keep your voice down. Now please tell me my merry prankster wife is pulling my leg."

"I don't see a problem," said Yohaba barely above a whisper. "What's the problem?"

"The last thing we want to do is meet the thin man. Are you nuts?"

"I thought you'd be pleased," said a crestfallen Yohaba. "You always said if he wanted you dead, he could kill you anytime. Now's your chance to talk him out of it for good."

"Or his chance to kill me—make that kill us—for good. What did Boris say about him when you were together in Zurich? Do you remember? He said even to be noticed by this guy is dangerous. Okay, my opinion counts for nothing around here. I got that. But now even your adoring minion Boris doesn't know what he's talking about? Is that what you're telling me?"

"Okay. So don't go," hissed Yohaba. "You can stay home and milk the cows. I'll go by myself. I'm not afraid of him." She pushed off the fence and stormed away.

Rulon violently threw his hat down in the dirt. At the sound, Yohaba stopped and walked back. Steenberg paused in mid-sentence to look at them, then continued. A few of the men turned from him to look at Rulon and Yohaba. Rulon smiled, and they refocused on Steenberg. Yohaba picked up his hat, brushed it off, and handed it to her husband. "We rarely argue," she said gently.

Rulon dusted off his hat some more and said, "Only because I'm patient, tolerant, forgiving, and hard of hearing."

"I need you there," she said. When Rulon appeared unmoved, she said, "Leonard has a relationship with this guy. That's why he was in Zurich just now. He had a meeting with him."

"What! Is he crazy?"

"They even played a chess game together. They're practically best buds. It's safe."

"He brought a chess board to the meeting!?" asked Rulon incredulously. "He told me he doesn't like to play chess. He would never play me."

"Oh, this is going to sting," said Yohaba. "No, he didn't bring a board. And he does like to play chess. He just doesn't like to play with people who have to use a board. It's just a thing with him."

"Of course. Who but us feeble dimwits would need a board?" said Rulon in exasperation. He paused and took a deep breath. "Okay. I'm a feeble dimwit. Forget the chess. The point is he should not be meeting with the thin man. The guy thinks Stalin was too soft. He can't be bargained with. He can't be reasoned with. He doesn't feel pity, or remorse, or fear. And he absolutely will not stop, ever, until I am dead."

"Oh, very cute. *The Terminator*, 1984. Michael Biehn. I'm not impressed."

"But you get my point."

"Leonard's going, and I'm going with him. End of story. They had a constructive meeting. If he wanted Leonard dead, he could have done it already. There is no logical reason to kill him now."

"Based on the information you have I'm sure you're right. But are you sure you have all the information? Face it. You have no way of knowing. Leonard thinks like an academic. He's logical. Reasonable. Fair. He believes in suffering the consequences of his actions. He's got a conscience. But the people he's dealing with are not like that. They spend their entire lives breaking laws and avoiding consequences. You're in over your head. So's Leonard. How come I can see this and you two can't?"

Yohaba put her hands on her hips. "I'm going with him, and we both know you won't let me go by myself. So, you're coming. I know it, and you know it. We are arguing over the inevitable. How come I can see that, and you can't?"

"I'm not finished. Your grandfather thinks this is a business, or worse, a game. A fun game and you keep score with money. He pays bribes disguised as salaries, invests his money, lets everyone keep a little piece of the pie, and thinks because he's being fair and he's happy that everyone's happy. He's wrong. None of these sides he's playing with are happy unless they're getting the entire pie. Every last crumb. These guys run businesses but they're not businessmen. When they don't get their way, they don't sit around a table and strategize about leveraged buyouts, currency fluctuations, and the derivatives market. Their tool kit has Zoldar the psychotic former Spetsnaz in it. They don't talk about price gouging. They talk about eye gouging. That's how they think." Yohaba tried to interrupt.

"No, no. Let me finish," said Rulon, now thoroughly worked up. "And it's worse with the thin man. He's got an entire secret, ultra-violent government apparatus under his control. He doesn't even have to hide his evil, because where he comes from, he's not breaking any laws. He is the law! Do you understand what I'm saying?"

"What are you going to wear? Don't forget to bring your toothbrush."

"I got a bad feeling about this. This is going to be CERN times ten before it's over."

"We can get your brother to help Dad with the ranch while we're gone."

"Good luck with that. I'm unburying Freya if I go."

"Fine, but I get the Glock 26."

"Fine," said Rulon.

"And the grenade launcher."

"Ha! Have fun getting it through airport security."

"Haha, smart boy! We're going in Vladimir's private jet. There won't be any security. You can bring your whole toy chest."

Rulon fumed, looked down, hemmed and hawed, and kicked the dirt with the toe of his boot. Finally, he asked, "What's the Prince of Blood gonna be doing?"

"He's coming, too. And stop calling him that."

"Fine. Well, he better be there. Everyone seems to have forgotten he's supposed to be MY bodyguard. It's about time he earned his keep around here. Look at this fence." Rulon tugged hard on the fence and a weakened fence rail gave way. "This should have been fixed a week ago."

"Hey, he's been sort of busy lately, don't you think? He does plenty of work. Anyway, Leonard is going to talk to him. He'll be there," said Yohaba and gave Rulon a kiss. "You won't regret this."

"I'm already regretting this," said Rulon. He frowned and sighed wearily. "I assume you were serious about the grenade launcher. I'll talk to what's-his-name about it. But hey, don't think I haven't noticed that you and your grandfather cooked all this up behind my back."

"The whole thing's been a moving target," said Yohaba unapologetically.

"And I want the operation to be called Operation Redfish."

"What!?" said Yohaba incredulously. "What on earth difference will that make?"

"It won't make a single bit of difference, but that's what I want. That's my condition. I realize I'm just an old boot around here, but I want to name the operation. Is it Redfish or not? Yes or no?"

"You're feeling sorry for yourself. Fine. We'll call it Redfish. I'm sure my grandfather won't mind."

Rulon gritted his teeth at that remark and said, "I'm going to go fix something now."

"Like what?" asked Yohaba.

"This fence. I'm going to fix this fence. Do something useful. I may even go speak with your grandfather again about how all the seams are bursting on his little project and how come I can see it and he can't."

"Good luck with that," said Yohaba.

"Then I'm going to dig up Freya."

They kissed lightly again then Rulon grumbled goodbye and walked over to the barn. Yohaba watched him go. She gulped. *Why Freya?*

Chapter 15

An hour after Leonard's speech, his people showed up in a blue Ford van. Wearing dark suits, white shirts, and single-color ties, they quietly and efficiently went about their work reassembling the computer equipment.

In the ranch house, Steenberg showed Brother-in-law the picture of Klendenin's daughter and waited for his reaction. "She's pretty," said Brother-in-law and handed the picture back.

"Do you want to rescue her?" asked Steenberg.

"Okay," said Brother-in-law.

Steenberg then went looking for Klendenin. He found him out by the Humvees that were now all parked in the yard. He pulled him aside for one last conversation. To Klendenin's amazement, true to his word, Steenberg had, in only a few hours, managed to locate his daughter. She was being held in a chalet outside Stein am Rhein in Switzerland an hour away from Zurich on the German border. Brother-in-law and a team would head there for the rescue right after the meeting with the thin man in Zurich. With any luck, they'd be back in Zurich with the girl that same day, pick up Rulon, Yohaba, and Steenberg, and then all fly home together. With any luck.

Flushed with the good news, Klendenin and his mercenaries packed into their three Humvees and left the ranch in a cloud of dust. All except Murphy, Dilly, Stringbean, and Benny. Those four stayed behind at Brother-in-law's invitation. Klendenin was off to put in place their plan for dealing with the Chinese. Wild Will and Russo, embarrassed at the mess they'd made of their mission, agreed to go with Klendenin as bodyguards.

Mr. Hurt sat on the porch swing watching all the comings and goings. Rulon saw his father, walked over, and sat down next to him. After a minute of silence, Mr. Hurt said, "Sounded like World War Three over here last night. The cows'll be giving us milk duds for a month."

Rulon unburdened himself to his father, sharing his misgivings about Steenberg's plans and the influence he was having on Yohaba. Mr. Hurt, despite his crusty indifference, understood very well the situation with Steenberg. And disapproved greatly.

Having been at Rulon's side just seconds after he'd been shot in the yard by a German assassin a year earlier, he also disapproved of but understood the dangerous world Rulon and Yohaba sometimes inhabited.

When Rulon told him they were going to Zurich to finally meet the thin man, his father suggested mildly that perhaps that wasn't the wisest thing to do. The conversation ended amicably, but Rulon, who knew his Dad's quirky ways very well, also knew the conversation wasn't over.

⌘

Later that night when Rulon was in the barn digging up Freya, the old man, tough as woodpecker lips, came over to talk. There was Rulon on his knees, small spade in hand, a two-foot hole in front of him, and a lantern hissing low on top of a small mound of dirt.

"Looking for gophers?" asked his father.

Rulon looked up. "No. Just resurrecting an old friend. We're heading out in a couple of hours. Be gone for a few days."

"Expecting trouble then?"

"Always. Don't bother cleaning out the ditch on the north side. I'll get to it when I'm back.

"Gonna save the world?"

"If it lets me."

"Is Yohaba going with you?"

"This time I'm going with her."

"I was thinking. I'll miss Yohaba's cooking and your dishwashing. Any chance you two can sit this one out?"

"I would if I could."

His father stuck his hands in his pockets and walked away. As he left the barn, he said over his shoulder, "Don't forget to fill up the hole. And while you're at it, fix the one in your head, too."

"Good night, Dad," said Rulon. His father waved without looking back.

Rulon watched his father leave then reached into the hole and pulled out a heavily wrapped package half again as big as a shoebox. With a small folding knife, he cut away the thick wrapping of duct tape, then the 30-mil plastic sheeting. Beneath that was a layer of black leather from an old jacket. At the sight of it, Rulon's breathing picked up like he was walking uphill. Through the leather he could feel the narrow, four-pound, forged steel head and the ten-inch rubber coated spring steel handle.

The martial arts experts all agreed that a hammer made for a poor weapon. If you missed, the follow-through left you wide open for a counter-attack. That made sense. But

Rulon was an anomaly, strong enough and fast enough that he could wreak havoc with short, controlled swings or if he swung too hard and missed could instantly follow through with a 360-degree spin like the hammer thrower he once was. It was all in the footwork.

Rulon peeled back the leather and there was Freya none the worse for time, the handle and narrow head still slightly discolored with blood, his and others. He stood up and let the leather wrapping fall to the floor. He slipped his hand through the hammer's leather strap and swung Freya back and forth in a series of slow figure eights, liking the feel and the weight of it. CERN came back in a rush and Rulon's breathing kicked up another notch. His right hand was now perfectly healed from CERN, and it confidently gripped the hammer with a memory all its own. He looked up and was surprised to see Steenberg standing by the barn door looking back at him.

"I thought you made a vow," said Steenberg.

"Desperate times," said Rulon. He knelt down again and began repacking Freya in the box.

Steenberg came over. "I just saw your father. He didn't look very happy. Would it be prying if I asked what you were talking about?"

"Just ranch stuff," said Rulon.

When Rulon wasn't forthcoming, but instead busied himself filling up the hole in the floor, Steenberg continued. "Yohaba said you wanted to talk to me."

Rulon got up from his knees with the spade in his hand. He seemed to fill the barn in the flickering light and shadows cast by the lantern. "Leonard," he said, "I hold you in the greatest respect, and I commend you for what you are doing. And good luck in your mission to save the world, but me and Yohaba are not going to be part of your plans after Switzerland. We'll get you through that and then it's adios amigo. Do you understand what I'm saying? We're done after that."

"Have you talked to Yohaba?" asked Steenberg.

"That's none of your business, sir. Frankly, you're in over your head and you're going to get yourself killed. And us too, if we're stupid enough to stick around."

"That has always been a risk," said Steenberg, "and that's why I need Yohaba. Don't you see? She is the only one who can take my place if something should happen to me. She is my heir, not just to my fortune, but to this enterprise. The stakes are almost beyond comprehension."

"Switzerland and then we're done," said Rulon. He tamped on the filled-in hole with his boot heel and then walked past Steenberg back to the ranch house carrying the spade and lantern and the box with Freya in it.

Steenberg was left in the dark. He started to teeter and reached out to steady himself on one of the stall posts. *I can't do this without her,* he thought to himself. *I can't. I can't.* After a few moments, his resolution returned along with the memories of all the doomed, humiliating pleas he had made in front of corporate boards in America and Europe. It was the humiliation compounded with the unmitigated stupidity of his audiences that had spurred him to eventually take such desperate measures. And then, as it had before, came the cold determination that at all costs he must do what needed to be done. *Rulon, don't get in my way,* he thought.

ↄ๏ↄↄ

Sawtooth National Recreation Area ranger Stanley Merryfield crouched over the remains of a huge campfire on the west shore of Redfish Lake. He held a timid hand over the coals and could feel a few calories of still rising heat. In front of him, there were traces in the sand where logs had been dragged from the forest and thrown on the bonfire. The sand was black over a fifteen-foot-diameter ring. It must have been an inferno.

Despite having zipped his heavy, dark green Ranger coat all the way up to his chin, the wind blew under his tan wide-brimmed hat and down the space between his collar and pencil neck like a chimney. He stood and stroked his protruding Adam's apple. What had begun as a phone call from a concerned backpacker had now become in his mind a "situation." Stanley unbuttoned the pocket flap of his jacket and took out a small notebook. He dutifully wrote his observations then took pictures of the scene with his camera phone. From another pocket, he removed a tape measure and precisely measured the size of the fire and its distance from the forest and the lake.

Next he searched the area around the fire, moving in ever-widening concentric circles as a bee would when searching for flowers. The academy training he'd completed just four weeks ago had been quite specific about that being the most efficient way to conduct a search. On his fourth concentric swing, ten feet out from the fire, something shiny caught his eye. He crouched down and with his pen poked into the hollow to pick up a spent shell casing. "Well, well," he said. He sniffed it and looked at it from several angles. Stanley didn't know it at the time, but it was the casing from the shell Rulon had test fired from his pistol.

The casing went into a small plastic evidence bag pulled from the supply Stanley kept in his inside jacket pocket. He wrote in his notebook: *ASYM Precision National Match ammo .45 ACP. Nickel plated brass, probably185 grains*. In Idaho it was against the law to discharge a firearm within one hundred fifty yards of a body of water.

The "situation" was now a felony crime scene.

Stanley Merryfield took out his forest service walkie-talkie and made his report to headquarters. His boss asked him if he was sure he wanted to make an issue of this. The question agitated Stanley so much, his Adam's apple bobbed up and down. Of course he was sure, Stanley stammered. His initial estimate was that the "perp or perps" had violated two federal and three state laws. His boss felt cornered into agreeing to something his experience told him was better left ignored.

On his way back to his beached Zodiac and its Yamaha outboard, Stanley noticed the markings of a canoe on the sand and two sets of footsteps leading directly to the fire, one small, probably a woman, and the other, a barefoot heavyset man. Barefoot?! In this weather? He also saw the imprint of a man's body on the sand where he'd lain stretched out like a snow angel. Like he'd been sleeping or more likely exhausted. Or maybe dead. He could see the impression of his belt, pockets, and shirt cuffs. Strangely, the man hadn't arrived in the canoe but had first come out of the water five feet from the canoe, barefoot but otherwise fully dressed. Then he'd pulled the canoe onto shore with the other person—had to be a woman—still in it. A really strong man.

Out again came the phone camera and measuring tape. He wrote down his findings and afterwards spent a few minutes studying the shape and width of the canoe's hull in the sand. He finally decided it was a Clipper Mac Sport canoe. The forty-inch beam confirmed in his mind that it was a Model 18. It was getting light now, and he needed to check on a report that a herd of elk had tipped over an outhouse in one of the campgrounds. He pushed the Zodiac away from shore, slipped, stumbled forward, and got soaked in the frigid lake water up to mid-thigh. Dang! Did it again! Fortunately, this time he managed to hang onto the raft. He scrambled over the side, got the motor started after a few tries, and took off.

On his way across the lake, the thought occurred to him that the use of a waterborne transportation vehicle in the commission of a felony in federally protected waters might be a violation of maritime law as well, perhaps even piracy laws. He'd research that as soon as he got back to his desk. Tomorrow he'd come back and make a plaster cast of the footprints and canoe outline and conduct a more thorough search.

❧❧❧

Chapter 16

There are 716 rooms in the China World Hotel on Jian Guo Men Wai Avenue in Beijing, just a few miles from Tiananmen Square and the Forbidden City. One of the suites on the eighteenth floor had been converted into an office. Sun Xiaofeng, Communist party member and second highest ranking employee in the Chinese Academy of Sciences, preferred the view from there to the one at the dreary, gray, five-story building where his 300-person staff worked fifteen miles away. Besides, the hotel was also closer to his home, and the hotel management gave him a special deal on one of the hotel's Grand Garden suites—a lavishly appointed 1,000-square-foot apartment. The room was free in exchange for not using the Party apparatus to totally screw the hotel over for some unfathomable, bureaucratic reason. Who could refuse a deal like that?

Sun Xiaofeng sat at his desk looking out through the floor-to-ceiling window at the window washers dangling from the roof of the skyscraper next door. It was like watching circus performers. The wind outside was treacherous. It howled and made the windows shudder. Three window washers were lowering themselves from the roof and obviously having trouble in the wind. They sat in little harnesses supported by a single strand of rope. They swayed back and forth in the wind as they washed the windows. One of them dropped a rag and reached for it, almost tumbling out of his harness. *This is better than a circus,* thought Xiaofeng.

Sun Xiaofeng pulled himself away from the window washers and looked down at the white paper on his desk titled, "Global Market Outlook for Photovoltaics until 2020," by the European Photovoltaic Industry Association. He adjusted his glasses and continued reading. Xiaofeng was sixty-six years old and still had vivid memories of the Great Leap Forward and the Cultural Revolution under Mao. These days his private little act of rebellion was to refer to the former as simply "The Great Leap" and leave off the "Forward" part. The latter he simply referred to as "The Revolution."

He was a lifelong Communist, but also a pragmatist. He didn't consider China's movement towards capitalism to be a betrayal of the memory of Chairman Mao. He looked at it as a natural evolution now that the untrustworthy parts of the population had been purged.

Xiaofeng was a patient man. And politically powerful. He was short and stocky, wore thick glasses, and had thick black hair, bad teeth, and a weakness for Armani suits. No one but the head of the Academy had any control over his career. These days he busied himself reading reports and staying abreast of trends where he could apply his country's vast natural resources—meaning its disciplined workforce—to making China richer. For the past several years, he had focused on solar energy.

China was already rich. Far richer than the world realized. According to the world's calculations, China was the second largest economy, roughly 70% the size of the U.S. even though it was going through a rocky patch right now. But Xiaofeng knew the real numbers. He knew that the Chinese currency was being deliberately undervalued and that regional authorities routinely under-reported their economic results so that development funds from the central government would continue to flow in. In a couple of years he'd have a few bookkeepers executed and bring the system back into line, but for now, this petty inefficiency served its purpose. It lulled the west into some degree of complacency.

Xiaofeng had the confidence of a man who didn't make mistakes, or rather, who couldn't make mistakes. Not only was he fully protected by his own internally recruited cabal within the Communist party, but, almost as importantly, the Chinese economic tide was raising all ships, including his own. It was almost impossible for him to make a business decision that didn't result in increased revenue and more jobs for China. He was particularly proud of what the Academy had accomplished with solar power. When he first stated that his goal for China was to be the world's number one solar panel manufacturer by 2022, his colleagues had thought him mad. Now, China was already number one and by an ever-widening margin, producing a full 50% of the world's supply of solar panels. That American inventor had been wrong. It wasn't a better mousetrap but a cheaper mousetrap that made the world beat a path to your door.

Unfortunately, China's cheaper solar panels had not come without cost. Polysilicon was a necessary ingredient in first generation solar cells. A byproduct of its production was silicon tetrachloride, a highly poisonous material whose safe disposal bumped the cost of its manufacturing in western countries up to $84,000 per ton. China, due to its low cost-structure, more efficient manufacturing processes, the ingeniousness of its scientists, its astute business leaders, and the firm visionary direction of Sun Xiaofeng himself, was able to produce polysilicon for only $23,000 per ton, thereby totally undercutting foreign competition. Or so went the propaganda cranked out and disseminated by Xiaofeng's creative marketing department. In fact, Xiaofeng had ordered the solar companies under his purview to ignore the environmental concerns and simply dump the silicon tetrachloride in the nearest open spot of ground outside their factories' fences…or wherever. Xiaofeng didn't really care. Rigid expense control was Xiaofeng's specialty.

Everything was going smoothly. Profits were rolling in. Complainers were neutralized. Sun Xiaofeng was widely admired. Life was good. His personal capitalist revolution was purring along. Then one day Leonard Steenberg showed up. Sun Xiaofeng still couldn't picture his face or even hear the sound of his name without grinding his teeth in fury. Leonard Steenberg. The Wily Devil, as he was now known within Sun Xiaofeng's department. That was the only name Xiaofeng permitted anyone in his department to use when referring to Steenberg. The fact that it was usually uttered with a subtle hint of awe by Xiaofeng's lieutenants, only added to his rage.

Steenberg had knocked on Sun Xiaofeng's door in the China World Hotel one day months ago. One fateful day. A tall man, by himself, matching Xiaofeng's penchant for Armani, a laptop case in one hand and an overcoat in the other. No appointment. No hat. White hair. Short white beard. Piercing eyes and a letter of introduction from Xiaofeng's son attending Dartmouth in the U.S.

Not a hint of a threat in that first conversation. Steenberg was famous in his field and a reasonable man with an engineering breakthrough in solar panel efficiency. He also had an intriguing business proposition. The screws didn't start tightening until the fifth visit. The threats were not directed at China or its interests but at Sun Xiaofeng himself. A wickedly big stick softened by an exceedingly big carrot. Grainy videos of barrels of silicon tetrachloride being dumped in ditches, fields, abandoned reservoirs, and being left to leak from derelict semi-trailers. Videos of chronically sick children. And as an added bonus, news articles about the fate of Chinese officials who brought disrepute on the Chinese economic miracle.

Personal ruin. Disgrace. Maybe execution after a one-day trial. But on the other hand, considerable personal wealth, power, and prestige if he cooperated. And then there was the knowledge that Steenberg had met his son. Knew where he lived. Had pictures of Steenberg and his son together on the Dartmouth campus, but always with a thin, sinister-looking, unkempt young man standing in the background wearing reflector sunglasses and a blue ball cap. Neither a student nor a teacher. But a threat. Wealth, ruin. Wealth, ruin. Actually, not a particularly hard choice.

In the end, Sun Xiaofeng chose wealth. Solar panels were sent at cost to a Russian manufacturer. Russian oil put up by a branch of the Italian mafia served as collateral. The deal was for five years. Then Sun Xiaofeng would get the videos and the formulas for increasing the energy efficiency of solar panels from the current top rate of fourteen percent to forty-seven percent. World domination in energy.

Of course, things did not go smoothly at first. Xiaofeng had tried a face-saving counter maneuver, siphoning off workers trained by Steenberg's engineers and taking them to build identical solar panels in one of Xiaofeng's private factories. Disaster! Steenberg had anticipated this duplicity and inserted a fatal flaw in the design that went undetected until it had rendered over $80 million of black-market panels useless. The flaw, though fatal, could be undone but only in a factory near Kiev run by some Russians in league with Steenberg. The Wily Devil.

"How will I know you will keep your word?" asked Xiaofeng at their last meeting.

"A deal is a deal," responded Steenberg as they shook hands. And strangely, though he hated him fiercely, and despite himself, Xiaofeng believed him.

Sun Xiaofeng recalled the various counterplans he had concocted as the negotiations had dragged on. He fumed over his counter-threats that bounced off Steenberg like a child's spit wads. It was Steenberg's patience most of all that galled him. The man was inscrutable. Xiaofeng laughed as a thought popped into his head. *I've been out scrutled.* Just then his phone rang. It was Becker.

A groggy voice said, "Steenberg is here."

"You sound drunk." said Xiaofeng.

"They drugged me. My heart can't take this. These people drugged a priest. They're barbarians."

"But you're not a priest," said Xiaofeng, suppressing a smile. "Where is here?"

"The Hurt ranch in Idaho."

"Not a total surprise."

"You'll have to move fast. He has repaired the alliance with the Russians. I don't know how much longer he'll be here."

"Is he wearing a disguise?" asked Xiaofeng.

"No. Wait. Someone's coming. I'll call you back."

Ten minutes later Becker called back. "I just spoke to the father. He doesn't know anything. There's a few others around, but no one I recognize, and they won't talk to me. This is weird. I don't know what happened to everyone. I've been knocked out for days, I think. Maybe they're coming back. I don't know. I need to lie down."

"Go back to the father. Find out."

"He doesn't know anything. He asked me if I knew how to milk cows. I've got to get out of here. I…"

"Wait there," interrupted Xiaofeng. "I'll send someone to pick you up." He hung up.

Becker, sitting on Rulon's bed, slowly lowered his cell phone. He had been just about to tell Xiaofeng about Klendenin and the Americans who had attacked the ranch. Instead, he shrugged and thought, *Serves him right*. He turned off the phone and lay down on the bed. *I'll just rest for a few minutes*, he said to himself. Within seconds he was fast asleep again.

☙☙❧

From his office in the China World hotel, Xiaofeng speed dialed a number on his desk phone. A young woman answered. "Good morning, another glorious day for the new China. My name is Cao Li. How may I help you?"

"How many agents are currently in Idaho?" asked Xiaofeng, and heaven help the agent who didn't instantly recognize his voice.

"One moment, sir," she replied. A minute later she took him off hold. "We have a two-man team working the Micron plant in Boise."

"Perfect. Have them call me right away," he said. "Who are they?"

"Zhao Yaobang and Yu Qing-Qiao," she said.

"Perfect. Email them a front and profile view of our agent *Clouds Over Idaho*. I want him picked up." He gave her Becker's location.

"And taken where?" asked Cao Li.

"Returned," said Xiaofeng.

Part 2

Chapter 17
Zurich

I'll take one dozen of those and also one of those." Rulon waited eagerly on the other side of the Sprüngli chocolate store's glass case while an elderly female clerk collected a dozen dark chocolate-glazed orange slices and arranged them neatly in a box. When she reached for only one of the plump, round, chocolate confections, Rulon corrected her. "No, I meant *one dozen* of the Luxembürgerlis as well. Actually, make that two dozen, and just mix them up. Yeah. None with alcohol, though, okay? That's great, Lily. All different kinds. That's perfect. And six of those chocolate gift boxes, yes, the Métal-Boîte Mädchens will do nicely. And, oh, why not! Throw in two boxes of the Truffles Grand Cru and a single Herzbonbonnière Rot for the little woman back home."

"Very good, Mr. Hurt," said Lily. "I will tie that one with a bow. Mustn't forget one's woman."

Lily packaged and bagged the chocolate cornucopia while Rulon kept up a steady banter in Swiss German. She put the finishing touches to a bulging bag of assorted chocolates, and said, "It's so very good to have you back, Mr. Hurt. And I'm pleased to hear you haven't forgotten the dialect. You make it sound so, so…cowboy."

Rulon touched the brim of his black cowboy hat, and said, "Aw shucks, Ma'am," in his best cowboy accent. Lily blushed.

He handed her a two-hundred franc note and waited expectantly for the change. Lily stood politely with the single bill in her hand, and Rulon smiled. Lily cleared her throat, and Rulon handed over another hundred francs. "Yes, you have been away too long," she said smiling.

"Well, Lily," said Rulon, quoting the Sprüngli company motto, "the art of chocolate since 1836 keeps bringing me back. And, of course, without my Swiss German how could I charm the lovely clerks at one of my all-time favorite chocolate shops." Sixty-eight-year-old Lily blushed again and handed over his modest change.

Outside, Yohaba and Brother-in-law, with his infamous duffle bag at his feet, were waiting cattycorner by the public bench outside the Blancpain watch store, where at eleven p.m., nine hours away, the thin man was supposed to be chatting with Leonard. They watched as Rulon exited the store carrying a shopping bag, paused to look around, spotted them, and walked over with a big grin.

"They still remember me," he said. "Can you believe it?"

"Darling," said Yohaba. "When you moved back to Idaho, they probably had to shut down a chocolate factory. How could they forget you? What on earth did you get?"

Rulon held the bag up and said, "Field rations." He reached inside and pulled out a box of chocolate-glazed orange slices for them to see. "Try to control yourselves," he said.

Brother-in-law cautiously reached inside and held up an orange slice for closer inspection. "Doesn't look like an M&M," he said and plunged it into his mouth. After a few chews and a swallow, he reached for another. Rulon grinned.

Yohaba said, "Now he's got you. He never charges for the first one." She greedily took one herself and sucked on the chocolate end. To a casual observer, they were three tourists standing on a street corner opposite Paradeplatz eating chocolate on an overcast misty day. If you looked closely, though, you would notice their eyes constantly shifting, checking out windows, following the pedestrians who passed, and that the three friends faced slightly outward from each other, seemingly together but in reality focused outside their tight little circle.

As Rulon scanned the nearby rooftops for likely sniper positions, he munched away and said, "For its Grand Cru chocolate, Sprüngli uses cacao beans from Madagascar and sometimes South America. But on days like this, I don't know, I think I prefer the taste of Forastero cacao from Ghana. What do you guys think?"

"No one knows chocolate like Rulon," said Yohaba, who was rifling through the bag looking for the Luxembürgerlis. "Ah-ha!" she exclaimed when she found them. To Brother-in-law she held out a chocolate, wafer-like concoction the size of a slightly flattened ping pong ball and said, "Try one of these." The three friends ate in silence for a minute.

Yohaba paused just as she was about to sink her teeth into her third Luxembürgerli. "When it comes to chocolate, my cowboy's worse than a wine connoisseur. Watch. Tell Brother-in-law what the Aztec word for chocolate is."

"You mean *xocoatl*," said Rulon.

"And these chocolates here," she said, holding up a dark chocolate orange slice. "Where is the cacao from?"

Rulon plucked it from her hand and popped it in his mouth. He savored the taste for a moment then said with an air of a man unlocking nuances inconceivable to the average person, "Somewhere in the southern hemisphere."

He continued relishing the chocolate. Suddenly, with a burst of certainty, he concluded, "Madagascar. Sun facing. North side of the hill."

"See what I have to live with," said Yohaba.

Rulon said, "Here's one I bet you didn't know. If an Aztec human sacrifice wasn't perky enough before the big moment, they gave him a gourd of chocolate to drink tinged with blood from previous victims."

"Cheery," said Brother-in-law. "And you're feeding us chocolate now?"

"You don't have to eat any more, if you don't want," said Rulon.

"I don't like this spot," said Brother-in-law, back to business.

Rulon said, "There's fifty windows with a clear shot, plus the church, plus trams unloading every few minutes, plus pedestrians, and people milling around store windows. And the side streets are so twisty, the Third Guards could be assembling a block away and we'd never know it."

"And if there's a firefight, the chocolate shop could get damaged," added Yohaba. "That's my husband's real worry."

"It won't be so busy tonight," said Rulon. "The Russians will have cleared it with the Swiss and you won't see any police. If they know there's going to be trouble, they might even halt the tram traffic."

"Loro Piana has some good-sized luggage in the window," said Yohaba. "If someone would create a distraction, I could probably slip the MP7 or the Vector into one of them." Rulon had brought the H&K MP7 because its standard cartridge did a better job against body armor than the MP5's pistol ammo. The Swiss-made Vector K-10 submachine gun was brought along for purely sentimental reasons.

"Always thinking. That's my girl," said Rulon proudly, "Personally, I'm liking the trash receptacles there in front of the windows. One of them could easily take the M79."

"Who collects the garbage and when?" asked Brother-in-law.

"Don't know," said Rulon, realizing that could be a problem.

Yohaba asked, "What if they come from the lake side and push us up the Bahnhofstrasse? They'll be pushing us away from our weapons."

"Then we'll also need some weapons stashed on this side of the street," said Rulon.

Rulon and Brother-in-law looked around. The Blancpain watch store next to where they were standing was the obvious next choice for a weapons stash. Rulon stepped over and put his hand on the store's glass window. "The glass is reinforced," he said. "I suppose I could shoot it here, here, and here…" Rulon touched three points on the glass with his finger. "…and then punch through with the hammer."

"We'll do it with a Claymore," said Brother-in-law. "Next problem."

Rulon took off his black cowboy hat and ran his fingers through his short brown hair. "You can't do that," he said slowly, drawing out every syllable. "No Claymores. I thought we agreed."

"Before you get your knickers in a knot," said Brother-in-law, "didn't you just say that if the Russians are planning any kind of direct action they'll clear it with the Swiss first?"

"So what?" said Rulon.

"So, the Swiss will make sure no one's around."

Yohaba added, "Yeah, but let's get real here. Just how are they going to do that? What about night watchmen, janitors, lovers out for a walk, people in the apartments above the stores, people coming off of trams. You think the Swiss police are going to gas the city and put everyone to sleep?"

"Fine," said Brother-in-law. "I'll use a Mini MS803 for the watch store then. They're smaller." The Mini was manufactured in South Africa and had only 300 steel fragments and a maximum 30-meter killing range, compared to a regular Claymore's 700 ball bearings and 100-meter range.

Hands on hips and eyes blazing, Yohaba said, "We've been through this before. This is my city not yours. You're not turning Zurich into ground zero like you did the ranch. You are so convinced this is an ambush. What if you're wrong?"

"Good question," said Brother-in-law calmly. "If I'm wrong, we all have a good laugh and collect our weapons tomorrow when the stores open. But the better question is *what if you're wrong*?" Brother-in-law gave them a few seconds to chew on that. "I'm going to make a prediction. This entire meeting is about getting Steenberg—" and now his eyes bored straight at Yohaba "—and knocking off his successor. Cowboy here's the bonus." He turned to Rulon and hurled in his face, "I don't even know why you let her come. If she was my wife, she'd be home with the kids right now. What were you thinking? Instead of worrying so much about saving everybody else, you should be more worried about saving your own wife."

Rulon's first reaction was to worry that Yohaba had been hurt by Brother-in-law's oblique reference to their not having children. His second reaction was to wonder if maybe Brother-in-law was right. Should he have put his foot down and told her she couldn't come? He looked at Yohaba and could see her wrestling with Brother-in-law's words, trying to make sense of the inexplicable turn this conversation had taken. But he could tell that though she was puzzling over something, Brother-in-law had not gotten to her in the way he had feared. They both knew Brother-in-law's history well enough to know what was really eating at him.

To ease the tension, Rulon made a joke. "It's overcast today," he said. "If you're suffering from seasonal affective disorder, I can buy you a sun lamp."

Brother-in-law met his gaze straight on and said, "That didn't come out the way I meant it."

"Okay. Works for me," said Rulon. He held out a bag. "Here. Have another Luxembürgerli."

Yohaba took hold of Brother-in-law's hand and held it in hers along with Rulon's. "What happened to your family wasn't your fault," she said to their friend, "and has nothing to do with what's happening here with me. If I stayed back on the ranch, I could be thrown from a horse and break my neck. The safest place for me is right here with the two of you." Brother-in-law didn't pull his hand away. He struggled to say something.

When he couldn't get the words out and gave up, Rulon said, "Amen, brother. Couldn't have said it better myself." Yohaba teared up, but before she could say anything more, Rulon clapped his hands together and said exuberantly, "C'mon. We'll all feel better once the machine guns and Claymores are in place."

They walked over to Loro Piana and Yohaba asked, "What about snipers?"

"I'm betting that's why we brought Benny," said Rulon. Brother-in-law nodded.

Yohaba asked, "By the way, how are we going to plant the Claymores without people spotting them?"

Brother-in-law said, "Murphy's got that covered."

"Okay, one last thing," said Rulon. "Let's put our hands together and on a count of three say, 'Go Redfish.'"

"That'll be the day," said Brother-in-law.

Yohaba grabbed Rulon's and Brother-in-law's hands and held them together with hers. "Please, just do it," she said to Brother-in-law. "Don't think about it. Just do it or there'll be no peace. Please." Brother-in-law frowned but didn't pull his hand away. Rulon counted to three and with Yohaba said quietly, "Go Redfish." A few passersby looked at them strangely.

Brother-in-law shook his hand free and spoke into his throat mike. "Did we give you enough time?"

From the Fraumunster church tower Benny replied, "Yep. Got observers on the third and fourth floor of Credit Suisse. Can't see any weapons. Could be they're just checking things out beforehand like us."

Cattycorner from the bank, Stringbean said, "I got another in the second-floor window of the hotel just up from the church. No weapons."

Murphy by the Sprüngli chocolate store said, "Looks to me like they've got a video team set up above the clothing store. Be sure to smile and point your toes tonight." Dilly by the Paradeplatz tram stop said everything looked normal from his vantage point.

"Okay, start heading back to the van, but don't make it obvious," said Brother-in-law. "Dilly, you go first." Then he said to Rulon and Yohaba, "Flushed out a few tadpoles. Let's head back."

"Well, can't say I'm surprised," said Rulon. "I guess we're pretty much good to go. Let's just make sure whatever happens tonight it stays out of the morning papers."

❧❧

Standing in the subdued light of the closed stores on a quiet Poststrasse, Rulon looked at his watch and marveled at how slowly time dragged by. It was six minutes before the thin man was due to arrive. The weapons, if needed, were in place. He, Yohaba, and Brother-in-law plus Palmer, Steenberg's body double, stood by the bench next to the Blancpain watch store. Edgy.

All except Brother-in-law, who slipped into his backwoods persona whenever he sensed they were tensing up. He even got Palmer laughing, and Rulon had to remind the actor more than once to act like the eighty-year-old he was supposed to be impersonating. Steenberg waited in a third-story room in the Savoy Baur en Ville Hotel thirty meters away. Once the thin man appeared and Yohaba signaled all was safe, he would make his appearance on the street.

As the time drew near, Rulon told Palmer one more time to stand still and stop fiddling with his hat. It wasn't Steenberg's style to be fidgeting like a crack addict. This was Palmer's first experience as Steenberg's double, and already Rulon decided it would be his last. He just wasn't cut out for this. He was scared and looked set to bolt any second. Like the others, Palmer was wearing a bulletproof vest. He asked what it would feel like if he was shot. A bad sign. *Like being hit with a baseball bat*, Rulon replied from experience.

Meanwhile Yohaba jabbered, as she always did when anxious. Rulon only half listened, and, as the time drew near, even Brother-in-law grew quiet. Murphy and Benny were at their stations. Benny had Rulon's Remington 700 AcuSport VTR .308 caliber rifle with the 5-R rifling. It was similar enough to the U.S. Army's M24 sniper rifle that Benny had no problem adjusting to it. The distances were so short, he felt he didn't need a spotter. Next to him on the ground was an M16 and ten 20-round magazines. Dilly and Stringbean waited in the Mercedes van three hundred yards away behind the Grossmunster cathedral just across the river from the Fraumunster. Vladimir,

Vadim, and Yevgeny and his team were waiting at the plane parked near the D gates at the Zurich airport poised for a quick takeoff.

A minute later, at precisely 10:55 p.m., Murphy, went into action from the grey stone balcony of his second-story room that was right below Steenberg's in the Savoy Hotel. He activated the first of three radio-controlled cars that had been waiting under a delivery truck parked down the street in front of the Gucci shop. The tiny Corvette buzzed past the bench at the corner of the Bahnhofstrasse where Rulon and the others were standing and made a U-turn. Taped to its hood was a Mini MS Claymore mine.

It angled towards the sidewalk on the opposite side of the street, slowed slightly, and tried edging over a low point in the curb. Instead it bounced and rotated sideways, getting hung up with its rear wheels spinning in mid-air. Rulon snorted and Yohaba rolled her eyes at Brother-in-law, who said, "If it ain't chickens, it's feathers." He gestured to them to be patient.

A few seconds later, a miniature Humvee with a similarly affixed Mini MS came whirring along the same route. It slowed as it approached its stricken partner, stopped, and then edged forward a few inches, then a few more, to gently nudge its partner over the curb. The Corvette took up its position between two phone booths on the sidewalk with its Claymore tilted slightly upwards, in front of the Loro Piana store front. The mini Humvee halted in the street right up against the curb facing outwards towards Paradeplatz.

Thirty seconds later, a miniature black Dodge Challenger came to a stop in the middle of the street with its Mini MS facing towards the church in case trouble came from that direction.

The cars in place, the street once again fell quiet until 10:59. A number 7 tram approached and stopped at

Paradeplatz. Two old women stepped off. The tram appeared empty except for the driver. It moved on, turned onto the Bahnhofstrasse and rumbled past Rulon and the team toward the main station at the end of the street 800 meters away. The streets were otherwise deserted. The stores had been shut since eight. A halogen streetlight flickered, and Rulon's hand inched towards the Colt in his shoulder holster. Something didn't feel right.

The two women had to be pushing ninety. They walked arm in arm, the sprightlier one helping her sister over the curb as they crossed the street. Gracious smiles were exchanged, a gentle pat on a fragile arm, they came together, a Norman Rockwell painting of sisters in their sunset years, their handbags big and heavy in the crooks of their elbows. Where were they headed this time of night? The Fraumunster? It was closed. To one of the apartments above the shops on Poststrasse? Fifty meters away, the Fraumunster bell resounded like Vulcan's forge. It was precisely 11 p.m.

The old women continued to approach. Twenty feet away now, chatting quietly with each other, rouged cheeks, feeling safe and secure—after all, this was Zurich. Now ten feet away. A familiar shape in the bulky cloth handbag. Suddenly, alarm bells in Rulon's head clanged louder than the Fraumunster, and without thinking he pushed Yohaba into the Blancpain doorway and drew his pistol. But froze. An instant later two shots from Brother-in-law's .22 popped and echoed in the narrow street, and the two old women sagged to the ground. Rulon yelled at Brother-in-law, then saw the silenced pistol slip from the one woman's bag as she folded down, down, down like an ironing board losing its legs. Yohaba yelled from behind him.

Brother-in-law said in a normal voice, "Here they come."

❧❧❧

In the moonless dark of the Hönggerberg forest just outside the city, the team paused to regroup and assess before continuing on to the airport and Vladimir's waiting Gulfstream.

They were little more than shadows to each other in the inky blackness between the tall trees. Steenberg sat by himself in the white Mercedes van writing on a pad of paper in the dim light of the van's cosmetic mirror. Rulon stood a few feet away with Brother-in-law rehashing what had happened. Yohaba sat by herself on the van's bumper. They were parked deep in the woods, one hundred yards from the nearest dirt road. As he talked, Brother-in-law poked a dejected Rulon in the chest a few times then grabbed his shoulder and gave it a friendly shake.

Rulon wrapped up their conversation and came over to Yohaba. She rested her head on his shoulder. Brother-in-law looked thoughtfully at both of them then disappeared into the darkness to go check on Murphy, Benny, Dilly, and Stringbean, who were out of sight somewhere in the trees keeping watch. All was quiet except for the clicking of the van's diesel engine and the soft, muffled sounds of Yohaba's intermittent sobbing. After a minute Yohaba wiped away her tears and sat up straight.

"He was a nice guy," she said.

"What did you say?" asked Rulon, still partly deaf from the explosions and gunfire.

"Nothing," said Yohaba. "We were almost away. I thought we were clear. If it wasn't for that guy in the window. How many were there?"

"What did you say?" asked Rulon again.

"What?" asked Yohaba sharply. Her ears were ringing too.

Rulon leaned close and whispered into her ear, "I'm not hearing so well." Yohaba repeated her question softly into his ear.

"There were two in the room where most of the shots were coming from," said Rulon.

"Did you get'em?" she asked.

"Brother-in-law," said Rulon.

"The cameramen?" asked Yohaba. "I thought you got the cameramen, the ones that shot Palmer."

"Yeah, yeah, that was me," said Rulon. "Sorry. I'm not thinking straight. Brother-in-law got the shooters over the Gucci shop. Everyone's dead. They're all dead. When a guy with a gun breaks into a room with guys with guns, everyone has to start shooting. There's no way around it. It's self-defense for everyone."

"Dead idiots," she said. For a moment, they both fell silent.

"We were lucky," said Yohaba, sad and beyond tired— her body's post-combat chemicals wreaking havoc with her emotions. "They were going to assassinate us all. An actual Russian hit team. Really. With everything that happened to have only one of us killed was a miracle."

"Yeah, poor Palmer," said Rulon wistfully. "John Sebastian Palmer." And then angrily he added, "But, dang it! It didn't have to come to this. Geez, we should not be messing with these people. They're insane."

"Do you think they'll be fooled?" asked Yohaba. "At least long enough to keep the Russians and Chinese off our backs?"

Rulon grew somber. "The store was still burning when we left. I doubt there was much left of the body. He was the right height and weight. Your grandfather took care of the dental records and fingerprints. Yeah, I think they'll be fooled for a while."

"He switched the DNA records, too," said Yohaba. "He thought of everything."

"If you say so," said Rulon angrily.

They both looked up and held eye contact, then like two planes approaching head-on before veering off, they looked quickly away, their minds soaring off into their own thoughts. Rulon took a deep breath, and the memories of what they had experienced only a few hours ago came rushing back like falling down a well.

Rulon's recollections were interrupted by Brother-in-law returning through the forest's drifting night fog. He sat on the bumper alongside Rulon and Yohaba.

"We need to go," he said.

"I feel bad that we had to leave him," said Rulon. "Just doesn't feel right somehow."

"Tactical necessity," said Brother-in-law.

"It was in the contract," said Yohaba, her voice heavy and tired. "Assassinated doubles get left behind. It has to be that way." Rulon looked up. Yohaba's emotional exhaustion was showing. She stood up. "If we move now, we can maybe take off before they lock down the airport." Brother-in-law also stood up and spoke quietly into his throat mic, summoning the rest of the team back to the van. Yohaba put her arm around him. "That was a very brave thing you did. You know, stepping out into the street for Palmer."

"It didn't save him," said Brother-in-law. "We need to go."

"No, it didn't. But what you did back there. You hardly knew the guy."

"He was part of the team. Fat Rancher did okay, too," said Brother-in-law.

The van door opened and Steenberg stepped out holding a computer tablet. He walked over to where the others were sitting. "Operation Able Archer is quite instructive," he said. Rulon and the others looked at him, puzzled. Steenberg continued, oblivious to their reaction. "Able Archer was a 1983 NATO exercise in Eastern Europe that brought the world closer to nuclear war than the Cuban Missile Crisis, and yet very few people have ever heard of it."

"Wow, this is the perfect time for a history lesson," said Rulon with a tone that earned him a warning squeeze on the arm from Yohaba. Rulon was furious with Steenberg for using doubles, a sure sign that while Steenberg knew the situation was dangerous he didn't want to risk his own life. It struck Rulon as cowardly. Sure, Steenberg was indispensable to saving the world, but, geez, thought Rulon, what an ego to think your life was more valuable than someone else's.

Steenberg cleared his throat. "Able Archer was a tragic comedy of coincidences. America had completely modernized its European Pershing ICBM arsenal to counter the Russians' new SS-twenties. The Soviets reacted with their typical epic paranoia."

"What a shock," said Rulon, this time earning a withering look from Yohaba.

"Exactly," said Steenberg. "But a computer program exacerbated the problem. It measured thousands of variables every second. Economic results, military readiness, troop movements, agricultural output, plus psychological profiles on foreign politicians—all of this was measured to determine Soviet vs. U.S. weaknesses and intentions, and that program came within a hairsbreadth of recommending a first strike. Can you see the beauty—the colossal beauty—of this blunder?"

"Yes," said Rulon. "I am very much attuned right now to the beauty of colossal blunders."

Yohaba stood up and put a hand on her grandfather's arm. "We really need to go," she said, sensing that Rulon was about to explode, but Steenberg stood firm.

"The Russians armed thousands of nuclear warheads, put their entire nuclear arsenal on extreme high alert and cancelled all military flights except reconnaissance. They were convinced America was planning a nuclear first strike against them, and they came..." Steenberg held a thumb and index finger a fraction of an inch apart. "... this close to launching."

"To really screw things up takes a computer," said Rulon drily. "Okay. I'll bite. Why didn't they launch?"

"They didn't launch." explained Steenberg, "because the U.S. Air Force's assistant chief of staff at the time forgot to change NATO's alert status. If he had, the Soviet computer would have picked it up and reacted. There would have been a nuclear war with millions of casualties in a matter of hours."

"So, it was incompetence that saved the world," said Rulon irritably, "not some giant brain that thought he knew all the answers and had everything figured out."

Steenberg raised an eyebrow at Rulon's surly retort and said gently, "Yes, clearly incompetence can also serve a purpose. In our case, it was our competence that incited our Russian partners. I need to get a message to my chess partner so this doesn't escalate."

Yohaba tugged on Rulon's sleeve to stop, but he was in the mood for a good argument. "No," he said very slowly and drawn out. "You don't need to get a message to the thin man. He thinks you're dead. That's a good thing. That's why Palmer died. Remember? You need to run and stay hidden. We all need to run. I will make a prediction. We are all dead or in somebody's version of a rendition site within twenty-four hours if we don't start making some right moves now."

When no one responded, Rulon gathered himself for another go at Steenberg. "We're not going to get a message to the thin man. He's through talking. That's his message to you. He now understands how the money flows. You've been waving lots of it around and your Russian chess buddy wants more of it. Actually, he wants it all, and you're in the way. That's it. It's not complicated. He makes more money with you dead than you alive. Oh, he'd like to kill the rest of us too, but we're just bonuses in his little private spy game. There, I solved it for you. The only thing he wants to read from you is your death certificate from Zurich's Funeral and Cemeteries Office. As soon as he finds out it was Palmer and not you lying on a slab in the Leichenschauhaus, it's going to be Paradeplatz times ten all over again." Rulon turned away, too angry to even look at Steenberg.

"You need to wrap this up," said Brother-in-law. "The boys are on their way back, and I don't want them hearing this."

"Rulon. Are you still with us?" asked Steenberg sadly. "I don't have to worry about you too, do I? What I'm trying to do is almost beyond my strength. I can't do it if the people around me aren't totally committed and supportive. I simply can't."

Rulon turned to face him. "I can't get a straight answer out of you," he said angrily. "With everyone else in my life, I ask a question, and I get an answer. With you, all I get is a load of pixie dust that wears off after thirty minutes. Then I've got twenty more questions and you're right there with the pixie dust again. And you're pulling Yohaba into something I don't like. She loves you and you're using that to make her break promises she made to me. I told you that I would help protect you, but I won't get dragged into your schemes. And I won't let Yohaba get dragged in either."

"Rulon," said Steenberg, "I need you, but I need Yohaba more. Sorry to be so blunt. But I can't do this without her. I need her full support. If you undermine that, it puts the entire operation in jeopardy."

Rulon looked up at Steenberg and said low and dangerous, "Is that a threat?"

Yohaba gasped and yelled, "Rulon! Stop it!"

Steenberg quickly said, "No, no, no. Of course not." He and Rulon locked eyes for a moment. Then Steenberg said, "I also mourn John Palmer." He handed Rulon his tablet.

"What's this?" asked Rulon.

"It's my letter to John's stepson," replied Steenberg. "His only surviving family member. They were estranged. I chose John specifically because he had so little family."

Rulon flipped on the van's dome light and read. After fifteen seconds, Brother-in-law said, "We haven't got time for this."

"Yeah, we do," said Rulon. After another minute he looked up. "Well," he said when he was finished. "I might have shot my mouth off a little. I apologize. This is beyond generous." When Steenberg said nothing but smiled at him benignly, Rulon added, "But the spirit of what I said is still true. If you knew it was going to be dangerous enough for a double, we should have used a cadaver and not a real person. I'm sure with all your connections you could have dug one up somewhere."

Yohaba said, "We still would have needed someone to be standing there to act like him. It was always going to be dangerous no matter what."

"We could have propped the cadaver up on the bench."

"Coulda, shoulda, woulda," said Brother-in-law.

"Well," said Rulon to Brother-in-law. "Next time when it's your body lying dead and burned on the ground that's what I'll say. You won't mind, will you?" Brother-in-law frowned but said nothing.

Yohaba put a hand on her grandfather's arm. "Listen to Rulon, please. I think he might have a point. We may be in over our heads. I'm not sure we're in control anymore. What do you think?"

Before Steenberg could answer, Murphy and the others came melting back through the trees. Murphy said, "We gotta scoot."

Chapter 18

On the way to the airport, Dilly drove the ten-seater van with Rulon next to him. Directly behind him was Yohaba. Next to her were Steenberg and Brother-in-law. Stringbean, Murphy, and Benny followed in a rented charcoal gray turbo 8-cylinder BMW. In the van, everyone nervously braced themselves every time a police car, fire engine, or emergency vehicle raced by. Strangely, the vehicles, sirens screaming and flashing lights blazing, were heading both into the city and away from it towards the airport. Every time a police car showed up in the rearview mirror, Dilly's hands went white on the steering wheel. One time a police car came up behind and followed them all the way through the Unterstrass district and onto the A1.

"If he pulls us over, let me do the talking," said Rulon. But eventually the patrol car sped off with nothing more than an aggressive look from the policewoman in the passenger seat as it went by. "That was weird," said Rulon.

Dilly pulled into the far-right lane to let an emergency truck roar by. "That's the eighth one," he noted. "I don't get it. Shouldn't they be heading into the city? And shouldn't there be roadblocks? What could be bigger than what we just came from?"

From behind him, Steenberg said, "Someone call Vladimir."

Yohaba called on her cell. "He's not picking up."

"Try the kid," said Rulon. Yohaba speed dialed Vadim. No answer.

"Try again," said Rulon. She did, and just as she was about to hang up, Vadim answered, hysterical, in Russian. In the background were the confused sounds of sirens and men's voices. "Put it on speaker," said Rulon. "And make him talk English." Yohaba hit the speaker phone button and spoke to Vadim. Eventually the young man calmed down enough to make sense.

"They're all dead," he stammered. "My grandfather is dead. The plane just…just…blew up. Just like that. I went to buy something in the shops. There was an explosion. I ran back with Yevgeny. I could see the plane. They were on fire inside." Yohaba let him talk.

"What about Tripod?" asked Brother-in-law, but Yohaba put her finger to her lips and hoped Vadim hadn't heard. This wasn't the time to be worried about a dog. Brother-in-law had a Remington model 870 Express pistol-grip pump shotgun on his lap, which he now pumped once. Steenberg kept silent.

Eventually Vadim stopped talking. "We're almost there," said Yohaba. "We're coming for you." She touched Rulon on the shoulder. "What should I tell him?"

"They'll shut down the entire airport for sure," said Rulon. "We can't go there. Let me talk to Yevgeny." Over the phone, Vadim could be heard talking to someone in Russian and then they all heard a familiar bark. Brother-in-law noticeably relaxed.

"Everyone is gone," said Yevgeny, shaken, once he had the phone. "Where are you?"

Rulon said, "We're almost at the airport, but we can't get in to pick you up. If we do, we'll be trapped and they're going to be searching every car. You have to get out of the airport. There's a gas station by the last airport exit. It's maybe a five-minute walk from Terminal 1. You have to get there. I don't think there's any sidewalks, but you're just gonna have to get there. We'll be waiting for you."

"Yevgeny," said Yohaba. "I'm so sorry. We were ambushed, too. Did you hear it over the news yet?"

"No," he said, "but there were police everywhere even before the plane blew up. We knew something had gone wrong."

"Get to the gas station," she said. "We're almost there."

⁊⁊⁊

Moscow, 05:15 a.m.—5 hours after the incident at Paradeplatz

Captain Gromanko of the Russian Foreign Service produced his photo ID then emptied his pockets into a gray plastic bin sliding along a conveyor on its way through one of the Kremlin's ground floor x-ray machines. He next sent along his computer and bag. Finally, he too passed through a metal detector. Afterwards, he stood patiently with outstretched arms while a young, grim-faced guard wanded him. This was Gromanko's almost daily ritual, though the times of day were never the same. The guards were familiar to him, but still his arrival drew no smiles and no greetings. After midnight everyone looks suspicious. While being frisked, he focused on a large painting hanging to his left of Putin framed by the Russian flag. It was a miracle how much younger and taller Putin looked than in real life. Gromanko thought about that and hoped this night the Kremlin held a miracle for him as well.

After a frisking that bordered on objectionable, he packed his computer back in its bag and walked over to a wall of elevators. He took the center elevator eleven floors down and endured another thorough search while being watched by two heavily armed guards standing behind bulletproof glass partitions. In this, the Kremlin's deepest and most secure, most bomb-proof level, the halls were deserted except for the guards.

A circuitous five-minute walk later, the captain reached the thin man's office down a long, drab, yet highly polished linoleum hallway. The mission in Zurich had been a disaster. The Foreign Service hadn't lost that many people since an incident in Lebanon in 1982, but just as disturbing was the threat that the Swiss might never work with them again. At least Steenberg was dead. A partial victory. Gromanko's brain was abuzz wondering if he would ever see the light of day again and whether his wife, when she found out, would forgive him for overseeing an operation that destroyed the Gucci shop.

Gromanko, a Spetznaz veteran with a thick skin and a hate for Rulon Hurt that was more than skin deep, grieved most of all, not for the career that may have permanently slipped through his fingers this evening, but for the blown chance to finally settle the score with Hurt. Hurt had a reputation for being the elbow that was close but could never be bitten. Gromanko was starting to understand why.

In Gromanko's bag was a DVD of the action which for four minutes and twenty-six seconds had turned Paradeplatz into a war zone. It was an exercise that had been planned and rehearsed for a month. Gromanko knew this was one ambush they'd be studying for years at the VITYAZ training center. It was textbook. No one ran. Everyone died doing their duty. Even the two armed cameramen stayed at their post guns blazing until the Cowboy found them on the third floor above the Blancpain watch store. What had gone wrong? Gromanko reflected on that. He had reviewed the tape three times. Nothing had gone wrong. Except everyone was dead.

The wooden door with the wired glass center panel was open but flanked by two guards with sub-machine guns. Gromanko adjusted his peaked visor hat and said in an attempt at friendliness, "He must like to start early." Behind one of the guards, Gromanko could see the thin man sitting at his desk in the light of a green-shaded desk lamp.

Out of the corner of his mouth the guard said, "He doesn't sleep."

Gromanko entered the room and stood at attention in front of the desk. The old man didn't look up but continued writing on a legal-sized note pad, a slight creak emanating from his ancient roller chair salvaged from the ruins of Stalingrad. He wore a white shirt, buttons, no cufflinks, and a plain red tie. His well-worn suit jacket hung behind him mounted on a wall hook. On the opposite wall facing the desk was an old and faded, framed black-and-white photograph of a young man standing in the center of a line of eight bright young females in tired, tatty clothes but looking happy despite the building rubble around them. *Stalingrad,* thought Gromanko, *and the thin man's angels.*

Gromanko waited dutifully. As always, the old man looked to be getting perpetually thinner like a piece of wood being varnished away. He finally looked up, piercing eyes behind thick wire-rimmed glasses, now staring at Gromanko as if the two men had been locked in conversation for an hour and he had just paused to form a reply.

"First, how did the two babushkas die?" he asked.

Captain Gromanko told how the two old ladies had gotten off a tram and crossed the Bahnhofstrasse arm in arm innocently on their way down Poststrasse in the direction of the Fraumunster. It was their mission to kill Steenberg and Rulon as they walked past with silenced

.22s hidden in their purses. But something gave them away and they were shot before they could draw their weapons. If all had gone well, snipers were then to take out Yohaba and anyone else who was around. Then the two blue vans were to drive up, and the bodies collected.

The old man asked, "Did they suffer?"

"No. They were shot in the head."

"I've known them since the Great War," said the thin man in an uncharacteristic revelation. "Was it the Cowboy?

"Maybe. We're not sure. He was the first to draw a weapon, but the muzzle flashes were obscured in the video. It could have been the other American. A U.S. Navy SEAL. Again, the video is inconclusive. We don't know what gave them away. Their hands were always visible, and their pistols were still in their handbags when they were shot."

Wearily, the thin man ordered, "Describe their handbags." One of them had a brown leather purse, the other a felt Russian valenki handbag. A peasant's purse. The thin man listened to Gromanko then concluded, "Their weapon was seen through the fabric of the valenki. Which one of them had it?" Gromanko gave a name. The thin man groaned and shook his head, "She of all, should have known better." To himself Gromanko wondered, *But still, to kill two old women without hesitation based on a bulge in a purse…who could have foreseen that?*

The thin man asked many questions, most of the time with his eyes closed and his almost hairless head resting against the back of his chair.

He betrayed no emotion, not even a blink when Gromanko described how each man had been killed but grew progressively more irritated at the story's increasingly exotic turns. The mention of the M79 grenade launcher stashed in the luggage in the Loro Piana display window caused him to open one eye and cock it at Gromanko, the sub-machines guns hidden in the watch store brought an irritated sigh, but it was the Claymore mines duct-taped to radio-controlled model cars that finally pushed him over the top.

"Have they no sense of proportion?!" roared the thin man, both eyes wide open, pounding the desk in fury, unable to take it anymore. "Paradeplatz is one of the most famous squares in all of Zurich, in all of Europe!" Gromanko waited in patient silence for the old man to regain his composure. Outside the door, the guards trembled.

Gromanko managed a partial recoup with the death of Steenberg, shot by one of the cameramen, a planned-for contingency in case all else went wrong. Before he left, Gromanko placed another DVD on the desk. "This one is from the live feed in the room where the film crew were killed."

"They killed the film crew," repeated the thin man slowly. "Interesting. This time the Cowboy?"

"Yes. After they killed Steenberg." Gromanko waited but when the old man didn't react, he placed on his desk a dozen still photos of the action. Brother-in-law's picture was on top. "This is the other man we thought might have killed the old women. He is an active-duty U.S. Navy SEAL. Served in the Congo. Our analysts are double-checking his record."

"Why?"

"It's not believable."

"What do you mean?"

"It reads like a Zaytsev comic book. His file is simply not believable."

"Neither is the Cowboy's," said the thin man drily. He picked up the photo and studied it. Then he laid it aside and picked up the next one. It showed Rulon Hurt, arm extended, sighting down the barrel of his Colt Gold Cup Trophy automatic. There was a larger weapon in his other hand, but it was obscured by the wreckage of a phone booth. "What's this?" asked the thin man.

"We believe that is the grenade launcher I referred to earlier, sir."

The thin man put the photos down, sighed deeply and quipped, "*Zurich. The spiritual home of natural spies.*" Then he added, "Steenberg is dead? There is no doubt?"

"It has not been 100% confirmed. The Swiss have promised us the forensic report by the end of the day. But we are very confident."

"How angry are the Swiss?"

"Very, but not as much as one might think. They're calling it a gas main explosion." Gromanko reached into his briefcase, pulled out a sheet of paper, and laid it on the desk. "Here is a draft of what's going to appear in *Die Neue Zürcher Zeitung* in a few hours."

Explosions Rock Downtown Zurich

Zurich officials say a contractor's cigarette caused a gas explosion that severely damaged the Paradeplatz tram station, vehicles, and nearby buildings, killing eleven people and injuring four others, two critically. One of the dead was Leonard Steenberg, retired director of CERN, the European Nuclear Research laboratory in Geneva. The series of blasts and small fires occurred at 11:01 p.m. and were felt throughout the downtown area. The injured were taken to the University Hospital on Rämistrasse.

Friday morning, investigators were still sifting through the charred remains of the Loro Piana, Montblanc, and Gucci shops on Poststrasse. The Armani and Ermenegildo Zegna stores in the nearby Credit Suisse building and the landmark Fraumunster cathedral were also damaged and will be closed indefinitely.

Eighty apartments in the area were evacuated. Panicked residents initially reported gunshots and a running gun battle between rival gangs. A police spokesperson dismissed the accounts but did report warning shots were fired at several looters who escaped and are still being sought.

Officials gave no date for the resumption of tram service on lines 2, 6, 7, 8, 9, 11, 13, and bus N6 to Paradeplatz. In what officials termed a minor miracle, the nearby Sprüngli chocolate shop was undamaged and will remain open per its usual operating hours.

The thin man read the article. When he was done he laid the paper down and said, "No one keeps a secret like the Swiss. And you think they are manageable?"

"With time, yes, sir," said Gromanko. "They had observers on the scene and clearly we did not fire the first shot nor resort to explosives. That we will pay for the damages also helped." The thin man asked how much that would be and when told, the twitch in his left eye came back.

"And our troublesome countrymen? The Swiss haven't tied us to that, I hope."

"No. They're blaming it on a feud between oligarchs. All were killed except the boy and one of his bodyguards who were in the terminal at the time." The thin man nodded. Gromanko continued, "Would you like them finished off? We still have assets there."

"I think not," said the old man. "Sparing the boy may actually work in our favor."

"A little mercy, then?" said Gromanko.

"Not at all," said the old man, as if the very thought was absurd. "Simply a reminder to the father that he still has something left to lose."

"Yes, of course." After Gromanko's answer, the thin man said nothing but studied his protégé in silence until the young officer couldn't take it any longer and blurted, "Regarding the others, should I leak their names and pictures to Interpol or the Swiss?"

"No," replied the thin man. "We will clean up our own mess. Give our assurances to the Swiss on that score. We don't want them interfering. Make sure they understand. And I want them kept in Switzerland if at all possible. I don't want to chase them all over the world. Make sure they understand that." Gromanko nodded. The old man waited an unbearably long time before continuing. "So, the entire mission was a great success, and Steenberg is truly dead." The thin man said this then waited.

Gromanko correctly judged that this last statement was really a question—the moment of truth. He swallowed hard. "Everyone played their roles impeccably at Paradeplatz. No one ran. No one shirked. All died doing their duty."

"It was the planning then?"

Gromanko, now clawing for survival, lost it in a torrent of words. "Every reasonable and unreasonable contingency was prepared for. But Claymores and grenade launchers in downtown Zurich!? The old women being shot based on a bulge in a handbag!? There are no plans for this. No one can plan for *crazy*. If you have to plan for crazy every operation would take ten years and a thousand people to implement." If Gromanko had stopped there his career would have been over, maybe even his life, but with a last gasp he threw in an old Russian proverb. "When God throws, the dice are loaded." His red face and blazing eyes that said, *Go ahead have me killed, I don't care,* said it all. He was at a loss to explain the failure. And, for the first time in many years, so was the thin man.

Perhaps a younger version of himself would have had Gromanko executed, or at least demoted, but the reference to God made the thin man reflect on his previous conversation with Steenberg, which somehow managed to come around to the subject of religion. He would miss not having a chess rematch, and even miss Steenberg's smug, untouchable faith. To his surprise, the old man felt a tinge of guilt over having ordered Steenberg's death and that is what ultimately saved Gromanko.

The thin man said, "The late Doctor Steenberg would have agreed with you." The captain was dismissed with a careless wave.

Saved by a hair's breadth. Gromanko strode to the door in a daze, knowing that somehow, inexplicably, his final answer had saved him. He reached the door and had one hand on the doorknob when the old man stopped him in his tracks. "Stay by your phone. There will be another mission."

"Yes, sir," said Gromanko.

"And you won't have ten years and a thousand people to execute it this time either."

"Yes, sir."

"But I suggest you make it appear so."

Ten minutes later Gromanko walked across Red Square to the GUM department store to buy a gift for his wife—a peace offering for the destruction of the Gucci shop—and two bottles of expensive vodka for himself.

⌘

Redfish Lake—the same day
Ranger Stanley Merrifield stood waiting for the plaster cast to harden around the imprint of the canoe bottom in

the sand, a process made more difficult by the early morning cold and the wind whipping off of Redfish Lake. *Yes, it was definitely a Clipper Mac canoe*, he thought. He gripped the canoe catalog tightly, fighting to keep the pages from fluttering, looking from it to the canoe impression and back again over and over. Yep! Stanley could feel the noose tightening around the perp or perps.

It occurred to him that the canoe had to have been beached somewhere else along the lake and then transported in a truck of some kind or perhaps a canoe trailer. The lake had eleven miles of shoreline, but with any luck he wouldn't have to search every inch. He would begin his search at the parking lots and work out from there. Fortunately, it was still cold and any impressions made in sand were likely to have remained visible. Perhaps even tire treads if blowing sand had drifted over some of the spaces. Plus, schools were still in session. This time of year the park was deserted except for the diehard locals. *There can't be many who bring canoes to the park*, thought Stanley. Stanley's hat blew off, and he raced after it into the trees.

Chapter 19

Winston Klendenin III's refurbished Boeing 737-200 circled Moffett Airfield in preparation for landing. From his window, Winston could see the San Mateo and Dumbarton bridges, and in the distance the towers of the Oakland Bay Bridge and the city of San Francisco with its landmark Bank of America pyramid. The plane was low enough now that the red towers of the Golden Gate Bridge had sunk behind the hills of the city. To his left, unseen on the other side of the Santa Cruz mountains that ran north-south along the peninsula, a fog bank was building up out over the Pacific. Also unseen was the always lurking San Andreas Fault that paralleled those mountains along most of its length.

"How can we be landing here?" asked Wild Will, who was looking through the window on the other side of the plane. "Isn't this a military airfield?"

"Not anymore," said Winston. "Technically, NASA owns it."

"And they let you land here?" asked Russo.

"Not out of kindness," said Winston. "It costs me $1.3 million per year."

The plane continued its descent and landed on a well-maintained airstrip that ran parallel to the Bay. The plane taxied to a small terminal where a landing crew was waiting. Once the plane rolled to a stop, a stairway on wheels came alongside, and Winston, Wild Will and Russo exited carrying duffle bags. A Cadillac Escalade ESV, its 420 HP engine rumbling, five doors open, waited just beyond the wing.

They threw their bags into the back and Winston jumped into the driver's seat. On the way off the base, they passed an immensely huge building shaped like a barrel cut lengthwise in half and Russo asked, "What's in there?"

"That's Hangar Two. It's for dirigibles," said Winston. "It's the size of six football fields and has its own weather." When Russo gave him a funny look, he explained, "It's so tall, fog can build up inside, and it will even rain sometimes. But look over there. There's Hangar One. That's the big one. Actually, the whole thousand acres here and the three hangars you see are run by Google. They paid a billion dollars to lease it for the next sixty years."

"Dirigibles," said Wild Will. "There's an old-fashioned idea."

"Or an idea whose time has finally come," replied Winston. He decided not to mention that he owned one of the dirigibles. "Someone's willing to bet their money on it, and that's either a sign of confidence or of too much money." Winston laughed at his own wit and the sound of it perked him up. There were times over the last few months when he thought he'd never laugh again.

"Where are we going?" asked Wild Will once they passed through the last security gate.

"I'm taking us to Bill's Place," said Winston. "Best hamburgers in the Bay Area." After leaving Moffat Field, Winston turned onto 101 heading towards San Francisco.

Somewhere over Nevada, Winston had disappeared for half an hour then emerged dressed in his European finery—a gray Desmond Merrion suit with a Hermes French cuff white shirt, red paisley Leonard tie, and New

& Lingwood black Russian calf shoes. A $40,000 ensemble. Dressed like that, he no longer seemed the bumbling, inept character who dressed in tailored Crey Combat camo and tried to be one of the boys. The new impression was not lost on Wild Will and Russo, who had also changed, but into jeans and casual wear. Both former soldiers sensed the pecking order rearranging the closer they got to California.

They drove in silence. It had been a long day. Before arriving at Moffatt, they had stopped in Dallas, Little Rock, Raleigh, and Portsmouth, Maine to drop off the four men who were injured at the ranch. Including downtime from a refueling stop in Chicago, it had been twenty-one hours since they flew out of Boise.

The firefight in Zurich had happened over two hours ago, but Winston and his companions were still unaware of it. At this exact moment, Rulon and the others, now including Vadim, Yevgeny, and Tripod, were crammed into the van and driving along the A1 in Switzerland towards Schaffhausen, a town on the German border and not too far from the village on the Rhine River where Klendenin's daughter was being held.

Winston had warned them not to contact him except in an emergency. The NSA was always listening. Suspected terrorists tended to get most of the attention, but billionaires also merited some listening time. Terrorism needed money to flourish, and billionaires had lots of it and were easy targets for blackmail, as Winston knew all too well.

From 101, Winston turned west on Highway 92, then north again on 280. As they drove through the 92/280 interchange, he stared straight ahead, the driving part of his brain on autopilot. The miles slipped by. *I'm finished,* he thought. *I'm a forty-seven-year-old billionaire would-be-murderer with a craving for a hamburger.*

Winston had learned over the course of his career that nothing ever went smoothly. Being successful simply meant being more willing than the next guy to pay the price, whether that price was more research, or investment, or time, or now…attempted murder.

During their walk back at the ranch, Steenberg had asked him to come up with a business venture to distract the Chinese—casually suggesting that something in solar panel technology would do nicely, though he left the final decision up to Winston. It didn't have to be real, just the threat of a competing product so cheap that even the Chinese would be screaming for trade protection. Solar panels were out of Winston's area of expertise, but in Silicon Valley world class expertise in almost any technology was within an hour's driving radius of Palo Alto.

Winston had asked if the Chinese could be dangerous. Steenberg answered honestly, yes. Winston almost backed out at that point, but Steenberg explained that this would be Winston's sacrifice to buy time for Steenberg's grand scheme to save the world. It would be his redemption for shooting that poor man in IQ's boardroom and leaving him in a coma. And in return—this was the kicker—Steenberg's people would save his daughter. The deal was done. It was Steenberg who arranged for Wild Will and Russo to stay on as Winston's bodyguards.

After meeting Steenberg and Yohaba, Winston was 95% sure Steenberg hadn't been behind his daughter's kidnapping. But as he drove, his mind couldn't help focusing on that 5% uncertainty. Steenberg bought IQ stock at just the right time. He spoke Russian and had lots of ties with the Russian underground. And Winston suspected his daughter was being held by Russians. Then there was Brother-in-law—Steenberg's Luca Brasi. The immense seriousness of Steenberg's mission meant that almost any result could be justified, plus Steenberg had demonstrated an uncanny ability to deceive individuals on both a personal and strategic level. On the other hand, Winston had met Yohaba and Rulon and seen how they interacted with Steenberg. They certainly didn't seem like the kind of people who would kidnap someone's child or even tolerate it. Winston trusted them, and that made Steenberg seem more trustworthy and had ultimately won his confidence.

On the plane, Winston had kicked around a few scenarios for tricking the Chinese. All were feasible except they would take months to implement. Steenberg had said time was of the essence. Winston thought of Patten's famous quote. *A good plan violently executed now is better than a perfect plan executed next week.*

Winston's mind wandered as he drove. He had left his Catholic high school in San Francisco heading for college and thinking he would reform soulless corporations from within. Now at forty-seven he was firmly in the ranks of the soulless. Could he make amends by helping Steenberg? What if he failed? Maybe he should just turn himself in to the police now for the sake of justice, and for Connie, that poor woman who had forked over a ten-million-dollar bail bond and was now wandering around her house with an electronic ankle monitor. No, he couldn't turn himself in. For his daughter's sake he had to follow through.

By now they were in the city, driving north along Sunset Boulevard until it ended in Golden Gate Park. He then weaved his way through the park, driving slowly past the large bison paddock on John F. Kennedy Drive, and came out on Fulton at the 25th Avenue exit. Ten minutes later he and his two bodyguards were sitting in Bill's ready to order with Winston feeling like the luckiest man in the world for having found a parking place only a block away.

After they ordered, he noticed an enlarged photograph on the wall of a couple of kite surfers in black wetsuits braving the frigid waters off Baker Beach with the Golden Gate Bridge in the background. Surfers seemed to always wear black wetsuits, which struck Winston as odd, especially in San Francisco waters. The largest white shark breeding ground in the world was in and around the Farallon Islands just thirty-two miles away. Who knew how many sharks were out there right now under the water looking for something to eat? And then there were the surfers all looking like big, fat, blubbery seals in their black wetsuits. Didn't they have any common sense?

But next came the question he couldn't drive out of his mind—why had he given in to his daughter and allowed her to live part of the year in Russia, of all places? A supposed first world country but with third world corruption? He thought about that fateful day when his family was kidnapped in St. Petersburg. And then the note, delivered to him by the local police chief. *Not all the sharks are in the water*, he thought...and not all the blubbery hapless seals either.

But he hadn't always been a hapless seal. *What happened to that old Winston? Where's that old fire?* he asked himself. He brightened a bit but then just as quickly got depressed again. Like stirring a dead campfire with a stick. A few sparks, the coals glowing, and then nothing. Poor Andy Oderhardt. Winston couldn't get him out of his mind. Boy, was he tired. Guilt was exhausting.

Their orders arrived. Winston looked at the picture once again and could feel the sand of his soul crumbling as the successive waves of stress and guilt pounded him. Still, the hamburger tasted good.

As they walked back out to the car after their meal, the phone rang. It was Yohaba. "Winston, it's me."

"Whoa, why are you calling?" asked Winston. "I thought we agreed, no cell phones."

"I had to. You're going to see some things on the news in a few hours. You'll hear that my grandfather's dead and that there was some kind of accident in Zurich. We're not exactly sure what kind of cover-up story they'll come up with, but it will be something like that. But the important thing is none of it is true. Well, some of it is true but my grandfather wasn't killed. It was one of his doubles, a really nice guy. Oh, never mind, I don't want to talk about it. But I just want you to know that the rest of us are all right and the plan is still going to work."

"What happened?" asked Winston.

"The Russians double-crossed us."

"Vladimir. That skunk. I don't believe it."

"No. It was the other Russians." Yohaba told Winston what happened including Vladimir's death in the plane explosion.

Winston let out a long whistle when she was finished. "I thought your grandfather said the meeting wasn't supposed to be dangerous."

Yohaba was getting nervous over of the length of the call. "Listen, we haven't got time for this. I don't completely trust this phone. I'm calling you because no matter what you hear, the plan is still moving forward. You understand? We're on our way now to get your daughter. You just have to stay focused on your part of the plan."

"Where's your grandfather now?" asked Winston.

"Saving the world in some inscrutable way," Winston heard Rulon say in the background.

"Don't mind him," said Yohaba. She then told a lie in case someone was listening in. "My grandfather's on a train to Munich right now."

Winston paused before asking. "Do you still have a good feeling about this?"

"Yeah, definitely," said Yohaba. "The hard part's over. Now we just have to get your daughter back. That'll be a piece of cake. Just remember what my grandfather always says—'a deal's a deal.'"

"Yes, a deal's a deal," murmured Winston. That phrase stirred a memory. It felt important but Winston couldn't quite place it. He put it on a mental back burner.

By the time Winston hung up, he was back sitting behind the wheel of his car. He gave Wild Will and Russo a quick summary, making sure to particularly emphasize Yohaba's assurances that all was well. Wild Will opened up his phone and did a quick search on Yahoo News. He found what he was looking for under the headline, *War Zone Zurich*, and read the first couple of paragraphs out loud. All three of them were astonished at the mayhem.

After a long ten seconds of silence, Winston said, "You know how these news agencies like to exaggerate. Twenty-four-hour news cycle and all that."

"Ah…I didn't sign up for this," said Russo, unconvinced.

"Not good," said Wild Will. "This is terrorist stuff. This is wrong. This is thirty years in a Supermax." He turned around from his position in the front passenger seat to look back at Russo. Without a word, both nodded to each other and reached for the door handles.

"Could you please unlock the back so we can get our things?" asked Wild Will politely but in a tone that brooked no interference. Winston complied and Wild Will and Russo got out and retrieved their bags. "Goodbye and good luck," said Wild Will, and slammed the liftgate shut.

As the two ex-soldiers walked past the van's passenger window, Winston said rather pathetically, "A deal's a deal." Wild Will only snorted in response. Winston watched them walk down the sidewalk, saw Russo hail a taxi, and they were gone. *Well, it worked on me,* thought Winston. Again, the phrase jarred. Why?

Winston sat there by himself for a good ten minutes. The parking meter was expired, and Winston could see a meter maid on foot in his side-view mirror working her way down the block car by car towards the Escalade. It was then he made his decision—actually two decisions. Amongst all the manure being shoveled back and forth in his head between Yohaba's phone call and the loss of his bodyguards, a mushroom of a strategy vs. the Chinese had sprouted and taken root in Winston's fertilized brain. A crazy idea. A bold idea. But maybe…just maybe…if he could pull it off…if he had the brains and the imagination…if he just didn't care anymore. If he were screwed anyway. Just maybe.

Fueled by adrenaline and a good hamburger, Winston's mind kicked into high gear. He would first attack the Chinese with a feint from a dummy solar energy company, but then really set the hook via an attack on their internet. Solar energy was a given. The Chinese might even be expecting an attack on that front. The Chinese warlord after Steenberg's head would be particularly vigilant against any threats to his solar panel profits. But the internet was definitely out-of-the-box, having the dual advantage of being both unexpected and highly profitable. This wouldn't be an attack by hackers though. Heck, the Chinese were state-of-the-art hackers themselves, especially their Deep Panda team in the Ministry of State Security. No, there was a better way. There were 299 undersea cables sunk deep in the world's oceans and seas, over which flowed 99% of the world's internet traffic. The remaining 1% transmitted over satellite.

Why attack just the Chinese solar energy industry when its entire export economy was leaning with its chin into an overhand right? By faking an attack on the undersea cables linking China with the rest of the world, Winston could really tie their knickers in a knot, and perhaps make a hefty profit off the rise in stock price of any companies peddling satellite transmission technology. Of course, it might also start World War III.

"It would have to be two acquisitions," he said out loud. Then remembering Steenberg's warning about time, he thought, *Well, not exactly acquisitions. More like joint ventures—first a company developing solar panels then a company knee deep in advanced satellite transmission technology. Both had to be buried deep in debt and desperate. If I can just find the right companies, some desperate start-ups run by greedy bloodsuckers—well heck, how hard can that be in Silicon Valley?*

Yes, sir, he thought, *I can do this with a small team. Everyone in the dark except me. I need a top-notch growth hacker, someone else experienced in responsive web design, deep linking, customer-centricity, and programmatic marketing, plus some good old native advertising. All localized, of course, for a Chinese audience. I'll handle the brand storytelling myself. I'll also need some actors.* Or maybe not, depending on the level of expertise in whatever startup he bought up.

Winston pushed the ignition button on his Escalade and swung into traffic just as the meter maid raised her foot to rest it on his bumper to write the ticket. And then quoting a line from one of his favorite musicals, he said out loud, "I have this timed down to the last wave of the brakeman's hand on the last train outta town."

એન્ડ

After Yohaba had hung up, she asked Rulon. "Was I too long?"

"Probably," said Rulon. "I'm sure somewhere a computer was listening, either at Fort Meade or Beltsville. But I wouldn't sweat it. The NSA's problem is they collect too much data. Their haystack has too many pins in it for them to find one that's useful. We'd have to be pretty unlucky."

"That's good," said Yohaba.

☙❦❧

In Camp Williams, just outside of Bluffdale, Utah, behind a heavily guarded fence sits the rather wordily named *Intelligence Community Comprehensive National Cybersecurity Initiative Data Center*. The site consists of nine buildings with associated power plants, fuel tanks, and water storage silos. Two of the buildings house Data Halls 1-4, square enclosures roughly two hundred yards on a side. Each hall contains a classified number of Cray XC30 massively parallel processing supercomputers, each capable of managing a million Intel Xeon processors. Each Cray can process one hundred thousand trillion calculations per second. The combined total compute power is enough to crack the human genome, predict earthquakes, discover the building blocks of atoms, predict the path of hurricanes, simulate the behavior of every active cell in the human body for medical research...or capture and analyze every phone call, Google search, email communication, and internet, cable, or satellite transaction on the planet.

The total capacity of the site is approximately twelve exabytes, in other words, 36,000 times the total written, digital, audio, and video content of the Library of Congress. And this is raw capacity calculated before the NSA invokes its sophisticated compression algorithms.

The site requires 65 megawatts of electricity, about what it takes to power Salt Lake City 20 miles away, at a cost of $40 million per year. An NSA homegrown software program connects all the servers and their storage together and provides the necessary redundancy in case of a hardware failure.

After Yohaba and Winston hung up, a highly sophisticated program running in Data Hall 3 analyzed their conversation searching for certain keywords—both pre-programmed keywords and keywords lifted from current news articles from around the world based on highly classified algorithms. In Yohaba and Winston's case, their conversation ticked all the level 5C security boxes and was relayed to an analyst sitting in a 4 by 6-foot Herman Miller cubicle in Beltsville, Maryland. The analyst was on his lunchbreak when the alert came through. He would get to it soon.

❦❦

Chapter 20

Schaffhausen has a population of 35,000 and is both the capitol and largest city in the Swiss canton of the same name. It is only a few miles from the German border crossing at Singen. Despite Switzerland's neutrality, Schaffhausen was bombed by the Allies during World War II. Two dozen B-24 Liberators dropped their payloads of incendiary and explosive bombs on the city. Their target had been the German city of Ludwigsshafen 180 miles away. Forty Swiss were killed and about 100 injured. Airplane navigational systems have improved a lot since then. Today there are approximately thirty hotels in the area. Rulon and the team only needed three of them.

It was deemed too risky for the entire team to stay at the same hotel, even though at that time of year all of the lodgings in town had plenty of vacancies and staying together had its benefits. Rulon knew the town well. Murphy, Benny, Dilly, and Stringbean got dropped off first at a hotel by the river, then Vadim and Yevgeny, missing all their luggage which had burned up in the plane, were let out at another place two hundred yards away. Rulon, Yohaba, Steenberg and Brother-in-law stayed within walking distance of the others at the Park Villa on Parkstrasse, a 115-year-old, family-run hotel with a stone façade, quirky rooms and sturdy nineteenth-century furniture as well as a well-regarded breakfast buffet Rulon had been wanting to try for years.

Brother-in-law took a room on the first floor and Steenberg on the second. Rulon used his Schwyzerdütsch to charm the ebullient proprietor into giving him a room on the third floor as far away from the train tracks as possible. As soon as Rulon and Yohaba were inside the room, he closed and locked the door, and Yohaba called the front desk to say they were not to be disturbed.

Later, afterwards, in the fading light of day, they lay in each other's arms under the sheets. "You are my good and ardent lover," said Rulon, a trifle breathless.

"Ditto," said Yohaba, also a trifle breathless.

The hotel was only half full and the quiet, after the terror and explosions of Paradeplatz, lay over them like a second blanket. Though springtime, it was cold. Rulon got up to retrieve an extra blanket from the closet. He unfolded it over the bed then climbed back in.

"You know, you're not really fat," said Yohaba, once Rulon was settled again. "You're just wide and big boned. I don't see why they call you Fat Rancher. You shouldn't let them say that about you."

"It's no big deal. If it ever gets to me, I'll just sit on them."

Under the covers, Yohaba felt him around the waist with both hands. "You don't even have love handles. You have girth. You are a man of girth. You're more like a rhinoceros or a big boiler, or like a…" Yohaba's voice trailed off.

"Go on, say it," said Rulon. "Say what you were going to say. You were going to say 'or like a brick outhouse' weren't you?"

"You're ridiculous," said Yohaba. "I was going to say 'like a brick love god.'"

"I stand corrected," said Rulon.

"Sometimes I can't believe my life," said Yohaba.

"Yep," said Rulon. "Life is a miracle."

"I think of what it was like before I met you, and I just can't believe all the crazy things that have happened since then."

"Don't look at me," said Rulon. "It's your grandfather and his grand delusions." Rulon tried to kiss her but she quickly tilted her head just enough to make it difficult.

"I'm talking here," she said.

"You were a real brat when I first met you," said Rulon, persisting. "But you're a much nicer person now and generally more cooperative." He managed to corral her and kiss her passionately. She responded with gusto.

After a long moment, they pulled apart to lie on their backs. A contemplative minute later, Yohaba propped herself up on an elbow and said, "I want to stay here. I never want to step out that door again. I love this room." In one corner, two windows at right angles to each other, both framed by heavy, ornately patterned tied-back drapes, filtered the last rays of light through white sheer curtains. A small antique desk half-filled the length of the wall at the foot of the bed. On it, a scented candle burned softly and a wooden lamp with a beige lampshade cast a dim, yellowish light across the room. Above the desk hung two paintings, one of the outside of the hotel and another of a bowl of fruit. On either side of the desk were two sturdy chairs with white fabric seat cushions.

Yohaba said, "I'm afraid if we walk out that door, the world will find us, and I don't want to be found."

"I hear you," said Rulon. He reached down and groped for something on the floor. He came back with a box of Luxembürgerlis. "But soon as we run out of these I'm leaving with or without you."

"You can buy them online and have them delivered," said Yohaba.

"But they wouldn't be as fresh," said Rulon.

"I'll pay for express delivery."

"If I ever win one of our arguments, you'll let me know, won't you?"

"Don't hold your breath," said Yohaba.

They munched together.

☙❧

Downstairs, Brother-in-law with Tripod at his heels knocked on Steenberg's door. Three knocks, a pause, then one knock. Steenberg said, "Come in."

Steenberg was sitting at a small desk with his laptop open. He closed it when Brother-in-law entered. He saw Brother-in-law look from the laptop to him with a scowl. "Don't worry," said Steenberg. "To anyone tracking the IP address, I'm sitting in a coffee shop in Johannesburg. Where have you been?"

"Prowling," said Brother-in-law. He walked past Steenberg to the window and looked outside.

"See anything?" asked Steenberg.

"Not yet."

Steenberg sighed and spoke. "I've decided my new chess partner will be having his chess career cut short."

"Don't look at me," said Brother-in-law. "I don't do suicide missions."

"No, but Chechnyans do," replied Steenberg.

Without saying a word, Brother-in-law's strong disapproval expanded to fill the room.

"I do what is necessary," said Steenberg with granite-like firmness. "When the world is at stake, a conscience is a liability."

Brother-in-law said, "Chechnyans you will regret."

Steenberg turned in his chair to more directly face Brother-in-law. "Not growing squeamish, are we?" he asked in a gentler voice after apprising his younger companion for a few thoughtful seconds. "I have big plans for you, if you can keep the faith."

"Don't worry about me," said Brother-in-law. "But I'm trusting you to keep your end of the deal."

"That's my boy," said Steenberg. "Rest assured. Your faith is well-founded. Now about the young lady. During the rescue, I don't want anyone hurt. This is extremely important. None of the kidnappers can be hurt, or heaven forbid, killed. There is one in particular, if he were to be injured in any way, it would cause enormous complications for our project. Can you do that?"

"What do you mean?" asked Brother-in-law.

"I mean I don't want any of *my* people guarding the girl getting hurt." Steenberg gave the word "my" particular emphasis, hoping that Brother-in-law would catch the nuance. He sat back in his chair and waited.

With no cracks in his outward demeanor, Brother-in-law processed the terrible implications of Steenberg's admission. "So, you really were the one behind Klendenin shooting that guy?" he said.

"Correct," said Steenberg. "A strategic necessity. I was under a considerable amount of time pressure." He carefully scrutinized Brother-in-law's reaction.

"And the reactor in Japan and the factories in Thailand?" asked Brother-in-law. "More strategic necessities?"

"Correct again," said Steenberg.

"I've underestimated you," said Brother-in-law.

"But you won't make that mistake again," said Steenberg. "Will you?"

"I reckon not."

"People don't really want to be in the know," said Steenberg. "Oh, they all say they do. But, really, it just disturbs their little world and presents them with all sorts of confusing consequences. Ignorance is bliss for most people. But you're not most people. Are you, Orin? I'm pulling back the curtain for you. So you can see. Can you handle it?"

"I reckon," said Brother-in-law.

"I would like you to become more involved in operations. I'm offering you an expanded role."

"I have no ambitions," said Brother-in-law. "All I want is your help getting my boys back."

"Ah, you say that now. But what happens next? Do you want your children to live forever in the Congo? Or do you think you can just walk into the U.S. embassy in Brazzaville with two black children, and they will believe they are yours? Will they even bother to do DNA testing? I can get you birth certificates and passports in a week. And what about when they grow up? Would you like them to go to college? Can you afford that? In Shannon County, Missouri? I believe that's where you were born? Average household income $24,835. They still have a copper mine. Maybe you can get a job there. Shannon County. I'm sure your children will fit in very nicely. Black population one-third of a percent. You see, I've done my homework. But at least you will be with family. You can introduce them to their grandfather in three years when he gets out of the Missouri South Central Correctional Center. And after what they've been through, your children will surely need counseling. Probably for years. How are you…?"

"That's enough," said Brother-in-law. "I get the picture."

"Good," said Steenberg. "Are you still in?"

"I'm still in," said Brother-in-law.

"Good. That pleases me immensely. You have become quite indispensable." Brother-in-law said nothing. After a moment, Steenberg continued. "Now let's talk about the operation. Can it be done without collateral damage? See," he said with a lighthearted chuckle, "your military expressions are rubbing off on me."

"Right now the team's like a porcupine in a balloon factory," said Brother-in-law. "They're likely to shoot first and ask questions later."

"We can't have that. What do you suggest then?"

Brother-in-law walked over to the desk and from his pocket took out and unfolded a hand-drawn map of the villa and the grounds. He laid the map flat and looked it over, touching it here and there as he considered various options. "It's doable if we keep it simple. If we have to break into the house for the girl, anything can happen. Our best chance is the girl outside with one guard. Have one of your people take her for a walk. There's a path there from the house through the garden to the woods. Make it after dinner, no later than ten. We'll be waiting in the woods. I'll dart the guard and take the girl. Simple and minimal opportunities for casualties."

"If it's that simple, let's get Rulon to do it," said Steenberg. "He and Murphy. They seem to make a good team. At least they laugh at each other's juvenile jokes. Two should be enough. Besides, I may need you here."

"I have to go with them."

"You should trust Rulon more. He's capable," said Steenberg.

"Yeah, he is," said Brother-in-law. "And that's why he'll be suspicious if we send him and tell him exactly where to wait for the girl."

"Perhaps you can just make a suggestion that he observe the home from the woods."

"If I make a suggestion, he'll do the opposite. No, I have to be there."

"I really wish there were another way. I would like you to stay close to me tonight. I have resourceful enemies. You know that."

"He's not stupid. That's why I have to go with him and fake it like we're doing surveillance. I'll have Dilly and Stringbean babysit you. You'll be safe. Do you want the girl taken without casualties or not? It's your call. We either do it this way or we storm the villa tomorrow. Those are your options, and if we storm the villa, there will absolutely be casualties."

"Yes, of course," said Steenberg. "I bow to your tactical sense. It's settled then. I'll throw in a bonus for the man who gets darted. I'll even ask for a volunteer. See, I'm not so ruthless." He laughed good-naturedly. "Now show me on the map where you will be waiting."

When they were done, Steenberg walked Brother-in-law to the door with his arm around his shoulder. Tripod hopped past them to wait in the corridor. Steenberg said, "I'm under a lot of pressure right now. Please excuse my previous bluntness. I've already made provisions for you and your children that are beyond your wildest dreams."

"I appreciate that," said Brother-in-law.

"With me a deal's a deal," said Steenberg. With a merry laugh, he added, "That's become my favorite phrase these days."

❦❦❦

Once back in his room, Brother-in-law lay back on his bed and flipped dog treats to Tripod, who sat upright on one of the antique chairs and caught the treats nimbly in his disfigured mouth. "What do you think, boy?" asked Brother-in-law, with every flipped treat another question. "Why would smarty pants want to know exactly where Rulon was waiting? If you were plotting to save the world would you even care? Maybe he's one of those micromanagers. Do you think? But why would smarty pants want just the Cowboy and Murphy to go? Don't he like us no more? Maybe it's you? Maybe you smell bad?" Tripod barked twice. Brother-in-law tossed him one last treat and said, "Shhh. They'll kick us out. Okay, maybe I'm the one who smells bad."

Brother-in-law pulled the photo of Klendenin's daughter out of his pocket. "She's pretty." Brother-in-law showed Tripod the picture, and he barked again. "What do you think, boy? Should we trust smarty pants?" Tripod growled and dripped saliva. "Think he plans to do the cowboy in?" Tripod growled louder.

The room phone rang. It was Steenberg. He'd made contact with his team in the villa and all was arranged. He wanted Brother-in-law to go with him to Rulon's room to explain the new plan.

☙❧

"Why aren't you more paranoid?" asked Yohaba after her sixth Luxembürgerli. "This is not like you."

"Two reasons. First, I'm proactive," said Rulon, still under the sheets, the strain of the day for him having melted away in Yohaba's arms. "While you were in the bathroom, I checked *Twenty-Minuten* on my cell."

"Ah," said Yohaba. "My favorite online newspaper."

"The Swiss are going to leave us alone. Get this. They're calling Paradeplatz a gas leak. Dang, that is so Swiss. Keep it simple, say it with a confident, jutting jaw, and everyone will believe you. If I'd spray-painted graffiti on a tram, I'd be in jail right now, but blow up Paradeplatz, and there's not even a manhunt. There's a lesson in there somewhere. Also, good news is no civilians got hurt." Yohaba knew the worry about that had been eating at Rulon.

"Anyway," Rulon continued. "I suspect they're letting the Russians do their dirty work, and the Russians are going to have to go back to the drawing board and fly in a whole new team. I figure we've got at least forty-eight hours to snatch the girl and get out of the country before the Russians come after us. Then they'll have to regroup and follow us to Twin Falls. But I've got that figured out too. I'll alert my pals in OCD and they'll track their flight plan and make them land at JFK and then send them back home. Heck, they won't even make it to Idaho."

"Hey," said Yohaba, "I just thought of something. How are we going to get home? We don't have a jet anymore. And the girl. Once we snatch her, she's going to need her passport if we're all going to fly home on Swiss."

"Oh, yeah. The plane was a glitch," said Rulon. "Let me think about that. Wait. What is wrong with me? Men died on that plane. It was not a glitch. It was a terrible tragedy. I liked those guys. In a different world we could have been friends."

"That's okay," said Yohaba. "I knew what you meant. So what's the second reason?"

"The second reason is, I strongly suspect our little buddy is out there somewhere on patrol with my dog."

"What makes you say that?"

"Did you notice he insisted on the ground floor? Why do you think that was?"

"So he could climb out the window with Tripod?"

"Very good, Grasshopper," said Rulon.

"Okay, this here's the last one," said Yohaba. She held up a lone Luxembürgerli. "Feast your eyes on the rich chocolate color. The smooth, creamy filling. Vanilla, I believe. Feel the light, delicate shell. Taste the perfection exploding in a symphony of erupting flavors."

"Ah, just for the record, this is a Luxembürgerli were talking about, right?" asked Rulon.

"Of course, you idiot. C'mon, I'll arm wrestle you for it." They arm wrestled and Rulon had her within an inch of being pinned, but Yohaba braced her feet against the bed's headboard, fought back mightily with two hands and won. "Ha!" she said. "Never, never get between me and the last Luxembürgerli. And I don't want to hear any whining about how you let me win."

"You won fair and square," said Rulon. Yohaba bit off half the confection, stuck the other half in Rulon's mouth, and kissed him.

So, when are we leaving?" asked Yohaba.

"Everyone needs to check out tomorrow before eleven so we don't get charged for an extra day."

"You are incredible," said Yohaba.

"Well, thank you, dear."

"You know what I meant. An incredible cheapskate."

"I'm not a cheapskate. Make sure you leave a tip for the maid."

Just then there was a knock at the door. Rulon grabbed the Colt off the nightstand and nudged Yohaba. "Go ahead."

"Who is it?" she asked sweetly.

"It's me," said Vadim. "I need to talk to you."

"She's indisposed," said Rulon through the door. "Go away."

"Give me a second," said Yohaba loudly, and then to Rulon she said more quietly, "He just lost his grandfather, for crying out loud. Give the kid a break."

"Yeah, give me a break," said Vadim through the door.

"Sorry," said Rulon sincerely, loud enough for Vadim to hear.

They dressed quickly and Yohaba and Rulon, armed and in their bulletproof vests, answered the door together. Vadim was there with Yevgeny. Rulon, Colt in hand, stuck his head out the door and checked the hall was clear. He nodded curtly to Yevgeny, who then turned on his heels to go downstairs and presumably wait in the bar. Vadim came in and sat on the unmade bed.

Rulon sat next to him and put his arm around his shoulder. "I liked your grandfather despite our earlier differences. I'm really sorry about him and the others."

"He died doing what he loved," said Vadim, which to Rulon and Yohaba sounded like a really strange thing to say.

"And what was that?" asked Yohaba, somewhat puzzled.

"You know, plotting and scheming. I think he planned to kill you both when you came back to the plane. I don't know. He hadn't decided yet when we left, but I made up my mind I was going to warn you." Rulon withdrew his arm from around Vadim and walked over to sit in the chair nearest the window. *Russians*, he thought.

"Okay, so what is it?" Yohaba asked Vadim.

"My father wants me to come home," he said.

"Good idea," said Rulon. "I'll order you and Yevgeny a taxi to the airport."

"But I've decided to stay," said Vadim, ignoring Rulon and focusing solely on Yohaba. "I want to avenge my grandfather, but also I want to make up for what happened back in Idaho. You know, that thing I said about 'you don't know what we're capable of?' I didn't really mean it. It's just that my father uses that expression a lot."

"Totally understandable," said Rulon. "You're just young and impressionable."

"Neither of us took you seriously," said Yohaba. "Don't worry about it. But your father's right. This is too dangerous." Rulon, by the window, held a curtain back and peered anxiously outside, indulging a tinge of paranoia that had crept into his soul.

"Actually, it won't be," said Vadim. "My father says the Swiss won't be chasing after us. That's good news, isn't it?"

"Actually, no, son," said Rulon, not bothering to turn around. "It means the Russians have struck a deal with the Swiss. They want us for themselves. Your government will now be parachuting people in with plutonium-tipped umbrellas. The Swiss would have taken us prisoners. Your countrymen won't be so squeamish. Your father wants you home because he knows your government is planning to kill us all, and he wants you safe."

"Oh," said Vadim. "In that case I want a gun."

Rulon snorted loudly.

"I know a secret," said Vadim. "I will trade you the secret for a gun."

Rulon, looking bored, said, "Go home, Vadim, just go home. Go home and grow up."

Vadim said excitedly, "All right, I'll tell you. This is good news. I know it will make Yohaba very happy."

"Drum roll," said Rulon.

"Your old friend Boris Zokolov works for my father."

"We already saw the messages on your cell phone," said Rulon. "Tell us something we don't know."

"He's coming to Zurich," said Vadim. "I'll bet you didn't know that."

"Yep, got us there," said Rulon.

"He's supposed to help Yevgeny keep me safe. Ha! He thinks he's bringing me back to Moscow, but I won't go. He lands in five hours. Isn't that great news? Yohaba, her former lover, the man who saved Rulon's life too many times to count, and the famous Rulon Hurt all together again. The three comrades. He told me all the stories."

"That is great news," said Yohaba. "Wow, I miss that critter. Gosh, the things we did together."

"He is not Yohaba's former lover," said Rulon through gritted teeth. "And he never saved my life. I saved his."

"Rulon?" said Yohaba sharply.

"Okay, once, he saved me once. From a beating. But he definitely was never Yohaba's lover."

"Haha!" laughed Vadim. "He said you would say that."

"Well, if it's the truth, what else would I say?" asked Rulon.

"It would be more convincing if the denial came from Yohaba," said Vadim smugly.

"Just shut up. I'm not in the mood," said Rulon, "Yeah, yeah, I know you're joking, but if you want to know why I would never give you a gun, there's your answer. You're immature." Vadim started to protest but Rulon cut him off. "One more word and the duct tape's coming out again, not just for what you are saying about Yohaba, but because you're making jokes and your grandfather and bodyguards were all killed just a few hours ago. Or have you forgotten?

"We weren't very close," said Vadim, sheepish and contrite.

"You need to go home," said Yohaba. "Rulon's right." There was another knock at the door. This time Rulon answered, still with the gun. It was Steenberg and Brother-in-law with Tripod.

"I don't remember ordering room service," said Rulon. He threw the door wide open and said, "You were supposed to wait till I came to get you." Brother-in-law and Steenberg brushed past him into the room. Rulon whistled and said, "Here boy," but Tripod didn't respond until Brother-in-law gave a curt command. Rulon sat down in the chair by the window, mildly disgusted. "See what I mean," he said to Yohaba. Tripod followed him and laid his head affectionately on Rulon's knee. Rulon rubbed his ears unenthusiastically.

Brother-in-law said, "I saw some cops poking around the hotel talking to the staff. Thought they had us painted. But then they drove off. What do you make of it?"

"Swiss efficiency," said Rulon. He explained to Brother-in-law and Steenberg his theory about the Swiss letting the Russians do their dirty work for them.

While Rulon talked, Brother-in-law laid out on the bed his map of the home and grounds where Klendenin's daughter was kept. "The plan still looks good," he said. "But we need more intel."

The first thing Brother-in-law and Rulon did after they landed in Zurich the day before was to drive up to Stein am Rhein and check out where the girl was being held. It was a white, ten-room, three-story villa with a brown slate roof on two-and-a-half acres of farmland just a few hundred yards from the river and about six miles from the old town. The house was surrounded on three sides by tall pine trees that cut off much of the sunlight but also maintained an extra layer of privacy. In the front of the villa was an open area for parked cars and a garden with a maze of hedges that abutted the forest. The windows all around the house were small and framed on both sides by green shutters. But the dining room looking onto the rolling farmland to the east was well exposed with large, wide sliding glass doors onto a roofed patio supported by carved while pillars. There was a garage detached from the main house that was most likely converted from an original stable.

It was assumed there was a state-of-the-art security system with outside motion detectors, cameras, and ear-splitting alarms. Not to mention armed guards inside. No guards had been on patrol outside the villa, indicating they had a lot of confidence in whatever electronic surveillance was in place. The girl might be held in the cellar, but more likely on the top floor, perhaps in one of the attic rooms.

All the windows would be secured, but only the top floor had its windows shuttered. Closing the shutters on all the windows would have been suspicious. The doors would be locked. Men with binoculars would be sitting in rooms with a view of the countryside. Probably with night vision. They would be bored.

The girl would have been their prisoner for three months. She would by now be a human being to them. Perhaps she was allowed to roam freely around the house. Perhaps even to take walks in the garden or into the nearby woods under guard. They would have taught her a few words in Russian. Perhaps she would have shared with one or two of them details about her life and hopes and dreams. Perhaps one of them had fallen in love with her. Perhaps she with one of them. All this was discussed between the team in the hotel room. Even Vadim chimed in. Only Steenberg stayed quiet, preferring to leave this phase of the plan "to the experts," as he put it.

"I want to do a little more recon tonight," said Brother-in-law. "Cowboy, wanna come? If you don't, you'll miss all the fun."

"Why don't you?" said Yohaba to Rulon. "Just recon, right, Brother-in-law?"

"Just recon," he answered. "How far is it from here to the town?"

"About fifteen miles to Stein am Rhein," said Rulon, "and then another six to the villa."

"Good. We'll leave in two hours. Let's take Murph too."

"Okay," said Rulon.

"Don't take Freya," said Yohaba. When Rulon hesitated, she said, "You're just checking out the place, right?"

"Okay," said Rulon.

Chapter 21

Rulon drove the van. Brother-in-law rode next to him in the passenger seat. Murphy was stretched out on the row of seats behind. On the floor behind him in front of the last row of seats, covered with a blanket, were two duffle bags filled with their equipment. Tripod was out of sight somewhere in the back. As usual, Brother-in-law had insisted they bring along enough munitions to level a city. Also, a couple of the Cap-Chur pistols just in case. And an IR Spotter Mini Thermal Surveillance camera which Rulon didn't even know they had. When Rulon asked about it, Brother-in-law, had again said, "Just in case."

Just outside the town of Stein am Rhein, Rulon had a thought. "I'm not so sure a second look around is a good thing."

"Why not?" asked Brother-in-law with barely concealed annoyance.

"It increases the chance of us being seen, in which case they'll tighten security and then the snatch tomorrow becomes even more difficult. Or maybe they'll see us and just pack up and move the girl, and we'll have to start all over. And there's no upside. We already know what the place looks like."

"Yeah, but the last time we saw it was in the day. I want to see it at night, too."

"Trust me. It looks the same as in the day, only darker."

"I want to see if we can spot their patterns. Shift changes. Smoke breaks. When they take the garbage out. Things like that."

"Okay, that makes some sense," said Rulon. "But after months of guarding the girl in the middle of nowhere, isn't it more likely they're all just watching TV at night. If you want to see them jumping around, you'll have to cut their TV cable."

Brother-in-law looked at Rulon. What he saw was a true friend. A brother in arms. Quirky. With a strong moral compass. Nobody's fool. Tough as oak. And a man with great taste in wives. He wanted to keep Rulon in the dark for his own good. What if his suspicion about Steenberg wanting to knock off Rulon was wrong? Or if he were right, maybe he could settle this without involving Rulon. But Rulon wasn't making it easy. He was like a bloodhound once he got on the scent. Brother-in-law gave it another try. "Klendenin said they sometimes let her go for walks after dark. I was hoping to catch a glimpse of her. To make sure she's still there and all right."

"Well, why didn't you say so?" said Rulon. "Man, you are so secretive."

They drove on in silence while Rulon processed everything. Something struck him as odd though. "When did Klendenin tell you all this? I never noticed you guys talking together, and I thought it was Steenberg who located her."

"For crying out loud!" yelled Brother-in-law. "Steenberg told him and he told me! Geez, man! Can you ratchet down the suspicion for just a few hours?" In the back, Murphy sat up and Tripod, from out of nowhere, jumped over the seat to sit next to him right behind Brother-in-law. For the first time ever, Rulon felt he actually had the upper hand with the normally unflappable

Brother-in-law. Part of him, the part that wasn't focused on what on earth could be causing Brother-in-law to be so jumpy, wished Yohaba was here to see it.

Rulon said, "Words are coming out of your mouth, but they are not making sense. Why is that?"

"All right. I sent Benny up ahead," said Brother-in-law, back to being his calm self. "I'm not expecting trouble. But I think there's a chance we can grab the girl tonight. There, that's it. Sorry, I didn't tell you sooner. I was hoping we could get lucky, but I wasn't counting on it."

"That's cool," said Murphy from the back seat. "I never liked the idea of assaulting the house. Too many little rooms in these old villas. Every one of them a potential ambush point. Better to just call in an airstrike and level the place."

"It's like peeling an onion with you," said Rulon to Brother-in-law. "Where's Benny?"

"He's on the hill above the house with that guy's twin." Brother-in-law nodded towards the thermal imaging camera sitting between them on the console.

"When were you gonna tell us all this?" asked Rulon.

"I hadn't decided," said Brother-in-law.

Three hundred yards from the villa Rulon cut the headlights and pulled onto a dirt road that wrapped out of sight around the property. They drove for another hundred yards and stopped just before a turn in the road that would have made them visible from the house. At that point the three men got out of the van, and Brother-in-law, with Tripod hopping along at his side, said he would call Benny.

He walked off by himself out of earshot—a strange behavior that wasn't lost on Rulon. Brother-in-law then called Benny on his cell phone instead of on his throat mike where the others could listen in too—a behavior that really raised Rulon's antennas. Rulon rubbed his chin and watched Brother-in-law with a mixture of curiosity and suspicion.

"Tell me the good news," said Brother-in-law to Benny once he was out of earshot.

"Well, that depends on your point of view," said Benny.

"How so?"

"There's six of them and these guys are no pilgrims. They want you dead, brother, that's for sure. They got a nice little ambush set up for you right where you said they'd be. And they brought some nasty stuff with them. And get this, they're not Russians, they're Chinese."

"They all bleed the same," said Brother-in-law. "What did they bring?"

"Uzis and Atchisson automatic shotguns with drum magazines," said Benny. Brother-in-law knew right then and there that Steenberg intended to kill Rulon. Or maybe even all of them. He considered that latter possibility but quickly dismissed it. Somebody had to be left alive to rescue the girl and hand her over to Klendenin. With that realization came clarity of purpose. Steenberg was a dead man. That was a given. Had to be. The world was going to end…for him. And it was going to come from something considerably smaller and slower than an asteroid, something that weighed about 1.9 grams and traveled 1045 feet per second. Brother-in-law patted the Browning .22 on his hip. He'd do it as soon as they got back tonight. But it was better to keep Rulon out of it. He wouldn't know what to do about Steenberg. *Well, he would know*, thought Brother-in-law, *but he wouldn't do it. He'd hesitate just like with the old ladies at Paradeplatz.*

"So, what's the good news?" asked Brother-in-law.

"That is the good news," said Benny. "I didn't say it was good news for you."

"Can you take them out?" asked Brother-in-law.

"Three of them for sure. Three of them not so sure. They're in a bunch of trees with no clear line of sight. I could sure use a spotter here."

Brother-in-law asked Benny exactly where he was. Benny told him and Brother-in-law walked back to the van and told Murphy to take a weapon out of one of the duffle bags and go spot for Benny. Murphy chose a futuristic-looking Belgian-made FN F2000 assault rifle.

When he was gone, Brother-in-law said to Rulon, "Pop quiz. What do we do?"

After a short hesitation, Rulon said, "We should hope she goes for a walk in the woods. She'll be out of sight of the house and probably only have a guard or two. We grab her there."

"What if there are already guards in the woods?" asked Brother-in-law.

"Why would there already be guards in the woods?"

"Just answer the question."

"Would the house be empty then?"

"Don't know."

"Well, then I'd still wait for her to go for a walk, but I'd take her just as she stepped out the door. Maybe wait for her to get a little way from the house so reinforcements couldn't reach her so fast. Then I'd rush the house, dart her and her guards, throw a couple of flash bangs through the windows…"

Brother-in-law cut him off. "Why would you dart the girl?"

"With all the craziness going around, she'd be likely to run off in the night. Couldn't have that." Brother-in-law nodded agreement. When Brother-in-law didn't say anything else, Rulon said, "I failed the pop quiz, didn't I?"

"Surprisingly, not entirely," said Brother-in-law. "Good catch there about darting the girl. But Redfish Lake ring any bells? Remember? If the primary ambush point is compromised, never, never, never fall back to the obvious second one. There's a good chance you're being setup. Sound familiar?"

"Vaguely," said Rulon.

"But don't feel too bad," said Brother-in-law. "It was a lesson I had to learn the hard way. I'll tell you the story someday."

"So where are we going with this?"

"If the ambush in the woods was blown, they'd expect you to take her by the house as far from the woods as possible. Let's assume there's an ambush waiting for us in the woods. What's our third best option?"

Rulon said, "I'd still take her on the walk. But I'd take her right at the edge of the woods where anyone in the house and anyone waiting in the middle of the woods would be equally far away."

"So would I," said Brother-in-law. He opened the van's side door and took out the two duffle bags loaded with weapons. Rulon always carried his Colt but was partial to Swiss assault rifles, so he chose the SIG SG 550 and four 30-round magazines. When he saw Brother-in-law grab one of the Cap-Chur pistols, he did the same.

While they waited for Benny and Murphy to check in, Brother-in-law asked Rulon how well he knew Steenberg.

"Hard to say," said Rulon. "At one time I had him pegged as either a saint-like genius or a delusional madman. But now I'm leaning towards saint-like madman."

"Me too," said Brother-in-law. Long silence. "Do you trust him?"

"Define trust," said Rulon.

"Would he keep his word?"

Rulon laughed. "You obviously haven't hung around geniuses enough. The problem with geniuses, you see, is that they can explain their way out of anything. You know.

I thought you told me it wasn't going to rain and here I am soaked. That's true, but the drops have to be at least .02 inches in diameter to be considered rain so this is only technically a drizzle. Blah blah blah. See what I mean? You can never win an argument with them. And they'll never admit they're wrong."

"You don't trust him."

"Oh, I trust him all right when the pixie dust is falling. The problem is the pixie dust eventually wears off. I'll have an argument with him then be painting a fence a week later, and I'll think, 'Wait a second, that didn't make sense.' Then I go talk to him about it, and wind up having another argument with him and Yohaba. Geniuses stick together."

"But Yohaba's not a genius, right?" said Brother-in-law. "I mean, she married you, right?"

"Good point," said Rulon.

"Have we got a problem?" asked Brother-in-law.

"I don't think he trusts people," said Rulon. "That's a problem. I think he trusts Yohaba though. Maybe just Yohaba."

"What about you? Do you think he trusts you?"

"I've never given him a reason not to," said Rulon.

"Who does he most remind you of?" asked Brother-in-law.

"Colonel Kurtz?" asked Rulon.

"Yeah, *Apocalypse Now*," said Brother-in-law. "But with a Ph.D."

"Actually, he's got three of them," said Rulon. "Yep. Yeah. Gonna save the world his way. Always the smartest guy in the room. The thing I don't like is the way he's got Yohaba wrapped around his finger. She promised me she wouldn't get too involved with his schemes. You know, just be his little gopher. Make a few copies. Check his spelling. Yeah right. I think she's in it up to her eyeballs, and I don't like it."

"So you believe it then," said Brother-in-law. "All this stuff about Elsa."

"Yeah, I do," said Rulon. "But it's not because of Steenberg. I don't think I ever told you, but Yohaba's got a brother in Switzerland with Asperger's syndrome. Now that boy is a scary-smart genius. He's the one who figured it out. Couldn't change a lightbulb without killing himself, but he spotted things that even Steenberg missed. But heck, what do I know. The Yellowstone caldera has blown every 600,000 years since forever and now it's 640,000 years since the last time, so it's way overdue. If it went off, there'd be a hundred-year winter over the whole earth and we'd all die anyway."

"But if something happened to Steenberg now, do you think Yohaba could take his place?" asked Brother-in-law.

"You're obviously going somewhere with this, and I'm not even gonna ask what, but to answer your question, yeah, I think he's groomed her to take over. Like that solves anything. Darling, could you please make dinner? Sorry dear, I'm saving the world. What do you say to that? See my problem?" Both men laughed, while all the time Rulon cast a discreet but worried eye in Brother-in-law's direction.

Benny came back on the mike. "Murphy's here. So what's the plan?"

Tripod's ears flicked. All the villa's outside security lights went dark an instant later. Now only the lights from the villa's windows illuminated the grounds, throwing long shadows across the circular driveway and over the gardens. A few seconds later the ground floor's inside lights went dark. Then the home's wide, carved oak door opened, and a man stepped out. He stood on the stone step and looked around. In his hand, menacingly, was an Uzi-Pro with a 20-round magazine. After a minute, satisfied all was clear, he went back inside but left the door open.

From their vantage point on the ground fifty meters away, their backs against the other side of the three-foot stone wall surrounding the property, Rulon and Brother-in-law could hear a man and woman talking. They couldn't make out the words, but the lilt of their voices sounded friendly. *Stockholm syndrome*, thought Rulon, and he was immediately glad they had brought the Cap-Churs with them.

Brother-in-law pushed Tripod out of the way, lowered himself prone and peeked around the driveway's stone arch entrance. The man and woman came out of the house and made a slow left-hand turn down the path that meandered through the hedge garden and eventually led up the small, wooded hill where the Chinese ambush was set. The guard's Uzi was out of sight, presumably under the man's jacket.

"I'll be danged," said Brother-in-law. "I do believe they're holding hands."

"Don't give up hope. Maybe she's fickle," said Rulon. Knowing that whatever alarms and motion detectors had been deployed were now assuredly turned off, the two men silently raced forward through the arch and on a track through the hedges parallel with the path the couple were on. A long row of rose bushes lay between them. For a big man, Rulon was inordinately stealthy. His bow hunting days in Idaho served him well. But Brother-in-law was a ghost when he moved. The shadows seemed to cling to him longer, his uncoordinated clothes disguised his human shape, and his smooth-soled Bata Vellies never broke so much as a twig.

They knew their path crossed that of the girl and her guard up ahead. Rulon and Brother-in-law hung back ten yards from the intersection of the two trails. There was no moon. Only the lights from the villa's upper windows still showed through the cracks in the shutters, shining a feeble yellow across the ground. Both men pulled their Cap-Churs and waited. Brother-in-law kept one hand on Tripod's neck. The dog and the man were so attuned to one another after their six months together patrolling the hills around Rulon's Idaho home that Brother-in-law could tell by the rippling of his fur exactly what the dog's incredible senses were picking up. A deer, a rabbit, a coyote, a snake, or a human. Tripod reacted differently to every one of them. Tripod could even sense emotions, especially danger, in his quarry. With one hand on his neck Brother-in-law could sense them too. And right now he didn't like what he sensed.

"Pull back," said Brother-in-law quietly. First to Rulon and then into his throat mike. Benny started to protest into Brother-in-law's ear bud but was cut short. "Pull back now."

Rulon looked quizzically at Brother-in-law but then nodded and frog walked backwards to stay below the level of the rose bushes but still facing forward in the direction from which any danger was likely to come. After a moment's hesitation, Brother-in-law and Tripod followed in his tracks.

Once back again behind the stone wall, Rulon asked, "What?"

Brother-in-law didn't answer but spoke to Benny, "Where are you now?" Benny and Murphy were together on the other side of the hill walking back to the paved road where Benny had parked the BMW. Brother-in-law told Benny to stop where he was and come around the hill to where he could see the front of the villa. And to turn on his thermal imaging camera again.

"No can do," said Benny. "The battery ran out an hour ago."

"Okay," said Brother-in-law, nonplussed. "We're all gonna meet back at the van. Tell Murphy it's in the same place." To Rulon he said, "It was a trap."

"What spooked you?" asked Rulon.

"Our little miracle dog here." Brother-in-law took Tripod's head in both hands. "Man, I love you, boy." As he talked, Brother-in-law rocked Tripod's head slowly back and forth. "You're the dawg! You're the dawg!" All in a whisper, of course. Then back to Rulon, he said in a surprisingly chipper voice, "Go figure. They were waiting for us at the first and third best ambush sites. That don't happen too often. You'd almost think we'd been ratted out."

"So let me see if I've got this right," said Rulon. "You're saying that my original idea to grab them coming out of the house would have worked? Wow, that must be a bitter pill. But tell me, how did you know there was also an ambush in the woods?"

At Rulon's question, Brother-in-law realized he'd said too much. But he consoled himself with the thought that Rulon was going to find out about the men in the woods from Benny or Murphy eventually anyway. But still, Brother-in-law was mad. He knew Rulon was even now putting the pieces together. Given enough time, Rulon could see through a brick wall.

"Benny spotted some guys in the woods. Looked like an ambush."

"Huh," said Rulon. "Benny saw guys in the woods, but he didn't see the guys in the garden just now?" asked Rulon. "That's weird."

"Benny's NVG battery died. The guys in the garden must have set up after he went dark. But man, you're doing it again. You're pushing and drilling down like you think I'm hiding something."

"So why are you?' asked Rulon.

Brother-in-law let out a sigh and changed the subject. "How are you gonna get the girl?"

"You're the Prince of Blood," said Rulon. "How are you gonna get the girl?" Brother-in-law chuckled. Rulon said, "They must have some surveillance technology we didn't spot."

"Yeah," said Brother-in-law. "A telephone." Before Rulon could react to what he said, Brother-in-law slapped him on the shoulder. "Let's get back to the van. The fun's just beginning, and we ain't leaving without the girl."

The night kept getting clearer and colder. Brother-in-law had been away for almost three hours. His last instructions before running off into the dark with Tripod and the remaining working thermal imaging camera were for the three of them to lay out a string of Claymores below their position on the hill then hunker down in a defensive perimeter near the van and stay awake.

Rulon was laid out flat at the edge of a thicket of trees with a view of the villa. Fifty yards to his right, just below the brow of the hill, Benny and Murphy, still the spotter, sat together behind a stack of firewood that was perfectly stacked, one meter high and three meters long. Very Swiss. Murphy had on the 4-barrel night vision goggles manufactured by L-3 Warrior Systems in New Hampshire that Brother-in-law had used back at the ranch in Idaho. The NVGs gave him 120 degrees of vision as opposed to only 40 degrees with the standard single tube model. All the men had throat mikes.

There had been no contact with Brother-in-law since he left, and no clue as to what he was up to. No muzzle flashes. No explosions. No screams. No dog barks. No hillbilly chatter. Rulon said over his mike, "It's been pretty quiet out there."

"Yeah, too quiet," responded Murphy with a touch of comedic drama.

"And it's mighty dark out there," said Rulon.

"Yeah, too dark," said Murphy.

"Shut-up, Murphy, will ya," said Benny. "You're driving me crazy."

"Ease up," said Rulon.

"Maybe he's captured," said Benny, only half joking.

"Not my hillbilly," responded Murphy confidently. "He's probably buried himself in a mud hole somewhere with just the whites of his eyes showing, waiting to pounce on some poor soul."

"Maybe his dog bit him and he died of rabies," said Benny, still not having made peace with Tripod.

"See anything?" asked Rulon for the twentieth time. Both men answered *no*.

Brother-in-law came over the microphone, "Easy does it, boys. I'm coming in. Don't shoot. Who's ever wearing the goggles, take 'em off quick. Just do it." Murphy ripped his off just in time. Down below, the tall windows on either side of the villa's front door suddenly lit up. An instant later, so did the villa's outside halogen floodlights. Now shouting was heard and men seen racing from the woods back to the house. Two men in black, holding shotguns, came out the front door and ran in opposite directions around the villa. More yelling. A third man stepped onto the front patio, a pistol in one hand and a cell phone held to his ear in the other.

"See that guy silhouetted in the front door?" said Brother-in-law. "He's a jerk. Benny, could you shoot him for me, please? Just a foot."

"Roger that," said Benny. Fifteen seconds later Benny's Remington cracked and the man in black camo did a painful face plant when his left leg shot out from under him. He tried getting back to his knees, tipped over sideways, and grabbed what was left of his foot. His yells reached the top of the hill. Three men rushed to his aid. After the shot, Benny and Murphy leaped up and raced to an alternate position thirty yards away.

"We're about a hundred meters away from your position," said Brother-in-law. "We're coming as fast as we can. On your right. Rulon, can you sweep the hill just to see if we're being followed? Dawg's acting mighty jumpy." From somewhere down the hill bullets zinged overhead and skipped up dust around where Benny and Murphy had just been. Then someone opened up with an AA-12 automatic shotgun.

"Gotta get me one of those," said Benny while he lay next to Murphy in a shallow depression.

Brother-in-law had assumed that Rulon had the NVGs, but they were with Murphy. Murphy came on. "Sweeping," he said. "Yeah, you've got lots of company. Looks like seven bad guys, and they're moving fast. They'll catch you before you reach us. The M18s are set up."

Brother-in-law said, "Then fire off one of those puppies. But not to kill. Just to warn. Can you do that? You didn't daisy-chain them together, I hope."

"No," said Murphy. "But I'm not firing till I know for sure where you are. Where are you?" Brother-in-law fired off three shots with his pistol and Murphy saw the flashes. "Gotcha," he said. "But just to be safe, lie down."

Murphy left the NVG behind, got up, and crouching low ran ten meters down the hill to the nearest of the three Claymores, the one guarding their own vector. He tilted it on its pegs so when it went off its ball bearings would fire down the hill but above ground level. While he was fussing with the mine, trying to get the angle right, a bullet kicked up dirt five feet away and then another hit a foot closer. Murphy got scared, hugged the ground, and low crawled back to his position with Benny. He thought the Claymore was anchored properly.

"They've got night vision, too," he told Benny. Then into his mike, he said, "Everyone cover your ears." Murphy grabbed the detonator, a device shaped like a staple gun, and squeezed. A huge, deafening explosion and blinding light followed shortly by silence immediately changed the nature of the battle. Everyone within five hundred meters felt the concussion. And got the message. Time had expired. The game was over.

There was one problem, though. The Claymore had shifted position in the soft ground and a goodly number of its seven hundred ball bearings had hit the villa's front façade, essentially turning the front of the home into something out of Berlin circa 1945.

When the smoke cleared and he lifted his head, Murphy realized immediately what had happened. All the lights and floodlights from the villa were knocked out except for a single light in a top floor window. "Oops," he said. Benny laughed. He was watching through the NVG as Brother-in-law's pursuers now raced pell-mell back down the hill.

"Sweet," he yelled. "Shock and awe!"

"Ah, I think we better go," said Murphy.

Unknown to the team, inside the villa, two men were seriously wounded and two were dead, including their leader, the man Benny had shot in the foot. He was Chinese, thirty years old, and the beloved son of Sun Xiaofeng, Steenberg's partner in the solar panel business.

When Rulon saw the aftermath of the explosion, he immediately put two and two together and thought it likely that more people's lives had just ended and another implacable enemy created. Suddenly with the force of a hammer blow, his stomach knotted with the thought that the girl might have been killed too. He grabbed his SIG and was already standing up and about to go down the hill when Brother-in-law's voice sounded in his ear bud. "Everybody back to the van."

"Wait for me," said Rulon. "I'm going after the girl."

"She's with me," said Brother-in-law, "get back to the van."

"Way to go," said Rulon, pleased that he didn't have to go find her. Rulon half ran, half walked the two hundred yards to the van and arrived puffing hard. Benny and Murphy were already there keeping watch. The van's motor was running but the headlights were off. It was just after 4 a.m. and the blackness was softening in the eastern sky. There was a figure in the back seat of the van, presumably the girl, slumped over with a blanket around her shoulders.

Brother-in-law had the side door open and was leaning over her when Rulon jumped into the driver's seat and said, "Nice to meet you, ma'am. Let's go, people!" The girl didn't reply, which struck Rulon as weird, but the others jumped in and slammed the doors shut behind them. Brother-in-law sat in the passenger seat. Tripod was somewhere in the van out of sight. Rulon could smell him.

Brother-in-law turned around in the front seat and asked, "You didn't leave any Claymores behind, did you?"

Murphy slapped himself on the head and said, "Geez, I knew I forgot something." Brother-in-law gave him a look that would have drilled through steel.

Murphy jumped out of the van, and Brother-in-law said after him, "Don't forget to put the safety pins back in." To Benny, he said, "Go with him." Benny raced after him into the dark.

Rulon turned to look at the girl and could see she had a set of handcuffs dangling from her left wrist. Brother-in-law saw Rulon staring and said, "Turns out they weren't holding hands." *Odd*, thought Rulon. *If you were going to unlock one side, why not hers.* But then he noticed the dangling half of the handcuffs hadn't been unlocked either. He also noticed the girl wasn't moving much.

"Is she okay?" asked Rulon.

"Yeah. No problem. Had to dart her to keep her from running off, that's all." And then he added, "And to get the handcuff off."

"But she still has the handcuff on," said Rulon. Behind them the girl moved and groaned.

"Right," said Brother-in-law. Before Rulon could ask his next questions, Brother-in-law said, "I was in a hurry." Which, of course, only piqued Rulon's curiosity further.

"How did you get the handcuff off the guard then?" asked Rulon.

"The usual way," said Brother-in-law.

Rulon grabbed the steering wheel with both hands and took a deep breath to settle down. He turned to look at the girl again.

Brother-in-law said, "I've already given her some of the antidote. Not a full dose. She'll come around in a few hours. I don't think she knows what happened. Let's keep it that way, okay?"

"Sure," said Rulon, his mind twirling with a hundred conflicting thoughts. "But the Claymore was a mistake. You know that, right?"

"It didn't have to be," said Brother-in-law. "Rookie mistake."

"Management's always 90% of the problem," said Rulon. Then with a start he said, "Oh, dang, I just remembered something. When you grabbed her, did you happen to grab her passport too?"

"No, and I didn't bring her cosmetic kit either," said Brother-in-law a mite testily.

"That's okay," said Rulon. "I sometimes expect too much from you."

"Dang it, Cowboy," said Brother-in-law, "people lose passports all the time. She can just walk into the U.S. embassy and get one. Switzerland's got a U.S. embassy, right?"

"They'll have no record of her coming into Switzerland. With what happened at Paradeplatz and now here, there's no way they're not going to scrutinize her up the ying yang."

"Then we'll get her old man to pull some strings. Maybe he's got another plane. But we're not going back down there, if that's what you're thinking."

"Ying yang," said a groggy voice from the back. Then a U.S. passport flopped over the seat into Rulon's lap.

Rulon picked it up and opened it. "It's hers. What a break! She had her passport on her all the time. What are the odds?" He turned around in his seat. "Thank you, Miss Klendenin." But she was slumped over again unconscious. "Just for the record," said Rulon to Brother-in-law, "I know a guy in Zurich who knows a guy in Zug who knows a guy in Wallisellen who could have gotten her a fake passport real quick. I was just funning with ya. It wasn't the end of the world."

Murphy and Benny came back with the two unfired Claymores. Rulon threw the van into gear and drove off.

After a few minutes of driving along a darkly forested road in silence, Rulon said, "All present and accounted for. And we've rescued the girl. I say group hug." Nobody laughed. Nobody spoke. Brother-in-law was thinking about Steenberg's plots. Murphy was thinking about his screw-up with the M18. Benny was sensing the weird vibes and didn't know what to think. *Uh-oh*, thought Rulon. The girl was still unconscious.

Rulon decided to have it out before they got back to the hotel. "Strange that guys were hanging around in both the garden and the woods," he said, trying to sound innocent. "I wonder if they do that every night or just tonight." The quiet in the car was deafening. "Strange, too, that the girl had her passport with her. I wonder if there's a connection here we're missing."

"Like you said, mission accomplished," said Brother-in-law. "Focus on your driving,"

"Just gnawing at a bone," said Rulon. "Benny, those guys you saw in the woods. What would you say? Were they set up like for an ambush?"

"Seemed that way to me," said Benny, now sitting up straight and sensing something was going on.

"But then they had a second ambush set up in the garden too, right? I guess that was just smart planning on their part. I mean, what are the odds we'd walk right into their only ambush seeing as we didn't have a reason to. Having two ambush points just made good sense, right?" Nobody said anything. Rulon continued. "But why set up two ambushes and then take the girl for a walk. Unless you are using her as bait, and you already knew the two most likely places for someone to try a rescue. You following me here? There's no way they could be doing this every night. It's like they knew we were coming tonight."

"When you put it that way, sure does, Miss Marple," said Murphy.

"Those guys in the woods were definitely expecting somebody," said Benny. "That means they were tipped off. But how?"

"You mean, but who," corrected Rulon. "Only a few of us knew. Right? We can start eliminating people right now. I wouldn't know how to reach them. Would you, Murph?"

"No."

"Would you, Benny?" asked Rulon.

"No."

"And Brother-in-law doesn't know how to use a cell phone, so he couldn't have done it." This was Rulon's small attempt at humor, but also a jab at Brother-in-law letting him know that his use of a cell phone to call Benny earlier didn't go unnoticed.

"Klendenin maybe," said Murphy. "He tracked them down in the first place. And he must have talked to his daughter if he knew about her taking walks." Inwardly, Brother-in-law groaned. It was all unraveling. Damn that Rulon.

"No, I'm not thinking Klendenin here," said Rulon. "Our plan tonight was a spur of the moment thing. Right?" The question was plainly one that Brother-in-law was supposed to answer. Instead he kept quiet.

A pregnant pause went by. Then Benny said, "Steenberg maybe. He's got enough money and connections. But he doesn't strike me as being that devious. And why would he do it? It doesn't make any sense."

"I hear ya," said Rulon. "But the really weird thing is the girl had her passport with her. It's like they were expecting her to be rescued, but also wanting to knock off the rescuers. How does that work?"

"Or maybe just one of the rescuers," said Brother-in-law, breaking his silence with a resigned sigh. "They'd still need somebody alive to rescue the girl."

"Now we're getting somewhere," said Rulon. Then, almost rhetorically he added, "Yeah, maybe they were after just one guy. But just the thought of it kinda makes you curious, doesn't it? I mean, which one of us was the one."

"My vote's on Murphy," said Benny. "He's the most annoying."

"It's Benny," said Murphy. "No brainer."

Rulon started to say something else, but Brother-in-law cut him off, "Just give me a minute here, okay? I have to think."

When after half a minute, Brother-in-law still hadn't said anything, Rulon said with a chuckle, "What? Was it your buddy Steenberg then? Was he planning on knocking *me* off or something?" With that Rulon, Benny, and Murphy all burst out laughing. But the laughing slowly died down as they each noticed that Brother-in-law didn't join in and his lips were clenched like a scar. A car drove past them on the other side and for a fraction of a second, Brother-in-law's tormented face was lit up by the headlights.

"Possibly," said Brother-in-law finally.

Murphy slapped Rulon on the shoulder. "There you go, Miss Marple. Possibly Steenberg wanted to kill you, possibly not. But isn't that just family? The husband's never good enough for their little girl." The van was filling up with some weird vibes. Benny, as surreptitiously as possible, slipped his Springfield XD semi-automatic pistol out of his small-of-back holster. It was his preferred weapon of choice because of its ambidextrous magazine release. He wasn't sure what was happening, but always felt better with his fingers wrapped around a weapon.

"Relax," said Brother-in-law, who knew exactly what was going on in the seat behind him. "We don't know anything for sure."

"Wow!" said Murphy. "That means it could have been me Steenberg was after. Finally, I have my own nemesis. And he's a genuine evil genius mastermind! Us superheroes only rise to the level of our competition. My momma will be bursting with pride when I tell her."

"No, I don't believe it," said Rulon seriously. "I won't believe it."

"I'm pretty sure it was Steenberg who ratted us out," said Brother-in-law. "But I don't think he wanted you dead. I found this on one of the guards coming in from the ambush." Brother-in-law took something out of his pocket and held it up for all to see. It was a syringe. "I had a taste. It's called Etorphine. Poachers used it in the Congo to knock out rhinos."

Murphy let out a long, soft whistle. "That clinches it, they were definitely after Miss Marple."

"And the guy also had some Diprenorphine. That's the human antidote. So, I don't think they wanted Cowboy dead."

"How sure are you that it's Steenberg?" asked Rulon.

"Sure enough that I'm gonna put a bullet through his head once we got back to the hotel. Heck, he's already listed as dead. There wouldn't even be an investigation. How 'bout it? Who's with me?"

It took everyone a few seconds to process the new reality. Benny spoke first. "No can do, bub. You're messing with my paycheck."

"Yeah, hold your horses, Buckwheat," said Murphy. "Benny's right. You kill him, and we don't get paid."

"Yohaba would still pay you," said Rulon. Everyone looked at him. Rulon looked sheepish and said, "I can't believe I just said that."

"Well, you did," said Brother-in-law. "You got something between your ears after all."

"Okay, let's back up a bit," said Rulon. "Who suggested I go with you tonight? Was it Steenberg?"

"Yeah. And he pressed mighty hard."

"Was I supposed to go by myself?"

"No. He suggested Murph, too. But he absolutely didn't want me to go."

"I'm sure he wanted me to be the one to rescue the girl," said Murphy. "I would have been the hero. I always knew he liked me best. No offense, Miss Marple, but you annoy the bejeebers out of him. We've all seen it. Right, guys?" Murphy was having fun with Rulon's new nickname.

"He's got a point," said Benny.

Rulon pulled over into a scenic turnout and cut the engine. "Bring us up to speed," he said to Brother-in-law. "We have to have a plan before we get back to the hotel."

Brother-in-law told them about his conversation with Steenberg and the plan to rescue the girl in the woods. It all seemed circumstantial until he related how Steenberg pressed him to know the exact location where the rescue would take place and admitted calling the kidnappers to coordinate their part in the rescue.

"But why two ambushes?" asked Benny.

"I think I know," said Brother-in-law. "He knew I was suspicious. He didn't have to be a genius to know I'd change my plan. But he's one smart dude, and he's a fast learner. He figured if I spotted the first ambush, I wouldn't go for the next best option." Brother-in-law turned to Rulon. "Did you tell him about Redfish, and how I chewed you out for heading to the second-best ambush point?"

"No," said Rulon, "but I'll bet Yohaba did, you know, just as a funny story."

"Anyway," said Brother-in-law. "He had them set up the ambush, knowing what I'd do."

"This is going to sound really paranoid," said Rulon, "but if you're right then I was probably the only target if the rescue happened in the woods, but if it happened in front of the house then you would have been targeted too, because he'd know then he couldn't trust you either. He'd want us both out of the way. Make sense?"

Brother-in-law didn't immediately answer. In the silence, Benny said, "Makes sense to me."

When Brother-in-law was finally through replaying for everyone every nuance of his conversation with Steenberg, Rulon said, "It's still a lot of circumstantial stuff. But even if there wasn't, we can't do this. We can't just execute someone. That is murder and that is a line I will not cross."

"He's off the reservation, brother," said Brother-in-law. "If he failed this time, he'll try it again. Do you really want a guy with his brains running around plotting to get you out of the way? And with you gone, Yohaba would be in his clutches. That suit ya okay?"

"For sure, it would make for some very awkward family holidays," said Murphy.

"Or worse yet," said Benny. "Maybe next time he decides to off you. For what? Really. For what? And what's to say in six months he doesn't come up with a screwed-up reason to off Yohaba, too? Maybe she becomes suspicious about what happened to you. Killing her would make as much sense as offing you. I'm telling you, he's flipped, man. Officers have been fragged for less." Benny quieted down, leaving the others to ponder what he'd just said. Then he added, "But I still want to get paid."

The sound of a far-off police siren getting closer snapped everyone out of their reverie. Rulon started up the van again.

"I think it's coming from over that hill," said Rulon. "I'm taking the long way home away from the town. I'm guessing any police would be coming from that direction."

"Your call, Cowboy," said Brother-in-law. As Rulon drove exactly the speed limit, everyone held their breath. A van with four men and a drugged girl this time of the morning after a shooting and an explosion at a remote villa would surely get pulled over by the police, and just as surely there would be a high-speed chase followed by a front-page shootout.

Murphy said, "I can see the headlines now. *Deranged Terrorists Rampage through Switzerland Leaving Wake of Destruction. They vow never to be taken alive. Cornered by police they kidnap an innocent tourist. All die in fiery explosion.*

"You can drop me off at the corner," slurred Klendenin's daughter.

"I'd almost forgotten about you," said Rulon. "Say, what's your first name again?"

In a very soft voice, she answered, "I'm Batu. This was a rescue, right? You're the good guys. Right?"

Chapter 22

randon Alexander Jefferson, a veteran of the first Gulf war with a squat body, bulldog face, and a voice that could unstick duct tape, was rich and he was for hire. He was also an analyst for the Alpha Group, Silicon Valley's most influential consulting organization. He charged $20,000 per day for his services and had risen to the pinnacle of his profession because he had the uncanny ability to vehemently disavow with a straight face all his previous inaccurate industry predictions and only remember the few he got right. In this regard, he was not entirely unique in his field. He was a large ego in an industry of large egos. And right now he was furious with Winston Klendenin III. Winston hadn't been listening. Hadn't been reading Brandon's weekly newsletter. Winston had been playing Mr. Jefferson for a patsy. Not confiding. Not sharing. Winston was officially a loose cannon.

Winston's offense was announcing a new technology without first consulting with Alpha Group. In other words, something was happening in Silicon Valley that didn't make Brandon richer. Had Winston gone mad? He'd even called Brandon to gloat about it. The last time they talked, Brandon had clearly told Winston that the energy wave for the next twenty years was to be clean coal, carbon capture technology. China generated 70% of its electrical power from coal and was set to bring 600 GW of coal-powered electricity online in the next twenty years, equal to the combined annual output of the U.S., Europe, and Japan. And what does Winston do? He comes out with an idiotic solar energy announcement.

Brandon's office was located in San Francisco on the forty-ninth floor of the Bank of America pyramid, and had large windows overlooking the bay. Visitors to his office typically found the view completely distracting. When they commented on it, Brandon, with false humility, would say, "Yeah, it's not too bad on those three days a year it's not foggy. Har har." But actually, it was a great view most of the time. From his heights, even on foggy days, Brandon could often see the two towers of the Golden Gate Bridge poking out of the dense grey cloud that enveloped the bay below.

His office was lushly carpeted and wood-paneled, but it was the massive oak desk that really put people in the proper frame of mind. That is, in the frame of mind to sit quietly while Brandon pronounced judgments like the Sun King from Versailles. The desk had once belonged to Cornelius "Commodore" Vanderbilt, the nineteenth-century railroad and shipping magnate. The rest of the office was stuffed with the usual assortment of gaudy chairs, flamboyant end tables, Tiffany lamps, expensive paintings, and bookshelves filled with books and reports no one would ever read. Behind Brandon's desk and his leather swivel chair were pictures of a younger Brandon playing golf with his father and President Bill Clinton at Pebble Beach.

Brandon picked up the Wall Street Journal for the tenth time, read again a paragraph that particularly annoyed him, and threw the paper back down on his desk. He almost called Winston but stopped himself. He looked at the phone. *Damn, this is going to bug me all day,* he thought, *unless I do something, but I can't call the little weasel. He has to call me.* Brandon thought and thought. He would put aside the research paper he was currently working on titled "Millennial Thought Leaders in Big Data." Instead, he would write a new paper, one titled, "The Solar of Things: A New Paradigm for Renewable Energy." Yes, it was a complete reversal of everything he had said for the past three years on the subject of energy. Yes, he would take some heat for it. But with any luck he'd be able to newsjack off the WSJ article and the flood of Twitter feeds it would surely generate to boost sales of his own newsletter. And then there were the consulting fees to consider.

Suddenly, Brandon felt a surge of power coursing through his body to the tips of his fingers. *This paper will save the world and end global warming!* he trumpeted inwardly to himself. Too bad he hadn't been able to pump Winston for more details. But Winston was holding a press conference on his new technology later that day on the steps of the Moscone Center in San Francisco. Maybe Brandon could learn more there, maybe not. No problem. Brandon had written industry-shaping papers on less.

❧❧❧

"Yes, you have to sign this non-disclosure agreement," said Winston with waning patience. "Yes, this is a bit irregular. But keep in mind it is only as irregular as the ridiculously high salary I'm paying you. There is a proportional connection here. You do see that, right?"

Peter was the only holdout. Sophie and Miranda had already signed their contracts, and with a smile at that. The four of them sat around a low coffee table in the lobby of Winston's Tri-Star Pleasanton headquarters. The ladies were also getting impatient with Peter the stickler. Around them the PR team and camera crew were buzzing.

"Wow," said Sophie suddenly. "Is that Wayne Adams?" Winston turned to look.

"Yes," said Winston after a quick peek over his shoulder. "He's the master of ceremony."

Peter, still looking unhappy, picked up the four-page NDA agreement and flipped through it one more time. "You're sure you're not asking me to do anything illegal? Because if you're not, why do I need to sign all this legal mumbo-jumbo?"

Winston pushed the pen closer to Peter. "Do you own an iPod?" asked Winston.

"Of course," said Peter.

"Did you agree to their terms and conditions?"

"Of course. I had to."

"Weren't you worried that somewhere in those fifty-two pages of iTunes legal mumbo-jumbo you agreed to something illegal?" Peter had no response. Winston continued. "Of course I'm not asking you to do anything illegal. Look. This mumbo-jumbo, as you call it, is for your protection, not mine. Do you think Wayne Adams would be involved in something that wasn't legit?" Peter made a face, and Winston lost patience. "Sign it, don't sign it. I'll just find someone else. I don't care." Which wasn't really true. Peter truly looked the part of a nerdy backend R&D manager. Tall, gangly, fortyish, bulky Dockers, and a dash of convincing redness behind the ears from excessive use of his Bluetooth device. But just as importantly, he had a Master's degree in Sustainable Energy Engineering from Kaplan University. Okay, it was an online degree, but he could speak the lingo and that would be important when he was answering questions from reporters in front of the Moscone Center. And even if he didn't have all the answers, the only reporter he had to convince was the one from the Chinese cable news show, China Central TV.

Peter signed the NDA, and Winston inwardly breathed a sigh of relief. Problem solved, move on. "Now run off and check in with my director," said Winston. He waved to a fiftyish, dark-haired woman in a pantsuit who was talking to the camera crew twenty feet away. "She'll polish up your roles for you. Go. Go now." The three actors left.

Winston sat back in the L-shaped sofa feeling a sense of accomplishment. In less than forty-eight hours he'd recruited a pliable energy company, planted a bogus energy story in the Wall Street Journal, baited a stuffed shirt from Alpha Group into jumping on the bandwagon, and set up a primetime press conference in front of the Moscone Center hosted by the local Fox News affiliate's top-rated weekend anchor.

The one glitch was having to hire actors. Winston had hoped that with enough money and pressure he could convince the executive team from some poor energy startup to tell white lies and jump through hoops for him. He naively thought he'd have to shoo the contenders away like flies, but instead found it surprisingly hard to find a malleable enough partner. He finally settled on Aurora Solar Energy, Inc., practically right down the street from his headquarters in Pleasanton, a three-year-old startup with eleven patents, one CEO, eight vice presidents, twenty-six engineers, a $27 million government backed energy loan, and a reputation for throwing extravagant Christmas parties. Last year's bash was headlined by Green Day.

When Winston first met Aurora's executive team, the CEO said next to nothing and appeared to be under the influence. Winston found that encouraging. However, even after he promised them $10 million as an angel investor, enough to completely fulfill their second-round funding requirements, there was a line even that team wouldn't cross. They had been working on developing a next-generation solar collector and would gladly make outlandish claims about its potential on the steps of the Moscone Center. However, no amount of urging by Winston could convince them to claim they'd been secretly testing solar panel technology at Upington, a town on the Orange River in South Africa's Northern Cape. But it had to be Upington.

Winston had chosen that spot for three reasons. First, it was very far away and in an awkward time zone for phone calls from California. Second, he had already bribed the local ANC-elected mayor there to support his claims if questioned by the media, and third, a half-minute's Google search showed it was the sunniest spot on earth—a logical place for solar panel testing.

But the actors would lie and do it convincingly, though technically they wouldn't be lying in any sense that wasn't protected by the first amendment. They would be following a "virtual script"—a script that only existed in Winston's mind. It was the next new thing, Winston had said. No one had time to write actual scripts anymore. The plot was simple. Small solar startup comes up with game-changing technology that would overnight make obsolete all other forms of energy production, including wind, coal, hydroelectric, fusion, oil, and even all other competing solar technologies. Peter was to be the proud but overly technical and sometimes rambling R&D manager. Sophie was the cautiously optimistic CFO, and Miranda the over-caffeinated marketing VP.

The first scene was to be a press conference at the Moscone Center. Everyone there including the police would be actors, Winston said. The cameras would roll and everyone was under an ironclad agreement to "act well their part." It wasn't possible to make a mistake, because there was no script. *Just stay in character*, he told them. No matter what. Never, never, never break out of character. Even if someone dressed like a policeman were to come screaming into your face that they once saw you in a car commercial, and they know you are an actor, and all of this is a fraud, still, never break out of character. Break character and you automatically forfeit your salary and the humongous bonus.

While Winston was playing things over in his mind, Anjie, Winston's dark-haired director, told the three actors to wait and walked over. "Is there something you're not telling me?" she asked Winston.

"Like what?" he snapped, leaning back on the sofa with both arms spread out wide signifying he had nothing to hide.

"Those actors," she said, "haven't seen the script, and they're fine with that. We don't have much of a script, I'll grant you that, but we do have one. Shouldn't they at least read the script?"

"A script is a good thing," said Winston, "but not for them."

"Go on," she said.

Winston patted the couch next to him. "Sit down," he said. Anjie sat down.

"How long have we known each other?" asked Winston.

"Seven years," said Anjie.

"And how many shoots have we done together, counting interviews, commercials, all-hands meetings, you know, everything?"

"I'd have to take off my shoes to count that high," said Anjie.

"Right. Have you ever known me to lie to you?"

"Never."

Winston scratched his ear. "Good. Those people are only pretending to be actors. They really are what they say they are. Peter's a brilliant engineer, Sophie one of the top minds…"

Anjie cut him off. "I've worked with them before, Winston. They're actors. The next time you ask me if you've ever lied to me, I'm going to have to say 'only once.' Do you want to start over?"

Winston thought hard before he spoke. "There is only so much I can tell you. You know I do a lot of work for the government. I'm working on a top-secret project. The Chinese have been stealing our solar energy technology for years, and I'm working with the FBI on a sting operation. This whole thing is a setup. We just have to do our parts and stay in character."

"Fine," said Anjie. "Have it your way."

Winston said, "The truth is, I can't tell you. Someday maybe, but not today."

Anjie stood up, looked down on Winston with a look that said *I hope you know what you're doing,* and then lifted her eyes to look out over the twenty or so members of her crew that were mingling in the lobby. "Okay, people," she ordered. "Saddle up."

⁙

From Winston's vantage point leaning against a light pole across the street from the Moscone Center, the press conference was going smoothly. For an event put together at the last minute, there had been surprisingly few glitches. Even the sound system that had caused so many problems at their last event had operated without a hitch. Each of the players had gotten up and done their piece and done it so convincingly they had Winston himself thinking he should be investing more in solar. And there were Miranda and

Sophie working the crowd like pros. Peter was to be the only one of the three who actually stood in front of the camera and answered questions, which was why finding an actor with his background was so critical. And so far even the reporters were cooperating. Powder puff questions. Until now.

Winston's ears perked up. Brandon Jefferson had shoved his way to the front of the crowd and in his bullhorn voice was lambasting Peter over something. Winston saw Anjie direct one of the cameramen to focus on Jefferson. *Good, good,* thought Winston. *That's all the little showboat wants.*

"Yes, yes, this has all been very interesting," said Jefferson, "but how about a few details? For example, how are you going to solve the intermittency, storage, infrastructure, and efficiency issues that have been plaguing solar energy for forty years, and what about..." Jefferson looked quickly down at his phone and then up again before he finished the sentence. "...solar grid parity?"

Winston almost burst out laughing. Perfect. Jefferson probably got that question five minutes ago off a Google search. He wouldn't know the right answer if it hit him in the head. *Just ramble on, Peter, old boy. Tie him in knots while he soaks up the camera time, then he'll waddle back in his hole like a satisfied crab.*

Instead Peter blasted him. "I've read your papers over the years, Mr. Jefferson, and what you and your carbon-capture buddies know about solar energy could fit on the head of a pin." Even from across the street, Winston could sense Jefferson's head about to explode.

❧❧❧

Ex-Father Becker saw them coming from his vantage point in the rocking chair on the Hurt ranch's front porch. His small, hastily packed suitcase was on his lap. The rooster tail of dust from their speeding vehicle could be seen for miles. For three days he'd been waiting at the ranch for the extraction team promised by his Chinese employer. He knew it was them because they'd called him thirty minutes ago on his cell phone to say they were almost there and to be ready for an immediate departure. It was about time. Just this morning, he'd finally run out of excuses for why he couldn't help out old man Hurt with the 4:30 a.m. cow milking. His forearms were sore and still cramping, and the second milking was due any minute. The team was cutting it close. Surprisingly they came in a pickup truck. Becker rubbed his sore forearms.

The pickup rolled to a stop in front of the porch. The dog came running over, curious. Two men climbed out. Tall for Chinese. Becker got up and started to say something like "What took you so long?" when with the impact of a punch in the stomach he realized something was wrong. They were both smiling..

Rulon's father came back to the house on his horse just as the truck pulled out of the driveway. He was leading a string of nine cows to the barn, where he planned to tie them to the milking stanchions and milk them by hand. He caught a quick glimpse of a pale-faced Becker sitting in the cab between two Asian-looking men. Mr. Hurt muttered to himself as he saw them leave, "Good riddance."

As he watched the truck drive off down the dirt road, his attention was caught by a second swirl of dust in the distance a couple of miles away. Another vehicle was coming down the same dirt road towards the ranch. It was also a pickup truck. He watched the two trucks slow as they passed each other on the narrow road at about the same spot where Rulon had knocked out Wild Will's two men four days earlier. Rulon's father sat on his horse watching. Now he could see the truck clearly. Government green. A single occupant. The truck with Becker in it had disappeared out of sight by the time the oncoming truck pulled into the yard, startling the bunched-up cows.

Sawtooth National Recreation Area ranger Stanley Merryfield turned off the engine of his forest service vehicle, took his wide-brimmed ranger hat off the dashboard, adjusted it on his head, and stepped out of the truck. He carried a bulging green man bag over his right shoulder. A wind kicked up and blew his hat off. He chased it around the yard in between the cows while Mr. Hurt watched, until finally it came to rest in front of the horse. Mr. Hurt stood up in the stirrups to look over his horse's head, saw the hat, thought it might blow away again, and urged the horse forward a step. Its hoof came down on the hat. pinning it to the ground.

Stanley rushed over, effusively grateful, and tugged at the hat but couldn't dislodge it. With a barely discernible touch on the reins, the father obligingly moved the horse backwards. Stanley snatched up the hat quickly, punched out the rumples in a dignified fashion, and reset it on his head, this time with the chinstrap firmly in place. By now the wind had died down.

"I'm Ranger Stanley Merryfield from the Sawtooth Recreation area," said Stanley.

From his perch on the horse, Mr. Hurt took the blade of hay he'd been chewing on out of his mouth, and said, "To get back to the Sawtooths, go back to the main road and then head east till you hit 93. Keep going until you reach Shoshone where 93 turns into 75. Then just go north on 75 for a couple of hours. Can't miss it."

"What?" said Stanley, confused for a moment at Mr. Hurt's unprompted directions. "No, no. I'm not lost," said Stanley. He looked around. "This is the Hurt ranch, isn't it?" Mr. Hurt nodded. His composure regained, Stanley said ominously, "I'm here on official business."

"You looked lost," said Mr. Hurt.

"I'm conducting a criminal investigation, and I would appreciate your complete cooperation," said Stanley. Mr. Hurt got off his horse. Stanley took an 8' by 10' color photo out of his forest green man bag and handed it to Mr. Hurt. "Do you recognize this?" asked Stanley.

Mr. Hurt took the photo and studied it carefully. After a moment's reflection, he said, "No, sorry. I've never seen this photo before."

"No, no. I didn't mean the photo. I mean the truck tire treads in the photo. Do you or anyone you know own a vehicle with tires with that type of tread?"

"What's this all about?" asked Mr. Hurt.

"We believe that a perp or perps vandalized protected beachfront property on Redfish Lake, and these treads belong to the getaway vehicle." When Mr. Hurt appeared unmoved, Stanley said, "And we have reason to believe they killed a grizzly bear and hid the body."

"That's hard to do," said Mr. Hurt.

"And we have reason to believe they may have cooked the body and ate it."

"That dog don't hunt, son. Grizzly meat doesn't even taste that good. Not near as good as bald eagle meat."

At Mr. Hurt's answer, Stanley stammered and sputtered an incoherent reply.

"Settle down, son," said Mr. Hurt. "I'm just funning with ya. Now what can I do for you?"

Stanley laughed wildly, a high-pitched laugh that set his Adam's apple oscillating. When he settled down, he explained to Mr. Hurt that the tire track came from a

BFGoodrich Long Trail T/A Tour tire that was on a truck parked at the lake the day in question. Stanley also showed Mr. Hurt a second photo, this time of the hull imprint of a Model 18 Clipper Mac sport canoe that was found in the sand at the scene of the crime in the vicinity of the suspect vehicle. Finally, out came a third photo of the spent shell casing from a 185 grain, nickel plated .45 caliber, ASYM Precision National Match ammo round.

"So?" said Mr. Hurt when Stanley was finished.

"Do you own a truck with BFGoodrich Long Trail T/A Tour Tire?"

"No," said Mr. Hurt. Stanley looked puzzled but pressed on.

"Do you own a Model 18 Clipper Mac sport canoe?"

"No," said Mr. Hurt. Again, Stanley was puzzled but continued.

"Do you use 185 grain, .45 caliber, nickel plated, ASYM Precision National Match ammo when you shoot?"

"No," repeated Mr. Hurt laconically.

"That's very strange," said Stanley. "Your name has been linked to the purchase of all three of those items. Items which are associated with a felony committed on federal land within 300 feet of a navigable water source punishable by a fine of up to $50,000 and imprisonment for up to twelve years."

"Yes, that is strange," said Mr. Hurt.

"Do you mind if I look around?" asked Stanley.

"Of course not," said Mr. Hurt, who waited just long enough for Stanley's expression to register joyous surprise at his answer before he added, "…as soon as I get my reading glasses so I can read your search warrant."

Stanley responded, rather deftly he thought, by casually hinting that where he came from non-cooperation carried a strong suggestion of guilt. When Mr. Hurt remained unmoved by that argument Stanley launched into a prepared dramatic monologue spouting regulations, federal statutes, legal precedents, and finally, in one final outpouring of righteous frustration, a vivid description of prisoner conditions at the SuperMax prison in Florence, Colorado. The old man stood there and let him jaw on until the skinny ranger ran out of steam.

When Stanley was finally done, Rulon's father handed back the photos, slowly got back on his horse, and drawled, "I'm going to go milk the cows now. Have a nice day." With that, he slowly turned his horse around and moseyed the cows and himself into the barn and out of sight.

Stanley was furious. Mr. Hurt had not only disrespected him with his ridiculous answers but the entire Sawtooth Recreation Area department as well. While Stanley could absorb affronts to his own dignity, the reputation of his Forest Service employer was nothing to be trifled with. How can one man be linked to all those items and not be the perp? he asked himself.

"We shall see, Mr. Hurt," yelled Stanley into the barn as a last parting shot on his way back to his truck. "We shall see what happens when the full might of the U.S. Forest Service turns your life upside down."

Mr. Hurt heard Stanley yelling but couldn't make out the words. He sat on his milk stool milking Amanda because she was the most ornery cow and would get tetchy if she didn't get milked first. As he milked, hands pumping, sinewed forearms working, occasionally swiping Amanda's tail away as she tried to knock off his hat, he muttered to himself. Amidst the muttering, the words "Rulon" and "flub-dubber" could occasionally be heard. But Mr. Hurt, being a religious man, was most concerned that perhaps he had lied to the earnest forest ranger. The more he thought about it, though, the more he felt vindicated. Technically, he didn't own those things. Just because Rulon bought everything in his father's name just to get a little extra discount from the store owners, who had all known Mr. Hurt for decades, well, Rulon had paid it all back. The tires, canoe, and bullets were all Rulon's. Technically and legally.

Mr. Hurt looked at his watch. Because his son had lived so many years in Switzerland, he was familiar with the time difference between there and Idaho. Eight hours. He did a quick calculation and decided to call Rulon when he was done milking the cows. Yeah, it'd be late, but dang that boy, why should he have the easy life while his eighty-year-old father had to take care of all the problems?

Later, after milking the cows, Rulon's father went to the house for his cell phone. It was then that he noticed ex-Father Becker's suitcase still sitting on the porch. *Am I the only person with a brain around here?* thought Mr. Hurt.

ം‍ം‍ം

Winston took the debacle philosophically. Anjie's last words to him after the camera crew had packed up were "Hey, any publicity is good publicity. Right?" When Winston just smiled, she awkwardly backed away into the night. Seeing her drive off in the camera van with the actors, Winston had kicked around the idea of stiffing Peter his salary and bonus, but then thought, "What the heck." He'd stayed in character. Unfortunately, it was the character of a paranoid, carbon-taxing, solar energy messiah.

It was 2 a.m. and Winston was alone with his third mocha in a diner on El Camino Real in Menlo Park. After much internal deliberation, he decided to scrap the idea of fighting a second front on China's internet capability. Too complicated. He considered calling Steenberg to ask about his daughter's rescue, but then, worried about NSA surveillance, thought better of it. Instead he turned around to signal the waiter for the check. When he turned back, Wild Will and Russo were just sliding into the booth across the table from him.

"I'm not even going to ask how you found me," he said.

"It was Steenberg," said Wild Will. "I think he's bugged your phone. Anyway, he said something's gone wrong and your life is in immediate danger."

"Plus, he's paying us a lot more money," said Russo.

"Thanks, I guess," said Winston. Suddenly Winston panicked. What if the something that went wrong was his daughter's rescue? "What do you mean 'went wrong?' What went wrong?" he asked.

Wild Will answered, "Somebody died who wasn't supposed to."

Winston snatched up his phone from the table. Wild Will reached over and grabbed his wrist.

"You can't reach him now," said Wild Will. "He said to tell you he has to disappear for a while, but your daughter's been rescued and is safe, and you just need to remember a deal's a deal."

And it was then like a thunderclap that Winston put it together. A deal's a deal. It was Simon quoting the director. As was Yohaba quoting her grandfather a few days ago. Steenberg. The former Director of CERN. That night, after he shot Oderhardt, Simon had said "a deal's a deal." Steenberg really was a director—a director of CERN. Storage IQ's stock had tanked after the shooting and Steenberg gobbled up the controlling interest. Two weeks later three of his people were on the board. Winston had heard IQ was now rejigging their Foxconn assembly lines in Manaus, Brazil to fit Steenberg's designs, just as Steenberg had originally wanted when he made his original proposal to Storage IQ. Where the designs came from, no one had any idea. It now all fit into place.

Steenberg. The fiend! Winston's first instincts had been right all along.

With a strength and a fury that surprised Wild Will, Winston shook his wrist free and speed dialed a special number on the phone Steenberg had given him to be used only in an absolute, life-and-death emergency. *Screw the NSA*, he thought while the number was going through. Someone picked up. It wasn't Steenberg. Wild Will considered snatching the phone out of Winston's hand but noticed the waitress staring at them. He smiled at her and relaxed back in his seat.

"Code in," said a voice over the phone. To Winston's surprise he recognized the voice. It was Simon. The same Simon he'd last met in the restaurant the night of the shooting.

"I know you," said Winston. Even over the phone, Winston could sense Simon's indecision and wariness. Apparently, he had recognized Winston's voice as well. "Simon, or whatever your real name is, put Director Steenberg on. I don't want to talk to you."

"One moment, Winston," said Simon. "I'll put you through." The phone went mute. Thirty seconds later Steenberg came on.

"What is the emergency, Mr. Klendenin?" asked Steenberg. Winston let loose with a string of profanities that had Steenberg holding the phone a foot from his ear until Winston settled down. When he did, Steenberg said, "Vulgarity Mr. Klendenin? A weak mind trying to express itself strongly. Now, please, let's not make this anymore unpleasant than it has to be. Actually, this should be a happy time. Your daughter has been rescued."

"You are pure evil," said Winston, this time with a measure of self-control.

"You say that only because you've never met pure evil," said Steenberg. "I have. Trust me, I've got a long way to go. Besides I'm only doing what's necessary." His self-justification left Winston at a loss for words. Steenberg continued. "I have kept my personal word to you, and I expect you to do the same. If not, there will be consequences. I hope that much is still clear. I'm not pure evil, but if I have to, I can do a reasonable imitation."

"You blackmailed me into shooting a man," said Winston. "You've stolen my family and my soul."

"The man is not dead, and your family has been returned to you. Your daughter is safe. I won't bandy words with you over this. Considering what is at stake, I should think you could be a little more gracious about your small role in the affair."

"Put her on," said Winston. "I want to talk to her."

"Unfortunately, that is not possible at the moment. She is with my granddaughter's husband, Rulon, the big chap."

"Yes, I know who he is. Where are they?"

"We've had a falling out. They're together somewhere. I'm sure they'll be in contact. Just remember, a deal's a deal. Goodbye, Mr. Klendenin." Steenberg hung up before Winston could ask about the danger he was supposed to be in. Winston tried calling him back but no one answered.

Winston sat there dumbfounded with the phone in his hand. Wild Will and Russo said nothing. Winston said finally, "You will tell me if he ever orders you to kill me, won't you?"

"You'll be the first to know," said Wild Will.

"Let's not take any chances," said Winston. "Whatever he's paying you, I'll double it."

"I was only kidding," said Wild Will, "but what the heck, we'll take your money."

❧❧❧

The NSA analyst who sat in one of the 4 by 6-foot Herman Miller cubicles in Beltsville, Maryland and had been at lunch when the alert came in on Yohaba's and Winston's phone conversation two days earlier had eventually come back from lunch. He did his analyst thing, filed his report, and sent it up the chain of command. His report had triggered a "three-deep" tap on Winston's phone. That phone tap had just picked up Winston's call to Steenberg and set alarm bells ricocheting off half the satellites over North America and Europe. To crack Winston's specially rigged Huawei phone, the NSA had worked its connections with the San Francisco police to use one of their StingRay devices coupled with a Hailstorm tower. Used together, they managed to jam Winston's signal and force it to drop from 5G down to a less secure and more crackable 2G connection. The virtual team assigned to the case was notified and immediately arranged a conference call. They filed a report after having determined that the entire conversation was an elaborate code. For what, they didn't know. More phone taps were authorized. More data collected. Now Steenberg's colleagues at CERN would be tapped as well as Winston's contacts in the Defense Department.

An industrious NSA FORNSAT foreign satellite interception analyst in Khon Kaen, Thailand pulled up Steenberg's travel records and noted his frequent visits to Beijing. Within twelve hours, U.S. embassy operatives in Beijing had tracked his visits to the China World Hotel and managed, with a discreet bribe of the hotel's grossly underpaid night manager, to gain access to Steenberg's elevator keycard history. His visits to the 18th floor were logged and cross-checked with the guest list. Leaving no stone unturned, Sun Xiaofeng's name was added to the TAP list just in time to catch his next call to Steenberg.

 споро

Sun Xiaofeng took the call from his team at Stein am Rhein in his office on the 18th floor of the China World Hotel in Beijing. As soon as he heard the voice, he knew something was wrong. The man was too low on the chain of command to be calling him directly. His son had been in charge of the operation. He was the only person who should be calling. As the story unfolded over the phone, Sun Xiaofeng remained silent until finally the phone slid from his hand, bounced once on his leg, then to his shoe, then to the floor. He could still hear the voice from the phone, but the sounds had no meaning. His oldest son was dead.

He thought he should call someone, but the only person he wanted to talk to was his wife. And she had died three years ago. He reached down to pick up the phone and held it again to his ear. He mumbled something about calling back later to hear the full story and killed the call. His secretary stuck her head in the door to ask if everything was all right. He waved her away and wept.

An hour later Steenberg's special phone sitting in Sun Xiaofeng's top right desk drawer played its melody. That Steenberg would call was a surprise to Xiaofeng. The phone was a Huawei Nexus 6P complete with a fingerprint sensor and an older version of RedPhone open-source encryption software that Steenberg himself had personally rewritten and enhanced. It ran only over WiFi and not even service providers could see the metadata. It was the same type of phone and encryption software Steenberg had given Winston Klendenin for emergency calls.

Xiaofeng retrieved the phone from the drawer. He looked at it for a moment before hitting the call button. "You," he said.

"I just heard the terrible news. You have my heartfelt condolences."

"I blame you."

"You are inconsolable right now. I understand that. I will personally arrange for his body and that of the other man to be flown back to China."

"I blame you and your grand plans."

"I believe you mean our grand plans. We have been walking a tightrope. Over a river filled with piranhas. Every blessed moment. And we are accepting these risks because we are saving the world. If not us, then who? If not now, then when?"

"Platitudes, Dr. Steenberg," said Xiaofeng. "Are we now reduced to platitudes?"

"Not platitudes, Sun Xiaofeng, but core values that separate the doers on this earth from the dreamers. These men that your son arranged to ambush, all under the plan we both agreed to, were quite frankly highly experienced and not in the least interested in being ambushed or having one of their members sedated. Given their background, the successful kidnapping of Mr. Hurt was never a foregone conclusion. I fully shared with you their unique backgrounds precisely to avoid any recriminations such as now. My instructions to your men were to set a trap and secure a member of my team who was becoming a liability. I gave him to your son on a platter. What more could I do?"

"I still blame you."

"At some point, when you are ready, I urge you to talk to your men again, but in more detail. I urge you to reserve judgment until you have spoken to them. I think you will find that everything that could have been done to ensure the safety of your son and the team was done."

"There's nothing you can say that will convince me. You will pay. I promise you. We are not partners. I work with you because you are blackmailing me. You as much as threatened to kill my youngest son in America. Now my oldest son is no more. And what kind of man arranges to have his only granddaughter's husband kidnapped?"

"We have invested too much in each other to sever our partnership now. We are men who are shaping history together. There were always to be risks. Even tragic sacrifices. I am truly sorry, but now we must be strong. We are so close. Your son must not have died in vain."

"Died in vain. You are worried that my son will have died in vain? How noble. Eventually every megalomaniac uses that phrase to justify the continued sacrifices of others. If in avenging his death, I rid the world of a monster like you then his death will have served a purpose. I will be in touch, Dr. Steenberg."

"Don't hang up," said Steenberg. "I have an offer." While Xiaofeng had been talking, Steenberg had been weighing his most persuasive options. The first and most obvious one was to remind Sun Xiaofeng of the catastrophe that would rain down on his head if Steenberg released to the Chinese government certain previously discussed DVDs. The second option was to win back Xiaofeng's trust by turning over to him all copies of the incriminating disks with no strings attached. This option, while noble, had no guarantee of success and might force Steenberg to take even more drastic action to secure Xiaofeng's future cooperation. The third option was exceedingly distasteful. Steenberg hoped he wouldn't have to use it.

"Tell me," said Xiaofeng, "what can you possibly offer me at this time? More money? A bigger cut of the profits? Please, by all means continue."

Steenberg decided to lead with option two. "I will destroy all the copies of the DVDs. In fact, I will give them to you. We will no longer be bound by threats."

"And here I thought I could never laugh again. You think I care about that now? I am going to take revenge on you, Dr. Steenberg, even knowing full well that you undoubtedly have some mechanism in place to release the disks to CNN in the event of your death."

While Xiaofeng was talking, Steenberg listened intently to his voice, trying to pick up the little nuances indicating Xiaofeng's degree of resolve. Reluctantly, he couldn't help but conclude that Sun Xiaofeng's resolve was absolute. With great reluctance, he threw option three on the table. "I can give you the names of the four men who attacked the villa when your son was killed, including the husband of my granddaughter. What greater proof of my heartfelt sincerity can you have than that?"

"What good are just the names?"

"And I have administrator access to their phones. On each of them I've installed a rootkit. You can track them any time they go by a WiFi hotspot. Revenge, Sun Xiaofeng. I am offering you revenge. Pure, sweet, uncomplicated revenge on the actual people who have caused your loss. My only condition is that you pledge me your word that there will be no repercussions to our joint venture."

"I cannot think now," said Xiaofeng.

"Say the word, and I'll send the data." said Steenberg. He waited patiently with only the sound of Xiaofeng's breathing betraying his continued presence on the phone.

"Send the data," said Xiaofeng finally then hung up.

As soon as Steenberg sent the data, he wrote a note to himself. *Tell Yohaba the team must destroy all its phones.*

∽∾∽

Eduardo Sanchez whistled as he methodically vacuumed the new beige carpet in IQ Storage's executive chamber in Palo Alto. Tonight's tune was *Strangers in the Night*. For twenty-eight years, whistling had been his trademark and a source of great irritation to his co-workers. However, he was on a first-name basis with the now retired founders of the company, had emptied their wastebaskets at 3 a.m. when they were working late and the company was just an ornery startup, and he was untouchable. Mention his whistling with anything but praise for its clarity and resonance and you would be invited to a "coaching" session with the HR director. So, Eduardo whistled away and vacuumed. Nice straight lines. Back and forth. Back and forth. Just after five a.m. No one around. Fifty minutes from quitting time. Back and forth.

The carpet had been replaced three months prior just after that crazy woman CEO had shot that nice man. There hadn't been that much blood but the memories had sunk deep into the carpet, and also the room, so not only the carpets but even the furniture had been replaced. The paintings too, as if the painted eyes had seen such horrors that even they needed to be spared the memories. Except for the two de Koonings. Appraised at over $500,000 each, like Eduardo they were untouchable.

As Eduardo vacuumed, he noticed one of the de Koonings hanging slightly crooked. He vacuumed around the heavy wooden, plushly upholstered chairs and the dark brown table legs of the sixteen-foot-long conference table, whistling as he worked. Back and forth. Back and forth. He stopped his vacuuming and stared at the painting. Its lack of symmetry was bugging him. Crazy gringos. *Buy an expensive painting then don't even hang it properly*. He stopped what he was doing and walked up to the painting and read the small silver-on-gold plaque that was underneath.

Willem de Kooning (American, b. Netherlands 1904—1997). Pink Angels, 1945. On loan from the Frederick R. Weisman Art Foundation, Los Angeles.

Eduardo's hand reached out to straighten the painting. And stopped a few inches away from touching it. He looked around. The door was closed and he was alone. He reached again and stopped again, wondering if the painting was perhaps protected by an alarm system. If so, would it be triggered by a slight movement? He tried looking behind the painting to see if there were any hidden wires or a device of any kind. He scrunched his face against the wall but he couldn't get his eyes close enough to see behind the picture. He pressed his face even harder against the wall but he just couldn't get the right angle. He pulled back from the wall exasperated. The crooked picture stared back defiantly. He set his jaw. "No guts, no glory," he murmured. Taking one more wary look around, he held his breath and carefully adjusted the painting by pressing down with one finger on the top left edge.

No alarm. He sighed in relief and stepped back to observe his work. He had corrected it too far. He made another adjustment. Almost there. Another small adjustment. Now it was worse. Another adjustment. No good. Now thoroughly frustrated, Eduardo grabbed the painting with both hands and manhandled it into position. Something fell to the floor from behind the picture. He picked it up and untangled two long black gloves. The label on the inside of one of the gloves read "House of Harlots." *What the…?*

Part Three

Chapter 23

Boris Zokolov thought of Yohaba. He often did when driving and his brain was on autopilot. The VW T5 9-passenger van he rented at the Zurich airport was probably overkill, but, at six-five and three-hundred-thirty pounds of bar-clearing, tattoo-covered, please-sit-anywhere-you-want-Mr.-Zokolov muscle, Boris needed the room. And so did the four armed, grim-faced Russians who rode with him—men who, like Boris, worked for Vadim's oligarch father, Anatoly Polykov.

At one time, between the criminally violent but well-paying life Boris had chosen after leaving the Russian FSR, which he knew Yohaba would disapprove of, and the long line of rhythmic gymnasts and assorted Bratva wannabees he'd consorted with over the years, which Yohaba would also disapprove of, he'd all but driven her from his memories. But then Steenberg and Polykov had struck a strange but lucrative deal, and for the first time in three years, Yohaba was a little bit closer.

For the past week, Vadim had been sending him the occasional surreptitiously taken cell phone picture of her. It was as close as he had expected to be until that early morning phone call from Anatoly that the plane had blown up and the old man and the other men, Mikhael, Tomas, and Ivan, men that Boris knew very well, were all dead. Boris would miss his comrades. Not so much the old man.

In the van, just past Dübendorf, Boris pictured again her angry but unafraid eyes as she talked him out of killing that little Italian in the alley in Zurich. And the look of relief in her eyes, no, more than relief, he was sure of it, when she later saw he was alive in the cathedral. And then, of course, when she later took the bullet for him. But most of all he remembered the feel of her forehead slowly rocking against his as they said goodbye. Funny how memories work. He thought of the other women he'd been with in the years since then…and shook his head. Boris wished no ill of Rulon, but if Yohaba were ever available, he'd be in Idaho wearing a cowboy hat, milking cows, and cheering for Boise State if that's what it took to win her.

⋘⋙

On the way back to Schaffhausen with the team, Rulon turned the thirty-minute return trip into a multi-hour excursion by taking what seemed to his passengers to be every single-lane backroad in the canton to avoid possible police roadblocks. The extra time gave Brother-in-law a chance to settle down a bit, but Rulon still wasn't completely certain he wouldn't plug Steenberg at the first opportunity. It was still dark and Rulon was driving slowly along the narrow country roads.

The tension in the van had been steadily rising for the past hour, and finally reached the boiling point when Brother-in-law spooked Rulon by dropping into his hillbilly persona, a sure sign he was contemplating something nasty. Rulon finally pulled off to the side of the road and refused to go any further until Brother-in-law promised not to kill Steenberg. But Brother-in-law remained noncommittal.

"I hear ya," he said, "but I'd be lying if I said I wasn't tempted," was the closest Rulon could get to a commitment. Benny and Murphy stayed out of it. Neither of them was exactly afraid of Brother-in-law, but when he went into hillbilly mode, staying quiet and unobtrusive seemed like the smart thing to do. Rulon didn't care and kept arguing. Finally, Brother-in-law cut him off and said heatedly, "I will take it under advisement. Can we just get to the hotel sometime this year?" At Brother-in-law's raised voice, Batu stirred under her blanket in the backseat.

"That's not good enough," said Rulon angrily. "Tell you what. Enjoy the walk back, because I'm not driving one more inch until you promise me that Steenberg is off limits. Look, we'll confront him, sure, and try to talk some sense into him, but no violence." Rulon turned the engine off, leaving the headlights on, and stomped out of the van with the keys.

"I'm going to take a nap," said Murphy. He tilted his seat back and pulled his ball cap over his face.

"Me too," said Benny and did the same.

At that point, Batu got out of the van with the blanket wrapped around her shoulders and walked over to where Rulon was standing about twenty feet away. She was still groggy from the dart but clearly had been listening to their conversation.

She was shorter than Yohaba but not short, maybe five foot six. Quite slender, but not frail-looking. Her skin was like a night in the Sawtooths, not chocolate brown, but deep, deep black. Her reggae-wild black hair hung in dreadlocks around her shoulders. Expensive blue jeans, running shoes, a gray hooded sweatshirt zippered halfway up, underneath it a white t-shirt with the words "Bring Back Our Children" on the front which Rulon assumed was a reference to some children kidnapped by the LRA or Boko Haram or some other group of murdering savages. High cheek bones, thin eyelashes above large brown eyes beaming from the whitest sclera—or maybe they just seemed so white because of the contrast with her skin—anyway, he surmised, she was African through and through despite her adopted parents being white billionaires. Somehow she'd grown up holding tight to her African roots. She walked up to Rulon, who was standing in the glare of the headlights. She stopped in front of him and swayed a little. He reached for her, but she steadied herself.

"Are you the leader?" asked Batu in a soft voice.

"Am I the leader? Now that's a good question," said Rulon. "Yes, I guess I'm the leader. The skinny guy lets me lead him wherever he wants to go."

Brother-in-law walked up too. "We need to get going. If you don't want to drive, give me the keys."

"You should promise him you won't kill that Steenberg guy today," said Batu to Brother-in-law.

"What?" said Brother-in-law.

"What?" said Rulon.

"Just promise him and then we can all go. Promise him you won't kill that man today. I'm sure he deserves it, but if everyone who deserved to be killed was killed and everyone who deserved to go to jail was in jail, the world would stop working. Maybe tomorrow that man will change his mind and be a better person. You don't know. If you kill him, you'll never know."

"That's a mighty interesting philosophy, Miss," said Rulon.

"Maybe he'll be worse tomorrow," said Brother-in-law.

"Maybe you'll be worse," said Batu. "Though I'm not sure how. I've been drugged and I think it was you."

"That's interesting," said Brother-in-law.

"Are you by chance a Star Wars fan?" asked Rulon. "You remind me of one of the characters."

"There is no try, only do," she said brightly.

"Ha," said Rulon. "You need to meet my wife. Her name is Yohaba."

"Sounds Chinese," said Batu. "Is she Chinese?"

"No, Swiss," said Rulon.

"What gives with the t-shirt?" asked Brother-in-law.

"My parents sponsored a school in Nebok, Nigeria that was hit by Boko Haram," said Batu. "They kidnapped 276 girls. I knew some of them."

Brother-in-law kicked at a tall clump of grass and let out an exasperated sigh. "Well, I can't argue against Yoda and Jabba the Hut together," he said. "Okay." He raised his right hand. "Being of sound body and probably unsound mind, I solemnly promise not to kill any mad geniuses today, and I solemnly hope I don't live to regret it." With that, Brother-in-law turned around and went back to his seat in the van.

Batu said to Rulon, "Who is he?"

"Navy SEAL, good friend. He's spent a lot of time in Africa, especially the Congo. Now he lives with me and my wife on our ranch in Idaho."

"He's not your brother-in-law then?" asked Batu.

"Him? No. We just call him that," said Rulon.

"Is that what I should call him?" asked Batu.

"Sure," said Rulon. "Just don't call him late for dinner." When Batu didn't react to his joke, Rulon said, "If you want to know his real name, it's better if you get it from him. Don't ask me to explain."

"I love a challenge," said Batu. "When can I call my parents?"

"Very soon," said Rulon. "I just have to sort out the phone situation. I'm not sure which phones we can trust right now. Are you all right?"

"Except for the kidnapping part and their leader, those men treated me well," said Batu. "But I'd like to get this off." She held up her hand and showed Rulon the dangling handcuffs. "But otherwise, I could work out and go on walks, and I even learned some Chinese."

"Why Chinese?" asked Rulon.

"Their English wasn't very good," said Batu.

"What?" said Rulon.

"They were all Chinese. Didn't you know?"

"No," said Rulon, fighting that feeling again that he was a cork bobbing on a very big ocean. "I thought they'd be Russian. But it doesn't make any difference. You're with us and we're gonna get you home." But inside Rulon was worried. Another puzzle piece that didn't make sense.

Once they were driving again, Brother-in-law rummaged through the glove box, cup holders, and door pockets looking for something. Once he found what he was looking for he climbed past Rulon into the backseat. While Benny held a flashlight, Brother-in-law managed to get the dangling handcuffs off Batu with a paperclip.

She said thank you and touched Brother-in-law's hand lightly. Their eyes met, and she said, "I sense Africa in you. I want to hear your story." Brother-in-law slowly pulled his hand away and said nothing. "Later, when we're alone," she said.

For the rest of the way back, Brother-in-law was calm, and there was no more backwoods chatter. They drove through the bucolic countryside in the gathering dawn. Rulon saw some cows in a field and grew wistful thinking how Daisy always tried to knock his hat off with her tail when he milked her.

At 5:30 a.m., at a point Rulon judged to be halfway back to Stein am Rhein, having finally come to terms with Steenberg's treachery, Rulon called Yohaba on her cell phone to warn her about her grandfather. She picked up immediately, having just slammed the door on her grandfather as he left her hotel room.

"An hour ago I would have been shocked," said Yohaba after Rulon told her how her grandfather had tried to have him ambushed, "but guess who just left the room with my handprint across his face. Yes, my noble grandfather. He said we needed to destroy all our phones, but he wouldn't say why. Oh, he also said he honestly felt he had to remove you from the equation and that it wasn't personal."

"That's a relief. I was worried it was personal," said Rulon. "I'm sure he made my sudden disappearance sound noble and necessary. I wonder what's the story with the phones. It probably has something to do with the NSA."

"I don't know, but I'm so sorry, darling," said Yohaba. "I've dragged you into my crackpot family, and you've always been so longsuffering. Yeah, and of all the gall. He actually thought he could talk his way out of it. He actually thought I would run off with him before you got back. If it's any consolation, I know he feels bad. Not just about you, but because somebody is dead who wasn't supposed to die. How's Klendenin's daughter? Is she all right?"

"She's okay," said Rulon. "She was passed out when we got her in the van. Brother-in-law had to dart her." Rulon suddenly realized what he just said and in front of whom. "Ah, oops."

"Sorry," said Rulon to Brother-in-law. At his side Brother-in-law shook his head in disgust.

"I knew it," said Batu.

"If you knew why, you'd thank me, Miss," said Brother-in-law in an "*I don't have time for this*" tone.

"Things got out of control there, didn't they?" asked Yohaba, bringing Rulon back to their conversation. "Admit it."

"It depends on your definition of 'out of control,'" said Rulon.

"Did you fire off any Claymores?" asked Yohaba.

"Maybe," said Rulon.

"If you look up the definition of 'out of control' in the dictionary, it says, 'See Claymore,'" said Yohaba. "But did you know that you killed the son of one of my grandfather's key partners back there? Somebody called him from the villa and told him."

"Yeah, well," said Rulon, "when you kidnap a girl and shoot at her rescuers sometimes bad things happen to you. Gosh, am I becoming jaded or what?"

"I think we all are," said Yohaba.

"How did your grandfather take it when you slapped him?" asked Rulon.

"He looked at me with what I would call grieved nobility," said Yohaba. "It was very annoying. You'd have to burn him at the stake to get a rise out of him. I'd say he was still undaunted and his determination in the rightness of his actions remains untouched."

"You realize we have to patch things up with him."

Yohaba heard the tire-on-gravel crunch of a car pulling up outside the hotel. "Hold on," she said. She rushed to the window with the phone in her ear and pushed the curtains aside just in time to see a man holding open the door of a black Mercedes S600 sedan and Steenberg brushing past him into the back seat.

"Well, Cowboy, there goes your chance," said Yohaba. "The man of the moment is driving off in a Mercedes. Geez, he's got minions everywhere."

"It makes you wonder," said Rulon, "how many plans, counter-plans, contingencies, and fail-safe fallback strategies your grandfather was juggling behind your back." For a variety of reasons, Rulon was relieved to hear that Steenberg had left the hotel. He quickly told Yohaba what happened at the villa and about Batu's rescue, but since Brother-in-law was sitting right there, left out the part about the problems he was having with him. Yohaba told him that Boris Zokolov had already touched down in Zurich. Vadim's father had sent him in one of his other private jets to take Vadim back to Russia. *Good riddance,* was Rulon's first thought. His second was, *Man, those oligarchs are rich.* His third thought was, *Boris Zokolov.*

"I'd like to see him again," said Rulon, a bit stiffly.

"Really?" asked Yohaba hopefully. "Me too."

"Yes. Just no Russian bear hugs with the guy. It's no secret he likes you more than he likes me."

"You have no reason to be jealous."

"Well, be sure to put that on my gravestone when he knocks me off so he can marry you."

"You better be nice to him. Get here quick," said Yohaba and she hung up.

☙☙☙

In Schaffhausen, Benny and Murphy were dropped off at their hotel first with orders to pack and wait for a phone call. Two minutes later, Rulon parked in front of the rough rock face of the Park Villa. Rulon wanted Batu to meet Yohaba but wasn't sure how it would go with Boris there. Plus, there were things he wanted to discuss privately with Yohaba first.

"You need to go with Brother-in-law," said Rulon to Batu. "Stay close to him. Make sure he packs his toothbrush. We'll meet back in the lobby in an hour."

Batu took a look at Brother-in-law, who was unloading his infamous duffle bag from the back of the van but heard what Rulon said. She shrugged. He shrugged. "I don't bite," said Brother-in-law as he slung the bag over his shoulder.

"I do," she said.

Rulon shrugged. Batu and Brother-in-law walked off together.

Rulon stayed on the sidewalk just outside the hotel's main lobby to make some calls. He called Dilly and Stringbean and then Vadim and Yevgeny, telling them they had the girl and giving them the same instructions he'd given Benny and Murphy. Wait for a phone call. Be ready to leave. When finished, he looked up at the leaden sky and sighed, then turned to face the hotel's front entrance, knowing Boris was probably already there with Yohaba. He liked Boris. He just didn't like him alone with Yohaba. He went inside.

In front of his room door, Rulon knocked three times quick, then twice slow—their code. When Yohaba opened, the smell was different. It smelled Russian. He brushed past her, and there he was, Boris Zokolov in living color sitting on the bed in his habitual black attire and seemingly taking up half the room. Before Rulon could react, Boris had him in a giant bear hug but, as big as he was, the monstrous Russian still couldn't get his arms all the way around the big cowboy. He tried lifting Rulon off the floor, all the while laughing and talking crazy Russian and breathing bratwurst in Rulon's face, but Rulon didn't budge. Finally, Boris gave up.

"You've put on weight," he said breathing hard and backing away a step.

Rulon sniffed and wrinkled his nose. "Same old cologne, I see. Sausage Obsession with a little tuna fish behind the ears." Boris roared with laughter.

"I miss you, Cowboy," he said. "No one dares insult me like Cowboy." Boris opened up his huge arms and clasped both Rulon and Yohaba to his chest. Suddenly serious, he said, "Yohaba, you have broken my heart and, you, Cowboy, have made me doubt my fighting skills. My friends, to compensate I have become a very bad man. It is your fault. I miss you. I miss you both."

"That's nonsense," said Yohaba to Boris. "You were no angel when we met you."

"True," said Boris. "Perhaps I exaggerate."

"Listen," said Rulon. "If things are that bad in your life, come back to the ranch with us. We can use you. We'll get you back on the straight and narrow."

"Where's the Klendenin girl?" asked Yohaba. Rulon told her and also brought her up to speed on the arrangements to meet later.

Yohaba had already packed for both of them, and their roller suitcases were sitting by the door. She stepped past them into the bathroom, and during the wait Rulon filled Boris in on the situation. When he was done, Boris said, "You know nothing. It is worse than you think."

"I think the world is going to end," said Rulon. "So whatever it is, it's not worse than I think." By now, Yohaba was there again sitting next to both of them on the bed with her arm draped over Rulon's broad shoulders.

"For three reasons, yes, it is," said Boris. "First take manure out of your ears. The Russian SVR wants you dead. No more pattycake with Russian agents in Idaho Karaoke bar. Ha! I think after Zurich maybe you agree with Boris, no? The thin man wants you dead, so you are dead. Sorry. And now probably Steenberg has Chinese Academy of Sciences also wanting you dead. Maybe you think—Ha! Rulon tough boy. Science Academy nerds don't frighten tough boy Rulon. But that would be stupid Rulon thinking. Military has hooks everywhere in China. Listen to Boris. The Chinese won't send science nerds after you. Maybe world will end in 2029, maybe not. But you definitely never here to see it happen if you don't get smarter faster. Maybe your world ends with no maybes if you don't listen to Boris."

"That's only two reasons," said Rulon.

"Okay. Now come real bad news. Vadim said Steenberg had big doomsday plan, yes?"

"I do have a vague memory about that," said Rulon.

"So," said Boris, "in one week, say goodbye to Western decadence."

"Good riddance," said Rulon. "So what's the bad news?"

"Very funny," said Boris. "You want bad news? Try this. Water and two nukes. Steenberg's giant brain thought up plan to nuke aquifer in Saudi Arabia and Libya."

Rulon thought about that for a few moments before turning to Yohaba and saying, "Darling, is this another one of those little secrets you've been keeping from me?"

At the mention of the word "aquifer," Yohaba immediately jumped to her laptop. "No," she answered Rulon as she typed, "but I've seen project invoices moving drilling equipment to the Kufra Lake region of Libya and to Al Kharj just south of Riyadh. I should have known something was up." She slammed her laptop lid down. "Shoot, shoot, shoot," she said. "He's already locked me out."

Boris fished through the inside pocket of his black leather jacket and took out a thumb drive. He tapped Yohaba on the shoulder and said, "It is all here. From Polykov himself. He speaks English like me. You will understand."

Yohaba stuck the thumb drive into one of her laptop's USB ports, did a few clicks and there was Vadim's father talking to them on the screen in bad but understandable English. She disconnected her laptop from its power cord and placed it on the desk so all could see.

"Greetings, my noble fools," Polykov said, then laughed heartily. Polykov said something in Russian, presumably to people behind the camera and much laughter could be heard. He began again.

"My dear Ms. Hurt and Fat Rancher. Haha! Yes, my son keeps me well informed. Greetings from Lakhta, Russia. My son told me you speak Russian, but I want your man to hear this too. But we know you are the brains. No offense to your man."

Under his breath Rulon murmured, "None taken."

"I think you are your grandfather's right-hand woman, so I speak this to you," Polykov continued in the video. "If you are listening then Boris Zokolov has found you. Good. Mr. Zokolov is there to bring my son home. Don't interfere. Your enemy, my enemy too in strange Russian way, the old man in Moscow, has given me window of opportunity. Forty-eight hours to bring Vadim home before he hunts you down. You see, you, your grandfather, and your husband must run. Good luck. You are marked people and are danger to everyone. I am sorry, but this is true.

"I am grateful that my son and Yevgeny are alive even if others are not, even my father. I mention this only to tell you I feel losses same as you.

"Now for information. Russians have many proverbs. Here is one. For mad dog, mile is not far to detour. That is your grandfather. He makes only great plans. He hides the truth easily and without blushing because he thinks his cause is great. But let me tell you. He is crazy and we are making big detour starting now even if we lose money.

"We have people who have people who know people in Bulgaria. From them we know your grandfather looked for nuclear weapons. We were disturbed but…"

Polykov broke off the English and spoke Russian for a couple of sentences, again to someone behind the camera. There were voices in Russian answering him then Polykov, looking at the camera again, said in English, "He was, how you say it, naïve. No one has nukes to sell, not even Bulgarians. But grandfather of yours is like pit bull. He finds nukes. This is how. When cold war, USSR agents smuggle small atomic weapons into Eastern Europe, even Switzerland. They hide them. These nukes are small for man to carry in backpack. Not too heavy. Some buried in earth and some in water. Your father found two. We know model numbers." He reads from a piece of paper in his hand. "RA-115-01s and 08s. Governments search them for years but mostly no luck. But your grandfather is genius, so he finds them. He looked only for ones in water. Why?"

Both Rulon and Yohaba exchanged desperate looks. Nuclear weapons. Death beyond belief. Horror of horrors. Steenberg forever mentioned in the same breath as Hitler, Stalin, and Mao. How could this be happening?

"Maybe, Mrs. Hurt, you know this already. Maybe you hear about Russian defector Vasili Mitrokhin. He tell world what Russia buries. The Swiss know Russians very well. They find one near small chapel near Bern. Maybe your husband knows this. Maybe not.

"Your grandfather wants nukes because solar panels are not endgame. Water is endgame. We laugh. We think him crazy, but water is crisis for many countries now. So, we think maybe crazy, but maybe we make rivers of money so we shut up.

"So, what is grandfather up to? He come to us one day with grand plan. He wants Russian factories to build for him. He tells us he has super technology to take salt out of sea. It comes from Einstein, he says. Who buys them? we ask. Where are contracts? Customers will come, he says. We say we love you but no.

"He says he puts one bomb in aquifer in Saudi Arabia. Boom! No more water to Saudi Arabia, Iraq, Qatar, and Syria. Maybe other countries also suffer. Second bomb in North Africa. In aquifer. Boom! Libya, Chad, Sudan now all get very thirsty. People must move. He thinks they move to Europe, He thinks Europe pay anything to keep them out. Even buy your grandfather's..." Once more,

Polykov broke off to ask something in Russian to someone out of view. When the answer came back, he said, "…desalination technology at crazy prices so people have water where they live and not come to Europe. They pay anything. Your grandfather is very clever man. Crazy but very clever. But so crazy he makes us sweat. Do you understand?"

At this point, Yohaba stopped the recording. "I can't listen anymore," she said. "This can't be happening."

Rulon put his arm around her and said, "Take a deep breath. We will fix this one way or another. It's not going to happen. I promise you." Rulon reached over and clicked "play" on the laptop.

"They buy water plants by hundreds or Europe and EU borders and culture are no more. Millions on the move. You see. We tell him bombs too small. He says bombs not too small anymore. Einstein again.

"This is why thin man wants him dead. Why he blew up my plane I don't know. I think it was old score. My father made many enemies during life. But my son is safe and we have new guarantees so business goes on. Thin man hunts for grandfather and will kill him unless you stop him. He will kill you too if you take his place. That is his message to you. I am delivery messenger. But Rulon Hurt is dead man no matter what, I think. Sorry. Thin man hates him.

"We know you are together now, and you are close to Steenberg. He will listen to you or maybe your Rulon will do something. My son says you and your husband are good people. Or maybe the hillbilly will do something. I should like to meet the hillbilly someday. Hey, he can work for me anytime. I am Polykov."

When the recording was over, everyone was quiet. Yohaba took out the thumb drive and stuck it in her pocket. She put down the top of her laptop. "I have to ask this," said Yohaba to Boris. "Can we trust your boss?"

"In this case, yes," said Boris.

Rulon started to say something, but Yohaba cut him off. "Don't say it," she said. He started to talk again, and again she said, "Don't say it. Don't even think it." She stared hard at Rulon until he appeared to relent. Then she got up and walked over to the window.

Rulon blurted, "I told you."

Yohaba was too beaten to react. "I can't believe I've been helping him," was all she could muster. Rulon came over and put his arm around her. "I can't believe he's doing this to us," she said. "We were supposed to be family."

"We'll find him and talk some sense into him," said Rulon. "It's not your fault. You thought he was doing good, and in fairness to him, he thought so too. And you are his granddaughter, so you were going to help him. That's all there is to it." Yohaba started to cry. Rulon said, "Ah, baby. We'll fix this. It's not the end of the world." At that last comment, Yohaba paused in her sobbing to look up at him. Rulon mumbled something about poor choice of words. At last the sobbing trailed off to a few sniffs and Yohaba wiped away her tears with her sleeve.

"I'm tired of being right," said Rulon. "Your grandfather is nuts. There, I've said it. I didn't tell you, but Brother-in-law was going to kill him when we got back but I talked him out of it. I'm feeling sorry now that I did."

"What are we going to do?" asked Yohaba.

"I must go now," said Boris, "and invest money in desalination technology."

"Please don't joke," said Yohaba.

Rulon said, "We need to get everyone together."

There was a knock at the door. "I know you're in there," said a young male voice.

Rulon opened the door and Vadim and Yevgeny walked in. At the sight of Boris, Vadim rushed to his side and even

Yevgeny looked pleased when he saw him. They all hugged and spoke in hushed Russian. Tears streamed down their cheeks. The losses in the airplane bombing had cut deeper than they'd ever let on to Rulon and Yohaba. Yevgeny's face was still marred from the fighting at the ranch. Boris asked him about it. The three Russians commiserated, and, despite the urgency, Rulon and Yohaba didn't have the heart to interrupt. Finally, though, Rulon couldn't hold off. He cleared his throat loudly. The three Russians, who by now were all sitting on the bed, looked at him.

"We need to check out or they'll charge us for another day," said Rulon.

Boris stood up. "Of course, my American…" He looked to Yohaba for help.

"Tightwad," she offered.

"I was going to say *misanthropist*," said Boris, "but, yes, cheapskate. Thank you. No problem. We're all going now. Back to airport. Back to Russia."

"Have a nice trip," said Vadim to Boris. "I'm not going. You can do what you want, but I'm staying here with them."

Boris grabbed Vadim by the ear and yanked him hard off the bed. While Vadim was standing on the tips of his toes, squirming, and grabbing at his hand, Boris said to Rulon and Yohaba, "I'm sorry this is quick. I will come to you in Idaho if you now have bigger horses."

"We've got a Clydesdale on order," said Rulon.

"I'm holding you to that promise," said Yohaba to Boris.

"Come in the fall," said Rulon. "There's lots of work to do then." Boris managed to give Rulon and Yohaba one more massive hug despite still having to jerk a clutching Vadim around by the ear, then turned to leave.

As he was half dragged out the door, Vadim yelled, "I love you, Yohaba. I'll come, too," and waved goodbye.

Yevgeny started to leave too but hesitated by the door just long enough to say, *"Poproshaisya s sumasshedshey Khilbilli za menya."* Yohaba laughed.

"Translation please," said Rulon after Yevgeny left.

"It was a bit of an idiom," she said, "but went something like, 'Say goodbye to the crazy hillbilly for me.'"

"Yeah, crazy like a fox," said Rulon. "Speaking of which, we need to make a plan."

Chapter 24

Thirty minutes later Rulon and Yohaba stepped out of the hotel elevator with their roller suitcases and looked around the hotel lobby. The rest of the team was already there, also with their luggage, either sitting on the brown leather Chesterfield sofa or leaning up against the far wall with a view of the entrance. Brother-in-law in jeans, jogging shoes, windbreaker, and blue ball cap, and Batu, still in the same clothes, stood off by themselves talking in the streaming sun of the garden doors. Yohaba nudged Rulon, nodded towards the couple, and whispered, "Would you look at that, Cowboy?"

"Are you going to warn her, or does it always have to be me?" said Rulon. Yohaba gave him a sharp elbow and walked over to Batu while Rulon went around the lobby gathering up the rest the team.

"I'm Yohaba, Rulon's wife," said Yohaba. She held out her hand. "Are you all right?"

"Yes," said Batu. She warmly grasped Yohaba's hand with both of hers. "I think so. I haven't got a toothbrush or anything else to wear, but I'm not complaining. Thanks to Orin I'm safe." When she used the name "Orin," Rulon on the other side of the room did a double-take.

"I can't take all the credit," said Brother-in-law. "Rulon helped too. He drove us there and back." Again, Rulon's ears pricked.

"Your mother and father are going to be ecstatic," said Yohaba. "Have you talked to them yet?" Rulon walked over.

"My mother, yes," said Batu. "But not my father. He's on a plane somewhere. My mother said the police found a glove that links my father to a shooting and now they want to arrest him. She also told me the NSA was tapping his phones, and I had to be careful about calling. She doesn't understand who you are and why the police weren't involved in my rescue? I didn't know what to tell her. I'm so out of it, but Orin helped me understand. He says my father hired you."

"Yes, your father arranged for your rescue," said Rulon. "He's the real hero. You need to call him. I think we can outfox the NSA one time." He turned to Yohaba. "Wait here. I'll check out. And I've got us a conference room." Rulon walked over to the front desk and talked with the assistant hotel manager, which culminated in Rulon handing over his credit card, then, remembering his tradecraft, quickly taking it back and handing over cash instead. He came back to the group with the conference room key in his hand and led them through the restaurant to the meeting room in the back of the hotel.

The Louis XVI conference room was set up to be a spillover area from the hotel restaurant. People could sit down there, doors could be closed, and there was a sufficient measure of privacy. A long, polished wood dining table covered with a white tablecloth and twelve place settings dominated the center of the room. Two smaller tables for two stood by the large windows on either side of the double doors that led into the garden. An ornate golden chandelier hung from the ornately inlaid ceiling.

As they entered, each member of the team stacked their luggage in a corner then spread out among the thinly upholstered, wooden chairs around the large table. Rulon gave Batu a burner phone, instructions on how to call her father, and asked her to wait in the garden.

Once Batu was sorted out, Rulon stood next to Yohaba at the head of the table waiting for the movement of chairs to subside, and for a young hotel worker to wheel in a whiteboard. Everyone now knew about Steenberg's treachery. It was a somber reunion. It wasn't a good feeling knowing you had a target on your back. Rulon observed his team and once again fumed at the mess Steenberg had gotten them into. Brother-in-law stood by the garden door just inside the room, keeping an eye on Batu as she spoke to her father. Tripod was with her. Brother-in-law looked at Rulon and nodded. The hotel worker bowed slightly and left.

"We are in deep kimchi," said Rulon once they had the room to themselves. "But first I need everyone to destroy their cellphones. Everyone except Yohaba. She needs hers for one more call. I'll explain later. You need to not just take out the battery, but actually destroy the thing so the speaker can't work. This goes especially for the special jobs Steenberg gave us. Sorry. You'll understand why when we tell you what's going on. I've got a few burners we can share that I'm reasonably sure aren't compromised." Rulon set the example by opening up his phone, removing the battery, and crushing the device under the heel of his cowboy boot against the tiled floor.

Murphy held up his Huawei Nexus 6P and said with a sigh, "Man, I love this thing."

"So does the NSA," said Rulon. "They can track you through it anytime they want and listen in on all your conversations. Plus, they can remotely turn on its mike and listen in to this meeting if they want. Even with the battery out in some models. There's no escaping them. Please destroy your phone."

Murphy looked at his phone scathingly and said, "Why, the little tramp." He ripped off the back cover, tore out the SIM card and battery, and stomped the phone into pieces. The others did the same, and Rulon passed around a wastebasket for the pieces.

When the phones had been dealt with, Rulon continued. "For various reasons, a powerful and ruthless, mostly secret Russian intelligence agency that has proven to be a real pain in the neck in the past wants Steenberg and me dead. Steenberg because of his plan to save the world by destroying it, and me on general principles. Plus, I'm not pointing fingers here, but when we rescued Batu, the son of the director of the Chinese Academy of Sciences was accidentally killed and now the Chinese are after us too. Fortunately, with layovers, it's at least a fifteen-hour trip from Beijing to Zurich, so I think we've got some time before they get here. And finally, Dr. Steenberg is upset and wants me kidnapped and out of the picture for undermining his life's mission and is probably less than pleased with Brother-in-law for not letting him do it. There's been a complete falling out with the guy. As far as we know, he doesn't wish any harm to Yohaba, but, heck, a few hours ago, I would've thought I was on his Christmas card list, so what do I know." Rulon looked at Yohaba. "Have I left anything out, baby?"

"Don't forget the aquifer," she said.

"Right, right," said Rulon. "The aquifer." He clapped his hands together. "You're gonna love this. Dr. Strangelove, I mean Steenberg, has come up with a plan to overrun Europe with refugees by using nuclear bombs to destroy a couple of aquifers in the Middle East and Africa." Rulon looked around the room and saw disbelief. "I am not making this up, guys. There it is again. Some genius thinks he's the smartest guy in the room, and in this case he may be right. But that's beside the point. Nobody is this smart. Nobody can foresee all the twists and turns and ups and downs of every situation. Nobody can know how other people are going to react when an entire region's water supply is cut off. This could start a nuclear war. And how ironic would that be? We're all wiped out during a nuclear war started by some genius who was trying to save the world from being destroyed by a meteor. I mean is that just one big ironic cow-pie or what? Think of it this way, if just one of us here…"

Rulon stopped in mid-sentence. He looked at Yohaba and said, "I'm ranting, aren't I?"

"A bit, darling," she said kindly.

Rulon turned back to the team. "Well, you get the point," he said. "No use getting worked up any more than we have to. There's your steaming bowl of kimchi. I hope you brought hip waders. And there's more." He also went on to explain how Steenberg had blackmailed Klendenin and had a hand in the Japanese reactors, dikes in Vietnam, and other disasters around the world. When he was done, he asked, "Any questions?"

No one moved. No one blinked. Slowly, the men stirred in their chairs. Brother-in-law seemed more intent on Batu in the garden than anything Rulon was saying.

"Ahm…this is getting out of our league," said Benny. "Maybe we need to bring in Interpol, or the U.N. or the U.S. Air Force, or something."

Before Rulon could answer, Murphy interrupted. "I just have one question," he said. "Has the money transferred yet? Just yes or no. That's all I need. Just a yes or no." Rulon looked at Yohaba.

"No," Yohaba said. "As promised, half the money is already in your account, but no, the rest of it has not transferred yet, and unfortunately my grandfather has locked me out of his systems, so I can't do it. You'll just have to trust him to do it."

"No problem," said Murphy. "Just because he's a mass murderer doesn't mean he'd oppress a hireling in his wages."

"Lighten up, Murphy," said Yohaba. "He's still my grandfather."

"The prince of darkness is a gentleman," said Dilly.

"What?" said Yohaba.

"Shakespeare, *King Lear*," said Dilly. "Never mind. Go on."

"I know it sounds funny," said a tired Rulon, "but Yohaba's right. It's the way he rolls. And I have no doubt that after he transfers the rest of the money as agreed, if he had a good reason, he would immediately pick up the phone and hire another team of homicidal maniacs to track us all down and kill us, and then see that the money goes to our next of kin."

"Don't sugar coat it, Cowboy," said Brother-in-law with a short laugh.

"Rulon is exaggerating," said Yohaba. "You're all going to get your money and, yes, our lives are in danger, but my grandfather wouldn't do anything out of revenge or spite. Everything he does is because he thinks he has to in order to keep the 'Great Plan' on track. He genuinely believes, and I do too, that the world is going to end in 2029, and he has to save it. He doesn't even want to kidnap Rulon anymore. There's no need. He's not a vengeful or irrational person. I've quit and removing Rulon won't make me start working for him again. He knows that."

"Okay, so there's still hope we'll get the money," said Murphy.

"Yes, definitely," said Yohaba, "but the money won't do anyone any good if they're not alive to spend it. So, here is what we're proposing. If you step back, Dilly and Stringbean, you're not on the Chinese hit list and maybe not even on the Russians'. No one saw your faces at

Paradeplatz. You could probably make it back home pretty easily, probably even on your own passports."

"Yeah," said Rulon, "but we were hoping you'd hang around the Zurich airport for a few days before you leave and let us know if the Russians and Chinese show up. Will you do that?"

Dilly and Stringbean looked at each other. "Sounds like easy money," said Dilly after a confirming nod from Stringbean. "Sure. What'll everyone else be up to?"

"We're coming to that," said Rulon.

"What's Brother-in-law think of all this?" asked Stringbean.

"You know what my first option would be," said Brother-in-law. "If it was me, I'd keep us together and hunt down Steenberg, the thin man, and the Chinese. End this once and for all. But what do I know?"

"Have you ever noticed," said Rulon, "that in life, every time you violently eliminate one enemy you create two others?" The team members looked around at each other unconvinced. Rulon saw their skepticism and said, "Just hear me out."

Rulon and Yohaba's general plan was still to reason with Steenberg, and get him to call off the madness. That was why Yohaba still had her phone. She wanted to make one more call to Steenberg. The only problem was that no one could come up with an argument that was likely to dissuade Steenberg from his course. Again, there was that conundrum. If Steenberg truly was convinced that every living person on the earth was at risk, what action could he not justify and what counter argument could possibly convince him to desist? After hearing all the arguments, Brother-in-law's contribution was again to offer to put a bullet in Steenberg's brain, and the idea was about to carry the day until Rulon spoke up.

"That's the easy solution," said Rulon. "And it may not solve anything. We don't really know if Yohaba was his only backup plan. Maybe he's got someone else ready to take over who's crazier than he is."

For the past ten minutes, Yohaba had been sitting silently. At Rulon's mention of her name, she stirred. "We have to convince him that his calculations are wrong," she said.

"Good luck with that," said Brother-in-law.

"True," said Rulon. "He's been the top man at CERN, holds thirty-eight nuclear engineering patents, has been a Nobel prize finalist seven times, has three Ph.D.s, and was mentored by Albert Einstein, but he still puts his pants on one leg at a time just like the rest of us."

"Ah, actually," said Murphy, "he doesn't. The day we left, he twisted his back carrying a milk can and I had to help him get into his suit. He puts both feet in at the same time then kinda pulls both pant legs over his ankles then stands up. But go on. I'm still listening."

"Very funny, Murphy," said Yohaba. "Anyway, my brother Alex is the one who discovered this whole asteroid thing in the first place. If we tell him Alex now believes he was wrong, I think he'll reconsider what he's doing."

"He won't believe you," said Benny.

"Maybe," said Rulon, "but we're hoping that deep down inside he'd love to be proven wrong. He's a good person. This has got to be killing him, the things he's been doing."

"He will insist on talking to my brother," said Yohaba. "And then when he does, we'll be there, too."

"You still won't get near him," said Benny. "He won't be that stupid. He'd just call. Your brother knows how to use a phone, right?"

"My brother suffers from something called Asperger's Syndrome," said Yohaba. "You can't talk to him on the phone. I mean, you can try, but it never works. He can't stay focused."

Rulon interjected, "She's right and Steenberg knows this. He knows he'd have to talk to him in person."

"He'd smell a trap," said Benny.

"Probably," said Rulon, "but he'd still come. He can't do what he has to unless he is one hundred percent sure. He will come." Rulon paused. "We think."

"Where does Yohaba's brother live?" asked Murphy.

"This is the beauty of it," said Rulon. "He lives right here in Switzerland near Bergün with his grandmother. That's less than three hours away. If we leave in the next hour, we can be there in time for an early dinner, and if Steenberg is still in Switzerland we could have this wrapped up by the end of the day."

"But the Chinese still want us dead," said Benny.

"Yeah," said Rulon.

"And the Russians," said Yohaba. "We can't forget the Russians."

"Yeah," said Rulon. "Them too."

"Hey," yelled Murphy, who every few minutes had been checking his bank account. He held up his new cellphone. "He did it. The old guy actually paid us the money. I'm gonna have to take back everything I've ever said about mass murderers."

∾∾∾

Chapter 25

After the meeting, Benny, Murph, Dilly and Stringbean left together to have breakfast in the hotel restaurant. Batu had finished her call forty-five minutes earlier and waited patiently on a bench in the garden for the meeting to end. When Brother-in-law opened the garden door, she came back in with good news. Her father was arranging for a long-range jet to pick her up in Zurich. The plane would arrive late the following day. Rulon asked if she wouldn't mind waiting a few extra days for Dilly and Stringbean to get their new passports and then take them home with her. It seemed like an obvious solution to Rulon, but to his surprise she asked, "What about Orin?"

"He'll be with us," said Rulon. "Just a little mopping up work."

"Sorry then," said Batu. "I'm staying with Orin. I'll leave Switzerland when he does."

"That's really cute," said Rulon. He turned to Brother-in-law and said, "Talk some sense into her, please."

"A body oughta make up their own mind," said Brother-in-law, "don't you think?"

"No, I don't think," said Rulon.

Rulon tried reasoning with them both. Got nowhere but got darn angry when Brother-in-law said, "She can go home when Yohaba goes home. That sound fair?"

"Please step into my office," said Rulon. "I'd like a word." He stormed off into the garden and Brother-in-law followed. Tripod trailed along and stood next to Brother-in-law with his ears perked listening attentively to the conversation. They stood under a spreading maple tree in the far corner of the garden.

"What's going on?" asked Rulon. From his vantage point, he could see Yohaba in the conference room talking to Batu. It was almost ten a.m. now and the day was heating up.

Brother-in-law took off his blue ball cap and raked his fingers through his long hair. He set his cap back on his head again and said, "I don't rightly know."

"Please don't tell me she's in love with you," said Rulon, "because if she is, there is an easy remedy. Just give me a few minutes with her."

Brother-in-law laughed softly. "I don't rightly know. I just know I don't want her to go either."

"Did you tell her your story?" asked Rulon. "The whole story?"

"Yeah, she beat it out of me," said Brother-in-law.

"I thought you were trained to resist interrogation," asked Rulon.

"Yeah, well," drawled Brother-in-law, "I guess I was, but the SERE instructors didn't look like her."

Rulon slapped Brother-in-law on the back. "Well, maybe it's time you got back on the horse that throwed ya. Anyway, make sure you build a constructive relationship based on mutual respect and adherence to good principles. I'll send you a link to a church talk on the law of chastity."

"You just can't help being you, can you?" said Brother-in-law.

"Nope. But you do know, don't you," said Rulon, "it's safer for her if she goes to the airport now and doesn't stick around you? Right? You know that."

"Actually, I don't. This is chambers-of-the-human-heart stuff," said Brother-in-law. "I can't explain it. But if she wants to stay with me, well, being away from me don't necessarily make people safer." Rulon knew immediately that Brother-in-law was referring to the massacre of his family in Africa while he was away hunting the LRA. And for that Rulon had no answer. He'd felt the same way about Yohaba when they'd first met, and the two of them had traipsed all over Switzerland together with the Russians on their tail. Didn't make sense then either, but things had turned out all right in the end.

"Besides," said Brother-in-law, "you don't know you're in love till you do the first stupid thing. Isn't that what you always say?"

"Then you must be head over heels," said Rulon. Changing the subject, Rulon said, "How'd you get the handcuffs off that guy without a key? I assume you didn't have a key."

"A key," said Brother-in-law thoughtfully as if considering the idea for the first time. "Wow, they have keys for handcuffs?"

"Did you cut off his hand?"

"No. But I'm glad we're alone. I've been wanting to talk to you about those two old ladies at Paradeplatz. You need to hear this."

"Oh, you make me laugh," said Rulon. "Here it comes. Another one of your non-linear diversions. Fine. But be warned, I'm circling back to the handcuffs when you're done." Rulon, hands on hips, smothered his smaller friend with his looming size. "C'mon. Out with it," he said.

"You spotted them first," said Brother-in-law, taking a step closer to Rulon just to show he wasn't intimidated. "That was pretty nifty. You zeroed in before me and even Tripod."

"Did I?" said Rulon.

"Oh, you most definitely did," said Brother-in-law. "You even went for your gun. What stopped you?"

"They were two old ladies," said Rulon.

"So?" said Brother-in-law. When Rulon didn't respond, Brother-in-law asked him, "What gave them away?"

"I saw the outline of a gun butt in the one gal's cloth purse."

"Cowboy," said Brother-in-law, genuinely impressed, "that is outstanding craft. So why didn't you shoot 'em?"

"Look, Prince of Blood," said Rulon, "they were two old ladies. Maybe the one gal had just bought a toy gun for her grandson. Maybe it wasn't a gun butt at all. Maybe it was a box of chocolates. Geez, man. This is exactly what I've been talking about all along. People making life and death decisions as if there were no possibilities of them ever making a mistake and like there was no possible other explanation for anything. The question you should be asking is why did you shoot 'em before their guns were even out? Don't lie to me. I saw your face. You were mighty relieved to see that gun spill out on the ground."

Brother-in-law smiled. "Maybe. But when *you* saw that gun on the ground, you were mighty relieved that I'd shot. Steenberg was target number one, yeah, but Yohaba was surely number two. Admit that too, my friend."

"You've got an answer for everything," said Rulon, irked. "What made you so sure, sure enough to shoot?"

"They reacted like professionals when you went for your gun," said Brother-in-law. "Both hands went to their purses and their knees bent into a shooter's position. Talk about a couple of tough babushkas. I'll bet those two never baked a chocolate chip cookie in their life." Brother-in-law started laughing. Rulon refused to join in.

When Brother-in-law couldn't stop laughing, Rulon said firmly, "I'm not laughing. I'm not laughing with you. Not about two old ladies getting shot."

"It was like watching a training video," continued Brother-in-law in between cracking up, "only they were ninety years old and not very spry. They were trying to move as fast as they could. You could practically hear the tendons snapping." Brother-in-law was laughing so hard he couldn't get the words out.

"Get a grip," said Rulon, tired from not having slept all night and from the constant adrenaline rushes when rescuing Batu. "I'm going back in." He looked around. "Where are the girls?"

"Wait, wait," said Brother-in-law, his eyes alight with mirth and with one hand on Rulon's arm. "Did you catch the look on their faces? It's always the same when an ambush goes bad. The eyes get real big and funny looking, the jaw twists and the mouth drops open." Brother-in-law mimicked the expression then burst out laughing again.

"Fine. Get it out of your system," said Rulon while stifling a yawn.

"I tell you, there is no more satisfying feeling in the world than turning the tables on an ambush and seeing that look. I've seen it more times than I count. It's like some kind of universal human response, like sneezing or something. I've seen it in a half-dozen different nationalities and cultures. Always looks the same. Always." Brother-in-law made *the look* again.

Rulon suddenly couldn't take it anymore. The pressure, lack of sleep, betrayals, Claymores, death, the end of the world. He burst out laughing and bent over double, paroxysms of laughter heaving through his body. "At least they died doing what they loved," he bellowed during a fleeting moment of control before he went back to laughing so hard the tears rolled down his cheeks. He stammered, "That's what Vadim…that's what Vadim…that's what Vadim said about his grandfather. When the plane blew up, he said he hadn't decided whether to kill us all or not, but at least…at least he died doing what he loved." Rulon's laugh was a roar.

Yohaba and Batu interrupted their conversation in the conference room to stare at the two men in the garden.

"Tough call. Should have just flipped a coin," said Brother-in-law, now pounding Rulon's back as he lost it again. "They always say that." He and Rulon were now both doubled over laughing. "Whenever somebody kills himself doing something stupid, they always say that. He died doing what he loved!" Slowly the laughter died away. When they both finally settled down again, Brother-in-law poked Rulon in the chest and said, "Next time trust your instincts. They're working just fine. Next time you pop the old gals. Action beats reaction every single time. Don't forget that."

"So how'd you get the handcuff off the guy without chopping off his hand?" asked Rulon, now fully composed and determined to circle back like he said he would.

"I stomped on his hand till all the bones broke," said Brother-in-law. "Then it was easy to slip it through the cuffs. Got the idea from you, my friend."

"Right," said Rulon. In CERN a few years back, Rulon's hand had been freed from a leather restraint in a similar way. Alex, Yohaba's brother, had been the one to figure that out.

"It was better for him than the alternative," said Brother-in-law.

"I'm sure he was grateful," said Rulon.

"It was hard to tell at the time. But I didn't do it to be nice. You can't hardly cut through the ulna and radius. They're too tough. And if you go for the wrist and don't do it just right, your blade gets caught in the scaphoid and lunate bones. Believe me, I've been there. Anyway, I didn't have time to fuss. He got what he got."

"And you knocked out Batu so she wouldn't have to watch the world-famous surgeon in action. Right?"

"And the guy. Don't forget the guy. Had to knock him out too. He looked like a screamer." Brother's last comment set Rulon to laughing again.

"Of course," guffawed Rulon. "Couldn't have him screaming. Would have upset Batu." Brother-in-law watched until Rulon once again composed himself. When he was done, he said, "Whew. I feel better now. Where were we?"

"I like her," said Brother-in-law.

"I can see that," said Rulon. "I'm grabbing some breakfast. Wanna come?" The two men had been standing near a tree at the end of a row of rose bushes. They turned to leave the garden just as Batu and Yohaba walked up to them smiling.

"You two seemed to be having a good time," asked Yohaba brightly. "Everything settled? Is Batu staying or going?"

"Ask her," said Rulon.

"I'm staying," said Batu. No words of objection from the two men.

"Okay, then," said Yohaba. "We're starving. Let's go eat." She kissed Rulon. Brother-in-law and Batu stood a few feet from each other looking straight into each other's eyes.

"I wonder if they serve fried bananas," said Batu.

Rulon turned to her when she said that. "I love those too, but, nah, no chance. Switzerland isn't as gastronomically advanced as one might think."

"I'll see if the kitchen can rustle some up," said Brother-in-law. "I like 'em too."

Over breakfast in the hotel, Yohaba offhandedly mentioned to Rulon and Brother-in-law that Batu was good friends with the young daughter of the Kremlin's security director. They were both rhythmic gymnasts and had trained together once upon a time at the same gym in St. Petersburg.

"That's interesting," said Rulon.

⁊⁊⁊

That's interesting," said Jurgen Altheuer. "Did you know that Klendenin's daughter is good friends with the daughter of Viktor Nemtsov, the head of Kremlin security? It seems they went to a sports school together."

"No, I didn't," said Leonard Steenberg. "How fascinating and potentially useful."

Leonard Steenberg's BMW was stuck in a traffic jam going across the border into Germany near Schaffhausen. Simon, his driver, had warned Steenberg about the delay, but Steenberg needed to get to Munich as quickly as possible in preparation for an appointment the next day with the board of Siemens. Next to Steenberg in the back seat was his smartly dressed chief-of-staff for European operations, Jurgen Altheuer, and now that Yohaba had resigned, his new right-hand man. Altheuer had previously been a managing director at Siemens and was there the day Steenberg had his initial disastrous meeting in front of the board to elicit their help with Elsa. That day, only Altheuer had championed Steenberg's cause and after the meeting, Steenberg, always looking for allies, invited Altheuer to join him for dinner at the Koi Japanese restaurant just a short distance from Siemens's headquarters on Wittelsbacherplatz. They hit it off. Three days later, a considerably richer Altheuer tendered Siemens his resignation and began working full-time for Steenberg. He had never met Yohaba. Had never even heard of her. Steenberg believed in compartmentalization.

"This is the only phone that works," said Altheuer as he listened through his earphones. "I can't even raise a signal from the others." On his knees was a busy laptop. He paused just long enough to loosen his tie and then continued typing and listening.

"I think I know which one it is," said Steenberg. "I suspect we'll be getting a call soon."

"An apology?" asked Altheuer.

Steenberg laughed and touched his face, still red from Yohaba's slap. "I think not. More likely to persuade me from my course of action."

"Surely they know you better than that."

"Oh, it wouldn't be a frontal assault, I assure you. Hmm… but I am curious. What will she come up with? I wonder."

"She?" asked Altheuer.

Steenberg sighed. "Never mind."

Altheuer said nothing but went back to trying to access the other phones. After a minute's effort he said, "Except for that one, I still can't even get a return ping. I think the batteries have been removed."

"What can you hear?" asked Steenberg.

"Now? Nothing really. Even on that one phone. People are talking but it's too faint. Like the phone is wrapped in a blanket."

"Rulon," said Steenberg.

"Who?" asked Altheuer.

"Never mind," said Steenberg. "But someone is definitely up to something. Forget about the other phones. They are destroyed. I had a second tiny battery installed in case they were clever enough to remove the main battery. I sometimes think I underestimate my granddaughter's husband."

"Excuse me, Chief?" said Altheuer.

"I suppose I should tell you," said Steenberg. "Your counterpart in North America was my granddaughter, but she is no longer an employee. Her husband objects. His name is Rulon. Rulon Hurt. Quite a rough-hewn fellow. A bit of an oaf. No, that's not fair. Actually, he's hard to classify. But he has been quite the gadfly lately. I suspect the phone in question is my granddaughter's." Altheuer processed this information in silence while he studied Steenberg's troubled expression.

"Rulon," said Altheuer. "Sounds like a name out of a fantasy comic book."

"No," sighed Steenberg. "Out of Idaho."

"Would you like me to take further action?" asked Altheuer.

"No, Jurgen," said Steenberg. "If you can't raise a signal then they are most definitely destroyed. But don't lose track of the one phone that still works. Unfortunately, I'm not dealing with idiots."

"Neither are they, Chief," said Altheuer. "But I thought you relished a good challenge. Why so glum?"

"Oh, is it obvious?" said Steenberg, "Right now my conscience has reared up, and my patience is wearing thin. I did something I regret. I hurt people I dearly love. Both my granddaughter and her gadfly husband Rulon. Yes, he's annoying, but he does have a way of ingratiating himself into one's affections. Like a giant St. Bernard." Steenberg sighed. "Perhaps a little repentance is in order and perhaps a little penance as well."

"Do you want to call your granddaughter on that phone?" asked Jurgen sympathetically.

"No," said Steenberg. "Let's see what they come up with first. I'm sure they've made a plan, and frankly, I'm curious."

"Sure, boss."

"Oh, what a bother. A few of my formerly loyal conspirators now have doubts and seem to have trouble prioritizing. Tell me, Jurgen, is saving the world from total annihilation not a noble enterprise?"

"Of course it is."

"Off the top of your head, can you think of anything more important?"

"No, sir. Nothing comes immediately to mind."

"I agree," said Steenberg. "So let us proceed as we have been proceeding." He looked out the car window at the trees very, very slowly rolling by. The car had hardly moved in the last ten minutes. *Et tu, Yohaba*, he thought to himself. *Can I ever trust you again?* He closed his eyes and when Altheuer tried to interrupt, silenced him with an impatient "shush."

Thirty minutes later Steenberg opened his eyes again. They were still in Switzerland, but traffic had by now advanced enough that he could see the German border crossing just a hundred yards ahead. He said, "Jurgen, my good man, congratulations. I've just moved you up in the organization."

"A promotion, Chief? Thanks. To what do I owe this honor?"

"To disloyalty," said Steenberg, but then shook his head. "No, no, that's too harsh. Not disloyalty, but rather to a disheartening lack of foresight."

Chapter 26

Granny stood in her garden on the side of her home in Bergün that got the most sun, gloved hands on hips and dirt on the knees of her Round House bib overalls, a present from her aggravating grandson-in-law, Rulon Hurt. Swiss gardeners didn't normally wear bib overalls, but sometimes there is no resisting an idea whose time has come. The blue overalls had a deep chest pocket, material that was nearly indestructible, several side pockets for various tools, and even a hammer loop. Rulon had sworn by them. Now, three of her neighbors had a pair and liked them so much Granny was thinking of becoming a Round House reseller, the first one in Switzerland.

The garden wasn't doing too well this year. The winter lasted forever and now there was too much rain. Her Ditta potatoes might never make it, but she still had hopes for the carrots, onions, celery, beetroot, and cabbage stretching in ten-meter rows in front of her.

Granny adjusted the straw hat on her head, another gift from Rulon to replace the one he'd sat on three years ago when he and Yohaba visited. Granny's white hair hung in a long ponytail down to the middle of her back. She squinted up at the sun, now shining through the pine trees around her home through a break in the clouds. She suddenly realized how quiet it was and looked around. Where was that dang boy? Turn your back on him for a second and he was gone.

"Alex. Alex," she called. No answer. Granny stomped entirely around the two-story brick house looking and hollering for her lazy-bones grandson. Each step made a sucking sound and left deep footprints in the muddy ground. She walked over the gravel driveway, over the curved, stone walkway that led to the front door, over the patch of grass that constituted the front yard, pausing for a second to look into the living room window to see if he was hiding there, around the back past the door to the cellar, through patches of overgrown wild grass, and finally back to her garden.

She shouted, "Alex. Alex. Where are you? Answer me!"

The brown boards that trimmed the windows gave the home a Tudor feel, but the two miniature turrets with small windows that graced the top story suggested something more Gothic. Granny heard a window open. She looked up.

"There you are," she said.

Alex's head poked out the left turret window. "I'm up here," he said. "I live in the woods for peace and quiet. Except for you."

"Did you finish your chores?" asked Granny.

"Forty-two percent of your sentences to me are questions. That's not normal," he said.

"How do you know that?" asked Granny.

"There. You proved my point again," said Alex.

"It is so normal to ask people questions forty-two percent of the time," said Granny.

"No, it's not. You only ask Rulon questions twelve percent of the time and Yohaba twenty-two percent."

"They're not normal," said Granny, "that's why."

Alex stayed quiet for a few seconds, while Granny stood there astounded at the idea that she might have actually won an argument with her grandson. Then he said, "I'm telling them you said that. They're coming. They just told me on the phone. They'll be here in two hours. I think they want to apologize for blowing up Zurich."

"That's ridiculous," said Granny. "Nobody blew up Zurich. It was a gas main that blew. I read it in the papers. You did too. I thought you liked Rulon. He likes you. Did he tell you he was the one who blew up Paradeplatz?"

"No, but the Sprüngli chocolate store was undamaged. Plus the gas lines there stop at Paradeplatz. If it were a gas main, the damage would have been south and east of Paradeplatz not north. It wasn't a gas main and the chocolate shop was untouched. Can't you see it?"

"Did you finish your chores?" asked Granny.

"No. I had to answer the phone," said Alex. "Rulon wants you to cook something. He likes your rösti and apple strudel."

"Is that what you would like me to make?" asked Granny.

"I would be much happier if you could find out what I like without asking me questions. Our relationship is lopsided. You need to get the questions down to seventeen percent. I want to be halfway between Rulon and Yohaba. That's normal."

"Will you get the…no, no. Let me rephrase that. Go get me six Dittas and eight apples out of the cellar. There, are you happy now?"

"Even when trying to do well, you are at thirty-three-point-three percent," said Alex. He ran off leaving the window wide open. Granny could hear him running down the stairs. There was a moment of quiet as Alex ran over the entrance throw rug, then he burst through the front door and ran around the house to the cellar.

"Slow down," called Granny. "You'll hit your head again." A long, loud howl came from the cellar. "When will you ever listen?" *Oh well, the boy's excited*, thought Granny.

She walked over to the open front door and sat on the doorstep. She awkwardly unlaced her muddy boots, her mildly arthritic fingers fumbling with the knot, and left them by the front door before going inside to cook. The rösti she could fry while they were all standing in the kitchen chatting, but the apple strudel wouldn't be ready in time unless she leaped into action now. Did she have vanilla ice cream in the freezer? Rulon liked it on his oven-hot strudel. Up above, the wind picked up and rustled through the trees. It picked up more and the taller trees bent. *Whenever the wind picked up, the weather always changes*, thought Granny. Whenever Rulon and Yohaba make a surprise visit, life changed too. *I wonder what they are up to*? she thought. *I wonder if it includes Leonard.*

Leonard Steenberg, former Jesuit scholastic and Einstein protégé, had suffered a single, uncharacteristic moral lapse in 1954 when he first met Granny in New York. Yohaba's mother was the result of that lapse. Yohaba the grandchild. The grandchild of Leonard and Granny.

Now as Granny sat on her front step her mind raced through the stages of her life. A pretty boring life, she thought, though there had been moments. There was the life she had first lived, which then became the life she learned from and had to live with after that. That was one of Rulon's expressions. He said it came from a movie about baseball, of all things. When Yohaba and Alex's parents had died in a car crash, the burden of raising the young children fell on her shoulders. Yohaba had been a blessing. Alex a responsibility. But she loved them both. And then six years ago Rulon had come into their life along with Einstein's trunk, and the connection with

Leonard Steenberg was once again established. Rancher Rulon with the Colt automatic and a phlegmatic attitude about everything except the price of milk. What Yohaba saw in him, she had no idea, though the man was handy around the house when he visited. Always fixing things and working like a field hand. Problem was trouble circled around him like vultures. But for some crazy reason, Yohaba loved him, so what was a grandmother to do?

Granny went into the kitchen and began making the apple strudel. A few minutes later Alex came in with the potatoes, and she set him to peeling them for the rösti. When he was done, she sent him back to the cellar for more. Rulon and Yohaba would be there in a couple of hours and Rulon was a big eater.

❧❧❧

Dilly and Stringbean sat in the open-space Aviolino restaurant by Observation Deck B in the Zurich airport, working on their third cup of coffee. They were both dressed in newly purchased Brax casual trousers and long-sleeved shirts rolled up to the elbows. The heat from the tarmac seeped through the lightly tinted observation windows and reflected off their glass tabletop. A jumbo from Shanghai was due to touch down in forty minutes. They'd be waiting at the arrival gate to see who came off. So far two planes from Russia and one from China had landed on their watch and nobody disembarking had seemed threatening.

A man and a woman, both in white aprons, were working behind the restaurant counter. Three other people sat scattered among the half-dozen tables around them. There was an older woman in a maroon dress with a small, brown roller suitcase next to her metal chair and two businessmen in suits, both on their cell phones. Dilly and

Stringbean kept one eye on their fellow diners and one eye on the people in the terminal hurrying here and there to catch a flight or to get home.

Dilly said, "Have you noticed how pulled together all the women look?"

"Yeah," said Stringbean. "And people here aren't fat. You know, not like Americans. Have you noticed that?"

"Yeah, I have. Here's my theory. I think the Swiss spend so much money on clothes they have nothing left over for food. What'd'ya think?"

"Could be. Or maybe the food's just so expensive."

"Yeah. Maybe."

Just to their right a sturdy-looking gentleman in an unbuttoned, blue sports jacket sat down at a table with a cup of coffee and a copy of *20 Minuten*, the free Zurich daily newspaper. The man took a sip of his coffee and opened the paper for a nonchalant read. Dilly kicked Stringbean under the table. "Stranger-danger," he said and nodded imperceptibly in the direction of the newcomer.

"Swiss fuzz," confirmed Stringbean after a surreptitious glance.

"The newspaper's a nice touch," said Dilly.

"Yeah. I'm totally fooled," said Stringbean. A chair scraped the floor behind them and Stringbean turned to see two men in their mid-thirties just sitting down. Once seated, the shorter, stockier man of the two took off his glasses and meticulously cleaned them with his tie. The other, a bit taller and a lot lighter, took out his cell phone and immersed himself in its wonders. Stringbean turned his chair slightly so he could watch the two men without straining his neck. The strangers engaged in whispered conversation for a minute, then the shorter one walked over to the service counter to place an order. He came back with two coffees and two jelly pastries.

Stringbean asked Dilly, "What's the Swiss equivalent of a donut?"

"Probably a Berliner, a donuty thing without a hole in the middle," said Dilly. "Rulon likes them. Why do you ask?"

"I don't know," said Stringbean. "Have you ever noticed that deep down, cops are the same everywhere?"

"Yeah," said Dilly. "Except for South African cops." Two tables over, the older woman got up and walked off with her roller suitcase, presumably to catch a flight. A tall man in a windbreaker and track shoes carrying a COOP shopping bag took her place. Next, the two businessmen left, still talking on their cell phones. A few seconds later two other men with no luggage seemed to spring out of nowhere to immediately grab their table.

"Did you ever see the movie *The Birds*?" asked Dilly after a minute.

"Of course," said Stringbean. "A classic."

"Do you remember the scene where the gal is waiting outside the schoolhouse and then a single bird comes and perches on the monkey bars?"

"Yeah, and then another and another…"

"…until finally there's like hundreds of birds sitting there and you know there's going to be trouble."

"Yeah," said Stringbean. "Really creepy. And that nursery rhyme the kids were singing. *Knickity-knackity.* Remember that, over and over? *Knickity-knackity. Knickity-knackity.*"

"Yeah. Hitchcock was a genius," said Dilly. "Knickity-knackity."

Both men remained silent for a minute until Stringbean added, "At times like this I always like to ask myself, 'What would Brother-in-law do?'"

"He'd probably blow up the terminal," said Stringbean.

"Yeah, probably."

After a few seconds Stringbean asked, "How do you want to handle this?"

"They got us," said Dilly. "You've heard of the Prisoner's Dilemma, haven't you?"

"Of course," said Stringbean. "Fell for it every time in SERE training."

"Ah…this isn't as funny as you might think. They'll try to link us to Paradeplatz…"

"Ease up, brother," said Stringbean. "I'm only joking. I won't sell you out. My oath as a SEAL."

"Mine too," said Dilly. "Here's our story. Our plane blew up. We got scared and wandered around sleeping on trains for a couple of days. Now we're buying a ticket to get out of here." They quickly put together an imaginary itinerary that didn't include going anywhere near Paradeplatz or Stein am Rhein.

From the far side of the terminal, the two SEALs watched as three tieless men in sports jackets wove their way briskly through the late afternoon airport crowd and advanced directly towards the restaurant seating area. There was a no-nonsense aura about them that had the crowds of travelers parting for them in unconscious compliance to authority and then following them briefly with curious eyes. At the same time all the other men at the tables around Dilly and Stringbean stood up, scraping their chairs against the floor.

"I'll bet Swiss jails aren't so bad," said Dilly. "Chocolates on the pillow and all that."

"Rehabilitation through yodeling," said Stringbean. They laughed nervously.

"The only easy day was yesterday," said Dilly.

"Amen, brother," said Stringbean. Dilly and Stringbean both spat in their hand and shook on it.

The three tieless men walked directly up to their table and stopped. The one in the middle, who appeared to be the oldest, opened his mouth to speak but paused. Dilly and Stringbean stared back. "Guten Tag," said the man finally. Dilly and Stringbean drained their coffee cups and set them back on the table. *"Es tut mir leid, aber sie werden ihren Flug verpassen. Bitte, stehen Sie auf."* Dilly and Stringbean didn't understand German, but they knew the drill. They stood up. The man motioned for them to raise their hands. They complied. He nodded to someone behind them, who then expertly patted them down before they were handcuffed and taken away.

Forty minutes later the plane from Shanghai landed and of the 348 passengers who disembarked, none of them looking threatening. But ten minutes after that a plane arrived from Tehran and eight East Asian males in slacks and Tommy Bahama shirts disembarked, all of whom, indeed, would have pegged out on Dilly's stranger/danger meter. Especially the last one who, at six foot-five and two hundred ninety-five pounds, towered over the others. His name was Ri Myung-rok, and his nickname in simplified Chinese was 金刚. King Kong.

ⱷↃⱷↃ

A cold wind swept over Redfish Lake. Storm clouds darkened the northern sky, casting ominous shadows over the south face of the Sawtooths and the north end of the lake. Still, hardy campers dotted the shoreline undeterred by the threat of bad weather. Parents sat on logs or lawn chairs on the pebbly beaches in sweatshirts and lightweight, down jackets watching their children play at the water's edge.

One intrepid family with two children had canoed across the lake to a small inlet formed by a twenty-foot-tall promontory that jutted into the lake. The mother sat on a cheap, plastic lawn chair reading *The DaVinci Code,* while struggling to keep to her page in the wind. The father crouched in front of his twin nine-year-old boys with a smooth stone in his hand demonstrating the correct way to skip rocks.

"Watch," he said and sent a stone skipping smoothly across the water.

"Wow, Dad," said the taller of the two boys. "That was a sixer!"

The boy with glasses, as was his nature, said little but peered curiously and suspiciously at a log, which suddenly wasn't a log, floating twenty feet from shore. "What's that?" he asked.

His father and brother followed the direction of his pointing finger and saw something bobbing in the water. The father said nothing but walked closer to the water's edge to get a better look. The other boy tried hitting the floating thing with a rock.

"Stop that," ordered the father. The mother put down her book and joined her husband.

"Looks like a hairy log," she said.

"It's a gorilla arm," said the boy who threw the rock.

"No, stupid," said the boy with glasses. "You can't grow bananas in Idaho, so how could there be gorillas?"

"Maybe one escaped from the zoo," said his brother.

"Yeah," said his brother, "and swung from tree to tree all the way from Boise for two hundred miles. Yeah, I'm sure."

"Dial it down, sons," said the father calmly. "It's got claws. It's only a bear leg."

"Maybe you should report this to a ranger or somebody," suggested the wife.

☙❧

Jim Anderson had been a pilot for United for twenty-five years before switching over to flying chartered planes for people with too much money. The pay was so much better. He was silver-haired and eagle-eyed, and his head looked like a bust of Marcus Aurelius. The kind of pilot you'd expect to see flying Air Force One. He liked his job. Bay Area billionaires were actually a pretty good lot. At least the ones who made their money from starting their own companies. The professional managers who came in later and fed off other people's genius, well, they were a different, more arrogant breed. Klendenin, he judged, was an entrepreneur and one of the good ones.

"Hey, boss," he shouted from the cockpit of Klendenin's 737. "Looks like you've got a reception committee waiting for you at Wayne County."

"What makes you say that?" yelled back Winston from his ultra-plush seat over the right wing.

"A little birdy from the tower told me," said Jim. "And he says they're wearing dark suits and reflector sunglasses."

"Dang it all," said Winston. He got up with a beer in his hand and stuck his head in the cockpit door.

"You can run but you can't hide, boss," said Jim. "Hold it for a sec." Jim exchanged communication with the tower at Detroit's DTW airport and then came back to Winston. "My little bird tells me if we land, you're getting cuffed and thrown into the back of a Crown Vic."

"Dang it all," said Winston again.

"There you go, boss, talking cowboy again," said Jim.

"It's infectious. How about Dallas? Have we got enough fuel to reach Dallas?"

"Maybe with a tailwind. But I've got a better idea. Let's drift over Lake Michigan, declare a mayday and then land at Windsor airport in Ontario. They can't get to you in Canada. At least not so quick."

"That's why I pay you the big bucks," said Klendenin. "Go for it." Klendenin went back to his seat. Wild Bill and Russo were sitting further in the back of the plane watching a movie. "Hey," he yelled. "I hope you guys have your passports with you." Wild Bill and Russo had earphones on and didn't hear him.

☙❧

Beltsville, Maryland. NSA regional headquarters. The meetings here that might lead to an uproar all take place in the glass-walled offices two stories below ground adjacent to the data center. For this meeting, among other analysts and observers, Angela, the office sceptic was invited.

"When he refers to the end of the world, he obviously means something else," said Bob. Bob held a degree in cognitive science from Yale and had been recruited by the NSA straight out of college. He was so good at his job they let him wear shorts and sandals to work. When it was winter, he wore a hoodie all day.

"Like what?" asked Angela, a somber-faced, middle-aged, middle manager in a gray pantsuit whose team focused on Switzerland and Germany. She was intently reading the briefing folder in front of her and made her comment without looking up.

"And he uses the word 'kidnapping' a lot," chipped in Bob's boss, a political appointee three months on the job. "Are you saying that's a red herring too?" Angela was used to her comments being ignored.

"Absolutely," said Bob. "Let me give you an example. Years ago a terrorist organization was plotting an attack in London, and they thought they were so clever. Whenever they used their cellphones, they always referred to a 'wedding cake,' as in, 'is the wedding cake ready?' Our software nailed them by the third phone call. 'Wedding cake' was code for 'bomb.' Who keeps talking about a wedding cake but never uses the word 'reception' or 'celebration' or 'bride?' It's the same thing here only more sophisticated. Nobody's been kidnapped. The world isn't going to end from some asteroid. There are no renegade military units running around in Idaho, and…"

"You obviously haven't spent much time in Idaho," said Angela, looking up for the first time.

"Please, Angela," said Bob. "Do you mind?" Bob cleared his throat and continued. "And the Chinese aren't sending hit teams to Switzerland. Think about it. It's just too ridiculous. It's a misdirect. A classic misdirect."

"Make up your mind, Bob," said Angela. "Is it a misdirect or is it a code?"

"Why can't it be both?" said Bob. "We're dealing with very sophisticated players here."

Angela kept quiet. It was stupid to argue with these wunderkinds when they had management on their side. She had seen so many of them come and go over the years, she had lost count. The bosses loved them, though. The wunderkinds wallowed in swamps of complexity. Such wallowing tended to expand budgets and give the middle managers something to talk about to their bosses. Who then had something to talk about with their bosses. *Oh, what the heck*, thought Angela. *I think I'll be a jerk today.*

"Whoa, whoa, whoa," said Angela. "I'm hearing Twilight Zone music. Why on earth can't you take this guy's words at face value? Has anyone even checked to see if this guy's daughter is missing?" Silence all around. "I thought not," said Angela. "And in case you haven't read the papers, there was a huge explosion in Zurich the other day. There were reports of gun fire and lots of foreign dead bodies. Were any of them Chinese?"

"The Swiss said it was a gas main explosion," said Bob. "It happens. Please, Angela, for once, no conspiracy theories."

"Fine, but ease up on the nuances," said Angela. "Why is it so hard to take things at their face value? This Klendenin guy's daughter was kidnapped to blackmail him into something he doesn't want to do. This director guy is pulling the strings and the Chinese want a piece of the action. Duh? And by the way, I looked it up and there really is an asteroid out there named Elsa something. Einstein named it."

"Listen to yourself," said Bob. "Just listen to yourself."

Bob held his arms out wide and looked around the room. "Everyone knows we're listening. Right? Therefore, they'd have to be pretty stupid to say anything we could use against them. Right? And we're not dealing with stupid people here. Right? So, it's a code and we need to collect more data, that's all. Then all will be revealed. With more data, the patterns become easier for our software to identify."

"Hold it a second," said Angela. "If Klendenin knows we're listening and is speaking in code, why then does he go to the trouble of buying these matching sets of military-grade uber-phones then slap on his own homegrown encryption that's some of the slickest stuff we've ever come across? All of that extra hassle is a waste of time if he's speaking in code."

Everyone looked at Angela and no one spoke. "We need more data," said Bob when the silence in the room became unbearable.

❧❦❧

Chapter 27

The Swiss town of Bergün sits at the foot of the Albula pass in the Engadin region of Switzerland near the Austrian border. It can be reached by car and train, but also via the well-maintained hundred-year-old Albula railroad with its bridges, viaducts, and three spiral tunnels through the mountains. An 800-year-old Romanesque church is perhaps the town's most striking feature, but the town itself is stylishly quaint and vaguely medieval. During the winter, the five-kilometer-long Preda-Bergün sledding hill, one of the longest in Europe, attracts many visitors. Winter enthusiasts can rent sleds in the local train station, ride the train to the top of the mountain, then get off and descend on a groomed, twisting, and sometimes perilously fast downhill track through the Albula pass. Once at the bottom, sleders can walk through the village back to the train station and do it all over again. Or perhaps, they stop at a charming cafe and order a hot chocolate. Or, if a close relative is in the area, perhaps they pay a visit and plot to save the world.

Somewhere the sun was still high in the sky, but there in the small glade a few miles from Bergün where Granny's house stood the shadows were already long. Tall pine trees and the even taller rock faces hemming in the valley made for late sunrises and early sunsets. A circular, white-pebbled driveway unwound itself in front of the house and extended as a narrow, graveled road a half-mile through the deep forest all the way back to the rural main highway.

Rulon cut the engine a hundred meters out and let the van roll silently into a parking place in the yard next to Granny's twelve-year-old Toyota Camry. A small precaution, perhaps pointless, but Rulon never liked to announce his arrival any earlier than necessary. Old habit. Batu was still with them, but Brother-in-law with Tripod and his infamous duffle bag, along with Benny and Murphy, had jumped out of the van back in the woods just as they turned off the highway.

"We're just gonna put up the welcome banners for any visitors," Brother-in-law had said. "We'll catch up."

Dilly and Stringbean had missed their last four scheduled check-ins, and when Rulon broke protocol by calling them, a strange, official-sounding male Swiss voice answered. Rulon improvised and said, *"Ist dies die Person, mit wem ich spreche?"—Is this the person to whom I am speaking?*—and when the man on the other end got flustered and didn't know what to say, immediately hung up. Now everyone feared the worst.

The drive to Bergün had been somber. On her phone call to her grandfather, Yohaba had lied like she'd never lied before, telling him she had new information that would change everything and that he needed to come to Bergün to hear it. Why couldn't this be done over the phone? he asked. Yohaba used all her cards. This new information had to be delivered face to face, or he wouldn't believe it. Alex had discovered something. It changed everything. And, for her sake, Steenberg had to speak with Rulon and clear things up. Was it safe? Of course it was. *You know Rulon. But you have to patch things up with him,* she pleaded. *It's not Rulon I'm worried about,* said Steenberg. Yohaba told him that Brother-in-law promised with his hand over his heart that he harbored no evil intentions. It ended with Steenberg saying how much he valued family. He was so very, very sorry about what he'd almost done to Rulon. He hadn't been himself lately. He would come.

After Yohaba hung up. Brother-in-law held up two crossed fingers and said, "Don't worry, I'll make it quick." Batu elbowed him in the ribs.

Yohaba said coldly, "If you harm him…even a hair on his head. I'm not joking about this."

"I won't touch him unless you order me to," said Brother-in-law. "That's a promise." He held up both hands to show no fingers were crossed.

When the van was settled in Granny's yard and all was quiet except for the ticking of the engine, Rulon, Yohaba and Batu sat for a moment waiting. No one came out of the house to greet them. Rulon slowly opened the driver's side door and stepped out. Yohaba and Batu did the same on the passenger side.

"I can smell rösti," said Rulon, "and the pine trees. Feels like Redfish a bit. Wait…wait…and apple strudel. What a great combination of fragrances. You know, they say for every sense there is an art. Well, on this canvas on this day, Gran has created a fragrant Mona Lisa masterpiece for the old schnoz." Rulon took in a big breath through his nose, his chest expanding till he almost popped the zipper on his brown leather jacket.

"In the history of the world," said Yohaba, "I don't believe the words fragrant, Mona Lisa, and schnoz have ever been uttered in the same sentence."

"For everything there is a first time," said Rulon.

"Leonard Nimoy as Spock to that lady Vulcan," said Yohaba.

"Saavik," said Batu. Rulon and Yohaba both slowly turned to look at her in partial wonderment. "Actually,

Lieutenant Saavik," said Batu and shrugged. "My father is a big *Star Trek* fan. It was our thing together when I was a kid."

"Anyway," continued Yohaba. "Lieutenant Saavik in *Wrath of Khan*, 1984."

Batu coughed and looked down. "Could have been 1982," she said.

Yohaba looked to Rulon for support. He looked down and hemmed and hawed. "Well," he said, "at least you got the right decade."

"Fine," said Yohaba in a huff, "1982. But Rulon's not using the quote properly. Spock meant it as someone doing something for the first time, like driving a car or jumping off a ten-meter diving board. Not garbling the English language worse than anyone before."

"Point taken," said Rulon. "But that's not important. These are the moments a man lives for." With sudden enthusiasm, he said, "Where is your grandmother? I need to honor her for creating an olfactory chef-d'oeuvre. There, satisfied? No mangling."

The house door opened. "I knew I heard something," said Alex from the doorway. "It's two-thirty. You're late." He walked over and stood in front of Yohaba. She knew better than to hug him. "Hi, Sis," he said. Alex hated to be hugged. Everyone who knew him knew that.

"Hi, Bro," said Yohaba. "You look good." They shook hands quickly, then Alex wiped his hand on his trousers.

Alex turned to Rulon. "Coasting in neutral uses the same amount of petrol as if driving at a fuel consumption rate of ten kilometers per liter. You weren't saving money."

"But I also turned the engine off while coasting," said Rulon. "So, yes, I did save money."

"But what if you needed to accelerate quickly to avoid a small animal?" said Alex. "Turning off the engine is a dumb thing to do then."

"Then I would have turned on the engine and accelerated out of danger, thus saving our little woodland friend," said Rulon.

"Then you would be wasting petrol," said Alex. "When rolling downhill with the engine off to save fuel, it's more efficient to put the car in gear and let the transmission start the engine. That way you don't have to expend extra power to the starter."

Rulon paused with his mouth open before saying slowly, "Well, Alex, I'm not conceding defeat, but I will have to get back to you on that one." Then speaking exuberantly, he said, "Here. Get over here." Alex walked tentatively over. "Let me look at you," said Rulon. He grabbed Alex's shoulders and held him at arm's length. "You are a sight for sore eyes. And, yes, I am going to hug you." Rulon encircled Alex in his burly arms and gave him a hug that lifted him off the floor—all hundred and thirty pounds of him. "Darn good to see you, Alex, my boy. I've missed you. We've all missed you. Isn't that right, darling? C'mere."

Rulon flung one arm out wide as an invitation to Yohaba, but with the other hand, held tight to Alex's collar so he couldn't get away. The three of them came together in a hug and held it for several seconds. They had once been together in the single most harrowing time in their collective lives—deep in the tunnels of CERN. An unbreakable bond was forged that day.

Granny came out and hugged Yohaba. "My, look at you," she said. She held Yohaba at arm's length and appraised her. "What you can do with jeans and a black leather jacket. I wish I had your figure. And you," she said turning her attention to Rulon, "I hope you've been taking good care of my girl."

"He is, Granny," said Yohaba. "Now don't pick on him."

"Why can't he answer for himself?" asked Granny. "Say something, Rulon. Defend yourself for heaven's sake."

"What's for dinner?" asked Rulon. Granny punched him in the arm. "Ouch," said Rulon a second later.

"Ouch, my foot," said Granny. "Hitting you is like hitting the side of a Brown Swiss. Too bad you don't eat grass like one. Rösti, that's what we're having."

"And your apple strudel," said Rulon. "I can smell it from here. You are Michelangelo in an apron." Rulon hugged her, and her hat fell off.

"Stop that," she flustered. Rulon put her down, picked up her hat, dusted it off, and handed it to her.

"Yes, and my apple strudel," said Granny. "What brings you here? I didn't even know you were in Switzerland. I hope you haven't gotten my girl into any trouble."

"It's always been the other way around, and you know it," said Rulon with a big grin.

Tears flowed. Yohaba introduced Batu. When Alex heard she was from the Congo, he asked if she was a Bakongo, Sangha, or M'Bochi and did she believe that Nzambi created people by vomiting them out when he was sick. The conversation went downhill from there until Granny ushered Alex away and the little group broke up to go inside. At Yohaba's urging, Rulon stayed behind. Batu was hungry and went in with Granny.

"Just like old times," said Rulon when they were alone.

"He's getting worse as he gets older," said Yohaba.

"He's okay," said Rulon. He knew it was hard for her to see her brother. They had grown up together and there had been more painful times than good because of his condition. Alex had been driving the car the day it crashed and killed their parents. Yohaba tried to forget but sometimes it was hard. "Why are we hanging back?" asked Rulon.

"What's Brother-in-law up to?" asked Yohaba.

"Just normal stuff," said Rulon. "You know, laying out Claymores, setting up fields of fire, trying to anticipate how they'll attack the house, devising counter ambush plans. Will they drive right up to the house guns blazing or sneak in on foot through the forest? A lot of factors to consider. The usual."

"So you think the Chinese are definitely coming?"

"Yeah, they're motivated. Or the Russians."

"How would you do it?" asked Yohaba.

"I'd come in through the woods on foot. Before dawn. Throw a few flashbangs into the home, then burst in with machine guns and kill everyone. Then burn the house down afterwards. Oh, and I would try to take me and Brother-in-law alive to torture us to find out who else was involved in killing the son. If that didn't work then…"

Yohaba cut him off sharply. "All right, all right. Enough already. I can see you've thought this through."

"Why so testy?" asked Rulon.

"Why so testy?" thundered Yohaba quietly so no one in the house would hear. "My family is in that house. You are calmly discussing the murder of everyone I love including you."

"That was me being insensitive, wasn't it?" said Rulon after a moment's contemplation.

Yohaba groaned. "Do you think we can get Alex to lie? And what should I say to my grandfather when he gets here? He could be here any minute. C'mon. You've got to help me."

"Tell him about Pericles," said Rulon.

"Why Pericles?" asked Yohaba.

"Pericles convinced Athens to start a war against Sparta. He told them if they all stayed behind the walls of Athens, Greek ships could keep their city fully supplied while blockading Sparta. It was foolproof, he said. And it was, except for one variable he couldn't control. Ships brought the plague to Athens and killed a third of the city. He died in the plague and they lost the war. There went another genius with a foolproof plan."

"It was more likely typhoid or typhus fever," said Alex, who had crept up quietly behind them and was listening.

"Stop sneaking around!" blasted Yohaba, spinning around and facing him. "What's wrong with you?! Why do you that?"

"Ease up, darlin'," said Rulon. He took her hand and squeezed it gently. "Alex, I'm gonna buy you a cowbell to hang around your neck."

"My grandmother says the same thing," said Alex. "She should wear hearing aids. So should you." At that, both Rulon and Yohaba had to laugh.

"And I'm not going to lie," said Alex. "You can torture me, but I won't lie."

"Here we go," said Rulon. He turned to Yohaba. "He's all yours, darlin'."

Yohaba looked steadily at Alex before she spoke. "Alex, listen to me. No one is going to torture you."

"Even if Rulon bashes my hand with a hammer, I'm not going to lie."

"We're not going to ask you to lie," said Yohaba. "It's more like using your imagination. It'll be like writing an exciting novel. But if you don't do it, the whole world will be destroyed, and it will be all your fault."

"Darlin'," said Rulon. "Really. All his fault? C'mon. Lighten up."

"Okay. Alex, it will only be forty-three percent your fault," corrected Yohaba. "But that's still a lot."

"This is going nowhere," said Rulon. "Just explain it to him. No, never mind, I'll do it. Listen, Alex. Your grandfather is trying to save the world, but in the process of trying to save it, he's going to destroy it. He plans to blow up a couple of aquifers in the Middle East, causing a mass migration to Europe unless they buy his desalination technology, which he will then use to pay for the program to stop Elsa. Are you with me?"

Alex thought for a moment. "If he blows up the Arabian Aquifer and the Murzuk-Djado basin in North Africa that would do it," he said.

"Yes, yes," said Rulon impatiently, no longer surprised at Alex's knowledge of obscure and unrelated information. "Yes, we know it would work. What we want to do is stop him. This is getting out of hand. He thinks he can control all the variables in this but he can't. Just like Pericles couldn't anticipate the plague or whatever hitting Athens. Yeah, he may end up saving the world, but this will cause incredible suffering and consequences no one could possibly anticipate, and maybe there's a better way. Do you see what I'm getting at?"

"We need you to invent a story," said Yohaba. "We need you to tell him you were wrong, that Elsa is not going to hit on April 13th, 2029. And you need to come up with something convincing. Something technical sounding. Just enough to get him to doubt his course of action. Can you do that? Of course you can. Tell me you'll do it."

"I won't lie," said Alex.

"It won't be a lie," said Rulon. "Think of it as a chess game. You're making a feint. A trap. A sacrifice. A strategy that will lead to ultimate victory if your opponent falls for it. We're not asking you to lie really. We're asking you to help us outmaneuver him. Temporarily. Just until the game is over."

"Why were you talking about Pericles and the Peloponnesian War?"

"I was trying to come up with an example for your grandfather of other great men who thought they had everything under control right up until the time everything went to heck in a handbasket."

"Pericles declared a trade embargo on Megara. I think he was right."

"What?" said Yohaba.

"Megara can't just take land for itself if it belongs to the god Demeter. Athens had to do something. And if Sparta threatens war if Pericles doesn't lift the embargo, what choice did Pericles have? Would you want Sparta to be the boss of you?"

"I guess not," said Rulon. He looked imploringly at Yohaba.

"Alex, listen to me," said Yohaba. "That's the same problem we have. If we let Leonard nuke the aquifers, how do we say 'no' next time when he wants to melt the polar ice caps?" Yohaba shot a helpless look at Rulon. Was this conversation even making sense anymore? Alex tended to have that effect on people.

"I don't want you to blame Pericles," said Alex. "He was just looking into the future and seeing the ultimate outcome. He had to do something. You should talk about Thomas Midgely instead."

Rulon and Yohaba exchanged quick, worried glances. "He's your brother," said Rulon resolutely. He folded his arms across his massive chest and waited.

"Okay. Who was Thomas Midgely," asked Yohaba, "and what great, unpredictable factors did he unwittingly unleash?"

"He invented leaded petrol in 1921 so combustion engines wouldn't knock anymore."

"Hmm… world-wide lead poisoning. That's a good one," said Rulon.

"Then someone wanted to replace methyl chloride in early refrigerators, so he came up with worse stuff. Freon."

"Goodbye ozone layer," said Yohaba.

"Hello skin cancer," said Rulon.

"Okay," said Alex, "you can mention Pericles as long as you tell my grandfather that Thomas Midgely was worse."

"I can honor that," said Rulon.

"But Freon wouldn't destroy the world before April 13th, 2029, so maybe that's not a good example," said Alex now sounding doubtful.

"It's a good example, Alex. Thanks," said Yohaba.

"Thomas Midgely, it is," said Rulon. "Alex, you are worth your weight in Luxembürgerlis."

"I guess you could talk about Pericles a lot too," said Alex. "I wouldn't mind so much, I guess."

"You already said that," said Rulon. "But thanks. It's always nice to have options."

"When will the game be over?" asked Alex.

"We'll tell you when it's over," said Yohaba.

"He's very smart," said Alex.

"Yes," said Rulon, "but you're smarter. You can do this."

"Did you blow up Paradeplatz?" asked Alex suddenly. Rulon laughed like a lunatic at the question. "I thought so," said Alex.

"Alex," said Yohaba. "Can we please just concentrate on saving the world?"

"I will do it, but I won't lie," said Alex. He abruptly turned and walked stiffly back to the house in his usual way, hands hanging straight at his side. "Einstein is an idiot anyway. It was all a mistake," he yelled just before he went through the doorway.

"Thatta boy, Alex," shouted Rulon after him. "Good start. You're the man." When Alex was inside the house, Rulon turned to Yohaba and said. "That went better than I thought it would."

"I wonder what he's going to come up with," said Yohaba. "But that sounded promising, don't you think?"

While they were standing there in Granny's front yard, Rulon's cell phone rang. "That's weird," he said as he struggled to extricate the phone from his jacket's inside pocket. "Who's got my number?" He gave Yohaba a troubled look and answered very slowly, "Yes." Then his face brightened a bit. "Oh, it's you. Okay. Why? Only if you say please. Okay. Where are you? Sure." He hung up and looked at Yohaba. "That was Brother-in-law. He wants to know if your grandmother has a chainsaw."

∽∾∽

Brother-in-law sat with his back against an alpine spruce. He was in the forest about forty feet in from the winding, half-mile-long, private gravel road that led to Granny's house and about a hundred yards in from the main highway. Murphy and Tripod were with him. Benny was on the other side of the road planting a Claymore. Brother-in-law was drawing its location on a piece of paper along with a number, so he'd know which one he was detonating when the time came. Just like back on the ranch in Idaho. While he was writing, Benny shouted something.

"Looks about right," shouted back Brother-in-law. Benny gave a thumbs-up and walked over.

"How many Claymores left?" he asked.

Brother-in-law peered into his duffle bag. "Four," he said.

Murphy said, "You've sure got a thing about Claymores."

"Poor man's shock and awe," said Brother-in-law. "And they're good for letting you know where you stand. When the first one blows, if they don't start running, you know you got a badger cornered."

"I never liked them," said Benny. "Too random."

"Spoken like a true sniper," said Murphy. The three men chewed the fat quietly in the fading light, talking about guns, women, and other missions. Tripod listened attentively, always at Brother-in-law's side.

"I wonder what Dilly and Stringbean are up to," said Murphy when everyone fell silent.

"Probably sitting in a Swiss jail," said Benny. "Safest place to be right now."

"As long as they don't connect them to Paradeplatz," said Murphy. "That would be bad."

"Yeah," said Brother-in-law.

"Yeah," said Benny. The group went quiet for a few minutes. Brother-in-law rubbed Tripod's ears. Every now and then a car would go by on the highway and everyone would tense up.

"He doesn't growl at me anymore," said Benny after a car had passed and everyone relaxed again. "I wonder what he's thinking now when he looks at me."

"Probably *I wonder if he tastes like chicken*," said Brother-in-law.

Benny chuckled. More silence.

"I was there right along the track in 2009 in Berlin when Usain Bolt set the world record in the hundred meters," said Murphy. "Man, that was the single most impressive thing I ever saw. It was like watching a force of nature. I didn't think a human being could run that fast, generate that much power. Every step was an explosion. I think about it and I still get chills. Can anybody top that?"

"There was this guy in Iraq," said Benny after a few quiet seconds. The voices of the three men hardly carried in the muffled texture of the forest. "A sniper. He made this shot. The target was like nine hundred yards away and only visible through a bunch of busted beams in a bombed-out building. But it wasn't the distance, it was the wind that made this shot so tough. Sand and junk flying around. I mean really howling. Later we calculated our shooter had to be aiming thirty-eight feet high because of the distance and fifty-six feet to the left because of the wind. But he got the guy right in the chest. And get this, the sniper wasn't even American. Does that even make sense? He was from the Welsh Royal Marines. Who ever heard of them? But, man-o-man, best shot in the history of gun powder."

"Rulon once took out a guy in a car," said Brother-in-law, "in the Hönggerberg forest right near where we parked the other night. He was doing a hundred, the other guy braking hard in the other lane so Rulon wouldn't get a shot off. Got him with that Colt automatic he always carries. One hand on the steering wheel, him starting to brake too, the other hand with the gun shooting through his open passenger window. Right between the eyes. Yohaba was in the other car. Saved her life."

"That's impossible," said Benny. "People always exaggerate their own stories."

"Yeah, but I didn't hear it from Rulon," said Brother-in-law, "and not from Yohaba either. Heard it from a Serbian. It was in a bar in Kinshasa way before I ever met the cowboy. Rulon's got more enemies than all of us put together."

"Is that your contribution then?" asked Murphy.

"Now, now, don't rush me," said Brother-in-law. "I was just priming the pump. Okay, here it is. Ronnie O'Sullivan, fastest 147 snooker break in history. Nineteen-ninety-seven World Championships, Sheffield, England. Five minutes and twenty seconds. Check it out on You Tube. I've watched it so many times, I've lost count. On that day, O'Sullivan was an extraterrestrial. No hesitation. No nerves. Just pure calculation, every muscle fiber under his control. The whole world slowed down. The pockets the size of basketball hoops in his head. I don't think he hit the side of even one pocket. The stick, the balls, the table, his eyes, and hands all one thing for five minutes and twenty seconds. It's what every soldier needs to be. Slow everything down. See everything. See the dust on the barrel. The finger twitching on the trigger. Hear the click of the flexor tendon just before the guy pulls the trigger so you know when to twist outta the way from the shot. For the generals, maybe, war is chess. But for us getting our hands dirty in small team combat, it's snooker."

"Snooker. That's like pool? Right?" said Murphy.

"Yeah, somethin' like that," said Brother-in-law with a tolerant smile as he slouched back down against the tree and went back to rubbing Tripod's ears with his eyes closed. Suddenly Tripod's ears pricked. "Rulon's coming," said Brother-in-law without opening his eyes.

"How do you know?" asked Benny.

"The dawg told me." Brother-in-law sat up and cupped Tripod's head between his two hands. "Didn'ya, boy. Didn'ya. Didn'ya." Brother-in-law stood up and walked onto the road. A few seconds later the white van came around a curve, Rulon at the wheel.

Benny and Murphy also stood up. Rulon stopped in front of Brother-in-law. He got out, went around the back of the van, and came back with a chainsaw in one hand and a small red picnic cooler in the other. Before he could say anything, Murphy asked, "What's the most impressive physical feat there ever was?"

"You mean like in a sport?" asked Rulon surprised over the question.

"Yeah."

"That's easy. Yuriy Sedykh's hammer world record. There's not even a close second. You know about that, right?"

"Nope," said Murph. He looked at Benny and Brother-in-law, and they both shrugged as if to say, "What's he talking about?"

"C'mon. You're pulling my leg. Yuriy Sedykh. You know, his two hundred eighty-four-foot, six-and-three-quarter-inch world record in the 1986 European championships in Stuttgart. And get this. He did it with only three turns in the ring. Everyone else takes four. He did it with just three. Gosh, I'm starting to cry. Give me a sec." Rulon wiped his eyes, sniffed, and said, "What's this all about anyway?"

"Nothing," said Murphy. "Just killing time."

"Okay," said Rulon. "Hey, you," Rulon addressed Brother-in-law. "Yeah, I'm talking to you. Granny said I wasn't to give you the chainsaw unless you promised you wouldn't use it to cut down any trees."

"Okay, I promise," said Brother-in-law. "Now give me the chainsaw." Rulon handed it over and Brother-in-law propped it up against the tree and asked, "Did you try calling Dilly and Stringbean again?"

"Yep. No good."

"Damn. If they're in jail, I'm breaking them out. I swear."

"Well, then you'll be in jail, too," said Rulon, "and I will visit you every year on your birthday, I swear. But let's not go there yet. If they've been picked up and have sense enough to keep their mouths shut, they'll be okay." Rulon held up the red cooler. "Here, I thought you boys might be hungry."

"Do you want to hear the plan?" asked Benny later through a mouthful of Granny's egg and bacon sandwich. All four men were sitting among the trees in a circle around the cooler.

"Sure," said Rulon.

"We're expecting them to come by the road," said Brother-in-law, "but Murph's still gonna patrol around the house just in case."

"That is if they come tonight," said Murphy.

"'Cause if they come tonight, they won't have had time to make a proper plan," said Rulon. "I got it."

"Yeah, there'd be no time," said Murphy. "They land in Zurich. Somebody picks them up. They come here and drive up the road, guns blazing. Everyone dies, they burn the house down, then fly home in business class watching movies all the way."

"What if they don't come tonight?" asked Rulon.

"Plan B," said Brother-in-law. "Then they'll have had time to make a plan. We gotta spread out 'cause they could come from anywhere. They'll try and surround the house, get close, then flip a few flashbangs through the windows. Shock and awe. You know. A proper, professional massacre, then go home."

"Maybe they won't find us," said Benny. "Heck, this place is so remote, I couldn't find my way back to the airport without a GPS."

"They'll find us," said Brother-in-law.

"All they have to do is hack the rental car company's tracking system," said Rulon.

"Then why didn't we dump the van?" asked Murphy. "Or move it? Heck, give me the keys. I'll leave it at a police station."

"You wanna be looking over your shoulder for the rest of your life?" asked Brother-in-law. "Or do you want to end this here? Now."

"Guess not," said Murphy after a moment's reflection. "But that won't necessarily end it. Last I heard, the Chinese had a few spare parts."

"You staying out here all night?" asked Rulon. "It'll be cold."

"Better cold than dead," said Benny. Tripod, who was lying down between him and Brother-in-law, barked once in agreement. "Hey," said Benny. "Looky, here. I think we just had a communication breakthrough." He started to reach to pet Tripod but pulled back quickly when Tripod growled and snapped.

"It's a start," said Brother-in-law, "but I wouldn't push it."

"I think you better go back," said Brother-in-law to Rulon. "Murphy'll go with you. We'll be all right. But can you leave the van?"

"Sure," said Rulon. "Hey, what's that?" Everyone stopped for a moment and listened. Somewhere on the main road, cars were downshifting. Every sense alert, the men stood up.

Now the cars had stopped, their engines still rumbling. SUVs. Big Mercedes. Hard to tell. Through the trees long shadows played, and it was starting to get chilly. Cars. Maybe three of them had pulled off the main street onto the long road through Granny's property.

"You know the drill," said Brother-in-law. "Earbuds," he ordered. Benny and Murphy grabbed their weapons, activated their earbuds, and melted off into the woods. To Rulon, Brother-in-law said, "Better get back."

"No way," said Rulon. "Where's your bag?" Rulon wanted a bigger weapon than the Colt he always carried. Brother-in-law nodded towards the duffle behind a tree. Rulon rummaged through it and got aggravated.

"Where's the SIG?" he hissed.

"Probably in the van under the seat," hissed Brother-in-law back. "But forget about the SIG. You'll turn on the dome light and give us away." Rulon went back to rummaging and came out with a Thompson submachine gun. "Hey, a Thompson and a hundred-round drum magazine. This could be fun. Where's the bolt lock assist tool?"

"It *was* taped to the stock," said Brother-in-law, "but if you lost it, then forget it. You'll never get the drum loaded. Just use the stick magazines. There's four in there."

"Fine. I guess I'll just have to make do," said Rulon. He found the thirty-round stick magazines, rammed one into the Thompson, and stuck the other three under his jacket.

Brother-in-law sat on his haunches behind a large spruce. He had the remote detonator in his hand. Rulon came over and crouched next to him. "Everyone in place?" asked Brother-in-law into his mike. Everyone acknowledged. All was quiet except for the idling engines a little ways off and the swishing of the trees.

Five minutes went by. Murphy asked, "Anyone see anything?"

"No. They're probably arming up and getting ready to charge down the road," said Benny. "If they come spaced out, I think we should let the lead vehicle pass through, so the others will fit in the kill zone. I can handle the first one with the M79."

"No, can't chance them making it to the house," said Brother-in-law. "But we got the van blocking the road now. It'll be okay as long you got the minis spaced like I told you."

A few more minutes of silence. Somewhere down the road, a car started moving.

"Get ready," said Brother-in-law.

"I see it," said Murphy. "I'm letting it through. It's coming slow. Now it's stopped. Dome light just came on. Someone's getting out."

The next thing Brother-in-law heard was Murphy chuckling into his mike.

"What's up?" said Brother-in-law. He had one hand on Tripod's back trying to feel what the dog was sensing. "Someone coming?" he asked over his mike.

"Yep," said Murphy. "He just walked past my position. He's on the road. You'll see him in a minute. Looks unarmed. Definitely not Chinese."

A minute later, Rulon and Brother-in-law saw a blond man in a business suit walking down the road holding a stick with a white flag attached to the end. Every few steps, he stopped and shouted, "Don't shoot. I am unarmed. I am with the Director."

"This is anticlimactic," said Rulon.

Chapter 28

Leonard's three Mercedes were parked outside the house. Some of Leonard's men were in the house working with laptops at the kitchen table while murmuring solemnly into their cells. Others were outside guarding the house. Granny puttered around the kitchen being ignored by everyone but Batu, who seemed to enjoy her company and proved to be quite handy in the food department. Brother-in-law's team was still in the woods waiting for the Chinese.

When Steenberg had first stepped out of his car in Granny's driveway, his minions had immediately taken up protective positions around him. Yohaba and Rulon were there.

"You came," said Yohaba. "I wasn't sure you would."

"You underestimate my affection for my family," said Steenberg, looking stern and reserved in his grey William Westmancott suit, blue Charvet tie, and black Johnston and Murphy shoes. "You and Rulon."

"Possibly," said Rulon. "But if so, we underestimate it more now than we did a day ago."

"You were in the way," said Steenberg. "No harm would have come to you. But you were in the way. If I had asked you to leave, would you have?"

"With Yohaba, yes," said Rulon.

"My point exactly," said Steenberg. "She is too valuable. Sorry if that offends you."

They went inside the house and Steenberg first spent fifteen minutes alone with Granny in the living room. They spoke together in soft tones, too low for others to hear. Before he got up to join Yohaba and Rulon for their discussion, he kissed Granny three times, alternating cheeks, the Swiss way.

Alex stood in the doorway of his bedroom down the hallway from the living room. He was afraid to go in. It was too crowded. Rulon and Yohaba were in there sitting on the bed, Rulon on the edge with his feet on the floor, and Yohaba with both stocking feet curled up under her and her back against the backboard. Alex had made the bed in the morning and now it was wrinkled. Alex's grandfather Leonard Steenberg sat opposite them in the corner on a stuffed, olive green easy chair that Yohaba had given Alex three years ago for his birthday. Alex never used it. It made an annoying squeak whenever he sat down, though Leonard didn't seem to mind. Maybe he was hard of hearing, thought Alex.

A woven, rust-colored, oval throw rug added color to the room. There was a four-drawer, blond wood dresser against the far wall. Next to that was a curtained window with a shutter that opened outwards. A blown-up, framed picture hung next to the window of Alex, Rulon, and Yohaba rafting down the Payette River in Idaho, orange life jackets, water spraying, and faces lit with exhilaration. That was the time Alex had fallen in and was sucked under what Rulon called "a strainer." Rulon dove in and cut his life jacket off him with a knife to free him. Rulon had said it would be safe but it wasn't. Rulon had lied. Next to the bed was a nightstand and an antique lamp. It didn't offer much light, but it gave off enough for Alex to read by late into the night.

Alex watched the three people in his room stare at each other. He wondered if they were waiting for him to say something.

"Make your case," said Leonard finally to Rulon and Yohaba. "If you have one. But please spare me any emotional appeals."

"Pericles," said Rulon.

"Ah, yes, Pericles," said Steenberg. "The student of Zenos the sophist. He who bribed the mob from the public treasury with amusements and financial distributions. Is that your point? Is that what I am accused of? Pandering to the mob?" Steenberg chuckled.

"No," said Yohaba. "But Pericles was a genius who thought he had all the answers. He eventually caused the downfall of Athens because he thought he had everything under control, but he didn't, and he didn't realize it until it was too late."

"Ah, yes, the plague of typhus," said Steenberg. "Think of me as Thucydides then, Pericles's adversary. I see the plague coming, and I'm determined to stop it. My adversaries better fit the role of Pericles than I. Besides, Pericles started that entire war with Sparta because he married Aspasia, a brothel owner, and she was accused of being impious to the gods and thus Pericles was implicated too. Then his accusers brought up the issue of mismanagement of public funds. He was to be tried, so he contrived a complaint against the Megarians to pull Sparta into a war that would divert attention away from himself. Again, I fail to see the comparison."

Yohaba and Rulon looked to Alex for help, but there was no reaction.

When no response was forthcoming, Leonard said, "I'm afraid you'll have to do better than that."

Yohaba stole a quick look at Alex and said confidently, "Thomas Midgely."

"Thomas Midgely. A gift from Alex, I suspect," said Steenberg. "Freon. Leaded gasoline. Destroyer of the environment. Inadvertent killer of millions. By all means, enlighten me. What is the connection with me you hope to draw? Mad scientist, perhaps?"

"I was thinking more, delusional benefactor of humanity," said Rulon.

Steenberg laughed. "As opposed to a delusional obstructionist like yourself. Elsa is coming. It won't stop. What will humanity do when that fateful day arrives? Perhaps we can all start a hashtag campaign. Or maybe we can hold up our cigarette lighters in the dark and sway back and forth while singing *We Are the World*. Or better yet, let's Twitter everyone to lock arms and blow in the direction of Elsa at the same time. Maybe we can blow it away."

"You're taking our perfectly reasonable position and expanding it to the absurd," said Yohaba.

"Am I?" said Steenberg. "Then please enlighten me. What exactly is your position?"

"We want you to save the world," said Rulon. "No one's trying to stop you. Heck, we've been working alongside you for the past couple of years helping you. So, ask yourself, what's changed now? No, let me answer that. You've changed. There is nothing wrong with your objective. It's the way you're getting there. You're becoming the very thing you hate. You're now this ruthless puppet master who has no regard for human life and believes the end justifies any means. For example, I saved your life four years ago in CERN. Remember that? Now try and square that with what you were trying to do with me yesterday."

Steenberg sighed. "My dear Rulon. While I sympathize with your hurt feelings, I must remind you what is at stake here. In fact, let me save us all a good deal of time." Steenberg paused for effect and spoke slowly and calmly. "If you want me to apologize for wanting to kidnap you and temporarily remove you from the equation, I will. I am truly sorry. Sorry that I had to do it. No, that is not quite right. Let me correct myself. I am genuinely sorry for what I did. There had to have been a better option. In fact, I'm sure there was. Mine was the sin of intellectual laziness.

"But there is something much more at stake here than a few lives or family relationships. There is nothing you can say that will dissuade me from my course. I am trying to save the world. I will save the world. My failure to act would result in the loss not only of billions of lives, but of human existence itself. If you can come up with an argument which supersedes that imperative, then please, I would like to hear it. I take no joy in what I have done, in what I have had to do. Yes, I have caused the loss of life. Hundreds of lives. And perhaps before my plan is fulfilled, tens of thousands more will die. If so, so be it."

At that point, Yohaba and Rulon both rose to interrupt, but Steenberg waved them off and continued. "But perhaps you will say, surely there is another way. And the answer is, yes, there is. In fact, there are eleven other ways, none of which have the same chances of success as the one I am currently pursuing. And all of them have the critical failing that if they are pursued and then found not to be feasible, it will be too late to try another alternative before Elsa strikes. Do you understand?"

Both Rulon and Yohaba nodded dumbly. *He's doing it again*, thought Rulon. *The pixie dust is suffocating me*. For a split second, he thought of making a counter argument with the Colt currently resting in his small-of-back holster, but quickly dismissed it.

"Or perhaps you would prefer taking a more theological tact," said Steenberg when he saw no response forthcoming. "Surely, you might say, God would intervene before such a catastrophe occurred. Has that thought ever crossed your mind? I think it has, because, frankly, it has crossed mine. Allow me to provide you with the answer—the answer you most certainly have already considered. God helps those who help themselves. If he has given us all the tools, and time we need to save ourselves, why should He intervene if we then refuse to utilize his providence?"

"Tell me about those other ways you mentioned," said Yohaba. "If we really work together, I'll bet we can raise the chances of their success beyond your current plan and not have to cost so many lives. So let's do it. Let's work together on this. I love you, but I hate seeing what this is doing to you. I mean how did you ever come to a point where blowing up aquifers in water-starved areas seemed like the right thing to do?"

"It will work," said Steenberg. "That is all the endorsement any plan needs in these circumstances. As sure as we are here in this room, blowing up the aquifers will cause Europe to fund the project to destroy Elsa whether they like it or not. I am already too old. I will die not knowing if my plan worked or not. But just do me this one honor. If it succeeds, I want a modest statue erected of me."

"Where would you like it?" asked Rulon.

"St. Peter's Square," said Steenberg after a moment's thought.

"If that can't be arranged, would you settle for Temple Square in Salt Lake?" asked Rulon. He and Yohaba looked at each other. They had no answers.

"The universe is full of mysteries," said Steenberg. "Why is there anything? Why us? Why the stars, why the earth, why the moon?"

"Moons," said Alex. Steenberg, Yohaba, and Rulon had forgotten Alex was there.

"Not now, Alex," said Yohaba.

"Yes, moons," said Steenberg. "There are many moons, aren't there, son? Why, 173 just in our solar system alone."

"That's wrong," said Alex. "There are 182."

Steenberg chuckled softly. "Oh, how I have missed our little conversations. Yes, I deliberately left out the moons around our solar system's dwarf planets. Ceres, Pluto, Haumea, Makemake, and Eris. Good catch, son. But those planets only have eight moons, so the total number in our solar system is 181, not 182. But excellent, Alex. I know only a few people who would have known even that much."

"I'm not talking about the dwarf planets," said Alex.

"Thank you, Alex," said Yohaba. "Isn't *Star Trek* on now? Don't you have someplace to be?"

"I'm talking about earth," said Alex. "You were talking about earth, and so I was talking about earth. I'm not stupid. Moons. Moons. Don't you know anything?"

Steenberg looked to Yohaba for help. "No one thinks you're stupid," said Yohaba. "Say goodbye to your grandfather. He has to go." Steenberg stood up.

"I hope we are back on speaking terms, Rulon," said Steenberg. "I am truly sorry. I give you my word, I will never harm you again. Never. I was wrong. We could have talked it out. I should have talked it out. Please don't give up on me." He gave Rulon a hug which Rulon reciprocated.

"I have a response on the tip of my tongue," said Rulon. "Just give me a week."

"Nonsense," said Steenberg. "You'll no doubt think of something to say just as my car pulls out of the driveway." They both smiled.

Steenberg turned to Yohaba. She made no sound, but tears rolled down her cheeks. "Now, child," he said, and hugged her too. "Take care of yourself and Rulon. If you ever wish to come back, there will always be a place for you." Lastly, he turned to Alex.

"Your breadth of knowledge never ceases to amaze me," said Steenberg. "By the way, my latest chess partner appears to no longer delight in my company. Perhaps you and I could play each other over the internet."

"The earth has two moons," responded Alex. Steenberg sighed, looked at his watch, then looked piercingly at Yohaba before focusing once more on Alex.

"I hope your sister didn't put you up to this," said Steenberg, his patience at an end. "Never mind. If this is about quasi-satellite 2003YN, then you need to know two things. First, Einstein knew about that very small moon, asteroid, quasi-satellite, or whatever you want to call it when he made his calculations in the nineteen-fifties. Second, it left the earth's orbit over ten years ago. It's no longer a factor. It was baked into the original calculations and now it is irrelevant. So, if there is nothing else. I have to go. I will contact you next weekend about the chess game."

Steenberg nodded to all in the room. Alex got out of his way and Leonard walked out.

"He doesn't know anything," said Alex after Steenberg had left.

"Alex, Alex, Alex," said Rulon, shaking his head ruefully. "When God made you, he broke the mold. But thanks for trying."

"Do you know what the word 'rude' means?" asked Yohaba. "If you look it up in the dictionary, it says, *See 'my brother Alex.'*"

"I don't believe you," said Alex. Behind them someone coughed, and everyone turned to look. Steenberg had come back and was standing in the doorway.

"Okay, Alex," he said with resigned patience. "I can spare you two minutes. Make your case."

"Technically asteroid 2016H03 is a moon," said Alex.

"I never heard of it," said Steenberg. "When was it discovered?"

"April 27th."

"By whom?"

"By the asteroid survey telescope at Hawaii University on Haleakala."

"How big is it?"

"One hundred meters."

Steenberg looked down, deep in thought. When he looked up again, he said, "Hawaii University. They're associated with the Center for Near-Earth Orbit at the Jet Propulsion lab in Pasadena. I know someone there. I'll make a call."

"I've done the calculations," said Alex. "Do you want to see them?"

"Yes. What do they say? Does Elsa react?"

"A little bit."

"How little?"

"Hardly anything. It's only a hundred meters long."

"Is Elsa still going to hit the earth?"

"No. It will miss by 327 miles," said Alex.

"Wow! Wow!" said Yohaba in astonishment. "When did you first realize this!?"

"A few months ago," said Alex.

"Well, why didn't you tell anybody? What were you thinking? Don't you think if the world is not going to be destroyed that you should tell someone?"

"No," said Alex. "The world wasn't destroyed yesterday either. I didn't call you. Are you mad at me about that, too?" Rulon burst out laughing.

"Fine," said Yohaba in exasperation. "But why didn't you tell us when we were talking about it just a few hours ago?"

"I did tell you," said Alex. "Oh wait. Maybe I didn't."

Steenberg's face was now an ashen grey. "Can I see your calculations?" he asked. Alex reached into his pants pocket and took out a piece of paper that had been folded and refolded down to the size of a matchbook.

"Here," he said, handing it to Steenberg. "You can have it. I don't want it anymore." Steenberg carefully unfolded the paper. The single-lined page was covered on both sides with Alex's incredibly small but precise handwriting. So many numbers and symbols the page was practically unreadable.

Steenberg looked at it for a half minute then asked Alex, "Are all these calculations pertinent to our new asteroid and Elsa?"

"No. Just this part," said Alex. He turned the page over in Steenberg's hand and pointed to a set of numbers separated from the rest by a drawn line.

"What's the rest of it?" asked Rulon.

"Private stuff that's none of your business," said Alex.

Steenberg said, "I'll need a few hours with this. If true, this changes everything, but I have to be sure. I have to go now."

Visibly shaken, he turned and left the room without saying goodbye. After a moment, Alex also wandered off.

Rulon was alone with Yohaba. They hugged each other and with their mouths close to each other's ears murmured words of relief and gratitude. "I feel like the weight of the world is off my shoulders," breathed Yohaba. "I know Alex is right. It has to be right. Oh please, let him be right."

"I knew the world wasn't going to end like this," said Rulon, and he squeezed Yohaba tighter. "It is right. I can feel it. This is what Alex does. He doesn't make mistakes about things like this, and he won't lie. Did you see your grandfather's reaction? He knows, too. Oh yeah, he'll double-check the numbers. Sure. But then it'll be mission accomplished. Our lives can go back to normal." Rulon pulled a little away from Yohaba. "I was thinking about this the other day. I've got a great idea for increasing milk production. It will require a little time and a little capital investment, but I'm sure it will pay for itself in a couple of years."

"My grandfather's got billions now that he won't know what to do with," said Yohaba. "Tell him you want that Fullwood Merlin milking machine you're always talking about. The robot one. He owes us. Besides, we're the only family he's got. We've earned a bonus. We'll use it to buy some better milking equipment." Yohaba was excited.

"My dad won't like it," said Rulon. "He'll put up a fight, but I won't back down this time. Dang it! I'm getting that Fullwood whether he likes it or not."

"You tell him," said Yohaba gleefully. "He's not the boss of you. And the world's not going to end. Yahoo!"

A gigantic boom shook the house. Rulon and Yohaba pulled apart. Then another boom. Alex, Granny, and Batu ran into the room.

"That thunder sounded pretty close," said Rulon with a nervous laugh.

"The forest is on fire," said Granny.

"I'll be right back," said Rulon.

❧

Just as Rulon tore out of the house with the Colt in his hand, Leonard's three Mercedes came roaring back into the circular driveway and skidded to a gravel-spewing stop. A man with an Uzi jumped out of the first car and yelled, "Your idiot friends blocked the road."

"Get Steenberg in the house," yelled Rulon without breaking stride. The man started to reply but by now others were emerging from the cars. The man with the Uzi turned to give them orders. Steenberg, looking anxiously backward over his shoulder at Rulon, was quickly ushered into the house by several armed men.

Rulon ran down the road but grew tired after a hundred yards and slowed to a fast walk. He called Brother-in-law on his cell phone as he marched. To his surprise, Brother-in-law answered.

"Where are you?" gasped Rulon. "I'm coming."

"Why, you sound nervous as a long-tailed cat in a room full of rockin' chairs," said Brother-in-law in vintage hillbilly.

"Don't hillbilly me," barked Rulon. "What happened?"

"That's two wrong questions," said Brother-in-law.

"Geez," groaned Rulon. "It never stops with you. Okay. Who are you with?"

"Better," said Brother-in-law. "Does Yohaba by any chance speak Chinese?"

"No, not that I'm aware of," said Rulon. "So, it's the Chinese then. Are any of them hurt?"

"So far mainly feelings, but you better get a move on. We pitched them a duck fit with a tail on it."

"What happened?"

"Walked right into it. Thought they were heading to a taffy pull. Boy, were they surprised when we unleashed hell on 'em." Brother-in-law chuckled to himself. "But if'n they figure out there's but three of us critters, they might get notions. Especially one of 'em. Man, he's like some kinda Commie-mutant-swamp-gator with a sore tooth. We got 'em all rounded up and disarmed. But they're getting edgy. Need you to come and sweet-talk 'em, or I may have to improvise. Can you do that? And I don't wanna be looking over my shoulder for the rest of my life either. I'm this close to shooting 'em and being done with it, so you better come up with somethin' good."

"We don't shoot prisoners," said Rulon. "I'll think of something. Where are you? Can I ask that now?"

"Just keep coming down the road." Brother-in-law clicked off.

Rulon stuck his phone in his jacket pocket. When a Claymore detonates, its C-4 gives off a distinctive tar-like smell. Rulon caught a whiff of it mixed with burning wood, which confirmed what he already suspected. He kept walking and now could clearly smell burnt pine trees. If there had been a fire, he couldn't see any evidence. Gotta love Switzerland. With all its rain, nothing burned for long. He kept walking until he came to a barrier made up of four big pine trees lying next to each other neatly across the road. He walked around to check their bases, and sure enough, they had been sawn cleanly through with a chainsaw. Dang that Brother-in-law.

Once past the improvised roadblock, Rulon broke into a jog. The sky was a rich blue and sunlight had turned the upper canyon walls purple. Rulon had come 500 meters by then but still couldn't see anybody. The smell of C-4 intensified just as Rulon rounded a bend and saw a green Skoda four-door sedan with four flat tires. The torn-up gravel showed where the tire spikes had once lain. Thirty meters further on was another green Skoda with a shattered windshield that had careened off the road into a tree.

He heard voices just beyond the second car. Brother-in-law was there with Murph and Benny. They had their guns trained on eight men dressed like civilians, sitting on the road with their legs crossed and their hands on top of their heads. One guy towered over the others, and Rulon wondered why he was sitting on a chair when it hit him that he was sitting on the ground too. The mutant swamp gator. Tripod was there as usual leaning right up against Brother-in-law's leg. Rulon had given up calling to Tripod when Brother-in-law was around. A little further down the road was a black Skoda 10-seater van with all the doors open.

"You missed all the fun," said Brother-in-law. Rulon walked around the brooding, bruised, and angry Chinese hit team. They all turned their heads and glared at him as he circled, particularly the big one.

"Oooh, I think they know you," said Benny to Rulon.

Rulon turned back to the group of men on the ground and held both hands up. "I come in peace.

I am your friend. I hold you no ill will, my brothers. You are all pawns in a bigger game. I know this is not personal for you. You are merely doing the bidding of your cruel master." None of the Chinese answered. Brother-in-law, Murphy, and Benny were too stunned to speak. "Oh, I forgot," said Rulon. "You don't speak English. Well, there goes any chance of solving this peacefully. I guess we'll have to start shooting them." Rulon scratched his chin. "Now, which one first?" At those words, the men in the group fidgeted nervously. "I'll be danged," said Rulon. "They speak English. They're just tongue-tied."

Rulon noticed seven of the eight team members all looking at the same man. *Ah-ha, the leader,* thought Rulon, *and most likely the most fluent in English.* The man was well muscled, with a mustache, a goatee and an intelligent face. His left sleeve was torn from elbow to wrist, but other than that he looked unhurt.

The man cleared his throat and said slowly but in accented but relatively clear English, "You cannot kill us all. There would be international incident. If you let us leave, we will leave quietly and not come back." He searched for more words and found them. "No hard feelings," he said and grinned.

Brother-in-law laughed out loud and said, "You'll also leave quietly if we kill you all. And actually we can kill you all. It's really simple. We won and you lost. And I don't give a flying…"

"Yeah," said Benny, "you weren't worried about an international incident when you came here to kill us."

"I know how Marshall Dillon would handle this," chimed in Murphy in his finest western drawl.

Rulon cut everyone off, "Hey, I'm the negotiator here," he said.

"Clock's tickin'," said Brother-in-law.

Rulon rubbed the bridge of his nose. He could feel a headache coming on. He signaled Brother-in-law to settle down and said to the prisoner with the mustache, "In situations like this I like to go for a win-win. For me that would be you leaving here alive and us being assured you'll never come after us again. What do you think? Can we get there from here?" At that Brother-in-law made a disgusted sound and gave the Remington shotgun he was carrying an emphatic one-handed pump, managing in the process to catch the ejected shell with his right hand. A neat little party trick that impressed everyone, including the Chinese.

"Look in the van," said Brother-in-law sharply.

"Wait here," said Rulon to the prisoners. "In the meantime, you guys can all take your hands off your heads. Just don't do anything stupid. Okay?" Looking wary the eight men slowly dropped their hands. "Wait," said Rulon. "Do I hear growling? Is one of you growling? It's you, isn't it?" Rulon looked at the giant, who had a smirky grin on his face and the body language of a man spoiling for a fight. Rulon shook his head in disbelief.

"The van," said Brother-in-law.

Rulon walked twenty meters over to the van and looked in the cargo space. "Wow, guns-R-us. And look here. Spare car batteries and cables with little alligator clips. And guys, c'mon. I'm pretty sure flame throwers are prohibited by the Geneva Convention."

"Just in civilian areas," said Benny.

Rulon knew killing them all wouldn't solve the problem. In fact, it would only up the ante and make things worse. Next time they'd be facing a dozen Chinese hit men with even more incentive to knock them all off. And if they were tied in with the Chinese government, which Rulon strongly suspected they were, the Chinese would hack every U.S. government database there was to track Rulon and the team down again and kill them one by one. It would never end until they were all dead. Rulon walked back to the group.

"I really would have preferred a peaceful solution based on mutual trust and respect," said Rulon.

"This ain't the knights of the round table," said Brother-in-law. "Why don't you just go back to the house and turn the television up loud. We'll take it from here."

"Excuse me," said Rulon to the Chinese. He walked over to Brother-in-law and together they walked a few more feet out of earshot of everyone else. "Okay, what's your idea, then?" he asked.

"I've thought it over very carefully," said Brother-in-law, "and we have to kill them all then kill the guy who wants us dead before he sends another team after us. We get the name from Steenberg, and if he won't tell us then we torture it out of him."

"Can't you think of a more violent way to handle this?" asked Rulon. He walked back to confront the prisoners again. He took off his cowboy hat and held it in his two hands while he spoke.

"We need to settle this here and now. We know why you are here. We killed the son of an important man. He sent you. But you need to know his son's death was an accident. We were trying to rescue a girl he had kidnapped, and a mine tipped over by accident and hit the house where he was. It was just bad luck for him. We didn't plan it to happen and didn't want it to happen, but, damn it, sometimes when you kidnap people bad things happen to you."

Rulon looked around at his audience but couldn't tell if he was reaching them or not. Behind him was Brother-in-law, the ticking time bomb. And then there was his own conscience pummeling him from the other direction. It didn't seem fair.

Rulon's next words came out faster and harder, like he was chewing on a tough steak. "Damn it! You came here to kill me, my friends, and my family." Rulon took his phone out of his pocket and flipped it to the leader. "So why don't you call your boss now and tell him from me to grow up and take the consequences for his own greed and stupidity."

The Chinese leader caught the phone, warily dialed a number, and held the phone to his ear. "That's enough," said Rulon. "Toss it back." The man, looking puzzled, ended the call before someone answered, and threw Rulon back his phone. Rulon verified their boss's phone number had been captured and tossed the phone to Brother-in-law. "Hang onto that," he said, and turned his attention back to the Chinese.

"If your boss hadn't been poisoning his own people by the thousands with his industrial waste, our boss never would have had any leverage over him in the first place. But maybe you don't know that part. Anyway, that's the guy you're taking orders from. Think about it, and while you're at it, try seeing this from our perspective. Why the big van? There were only eight of you and you already had two cars. Wait. I got it. You were planning to kidnap us and then what? Oh, that's right, the car batteries with the alligator clips. And let's not forget the flame thrower. What were you planning to do, burn us alive after you were done torturing us? Am I getting warm?"

The three Americans started clapping. "He sees the light. He sees the light," said Murphy in his best imitation of an old-time Baptist preacher. Rulon ignored him and slowly started unzipping his leather jacket.

"I don't think I can trust you," said Rulon to the leader. "It won't mean anything to you to swear on a Bible, and I haven't got a copy of Chairman Mao's Little Red Book."

The man said, "I give you my word as an officer in the Chinese army. If you let us go, we will take our things and quietly leave the country."

"Said the man with the car batteries and the flame thrower," said Rulon. He stared hard at the team leader. "You know, it just occurred to me," said Rulon. "There is a solution. How about we tie you up, take your passports, and dump you back in the van together with your weapons, a bunch of terrorist literature, and the floor plans of the Swiss parliament building, and drop you off at the local police station. How 'bout that? Think that might get you off our backs for the next twenty years?" Rulon was building up to something, and Brother-in-law, Murphy, and Benny exchanged approving looks.

"Oh, wait a second," said Rulon, suddenly calm while slowly taking off his jacket. "We don't have any rope. So how am I going get you to stay in the van when we drop you off?"

"You could say 'pretty please,'" offered Murphy.

Rulon was on a roll. He folded his jacket neatly then threw it carelessly over his shoulder in a heap on the ground. He was wearing a shoulder holster, but the holster didn't have a gun. It held a 4-pound Wilton Demolition model sledge hammer with a rubber coated, ten-inch spring steel handle and a leather strap. "I'm not gonna shoot ya. Nah, I can't do that. And I'm not gonna burn you alive. In fact, if you play your cards right, you'll be home for Christmas. That's December twenty-fifth in case you don't know. Someday you'll thank me for this."

The prisoners looked at each other, all talking feverishly at the same time. The leader tried to quiet everyone down but was no longer in control of his team. A well-built man in a black bandanna took charge, had everyone's attention, and began issuing commands. The prisoners spread out and faced Rulon in a variety of martial arts poses. They let out a collective shout which Rulon interpreted to mean, "Come and get it, fat boy!"

Rulon took his Colt out of his small-of-back holster and flipped it to Brother-in-law. Next, he took the hammer out of the holster, wrapped his hand through the leather strap, and swung the hammer back and forth a few times, liking the heft and feeling the power of it surge up through his arm like an electric current—a feeling he hadn't experienced since CERN and the Russians. The Chinese unconsciously drew closer together.

Rulon's breathing kicked up a few notches, and the hair on the back of his neck stood up. He closed his eyes for an instant. Memories of CERN came flooding back and also of the fight in the Marseilles bar when he first gripped Freya and together had torn that place to pieces before he was done. He held Freya to his nose now and inhaled the smell of leather, cold steel, and something he couldn't identify. Perhaps dried blood. He opened his eyes, and they were red. "You done got me worked up," he said calmly. "I hope you're satisfied."

In the same calm voice, Rulon said, "All I know is, I gotta think of some way to keep you in the van for the police to find." No one spoke. "Now, if you don't like my suggestion then you need to come up with something yourselves. I don't know why I have to do all the heavy lifting here just to save your hides. You see that guy over there?" Rulon pointed at Brother-in-law. "I suggest you think of something quick because he will kill you if I don't do something. You understand?"

The eight prisoners shouted something in unison again. Their blood was also up. The mutant pushed his way to the front and, sporting a gap-toothed grin, waved Rulon forward. "Okay then," said Rulon. To Brother-in-law and the others, he said, "Keep them in a tight circle for me, will ya, boys?" With all eyes on him, Rulon firmly sat his cowboy hat back on his head. Next, he rolled his shoulders a couple of times just to loosen up and took a few deep breaths. Satisfied, he charged into the group of Chinese hitmen like a message from Thor.

Chapter 29

Rulon wiggled his jaw back and forth and winced. "I wonder where this came from?" he asked to no one in particular.

From the middle seat of the white Mercedes van, Benny said, "I think I saw one of them catch you with a spinning back kick, Mr. Hurt." It was 11 p.m., and they were on their way home after dropping off the black Skoda van in front of the Bergün Gemeindeverwaltung, the government administration building that housed the local police station. Inside the Skoda were the eight Chinese trussed up with duct tape.

"Funny. I don't remember that," said Rulon.

"Fog of war, Mr. Hurt," said Murphy.

Brother-in-law was driving because Rulon didn't feel like it. His hands were bruised pretty badly, and he'd had to yank a couple of dislocated fingers back into place after the fight. Plus, besides the jaw, one eye was swollen shut, and his ears were ringing. "And would you guys stop calling me 'Mr. Hurt.'"

"Yes, God of Thunder," said Murphy. Benny and Brother-in-law cracked up.

"All right, dial it down, guys," said Brother-in-law when he stopped laughing. "Cowboy's got a lot to process. Like how's he gonna square this with Yohaba." To Rulon, he said, "Ya know, I wasn't really gonna kill 'em. I was just funnin' with ya. I had enough Midazolam to knock them all out for a week."

"Or maybe you're just funnin' with me now," said Rulon. "Look, the narrative for Yohaba is the following—you were going to kill them and…"

Brother-in-law cut him off, "Yeah, and you saved their lives by beating the living daylights out of them with Freya. Makes sense to me. How 'bout you boys?"

"If the God of Thunder says it's so, then so let it be written," said Murphy.

"Can we drop this?" asked Rulon. The van went silent for a few seconds until Brother-in-law spoke up again.

"We need to find a Walmart or something," he said. "I'm almost out of duct tape."

"Good luck with that," said Rulon. "This is small town Switzerland. Sidewalks get rolled up at six, and the people would be marching with pitchforks and torches before they'd let a Walmart come in here."

"I've got to ask," said Benny. "That hammer of yours. Where'd you come up with that? Any serious martial arts guy will tell you it's a terrible personal combat weapon."

"Yeah, yeah," said Rulon. "I've heard all the arguments. If you swing and miss, then you lay yourself wide open to a knife. Blah blah. But you just gotta swing coming down, you know, like chopping wood, and not try to take everyone's head off with one shot. You gotta trust the hammer. It's best to go for the legs. People can't stand on a compound fracture. Once that happens gravity takes over. It's simple Newtonian physics."

"Yeah, makes sense," said Benny. "But you're extra strong. The average person couldn't control the backswing, but you can. Right?" Rulon looked down humbly.

"What's your strategy for taking on a group?" chimed in Murphy. "Is it like you're an M1 tank with a hay baler in front, or do you think of yourself as more like a snow plow, sucking them up and spitting them out behind you?"

"Totally different strategy when there's five or more," said Rulon. "When that's the case, you've got to go for the toughest guy, not necessarily the leader."

"Is that why you took out the mutant first?" asked Benny.

"Exactly," said Rulon. "Make an example. Men don't fight so well when they see what you did to their buddy, and they start up-chucking. That's a known fact. And another thing…"

As Rulon described the finer nuances of hammer fighting to his eager audience, Brother-in-law drove with an easy smile on his face, listening. He thought about Yohaba and Rulon and the chance friendship of their first meeting. He loved the ranch life in Idaho. Loved Africa too. He gave a little click with his tongue and Tripod was immediately between the seats at his side. Brother-in-law reached down without looking and started rubbing his ears. He loved Tripod. Thought about his two kids still in the Congo. Thought about Batu. Thought about the thin man and the Russian Spetznaz team he was surely sending to find them. *The only easy day was yesterday*, he thought. The voices in the van seemed far away.

Brother-in-law turned left into the long driveway up to Granny's house and killed the high beams so as not to blind Steenberg's men guarding the road. He proceeded cautiously and was pleased to see the two damaged Skodas were gone and the felled trees had been sawed up and stacked. A man dressed in a dirty white dress shirt and suit pants stepped out of the trees. He was holding a SIG assault rifle that Rulon had loaned him. He peered intently at the van and then waved them through. Brother-in-law waved back and sped up.

Yohaba and Batu were waiting for them in the yard.

⁓⁓⁓

Once everyone was in the house, Batu let out a gasp when she saw Rulon's face. "He just does it for attention," said Yohaba. She walked up to Rulon and gave him a big hug and a kiss. Rulon winced in pain, but Yohaba ignored him. She reached inside his jacket, felt Freya, and shook her head.

"Hello, dear," said Rulon.

"Hello, dear," said Yohaba.

"Where's everybody?" asked Rulon.

"They're all together in Alex's room. Leonard's watching the thumb drive with Polykov's message. But guess what? Alex was right. Leonard worked the numbers, and I've double-checked them. It's a slam dunk. Divine intervention. The human race will muddle on."

"That's a relief," said Rulon.

"Would anybody like something to eat?" asked Yohaba to everyone standing awkwardly in the living room. "I'll bet you boys are hungry." Hearty agreement. "There's stuff in the fridge," she said.

"We'll get it," said Brother-in-law. He nodded to Batu and the two went off with Murphy and Benny, leaving Rulon and Yohaba by themselves. Rulon walked over and closed the door behind them.

When they were alone, Yohaba said, "That damn hammer of yours. Look at you. Just look at you. What have you done to yourself? How come no one else looks beat up? Why is it always just you?"

"I'm thinking of renaming Freya 'Florence Nightingale,'" said Rulon. "You know how many lives she saved today? Eight."

Yohaba came over to Rulon and threw her arms around him. "You big galoot."

"But I'm your big galoot," said Rulon, grinning through swollen lips. "But you should have seen this one guy," said Rulon once he got his bruised arms around Yohaba's slender body. "A fine-looking specimen. Trophy sized."

"Was it worse than CERN?" she asked.

"Not even close," said Rulon. "We're not going to talk about CERN. Remember? No one died today. We simply made them an offer they couldn't refuse."

"What was that?"

Rulon sat Yohaba down and told her what happened. In the end, he had tried to soften it for the Chinese, hoping to spark some sense of future gratitude. "Yeah, we took their passports. But we didn't drop them off with their weapons or plant any terrorist info on them. We could've really socked it to them, if we'd wanted. I think the way we left it, it'll take a couple of months, but it'll all get sorted out eventually."

"They'll turn you in," said Yohaba.

"That's the beauty of it," said Rulon. "They can't. If they do, out come the weapons and the terrorist literature. They brought some nasty stuff with them, all Chinese made." Rulon chuckled. "Can't pin that on us. We gave them a story. If they stick to it, they'll be okay. They were rock climbing, and all tied together when one of them fell off and dragged the rest."

"But where's their climbing equipment?" asked Yohaba. "No one's going to fall for that."

"I didn't have time to write them a script," said Rulon. "They're going to have to show some initiative."

"But you said you left them all wrapped up in duct tape," said Yohaba. "How are they going to explain that? *Uh, we fell off a cliff and got terribly injured then wrapped ourselves in duct tape then drove to the police station using our noses.*"

Rulon looked stunned for a few seconds, then blurted. "Well, they're just going to have to be creative. That's all there is to it." Yohaba gave him a look. He tried avoiding her eyes, but she grabbed his hurt jaw and made him look at her. "Ouch," he said. "It seemed like such a cunning plan a few hours ago."

"You've barely slept for two days," said Yohaba. "Classic case of battle fatigue. I'll cut you some slack. Do you think they might try to tie them to Paradeplatz?"

"Any other country but Switzerland, yeah, I think that would be tempting. Tie up the loose ends and all that. But here, no. Their passports said they only arrived yesterday. The Swiss will give them a hard time but play it straight. Once they check the plane manifests and security tapes and see when they arrived, they'll know it wasn't them at Paradeplatz. By the way, the big guy wasn't Chinese. He was North Korean. I guess he was with them on some kind of lend-lease program. Come to think of it, I hope I haven't added those loon buckets to our enemy list." Rulon paused to consider that.

"With our luck," said Yohaba sadly. But then perking up, she said, "What's wrong with me? The world's not going to end. For the first time in four years, we don't have to wake up with that hanging over our heads."

"Yeah, yeah," said Rulon. "Silver linings everywhere. You got any ice?" Yohaba left to get some from the freezer.

When she came back, Rulon was stretched out on the couch. She squeezed next to him and said, "Looks like everyone's gone to bed." She held a bag of ice against his swollen eye. He smiled with his eyes closed and rolled over. "My love," she said, but Rulon was fast asleep. She held the ice in place, feeling numb inside. Lack of sleep, too much worry, too many guns, too many enemies, the end of the world. It was all too much. She sat there, nodded off herself, and the ice bag slipped from her hand.

A half hour later, as Rulon and Yohaba were sleeping, Tripod came padding over and licked Rulon's face. Brother-in-law stood out in the hallway carrying an M16. He watched the sleeping couple for a half a minute, then softly slapped his thigh. Tripod immediately joined him, and they were out the door. Another night patrol.

ᏬᎾᏬᎾ

The thin man and Captain Gromanko walked together across Red Square. The captain wore a thick coat, the thin man only his suit jacket. No one who survived the battle of Stalingrad ever complained about the cold again. South was the Moskva River, in front of them was the GUM department store, and next to it the Kazan Cathedral. Lenin's mausoleum was behind them and the St. Basil's Cathedral was to their right.

"Does the date June 24, 1945 mean anything to you?" asked the thin man of his young protégé. "Does it swell your heart with pride, Captain?"

"Yes, Director-General," replied Captain Gromanko. "It was the date of the Moscow Victory Parade after we crushed the fascists. I believe it took place right here in Red Square."

The thin man stopped and turned around, holding out his arms to encompass the square. "When Moscow was under siege, men left from here directly to the front. It was glorious, though many did not return."

"Today," said the young captain, "we do not appreciate as we should the sacrifices that were made then."

"I was there that day. Standing right there." The thin man pointed to a spot near Lenin's Mausoleum. "I watched on that June 24th as they threw the banners of the defeated

German divisions at the foot of the crypt. You cannot imagine the pride of those of us who survived. I thought the sky would open that day and take us all to heaven. Yes, you heard correctly—to heaven. We had so much pride. It was Russian blood that defeated Hitler. Don't ever believe those liars. It was not the Americans, and it was certainly not the British."

"Yes, Director-General," said the captain. "And there was Stalin."

"Yes, Stalin the butcher," said the thin man. "A single death is a tragedy, a million deaths is a statistic. Who but a madman would ever say such a thing?"

"I don't know," replied the captain, not quite understanding the Director-General's opinion on the subject but not wishing to become either a tragedy or a statistic.

The thin man sensed his young captain's dilemma and chuckled. "Enough of this maudlin reminiscing. Let us now finalize *our* little tragedy. You are satisfied with the plan then?"

"Completely," said Gromanko. "Idaho is the surest chokepoint. He has a father there, and a ranch that he is emotionally attached to. It would be out of character for him not to return for the planting season."

"And the Chinese would not back off and leave him to us?" asked the thin man.

"No. They had a team already on the ground. They are very confident of success."

"So were we," said the thin man, "so were we." He raised a mildly accusing eyebrow in Gromenko's direction. "I am not a betting man, Captain."

"No, sir."

"But if I were, I would bet on the Cowboy. I think the Chinese have not met him before. They will have to learn like the rest of us."

Yes, sir."

"And the Swiss?"

"Not in a cooperative mood, sir. Not since Paradeplatz. But perhaps that will change. They have arrested two of his accomplices."

"Perhaps then," said the thin man. "Or maybe time will bring them around. But now back to work. Your plan is simple. Much simpler than last time."

"Too simple, sir?"

"A bullet is simple. Simplicity is not a flaw."

"Thank you, sir. I know eliminating Hurt is important to you."

"He is like gangrene to me."

👁️‍🗨️

Chapter 30

In the dark Brother-in-law first did a silent circle of the house. He was set to travel light and quiet. He wore his Bata Vellies, and carried a small backpack, his Browning .22, and an M16. Tripod hopped along beside. Brother-in-law stopped first to talk to two of Steenberg's men who were on patrol around the house. All of Steenberg's men wore suits and smooth-soled dress shoes. When the day started, none of them expected to be traipsing around in the woods. Brother-in-law told them to call ahead to the rest of their team who were out there somewhere and tell them he and the dog would be prowling around and not to get trigger happy.

From there Brother-in-law continued around the house, keeping just inside the tree line, when to his surprise he found Steenberg pacing the garden with Batu, deep in conversation. Steenberg's minion Altheuer was also there, standing near the cellar steps holding an iPad. Brother-in-law watched from the shadows for a minute and was about to continue his patrol when the dim light of a cellphone illuminated Batu's face, and he figured things were about to get interesting.

Batu spoke amicably then urgently in English into the phone before handing it to Steenberg and asking him to hold on. A minute went by, then another. Finally, someone picked up on the other end. Steenberg introduced himself over the phone in Russian. When it appeared it could be a long conversation, Brother-in-law lay flat and edged closer on his stomach. At one point Steenberg snapped his fingers to get Altheuer's attention and said, *"Machen Sie es,"* which Brother-in-law understood to mean *do it*. A minute later Altheuer nodded back, and Steenberg spoke into the phone a single phrase, *"Èto budet sdelano,"* and hung up. *It is done.*

Puzzled but with work to do, Brother-in-law and Tripod crawled on their bellies back into the forest. Once on their feet again, they made a couple of large concentric circles with every turn moving further from the house like bees searching for flowers. After two hours they came across the rest of Steenberg's men.

The forest was black as pitch and very still when Brother-in-law walked up to them, having first announced his presence so he wouldn't get shot. Two of the men were in a huddle with flashlights surrounding a third who was wounded and sitting bare chested on a log. His left forearm was wrapped in the remains of his shirt. A tinge of blood seeped through the white fabric. The two uninjured men had their weapons out—a SIG pistol and an H&K G36 assault rifle, the standard issue of the German armed forces. The injured man was on the phone.

"What happened?" asked Brother-in-law. A man in his mid-thirties with a German accent, shaved head, rolled-up sleeves, angry face, and the H&K spoke first. He appeared to be the leader. Their man had been walking back to the house when a Chinese guy came out of nowhere with a knife. Their guy had thrown up his arm in defense and taken three deep cuts before he could get his gun out. By then his screams had summoned help. The attacker fled but unfortunately with the gun.

Steenberg had brought eight guards with him. Two had been left to guard the house while the other six kept watch on the road and the woods. As soon as the attack occurred three of the guards in the forest rushed back to the house to strengthen its defenses. One of them would be coming back soon with the van to pick up the others.

The injured man looked at Brother-in-law, held out the phone, and said, "He wants to talk to you," in a thick German accent. Brother-in-law gave a command to Tripod and took the phone. Tripod hopped off into the dark on a proximity patrol.

"Orin," said Steenberg over the phone, "my man says there is a Chinese gentleman lurking in the woods. Do you think there is more than one?"

"Doubt it. Most likely, one got dropped off to watch the road before we ambushed them. Could be more, but I doubt it. And this guy wasn't much of a threat—leastways until he got your guy's gun."

"Why do you say that?"

"He never tried to rescue his buddies."

"Right. Of course," said Steenberg. "What are you going to do now, Orin?"

"Pest control."

"Orin?"

"What?"

"Were you really going to kill me when you got back to the hotel?"

Brother-in-law paused before answering. "I would have made it quick." He waited, then chuckled and said, "I doubt it. But I'd be lying if I didn't tell you for a while there it seemed like a real good idea. At least up until I found out you were only going to knock the Cowboy out."

"Orin. If it should ever seem like a good idea again, please keep in mind that I'm working to locate and rescue your two sons in the Congo. At considerable expense, I might add. That just might be a good reason to keep me alive."

"Yeah, that was one of the reasons."

"Was there another?"

"Your granddaughter's soft-headed husband talked me out of it. Look, I got work to do." Brother-in-law signed off and handed the phone back to the injured man. He stood looking at him for a second and said, "You'll live." He turned next to their bald-headed leader. "I'm going after the polecat who done this. Show me where it happened."

The man took Brother-in-law fifty yards down the road to a spot twenty yards into the forest. Both men shone their flashlights into the brush. The area of the attack had been thoroughly chewed up with the scuffle and by the men who had come to the rescue. Brother-in-law walked gingerly around the scene, stopping now and then to crouch down and touch the edges of a heel print. The forest bed of leaves and pine needles with large gashes of earth told a story. A life and death struggle in a hundred square feet.

"What do you see?" asked the German.

"He's five-foot-nine, weighs a hundred and twenty pounds, and is left-handed," said Brother-in-law.

"You can see all that?" said the German, astounded.

"Not really," said Brother-in-law with an easy grin. "But I know the shoes he's wearing now, and I know where he headed off. That's a good start."

"Can I help you?" asked the German. Brother-in-law considered the request. He'd be tracking someone through the woods in the dark, and he'd need to carry a flashlight and be constantly taking the NVG on and off. He decided he could only spare one hand for a weapon. He handed the German his M16.

"You can take this back for me," he said.

"Anything else?" asked the German as he slung the rifle over his shoulder.

"Nope, I got this one," said Brother-in-law. He gave an odd warbling whistle and Tripod barked somewhere to his left. The German headed back to his team carrying the M16 and his own H&K. He passed Tripod on the way and gave him a wide berth.

ᕦᕤ

Brother-in-law was on his knees rummaging through his pack when Tripod came up and stuck his nose in the opening. "Get outta here," said Brother-in-law in a furious whisper. "I only brought two zone bars, and they're both for me." Tripod pulled his head out of the pack and growled at Brother-in-law. "I've created a monster," said Brother-in-law. He grabbed Tripod by both his ears and held his disfigured face an inch away from his own. "All right. You can have half, but this is the last time." Satisfied, Tripod sat on his haunches and waited patiently while Brother-in-law unwrapped a bar and broke it in two. "Here," he said, and tossed half to Tripod, who caught it in the air and quickly devoured it.

Brother-in-law ate his half in silence, letting the dark curl around him, getting in the mood for a hunt. He thought about his adversary. Why had he attacked one of Steenberg's men? It made no sense except for wanting to get his hands on a gun. They were after Rulon, not Steenberg or his men. A diversion perhaps? A desperate act of suicidal madness? Brother-in-law decided he was after a gun and the house would be the ultimate objective. It had everything the desperate man wanted. Guns, food, a victim, and a chance to complete the mission. *Idiot*, thought Brother-in-law. *Doesn't know when he's licked.*

Brother-in-law took the 4-barrel NVG out of the backpack and put it on. He activated it, verified it was in working order, and out of deference to the limited battery power immediately turned it off again. He let it dangle by its strap around his neck. He next applied his camo face paint.

"Okay," he whispered to Tripod when he was done. "We're going operational. Now keep your pie-hole shut." Brother-in-law knew the direction the man had headed once the fight broke off. This didn't mean the man couldn't have circled off in another direction, but it was a place to start. Brother-in-law knew the man's shoe imprint, but also knew that in the dark with the smells of the wet forest floor mixed with the smoky smell of the earlier bush fire, tracking him was going to be tough even with Tripod. They set out.

Brother-in-law was wearing his Bata tracking shoes, brown and green woodland camo pants with a matching long-sleeved shirt and floppy-brimmed boonie hat. The forest was thick with trees and brush that would have been thinned out a long time ago by forest fires if there wasn't so much rain. Brother-in-law went slowly, not following footprints because most of the time he couldn't see any but stopping at every clear patch of muddy ground looking for where a footprint might likely be. When he found one, he would forge slowly ahead looking for the next likely place for an imprint, and so on and so on. In the first hour he made about half a mile then took a short break. Not bad progress considering. He used the NVG whenever needed and the flashlight when absolutely necessary, covering it with his hat as much as possible when he did. The moon was out and cast an eerie, dull, dark-silver pall, making the trees it touched seem as if made from stone and the bushes as if from twisted wrought iron. Somewhere out there was a desperate, trained man with a gun and a knife.

Brother-in-law had his Browning .22 out and ready. In a scabbard on his belt he carried an Ontario MK 3 with a 6-inch stainless steel blade. He didn't like knife fighting.

Generally, unless the guy you were fighting was a total idiot, in a knife fight you had to take one to give one. Usually that meant take one on the arm so that you could give your opponent one in a vital spot.

Brother-in-law had used a knife many times before but had been in only three true fight-to-the-death knife fights. The first time was in Eminence, Missouri, population 600. He was fourteen years old and had objected to the local meth dealer selling product to his cousin. Brother-in-law had gone to the hospital after that and the dealer to the morgue. The other two instances were in the Congo. Once in a public bus in Lubumbashi and once coming out of a hospital in Kisangani. From his experience, fifteen seconds was a long knife fight if the combatants fought with bad intent.

On the move again, he worked steadily and silently through the damp woods, moving branches gently aside and placing each foot toe first before putting his weight on it. Tripod stayed close without a leash, most of the time brushing up against Brother-in-law's leg, each of them exchanging some unspoken and unexplainable sensory data between them.

After another hour, Brother-and-law took off the NVG and looked at his watch. Two-thirty-eight a.m. He paused in a crouch in a flattened-out area of dirt. In front of him stretched a clear set of footprints from his wily adversary. Twice Brother-in-law had caught him walking backwards in his own tracks and then after a dozen steps jumping sideways into the bush and going off in another direction. He had spotted the trick because the toe imprint was deeper, which usually indicated a man was running, but his stride length wasn't any longer than usual, which meant he was still walking, that is, walking backwards with his toe striking first and taking most of the weight. But this latest trick was the cutest. The guy had put his shoes on backwards and was walking straight ahead with his shoes in the wrong direction.

At first, Brother-in-law couldn't figure out what the guy was trying to accomplish with that stunt. He sat on the ground, took off his pack, and retrieved the last energy bar. Tripod growled until Brother-in-law relented. "You don't know many words, do you?" said Brother-in-law. He tossed Tripod half the bar.

Brother-in-law chewed on his half in the dark. Something wasn't right. On a whim, he lay down flat on the ground and traced his finger slowly around the edges of each footprint within the little patch, crawling from one to another until after five minutes he'd thoroughly scrutinized all eleven of them.

"Well, I'll be danged," he said to Tripod when he was done. Slipping unconsciously into Swahili, he said, *"Sisi kuwa wili baja wenzangu."* We *have two bad guys.* The outgoing footprints with the shoes on backwards were deeper, much deeper than the ones coming in. Someone had carried someone on his back out of the patch. The shoes were on backwards so he could walk out the way he came in, step in the same footprints, and make it seem like there was still only one person. The problem was, besides the weight distribution being off, the new guy was a pronator while the first guy was a supinator. Though the soles were identical the heels on the two different pairs of shoes were worn down on different sides. Brother-in-law chuckled to himself. *Haven't seen that one before.*

He reached into his pack and pulled out a futuristic-looking Maxim 9mm pistol, with a built-in silencer. He sighted down the barrel once to adjust to the unusual weight distribution. Satisfied, he took two magazines out of the pack and stuck one each in a leg pocket. He closed his pack and put it back on. After a few steps, he and

Tripod were again mere silent shadows among the trees, Maxim 9 firmly in hand.

This was one situation where Tripod and his nose were invaluable. The Chinese agents would have a hard time backtracking to set up an ambush without the dog picking up a scent.

❦

In the house, everyone was asleep except Rulon and Steenberg. Rulon lay in bed next to Yohaba in her childhood bedroom. The bed was small and barely big enough for Yohaba alone, but Rulon didn't mind. He lay there thinking about Chinese and Russians and forest rangers. An hour ago, his father had called to tell him about the situation with Ranger Stanley Merryfield. Rulon would never deliberately want to worry his father, but it was all he could do not to shout over the phone, *"Do you have any idea what I'm dealing with here? I've got Russian and Chinese hit teams coming after me, and you're carrying on about a skinny forest ranger with a big Adam's apple."* But he didn't. He thanked his dad for the information and assured him he had killed the grizzly in total self-defense and built the fire so he and Yohaba wouldn't die from hypothermia.

"Can't you clear it up with him for me?" he had asked his father.

"I will try, son," said Mr. Hurt, "but did you have to slice up the bear like some kind of ancient Druid sacrifice? They're throwing the book at you over that. Something about cultural misappropriation of Indian rituals."

"Just try, okay?" said Rulon, his exasperation barely under wraps.

"Well, he seems pretty persistent," said his father.

"What's that sound?" asked Rulon.

"Hold on," said the father. "I'm just looking through the blinds to see if he's out there. Practically every day he drops off another subpoena or calls. I get the feeling he's watching us all the time or even tapping our phones. Is he allowed to do that?"

After they hung up, Rulon couldn't get to sleep. *It's always one more thing*, he thought.

In the living room, Steenberg was also on the phone. He had finally gotten through to Sun Xiaofeng. Xiaofeng's son's body was in a special coffin at the Zurich airport waiting to be flown back to China. Steenberg tried once again to convince him to drop the vendetta. He promised him all copies of the incriminating DVDs plus sole ownership of their joint solar panel operation in China. In other words, more wealth than he ever dreamed of. Over the phone, Steenberg could sense Xiaofeng softening.

"When anger arises, think of the consequences," said Steenberg at an opportune point, quoting Confucius.

"To see the right and not do it is cowardice," countered Xiaofeng with his own Confucianism, albeit with not much enthusiasm.

"If you harm Yohaba, you will make an enemy of her husband. If you harm the husband, you will make an enemy of his closest friend. I know the husband, and I know the friend. It's unlikely this would end the way you planned. Think of what happened at Stein am Rhein."

For a long time both ends of the phone remained quiet. Finally, with a voice so tired and beaten that Steenberg thought for a second someone else had come on the line, Xiaofeng said, "I spoke to your son-in-law an hour ago. I don't know why I listened, but I did. I have no more energy for revenge." More silence. Steenberg suspected Xiaofeng was weeping and wondered what Rulon had said to him. Xiaofeng finally pulled himself together and said,

"I will need more capital if I am to run the solar panel business properly. I have big plans."

"You shall have it," said Steenberg. "How much were you thinking of?" They discussed various figures and agreed on a princely sum.

Much relieved, Steenberg hung up. One problem solved. Now for the other. All this time Jurgen Altheuer had been sitting at his side.

"Well done, boss," said Altheuer. "It's amazing the things that money can accomplish."

At the sound of his voice, Steenberg turned to his chief of staff, as if woken out of a dream. "Ah…um…no…no. It wasn't the money exactly. It was exhaustion. He said my granddaughter's husband called him, and they spoke. I wonder how he got the number. Did you give it to him?"

"No, sir," said Altheuer.

Steenberg lapsed into reflection for a minute. "Well, it is very hard to keep such hate alive for very long. Our Chinese friend is greedy and mendacious, but he is not a hater. In the end, holding onto the hate was simply too exhausting."

"You're not worried he'll change his mind?" asked Altheuer.

"A little, yes," said Steenberg. "We'll keep an eye on him. But now," he said, fully alert and ready to tackle the next problem. "We're going to Munich to pick up a chess set."

Altheur looked puzzled. "What do you mean? A physical chess set? An actual board and pieces?"

"Yes, precisely," said Steenberg. "For a special occasion. I ordered it months ago. A present to myself."

"Seems like a strange thing to be flying all the way to Munich for," said Altheuer. "DHL could have it in Zurich by tomorrow if you want."

"Thank you, Jurgen," said Steenberg with a smile. "But I need you to call this number." Steenberg wrote a number from memory on a piece of paper and handed it to Altheuer. "His name is Robert Gunther Gerlach. Don't haggle over the delivery cost. I might have been a little parsimonious with him on this project. Tell him to meet me with the set at the Munich airport, Café Treffpunkt, Terminal one, precisely seven p.m. And tell him he must be on time. Intimate there will be a bonus if the chess set performs per specifications."

"What is going on, sir?" said Altheuer. "Chess sets don't 'perform per specifications.'"

"Well, this one had better," said Steenberg with hearty good cheer. "I feel in the mood for one more chess game with our friend in the Kremlin. There's nothing unusual in that, is there?"

"Actually, yes, there is," said Altheuer, "if the man just tried to have you killed. Besides, if it is who I think it is, you didn't use a board when you played him. What are you not telling me? Are you deliberately keeping me in the dark?"

"Yes, I'm afraid I am," said Steenberg. "Now please. Make the phone call. From Munich we'll be immediately flying to Moscow. Can you make sure the flight plan gets properly filed?"

Altheuer looked at his watch. "We're cutting it pretty close. I don't know if it can be approved in time."

"We're talking Russia," said Steenberg. "Bribe someone."

Chapter 31

Thirty minutes ago it had rained, which was a shame, since at the time, Tripod had been following a strong scent. Both man and animal could sense their quarry was close. But now the rain had washed the scent away. For the past half hour, Brother-in-law with Tripod sat on the wet ground listening, waiting, and periodically scanning with the NVG. Their enemies were out there somewhere, and they were close. Rain from the leaves dripped on Brother-in-law and Tripod in the dark. Where they were hidden, the vegetation was so thick and the air so humid that Brother-in-law could close his eyes and imagine himself back in the Congo. He could almost hear the sounds of the nightjars and the bee-eaters with their long, colorful tails. How many times had this same scenario been played out in forests and jungles before? The hunter and the hunted. The patient and the impatient.

He waited another ten minutes and then felt the hairs on Tripod's neck tense up. Brother-in-law smiled to himself. Patience wins again. Slowly and silently, he uncoiled from his sitting position into a half-crouch and slipped the NVG over his eyes. Thirty feet away, directly in his line of march, a man stood peering roughly in Brother-in-law's direction. He held a knife in his left hand, and Brother-in-law could feel him struggling with all his senses to penetrate the darkness. Brother-in-law had a clear shot but waited for the second man, the one who most likely had the pistol, to give himself away. He waited a minute. Then another. The first man had by now sunk into a crouch and only the top of his head was visible through the undergrowth. Suddenly an alarm bell went off inside Brother-in-law's head at the same instant he sensed Tripod reacting. He was being flanked!

Brother-in-law dropped flat just as a bullet whizzed over his head, He quickly rolled, and two more rounds ripped up the ground where he'd been a second before, peppering his face with a spray of mud pellets. He rolled twice came up shooting and rolled some more. Bullets tore through the bushes he'd just left. The forest echoed with the crack of the unsilenced pistol. Brother-in-law rolled and crawled while scattering off more quick shots in the direction of the shooter and his buddy from the Maxim's 15-round magazine, rolled some more, and fired off five more shots, emptying the magazine.

He pulled out his .22 and took off the NVG. Tripod came low crawling to him through the bushes. Brother-in-law slammed another magazine into the Maxim and reholstered the .22. He grabbed a flash-bang grenade from his belt and hurled it in the direction the last shots had come from. He covered his ears when the grenade went off then put the NVG back on and popped up quickly to check. Nothing. He reversed direction keeping low and didn't stop to reassess until he was a hundred yards away.

Once he judged he had successfully disengaged, he swung left through the woods with Tripod to outflank the flanker. Now he had no intention of breaking off, and he didn't think they did either. He heard a branch break up ahead and realized they had detected his movement and were running another flanking action of their own. He circled further right in an even wider flanking arc and came up behind both of them standing behind a tree, looking in the wrong direction, waiting for him.

Brother-in-law slowly took off his pack and silently laid down the Maxim. He stood up straight, unencumbered, gun-hand hanging free alongside the Browning.

"Hey, bros," he called from twenty feet away. They whipped around with a start and the one man brought his gun up. Fair game. Brother-in-law drew the Browning in a blink, shot twice, and both men slumped without a sound. Head shots.

He stood over them for a minute. Not happy. Not sad. Not proud. Well, maybe a little sad that he didn't feel sad. *What does that say about me?* Tripod sniffed at the bodies and pawed at a hand still gripping the stolen pistol. Brother-in-law picked up the pistol and stuck it in his belt. They were armed and had convincingly communicated their deadly intent. He went back to his pack and rummaged inside for his entrenching tool. He unfolded the shovel head, clicked it into place, and began digging. The ground was so soft he had two three-foot-deep graves dug out in less than two hours, just as the sky was lightening in the east.

⌘

Steenberg and his security team were driving down the long road off Granny's property when the lead car stopped. Up ahead, Brother-in-law was walking towards them with his pack on and Tripod hopping along at his side. Brother-in-law was muddy and grim. Steenberg, Altheuer and the bald-headed security chief got out together to meet him.

Brother-in-law continued approaching and never broke stride as he handed the security chief the pistol the Chinese agent had taken from his man. "Orin," said Steenberg, "Were you able to find him?"

Brother-in-law answered, "Yep," and kept walking along the road past the three-car motorcade.

"Who is he?" asked Altheuer when he judged Brother-in-law was far enough away.

"He is a friend of my granddaughter and her husband," answered Steenberg.

"No," said Altheuer, "I mean, *who* is he?"

Before Steenberg could answer, the security chief said, *"Er ist der Psychopath von dem Sie froh sind, er auf Ihrer Seite ist."*—*He's the psychopath you're glad is on your side.*

"Heard that," yelled Brother-in-law as he disappeared around a bend in the road.

ೋೊೋ

In Beltsville, Maryland, NSA analyst Bob was at his wit's end. The Anomaly program kept supporting his archenemy, Angela's original hypothesis. He'd run and rerun the program over and over on the captured phone calls from Steenberg, Xiaofeng, and Klendenin, as well as on the phone calls and surreptitiously recorded open-mike conversations from Rulon, Yohaba, and the rest of the team. The customized program from a U.K. based, big data software company had concluded that the targets were planning an imminent terrorist attack using nuclear weapons on two of the world's critical aquifers and that a world-wide conspiracy was in play to destroy an asteroid named after Einstein's second wife, which was due to hit earth in 2029.

"Give me a break," said Bob through gritted teeth every time the program came back with the same ridiculous answer.

He didn't know how she's done it, but obviously Angela had gotten one of the coders to monkey with the software just to embarrass him. He could imagine the howls of laughter around the table when he presented this absurd conclusion to the committee. It might even result in the entire Anomaly program being shut down. Angela and her band of merry pranksters in the European section of the NSA loved to play their little, infantile practical jokes, and Bob was usually the butt of them, but this had gone too far.

Bob stewed. Stewing turned into bitterness. Bitterness into paranoia. Finally, paranoia compressed in the isolation in a 4x6 work cubicle turned into desperation. He deleted one of Xiaofeng's conversations from the target package and reran the software. It still made no sense. He deleted all of Yohaba's conversations. Then all of Steenberg's, rerunning the program again and again on the dwindling number of target conversations. Finally a credible narrative took shape. An international ring of animal poachers operating in North America was harvesting endangered species body parts for sale on the Chinese aphrodisiac market.

There it was all the time, thought Bob, as he sat back in his chair with his hands clasped behind his head. *Right in front of us. But isn't that how it always is?* Bob liked to think of himself as a sculptor starting out with a block of unintelligible data and then patiently chipping away at the lies, mis-directions, and distractions to reveal the pure truth underneath.

He worked till three in the morning compiling his final report, complete with heavily redacted edits of the various phone conversations that best served his narrative. To help everyone pull the necessary pieces together with a minimum of effort, phrases were italicized, some were underlined, and others like—I SHOT THE BEAR…AND HACKED UP THE BODY—were written in capital letters. Included in the fifteen-thousand-word tome was a recommendation to coordinate the investigation with one Stanley Merryfield, a U.S. Forest Service ranger from the Sawtooth National Recreation Area who had first stumbled across the mutilated carcasses left behind by this criminal enterprise.

Before he sent off his report, just for grins, Bob looked up the kind of jail time the perpetrators would likely face. What a disappointment! Perhaps three-years probation, a few hundred hours of community service, loss of hunting licenses, and, as a first time offender, a $3,500 fine—if the judge was in a bad mood. No, no, no!

Bob was tired. He had worked half the night. His next shift was due to start in only five hours. He thought about going home and grabbing a few hours of sleep, but when a coffee-inspired bolt of righteous adrenaline surged through his body, he got his second wind. He went back to the Anomaly program and started adding in more of Xiaofeng's conversations one at a time until the narrative was sure to achieve a more fitting punishment for the criminal mastermind behind this international cabal of animal rights abusers—Rulon Hurt.

On a whim, Bob searched the web for a photo of Mr. Hurt and found quite a few. Rulon in college throwing something heavy. Rulon riding a bull. Rulon in a suit and cowboy hat standing next to Yohaba with the Swiss Alps as a backdrop. Rulon holding an M60 machine gun. Rulon winning first place in the pie-eating contest at the Idaho State Fair. *What a rube*, thought Bob. *How did he get such a gorgeous wife?*

തെയ

It was in Ontario that, much to his regret, Klendenin parted company with Wild Will and Russo. Despite their earlier disagreements, he liked their company and also liked the reassurance that if Steenberg was right and his life was in danger, they'd be at his side. But, they'd left their passports back home and Klendenin was determined to fly as soon as possible to Zurich to pick up Batu and the others. Adios amigos. Big regrets on Klendenin's side, much less so on the side of Wild Will and Russo who were scared to death of being linked to the Paradeplatz fiasco. As a last gesture, Klendenin rented them a car and a chauffeur to get them back over the easily crossed U.S./Canadian border.

Jim Anderson, the pilot, talked Klendenin out of flying to Europe in the 737-200. The wind would be in their favor heading there and, with a light load, they could probably make Zurich from Windsor without refueling. But coming back with the wind in their face would be a different story. They might have to refuel at an American airport, and who knew who would be waiting for them there.

So instead, Klendenin lay down a cool $147,000 to rent a 15-seater Gulfstream G450 to make the nonstop round trip to Zurich. Jim Anderson had suggested either a Falcon 7X, a Global 5000, or the Gulfstream. When the leasing company only had the Gulfstream available, Jim wasn't disappointed. They left Windsor at 4 a.m. after Jim had grabbed six hours sleep, and with helpful winds expected to be in Zurich by midnight local time at the latest.

એજ

When Brother-in-law got back to Granny's house it was dawn. He hunted around the outside for a hose, found one in the garden, and sprayed the mud off himself, Tripod, and all his things. Afterwards, Tripod ran off into the woods madder than a hornet while Brother-in-law stretched out on the lawn to let his clothes dry. The sun was just appearing above the peaks to the east. While he lay there, Rulon came out and sat on the garden bench.

"I see you're all painted up," said Rulon, referring to the waterproof face camo.

"Yep," said Brother-in-law.

"Want some breakfast?" Rulon asked.

"In a minute," said Brother-in-law without opening his eyes. "I'm thinking."

"What are you thinking about?"

"I'm thinking after this, I'll head back to the Congo."

"What will the Navy say?"

"They can say what they want."

"Then what will you do?" asked Rulon.

"Look for my kids, I guess."

"What about Batu?"

"What about her? She can't come if that's what you mean. I'll send her a postcard. We're in different galaxies anyway."

"Well, I'm coming. We'll find your boys. When do we start?"

Brother-in-law raised up on his elbows. "I thought you'd say that." He lay back down. "You're a good friend, Mr. Hurt, but no thanks. It wouldn't be your thing, if you get my drift."

Rulon broke into a song in his perfect Church choir baritone. *"I'm a lonesome cowboy, lonesome as I can be. Lonesome as a prairie tree."* Brother-in-law laughed and so did Rulon. The song just seemed funny.

It started to rain. Brother-in-law got up, looked himself over, and asked, "Do you think Granny will let me in the house?"

Rulon ignored his question and asked, "Did you get him? Is he sadder and wiser or sadder and deader?"

"Deader," said Brother-in-law. "I don't know about sadder. What's China like? He could be happier now for all

I know after living in a Commie hellhole. His partner too. And just so's ya know, they shot first. Scout's honor."

"Partner?" asked Rulon surprised. "There were two?" Brother-in-law nodded.

Rulon thought about that for a few seconds. "I hope this won't ever come back to bite Granny."

"Not unless someone goes looking for 'em with a backhoe," said Brother-in-law. Before Rulon could prolong the conversation, Brother-in-law said, "Let's get some breakfast." He turned to walk towards the front door just as Yohaba came out to meet him.

She gave him a big hug along with three quick kisses on alternating cheeks, and said, "Thank you for protecting us while we were sleeping."

❧❧❧

After breakfast and goodbyes to Granny and Alex, the whole team including Batu and Tripod drove to Zurich. Tripod was still fuming over being hosed down by Brother-in-law, so everyone kept their distance and gave the dog the whole cargo area to himself. Before they left, Rulon and Benny had placed all the weapons in an old trunk Granny donated to the cause and buried them way back in the woods. Except for the handguns. They kept the handguns.

Batu had been in touch with her father. His plane would be landing just before midnight. During the leisurely drive to Zurich, to everyone's great relief, Dilly and Stringbean called Rulon on his cellphone. They had been released thanks to the influence of some high-powered Swiss dignitary. The far-reaching influence of Steenberg seemed once again to be a silent partner on their journey.

Rulon told the two SEALs to take a taxi to the Glattzentrum mall in Dübendorf, a mid-sized city just on the other side of the hill from Zurich. They would meet them there in an hour at the Cha Cha, a Thai restaurant in the food court on the mall's third floor. The rendezvous took place on schedule. They stayed in the mall, hopping from restaurant to restaurant for the rest of the day, mostly just ordering drinks until the mall closed at 9 p.m.

The last thing Rulon did before leaving was check the *20 Minuten* website for news of the Chinese. He found what he was looking for buried deep in the Switzerland section of the online newspaper. The Chinese had all been injured in a freak climbing accident but managed to drive themselves to the only official-looking building they could find, where they bandaged themselves up with duct tape and waited for help.

"Ha," said Rulon. "What did I tell you? Necessity is the mother of invention."

After leaving the mall the team headed to the airport, turned in the van, and following Klendenin's instructions, waited for his jet at the airport's ExecuJet lounge for VIP flyers. While they waited, Brother-in-law pulled Batu aside and suggested she not mention their budding relationship to her father. When she asked why, he filled her in on what he'd done to her father back in Idaho.

Klendenin arrived on time looking like he hadn't slept in days. At the first sight of Batu, he burst into tears, and suddenly everyone saw him in a different light. He was no longer the foolish, special-op wannabe. Nor the shrewd, well-connected billionaire. He was a father who loved his daughter. After his tearful reunion with Batu, Klendenin profusely thanked the team for her rescue. He hugged everyone individually and spoke a few words of personal gratitude to each. For Batu's sake, even Brother-in-law endured a hug. When Klendenin got to Rulon, he held his hand and took a good look at his face. "What the hell happened to you?"

"Stepped on a rake," said Rulon.

Somewhere over England everyone fell asleep, even Jim Anderson, their silver-haired pilot. On the trip over, he'd already exceeded his maximum allowable flying time, and Klendenin had hired another pilot to fly them back on the Gulfstream. It had been a long week for everyone. Next stop Boise, Idaho. Klendenin figured the leased jet had thrown the government off his trail for a time, so he decided to take the chance and land in the U.S. From Zurich to Boise would be twelve hours.

Chapter 32

Altheuer rushed out of the big white rented Mercedes to come around and open the door for Steenberg. The man who would have saved the world now had smaller ambitions. He simply wanted to make things right for his granddaughter and her husband. There is no fool like an old fool, he said to himself countless times over the last two days, ever since he found out that Elsa wasn't going to strike the earth after all. Now, just a hundred meters away from the administrative entrance to the labyrinth known as the Kremlin, he said it one more time. In his right hand, he grasped a specially constructed, soft brown leather briefcase which held the special-order chess set.

"Excuse me, chief," said Altheuer. "Did you say something?"

"Yes, I certainly did," said Steenberg brightly. "I said, there is no fool like an old fool. If you are fortunate enough ever to reach my age, please be sure to remember that."

"I will, chief," said Altheuer. "Should I have the car parked? Will you be long?"

Steenberg put his long arm around Altheuer's shoulder and led him gently away from the car so the driver couldn't hear. They talked for ten minutes, and with every minute Altheuer's shoulders sagged a little more. At the end, Steenberg took a 128GB thumb drive out of his coat pocket and handed it to him. "Instructions. Please follow them to the letter," he said. "Now, leave here and don't come back. Get on the plane and head back to Zurich as quickly as possible. I will try to buy you two hours."

Altheuer protested but Steenberg waved him quiet and continued. "No. No protests. I will take a two-hour stroll across these magnificent historical grounds—no more. Did you know the Cathedral of Christ the Savior over there..." Steenberg pointed to the white, golden-domed cathedral a few blocks southwest of the Kremlin. "...was so beloved by the people that during Stalin's reign of terror people surrounded the church during the day to keep it from being blown up? Do you realize how brave they must have been?"

"From what I know of Stalin, I'm surprised he put up with that," said Altheuer

"He didn't," said Steenberg. "He had it blown up in the middle of the night on December 5, 1931 after all the faithful had gone home. One might say the spirit was willing, but the flesh was weak. He used the murals and marble to decorate the Moscow metro stations."

"Why are you telling me this?" said Altheuer. "Does this have something to do with your custom chessboard?"

"Perhaps." The two men shook hands and when Altheuer appeared hesitant to let go, Steenberg said, "Enough of this. Go now and don't forget the thumb drive. That is your priority now." Altheuer gave Steenberg's hand one more hearty squeeze then got back into the car and drove off. Steenberg looked at his watch, straightened his trademark black fedora, and began his stroll.

On the way to the cathedral he took from his jacket pocket an envelope Altheuer had given him while they were in Munich. It was a report on the progress of the search for Brother-in-law's two young sons. Steenberg, in response to some morbid premonition, had resisted reading its contents until now.

He sat on a public bench, opened the envelope, and unfolded the note inside. The two boys had died within a few weeks of each other over a year ago, one from cholera, the other from malaria. Steenberg refolded the note. He thought his quest to save the world had wrung all the tears out of him, but he was wrong. The news of the children hit him hard. Africa, so Africa. An all too common story. He wondered how Brother-in-law would react and decided to get it over with. He called Rulon on his cell and asked if Brother-in-law was there. He was. Steenberg gave him the news.

CO2CO2

After Brother-in-law ended the call and handed the phone back to Rulon, Rulon asked, "What was that all about?"

"Just tying up loose ends," said Brother-in-law. He leaned his head back and closed his eyes. They were sitting in a lounge in St. John's airport in Newfoundland. Klendenin, in consultation with Anderson and the pilot he hired in Zurich, had decided to land there and refuel rather than risk touching down in the U.S. with an empty tank and not being able to immediately take off again.

Yohaba walked up. "We're leaving in fifteen minutes. Next stop, the entertainment capital of the world."

"Sorry, babe," said Rulon, "but we decided not to land at Boise but to go straight to Twin Falls."

"Rats," said Yohaba. When the conversation died there, she said, "Hey, this is quite an airport. Did you know the space shuttle can land here in an emergency?"

"This is why she always beats me at Trivial Pursuit," said Rulon.

"Who'd a thunk it?" said Brother-in-law. "Say, what's that thing you're always quoting from that Goethe guy? You know that thing about comedy and tragedy."

"You mean, life is a comedy to those who think and a tragedy to those who feel?"

"Yeah, that's it," said Brother-in-law. Five minutes later, he asked Rulon for the phone then went off by himself and made a few calls.

ↄ∙ↄ∙ↄ

After talking to Brother-in-law, Steenberg continued his walk along the banks of the Moskva River to the cathedral. He walked inside the huge entrance then strolled casually to the center of the church and looked straight up into the cupola and the huge painting of the Savior surveying creation with outstretched hands. He then walked to a corner of the cathedral and stood admiring two huge paintings hanging on the wall there—one of Christ on the cross and the other of Christ being taken down by four of his followers.

One thing Steenberg liked about the Russians was that generally when they were bribed, they stayed bribed. But there were always exceptions. After ten minutes, a man of about fifty in a brown suit and a red tie, holding a newspaper, came over to admire the same paintings. Steenberg turned around to scan the church as the man settled next to him, but it appeared he was not followed. To Steenberg's chagrin, Altheuer had not succeeded in finding a photo of Batu's friend's father, at least not one that was recent. Steenberg sized the man beside him up and down. There was a certain similarity to the photo he had seen, but the resemblance was not ironclad. The first suspicion of betrayal.

"These painting are really beautiful," said the man with the red tie in cultured Russian, "and yet are often ignored by tourists. Why do you think that is?"

"Perhaps for some the paintings are too painful," replied Steenberg. "As for me, they are a reminder that my Redeemer lives."

"I believe you have something for me, Dr. Steenberg," said the man now that the code had been correctly exchanged.

"Yes, the briefcase. When will it next be in my possession?"

"First promise me again this isn't a bomb or something," said the man. He was sweating. Not exactly the man of stature Steenberg had been expecting. More like a paid actor who suddenly realized his life, despite assurances, might actually be in danger.

Well, actor or not, sometimes you had to give people a reason to stay bribed. "Of course it's not a bomb," said Steenberg. "I am a famous man. Surely after our phone call you looked me up on the internet. My Wikipedia page is particularly flattering. I represent certain interests that are best served through bribery not violence. Lift the case. Feel the weight. The pieces are made of gold. It is a bribe for a man who is extraordinarily difficult to access. Now tell me, after I'm through security, how will I reacquire the briefcase?"

The man looked around like a cornered ferret. Finally, he said, "Just past the first security screen, you will see three corridors like spokes on a wheel. Take the corridor to the left. At this time of day it will have a minimum of traffic. Go past two sets of double doors on the left. Turn into the third set. It will be on the right. It will be locked. In the room is a large wooden table surrounded by ten chairs. Ignore the equipment in the room. The briefcase will be there against the table leg closest to the chair that is slightly pulled out. Here is a key to the room. Leave the key on the table before you leave. This is absolutely critical. Do you understand?"

"I understand," answered Steenberg as he took the key, a non-descript key on a plain metal key ring.

"Here is a security card," said the man. "You will need it to get past security. This must also be left on the table. There can be no mistake with this. It must be left on the table with the key. Do you understand what I am saying?"

"Yes. It is all clear," said Steenberg. "Thank you."

The man picked up the briefcase. "You do realize this is all pointless. You cannot get past the second security checkpoint without a specially coded ID card and facial and fingerprint recognition. It would take me an hour to explain to you all the security measures. And the Kremlin has its own regiment. To reach the eleventh level would take a pitched battle. Do you understand?"

"Thank you again," said Steenberg. "Off we go."

"Do you have any idea what will happen to me if I am discovered?" asked the man. Bribing officials was always more art than science. Carrot or stick was a decision that could only be made in real time.

Steenberg looked to heaven for patience. He said, "Do you have any idea what will happen to your daughter if you don't comply? Let me make this easier for both of us. If you ask another question, I will pick up the briefcase and walk out of this church. I have people watching. If I walk out with the briefcase, your daughter dies within the week. I won't even have to make a phone call."

"Your Russian is very good," said the man, crestfallen. "The briefcase will be in the room for fifteen minutes starting in one hour." He looked at his watch.

"That is too soon," said Steenberg.

"Ninety minutes then, but no longer. The risk is too great."

"That will do," said Steenberg. "Off we go now. And do be extra careful with it. It is quite valuable. And it is not to be opened."

Steenberg watched him walk away with the briefcase. The bribe had been princely. The threat if he didn't comply equally vicious. Silver or lead. When he first embarked on his mission to save the world, Steenberg had suffered several early, painful lessons on the subject of bribery and betrayal. Now he understood exactly how these things were done. However, something rankled. The man had lacked a certain—how to put it—stature, thought Steenberg. Not exactly the type of individual you would think could rise through the corridors of power in the Kremlin to crush all rivals. *Perhaps the chess match has already begun*, he thought.

Steenberg waited twenty minutes then left the church. He retraced his steps along the Moskva River until he came to Red Square. He acted the tourist for a time then sauntered over to the Kremlin's administrative entrance.

෬෩෬෩

"These are good," said Captain Gromanko. "What are they called again?"

"Tortilla chili chips," said Lieutenant Joseph Andropov, the FSR's most decorated sniper. Gromanko looked at the writing on the package and tried pronouncing the word "tortilla" but got nowhere. Gromanko and Andropov were on a hill in Idaho overlooking the Hurt ranch. They had been there for two days already. The weather had been steady—warm and sunny with a bit of wind—which bothered Andropov. When the time came, he wanted to be closer to the house. They stayed in the hills to the east of the house, the hills on the other side of the ranch providing far less cover because of the recent fires. Lightning strikes, assumed Gromanko incorrectly.

Both of them wore desert camo and spent all of their time observing the main road into the Hurts' farmyard. The plan was to take out Rulon Hurt as soon as he appeared and to kill everyone else who happened to be around so they could buy time for a getaway. They'd gotten into position with dirt bikes, which were now hidden in the bush. They had enough food and water for a week. Their chartered jet and its Russian crew were cooling it in Boise. Their escape team was killing time in nearby Twin Falls.

"I could never be a sniper," said Gromanko. "All the waiting is oppressive."

"A hunter's wait seals a victim's fate," said Andropov. "Relax. I read his file. He's a rancher. I know ranchers. Right now it's driving him crazy that he's missing the planting season. How's he going to feed the cattle in the fall? My family were ranchers north of St. Petersburg. Believe me, he'll be here, and I will kill him. Or I'll kill his father. Either will do." At the moment, Andropov was looking through the scope of his Russian-made suppressed VKS sniper rifle and had Mr. Hurt senior squarely in his sights as he walked from the barn to the house. Just practicing.

Andropov had brought along plenty of 7.62mm shells, but also a box of newly developed 12.7x55mm, sub-sonic, armor-piercing rounds. Those shells could go through a meter of wood and six inches of brick or easily through a 5th or 6th class vest.

଼ଓଌଓ

There was a queue going through the Kremlin's security. One of the security scanners was broken, putting a double load on the one remaining. Steenberg was fourteenth in line, waiting patiently behind three men in military uniforms with picture IDs dangling from their necks. He looked at his watch and calculated the wait. At this rate he could miss his deadline. Then what? *The best laid plans of mice and men*, thought Steenberg. Which made him think of Rulon. If he ever made a list of people he regretted underestimating, decided Steenberg, Rulon Hurt would be at the top. Up ahead a woman was having her handbag put through the scanner a third time. Steenberg looked at his watch again.

When it was Steenberg's turn, he emptied his pockets into a dish, flashed his security card, and placed his hat and coat on the conveyor. The guards passed him through with hardly a glance. One of the benefits of being white, well-dressed, eighty years old, and absolutely fluent in cultured Russian was that you fit no one's idea of a threat profile. *That might change after today*, he thought.

Steenberg retrieved his wallet, pen, and key from the plastic dish on the other side of the x-ray conveyor and once again donned his coat and hat. He smiled benignly at the guard with the Bizon sub-machine gun and received not so much as a blink in return. Wishing to make it difficult for security cameras, he kept his head down and refrained from looking up at the portrait of Putin.

Once through security, he disengaged himself from the small crowd congregating in the security hall and walked slowly down the appointed hallway, key in hand. At the double doors on the right, he inserted the key and walked into the room without so much as a guilty glance to the left and right to see if he was observed. The hall was covered by security cameras, of course, but that could not be avoided.

The room was exactly as described. There was a large flat-screen TV on one wall along with a doorless cupboard that held a variety of audiovisual equipment. In the center of the room was a large, antique wooden table and ten chairs, one of which was slightly pulled out. He walked over and pulled the chair completely away from the table. There was the brown leather briefcase nestled against a curved, ornately carved leg.

He set the briefcase on the table, unzipped it, and laid both sides flat. There were the pieces, each in its own individual rabbit-fur pocket. One set yellow gold. One set white gold—gold mixed with 10% palladium. Altogether a kilo of gold worth over $55,000 plus $5,000 in palladium. He picked up the white gold king just to feel its heft and marvel at its buffed and timeless brightness. He replaced it and next examined the wooden board, snugly held in place by a leather strap and buckle. Satisfied, he zipped the bag shut again. Last, he opened up the briefcase's zippered outer pocket and pulled out a neatly folded piece of thin, legal-sized cardboard. Before he left, he placed the key and the ID badge on the table.

Once in the corridor again, he set the briefcase down, looked up at the security camera mounted on the wall, took off his hat, and for the first time, gave the camera and its facial recognition software a clear look at his aged, lined face. He waited a few seconds then unfolded the cardboard to its full size and held it against his chest in plain view of the camera. On it were written words in Cyrillic Russian. *Еще один шахматный матч? Ради старых времен? One more chess match? For old time's sake?* He maintained his position even while enduring the curious glances and smiles of two uniformed young women who walked by. After a minute he refolded the cardboard and waited.

Three floors down, a beep sounded in the earphones of a 24-year-old guard. He pivoted in his chair to a wall of screens and swung his attention to screen number 72 and its blinking red light. The subject's identity was quickly confirmed but, oddly, prompted a special security code—one the young guard had never seen before. He pivoted again in his chair and grasped a binder on a shelf behind him. He looked up the code, read the instructions, and hesitated. He interrupted the work of three of his equally young co-workers to confer about the situation. Still unsure, the guard made a phone call and within minutes the officer of the day, a Kremlin regiment lieutenant, arrived.

Together they read and reread the instructions. Finally, tentatively, and after a nervous gulp, the lieutenant dialed the indicated number. He stood rigidly at attention while speaking. After he hung up, he quickly made a hard copy of the security camera screenshot and placed it in a manila envelope. No sooner was he finished than a courier arrived. The envelope was handed over and everyone in the video surveillance department breathed a sigh of relief.

❧❦❧

In his Kremlin office eleven floors below ground level, the thin man studied the screenshot of Steenberg holding his sign. *Has he gone mad?* was his first thought.

Also in the room, sitting across the desk from the thin man, was an officer in full regimentals, Batu's friend's father, the Director of Kremlin Security himself, Viktor Nemtsov. Standing behind him, just to the right of the office door, was the man in the brown suit who had met with Steenberg in the cathedral.

"He's right on time," said the brown-suited body-double eagerly.

"Why is he still here?" asked the thin man without looking up. The man in the brown suit left immediately, head down, without a word.

After the man left, the thin man said to Nemtsov, "It was a sophisticated bomb, then?"

"Oh, yes," said Nemtsov. "The entire department was impressed. Four types of detonation triggers, a Magicube igniter, a backup lead azide detonator, an electrical igniter using a military squib, and a time-delayed sulfuric acid chemical detonator. Even a booby trap. Whoever built it hoped we'd find the obvious and quit. Oh, and I forgot. A mercury switch and a wireless remote detonator. It's a miracle it was transported without detonating. There are only a handful of people in the world who could have built it. We suspect the designer served in Afghanistan. We're going to track him down after this. This is one guy who needs to be taken out of circulation."

"No doubt about his intent, then?"

"None," said Nemtsov. "There was enough C4 to take down a building."

"And you're sure the device is absolutely safe now?" asked the thin man.

"The explosive component has been entirely removed and the entire device run multiple times through our most sensitive explosive detection scanner," said Nemtsov. "Yes, it is safe. I'd stake my life on it." He got up to leave.

"Good, you won't mind staying then," said the thin man. "Make yourself comfortable. The good doctor will be here shortly." The thin man settled back in his old worn chair. Nemtsov tried to make himself comfortable and failed miserably.

Five minutes later, Steenberg stood in the doorway clutching his briefcase. A nod from the thin man and the five-person, heavily armed escort turned on their heels and left. Steenberg was missing his coat, hat, suit jacket, tie, belt, watch, wallet, ring, and shoes.

The thin man came around his desk to greet him. "What an unexpected surprise," he said. They shook hands. "I thought we had you in Zurich, at least until I saw the forensic report."

"So this is your office," said Steenberg. "A bit like Hitler's bunker. Do you find it inspirational?"

The thin man turned to Nemtsov, who had also risen. "See. What did I tell you? The only living person who dares to give me grief."

Steenberg shook hands with Nemtsov. "Colonel Nemtsov, I presume," said Steenberg. "I must say, your impersonator didn't do you justice." Steenberg scanned the medals on his chest. "What have we here? The Order of St. George, second class, the Order for Merit to the Fatherland, first class, an Order of Suvorov and a Zhukov. And the second row is equally impressive. And how interesting, even an Order of Parental Glory. A sterling example of work life balance. You have had an extraordinary career, Colonel. You must be very proud."

"Before you answer, Colonel," said the thin man, "be aware. To the good doctor, pride is one of the seven deadly sins." The colonel laughed good-naturedly. "Please sit down, Doctor." The thin man gestured to a chair next to Nemtsov and resumed his own position behind the desk.

"I doubt you came all this way just to play a chess match?" said the thin man. "I mean smuggling a bomb in the chess board. The very epitome of a sore loser."

"You found it then," said Steenberg. "I assume it's been disarmed."

"That would be a safe assumption," said Nemtsov. "But dismantled would be a more accurate description. Did you really think you could bribe and threaten your way into the Kremlin with a bomb?"

"Guilty as charged," said Steenberg.

"My people were impressed with the craftsmanship," said Nemtsov, "but based on your reputation, I expected something more original."

"I am sorry to disappoint. But perhaps I can redeem myself." To the thin man, Steenberg said, "Just so my visit isn't a total waste, what do you say? Shall we set them up? For old time's sake? One last game? One more chance for all of us to redeem ourselves?"

The thin man laughed, something Nemtsov had never heard him do. "Why not? As long as you are under no illusions as to how this is going to end for you."

"None whatsoever, I assure you," said Steenberg.

"And you brought a board. How quaint. We didn't need one for our first game. On a public bench in Zurich. I believe the bench is no longer there."

"Collateral damage," responded Steenberg.

"Not just the bench," said the thin man, a pointed reference, not lost on Steenberg, to the two babushkas who were killed. He cleared away his papers and Steenberg unzipped the leather case and laid it flat on the desk. He took both kings out of their rabbit fur pockets and held them behind his back. The thin man nodded towards the right hand and Steenberg handed him the white gold king. Steenberg next unstrapped the board and set it between them. They set up the board in silence. The thin man made the first move.

"Who won last time?" asked Nemtsov. Good manners prevented Steenberg from saying. If it were not for a barely perceptible tightening around the thin man's eyes, Nemtsov's question would have gone entirely unanswered.

For the first forty-five minutes, there was very little action on the board. Then in a flurry of eight moves, three major pieces were exchanged. Nemtsov got up to use the bathroom. Steenberg had just made a move, advancing a pawn to within two spaces of being queened. The thin man told Nemtsov to sit back down. "Your presence reassures me," he said while concentrating on the board. Nemtsov knew exactly what he meant.

After ninety minutes of play, Steenberg glanced at Colonel Nemtsov's watch and saw the time. He did a quick calculation and judged that Klendenin's jet with Rulon and Yohaba aboard would have touched down in Idaho by now. He had bought his family and Altheuer the time they needed. For Steenberg, the game was now only an exercise in procrastination. He quickly precipitated a series of sacrifices that cleared almost all the pieces off the board, leaving him with only his king against the thin man's king, bishop and knight. Next, to the thin man's great annoyance, he artfully maneuvered himself into a stalemate position. The game ended in a draw.

"It looks like you can run and hide in chess as well as you do in life," said the thin man, irked, and irked even more that he could not hide it.

"But nevertheless a fitting end," said Steenberg.

"How so?" asked the thin man.

"We both lose," said Steenberg.

"Such negativity," said Nemtsov.

"Possibly," said the thin man. "But I rather think the doctor is about to make a point. You're absolutely sure the bomb has been defused?"

"Absolutely," said Nemtsov. "All verified with technology so state-of-the-art I doubt the doctor has even heard of it."

"It's been a long time since I've been 'out-state-of-the-arted,'" said Steenberg, "but please impress me. Tell me what you did."

Nemtsov looked at the thin man for permission to proceed, and when he received it, proceeded confidently. "First of all, the Kremlin has the very best bomb disposal and disarming experts in the world. We deal with

Chechnyan terrorists all the time trying to smuggle in bombs. We have seen every explosive device known to man. While yours was somewhat original in the sheer number of detonation technologies embedded in a single device, none of the technologies themselves was a mystery to us.

"Second, we use a variety of explosives detection equipment that in their aggregate simply cannot be evaded. We have ion mobility spectrometers, gas chromatographers and aerosol polymers that react with nitrogen groups. We also use computed axial tomography x-ray machines and nanowire sensing elements. Finally, you obviously were not aware that since the 1991 Montreal Convention all C4, in fact all plastic bonded explosives, must have a detection taggant added. Which means that in the end, we didn't need any of our technology, resources, or expertise to handle your pitiful assassination attempt. All we needed was a single bomb-sniffing dog, of which we have a kennel full. For your information, the dog who detected your bomb is named Pytor. Tonight he will eat steak." Nemtsov sat back proudly after his command performance.

"Pride goeth before the fall," said Steenberg.

"Yes, it certainly does," said Nemtsov. "And you are proof of that." *Touché*, thought Nemtsov.

The two Russians watched in silence as Steenberg slowly put the chess pieces and board away. When finished, Steenberg zipped up the bag and placed it firmly on the chair between his knees. "Very impressive," he said. "So, are you ready now?"

"Are we ready?" asked Nemtsov with a laugh. "What kind of question is that? You are about to be thrown in a hole that makes a CIA black site seem like a five-star hotel. Are *you* ready?" He chuckled. Again, the smugness.

"I mean, are you ready to start the negotiation?" asked Steenberg humbly.

Nemtsov started to speak, and the thin man laid a hand on his arm to stop him. "You have already made enough of a fool of yourself for one day, Colonel. Our distinguished visitor holds the patent for DMDNB, the taggant used in Semtex and C4. Isn't that right, doctor?"

"Oh, it's on a wall somewhere," said Steenberg.

"So maybe we should hear what the doctor has to say," said the thin man.

"I would like you to promise not to bother my family anymore," said Steenberg. "That's all. Let them live their lives in peace in Idaho. They mean you no harm." The briefcase was wedged between Steenberg's knees. As he spoke, he casually tightened his right arm around the leather case and intertwined his left hand through the handle.

"A totally understandable request," said the thin man, "but I'm afraid the answer is 'no.'" Nemtsov turned slightly in his chair to observe Steenberg's expression.

"Perhaps I can convince you to reconsider," said Steenberg. "Have you ever heard of Astrolite G?" Steenberg strengthened his grip on the briefcase. "I must warn you, any attempt to interfere with me now will result in the death of all of us." As an aside to Nemtsov, he said, "The bomb in the chess board was only a decoy."

"Astrolite G. Never heard of it," said the thin man dismissively.

"I have," said Nemtsov, not so dismissively. "It's an extremely volatile liquid mixture of ammonium nitrate and hydrazine…"

"…that maintains its explosiveness for four days," said Steenberg, "even when dispersed in soil. Even in the rain. Fortunately, under certain conditions, it also absorbs quite well into leather. Some say it's the most powerful nonnuclear explosive, but people in the defense industry are so prone to hyperbole one never knows what to believe."

Silence. Momentary confusion. Then the thin man started slowly clapping. "Bravo, doctor. Bravo. See, Victor. You wanted to take his briefcase away. See what we would have missed if I had listened to you? This little performance itself has been worth the price of admission, wouldn't you say? Now, Victor, this is your chance to redeem yourself. I suggest you don't waste it. Match wits with the doctor. Go ahead. Impress me."

Nemtsov cleared his throat. "You are bluffing, doctor. Astrolite G is a nitrate-based explosive. Our equipment would have found it."

"Your equipment probably did find it," said Steenberg, "but I counted on your technicians concluding it was C4 residue from the chessboard. Didn't anyone comment on how sloppily the C4 was packed? I also counted on your team imbued with their commander's arrogance and sycophantic tendencies—no offense, Colonel, but I've seen your psychological profile—growing lax in their search under the right conditions. The trick was to design a device that would stretch their bomb-detecting abilities just enough for them to feel brilliant and confident of impressing you."

Nemtsov swallowed hard. "But you have no way to detonate. We've taken everything metallic away from you, and even you can't detonate something without a power source. There may be Astrolite G in the leather, though I'm not even sure about that, but there is absolutely no power source in the briefcase. Of that I am positive." He started to reach for the briefcase to take it from Steenberg, but the thin man ordered him to stop.

"Let's see where this goes," he said.

"Very wise," said Steenberg once everyone was settled again. "Ah yes, the detonation. A challenge to be sure. Let me explain. You have an engineering background, Colonel. You might find this instructive. Zigbee. Don't worry if you've never heard of it. Not many people have. It's a wireless communication standard that requires very little power. Very, very, little power. There is a miniature Zigbee transmitter embedded in the strap handle of this case. One twist of the handle at a specified, unnatural angle and a signal is generated and the briefcase explodes with enough power to bounce cars on the street above."

"But there is no power source," said the colonel emphatically. "There is no power source! We checked for that. Please just hand over the briefcase, doctor. Let's end this with some dignity. Don't make me pull out my pistol and shoot you."

"It was a difficult problem," said Steenberg, ignoring the colonel's threat. "Gold chess pieces wrapped in rabbit fur produce an extraordinary amount of static electricity. But how do you harness it? Static electricity has a very high voltage but only a very low-current DC. Naturally I couldn't install a DC to AC converter in the briefcase. You would have found that. So there's the challenge. Surely you can appreciate that. But all I needed was enough of a discharge to power a five-watt light bulb for four-hundred-forty microseconds. A solution presented itself. The science was intriguing. Even overdue to my way of thinking. It was crude. Inefficient. Still several iterations away from what I would consider commercially viable. But enough static electricity could be harnessed for a Zigbee signal to reliably travel five-eights of an inch. That was sufficient."

Steenberg stopped talking and looked at his audience. He struggled to read their expressions. "With all that said, perhaps we can begin the negotiations again from a new perspective. I simply want your assurances that my granddaughter and her husband are safe. In perpetuity. I ask nothing for myself."

The colonel and the thin man exchanged glances. The colonel said, "Would you like me to handle this, sir?" His hand was on his pistol.

"Not yet, Colonel," said the thin man. "Let's give the good doctor one more chance to do the right thing." Turning to Steenberg, he said, "My dear Dr. Steenberg. We should have been playing poker all this time. You seem to have a natural flair for bluffing."

"You think this is a bluff, then," said Steenberg.

"Yes, yes," said the thin man. "A very well played bluff. When caught, double down. I will miss you. Now, allow me to make you a counteroffer. If you lie down on the floor now so the Colonel can shoot you without messing up my desk, I will only have Rulon Hurt killed. Right now, as we speak, there is a sniper team in place at his father's ranch. They will call me when he arrives. What shall I tell them? You have one minute to decide. For every minute you delay after that, I will add another of your loved ones to the list. First your granddaughter, then your grandson, and so on and so on. Do we understand each other?"

"Tell the colonel to take his hand off his weapon," ordered Steenberg.

"No," said the thin man. "Rulon Hurt must die. You too. Let me tell you why. Those two old women at Paradeplatz that Mr. Hurt killed, I have known them since Stalingrad."

"Rulon didn't kill them," said Steenberg.

"Oh, that's good to know," said the thin man. "Thank you. It was the Navy SEAL then. Colonel, add him to the list."

"With pleasure," said Nemtsov.

"As I was saying," said the thin man. "Those two dear babushkas served in the all-women 1077th anti-aircraft regiment during the battle of Stalingrad. They were mere girls then, had no infantry support, but for two days the 1077th defended the Stalingrad tractor factory against an all-out attack from the German sixteenth panzer division. They lowered their M1939 air defense guns to their lowest position and destroyed eighty-three German tanks, fifteen infantry vehicles, fourteen aircraft, and effectively annihilated three battalions of infantry. They were two of only eight women who by a miracle survived, and they have continued to serve the motherland honorably ever since. It is unthinkable that lives such as theirs should go unrevenged."

"Please spare me," said Steenberg. "You had already made the decision to kill me and Rulon at Paradeplatz, and probably Yohaba too, before anything happened to those women."

"True," said the thin man. "But perhaps if they hadn't been killed, I would have accepted the offer you just made."

"If they hadn't been killed," said Steenberg, "I wouldn't be alive now to make the offer."

"True again," said the thin man after a moment's reflection. He frowned then brightened. "Well, not everything in life makes sense. You really need at this point to be lying on the floor. I believe your first minute is past. People are dying, doctor."

"I am not bluffing," said Steenberg evenly. "The colonel here wears the Order of Parental Glory. To earn that requires that he have at least seven children. Do you really want his death on your conscience?"

"My good doctor," said the thin man. "You are bluffing. The great Dr. Leonard Steenberg trained by Einstein himself, holder of dozens of patents, Nobel prize finalist, would-be savior of the world. Oh, what happened to him? No one knows but it is rumored he died a fumbling, bumbling fool begging for his life. How pathetic. Lie down on the floor, Doctor."

"Goodbye," said Steenberg. He redoubled his grip on the briefcase and twisted the handle violently. The colonel jumped in his chair. The thin man sat there implacable. Nothing happened.

"In the early days of Stalingrad," said the thin man in the tone of a parent summoning all his patience, "the average life expectancy for a Red Army recruit was twenty-four hours. For an officer it was seventy-two hours. And yet here I am. You're bluffing. Besides, Doctor, I know you all too well. Your religious persuasions, quaint as they may be to me, would never allow you to take your own life. That would be—what do you Catholics call it?—oh yes, a mortal sin. You would go straight to hell. No, Doctor, if you are going to bluff, you have to be more convincing than that. Suicide? I don't think so."

The thin man laughed. The colonel hesitated then joined in. Steenberg locked eyes with the thin man until the laughter in the room died along with the conviction that Steenberg was bluffing. "Not suicide," said Steenberg. "Atonement." Once more he twisted the briefcase's handle.

Steenberg was right. Cars on the street bounced.

Chapter 33

After consulting with Klendenin, Murphy, Benny, Dilly, and Stringbean all decided to stay in Newfoundland and work their separate ways home. Klendenin was convinced the authorities were hot on his tail, and though he felt landing in Twin Falls was secure and worth the risk, he could make no guarantees. It was unreasonable to think all the mayhem in Switzerland would be swept under the carpet indefinitely. The four men parted with a smile. Steenberg had again given Yohaba access to his various banking accounts, and she paid the men in full along with a hefty bonus before Klendenin's plane lifted off from St. Joseph's.

Klendenin's plane touched down in the late afternoon at Twin Falls's Joslin Field without incident. No police, FBI, Interpol, CIA, rogue assassins or ATF agents were there to greet them. A pleasant surprise.

Stepping out of the plane at the top of the ladder, Rulon took a deep breath. "Idaho! I can't tell you how great it is to be back. Feel that air. Suck it in. It is the breath of freedom."

On a lark, Klendenin decided to rent a helicopter and fly everyone to the Hurt ranch. While they waited in the airport terminal for Klendenin to make the arrangements, Brother-in-law and Batu sat off by themselves with Tripod.

"Look at those two," said Yohaba from fifty feet away. "The little love birds."

"They're not even holding hands," said Rulon.

"But she's got Brother-in-law stringing multiple sentences together," said Yohaba. "It must be love."

"He told me he's going back to Africa and not taking her," said Rulon. "That doesn't sound like love to me."

"He's going there to look for his kids, isn't he?" said Yohaba. Rulon didn't respond. "What's wrong, Cowboy?" asked Yohaba. "You were so happy when we first landed. What happened?"

"It suddenly hit me hard. We're on the run and it's not going to stop. They're coming after us, babe," said Rulon. "They're coming after us with both barrels. They're coming after us from so many directions, they're going to have to get in line and take a number. We got the Russians, the Chinese, and the Swiss, and for all I know the North Korans gunning for us."

"Don't forget the Idaho Forest Service," said Yohaba. When that didn't even get a smile out of Rulon, she said, "My grandfather can help. He told me he would. I believe him."

"Won't hold my breath," said Rulon. "It's up to us. That's how I see it, anyway."

"Have you called your father yet?" asked Yohaba. "That might cheer you up. I know it'll cheer him up."

"Good idea." Rulon dialed his father's number on his cell. No answer. "He might be out on the tractor." He put his phone away. "Do you know what I want to do? I want to milk some cows. I want to fix fences, oil weathervanes, rebuild carburetors, re-shingle roofs, plow a fire break, and plant some corn. But you know what I want to do most of all? I want to take a three-turn spin and throw a sixteen-pound hammer out, out, out there farther than I've ever thrown it before. I want to keep throwing until my arms fall off. Does that make me weird?"

"No," said Yohaba. "That makes you Rulon Hurt, my husband." They held hands, and she rested her head on his shoulder.

"My grandfather was very depressed when he left," said Yohaba.

"He had a good reason to be," said Rulon.

"He was particularly depressed about how he treated you." Rulon rolled his eyes.

It was a beautiful, warm, late spring day. Coming over the hills to the south of the ranch in the helicopter, they hit some turbulence from the rising hot air. "The place needs more rain," said Rulon, worried, as he surveyed the brown landscape from the window of the Bell 427. "We got work to do laying irrigation pipe. Add that to the list."

"Yes, dear," said Yohaba over the noise of the helicopter's engines.

They approached the ranch from the west. Brother-in-law broke off his conversation with Batu to insist they circle the ranch a few times before landing. Klendenin looked at Rulon, who shrugged.

Klendenin said to the pilot, "Don't set her down just yet." The pilot nodded and banked the helicopter in a wide circle five hundred feet above the ranch house and barn. Everything looked fine. No sign of the father though, just cows.

Rulon looked at his watch. "It's milking time. The cows shouldn't be out. What's going on?"

"Make another pass," said Brother-in-law. "Wider this time." Klendenin relayed the instructions to the pilot.

"What's up?" asked Yohaba. Brother-in-law and Rulon, looking intently out the window, didn't hear.

"Two dirt bikes, there, on the south-east ridge," said Rulon, pointing.

"See the riders?" asked Brother-in-law.

"Nope," said Rulon. The pilot took them over the eastern hills and flew on a wide arc around the north side of the ranch. Nothing strange. After one more circle, the helicopter hovered over the barnyard for a minute. Still, nothing moving but the cows.

"Call your father again," said Yohaba. Rulon called and after a half-minute shook his head. Again no answer.

"Damn," said Brother-in-law, He reached into his duffel bag for his holster belt and gun and strapped them on. He drew the Browning and spun the cylinder. "Ready."

"I've got the Colt and five clips," said Rulon.

◈

"What is the problem?" said Andropov angrily. "Is the battery dead?"

"No, the phone's working fine," said Gromanko. "He's simply not answering."

"But you spoke to him just a few hours ago," said Andropov. "I'm going to take the shot if I get one."

"No, you mustn't," ordered Gromanko. "We have our orders. He gives the word. Only him. This is personal for him. It has to be that way. And we have to leave the phone on so he can hear the shot."

"They're getting ready to land. I'm going to take the shot. If you reach the old man later, I'll fire off another shot just to make him happy. He'll never know."

"No," said Gromanko. "We have our orders."

From his prone position, Andropov sighed, "Great." He took his finger off the trigger of the VKS, laid his head on his folded arms, and closed his eyes. "Wake me up if you want someone shot."

❧❧

Rulon was just about to tell the pilot to land when he caught a reflection of light off something shiny to the north. His first thought was binoculars or a rifle scope. "Over there." He had traded places with Klendenin and was now in the passenger seat next to the pilot. "I saw something."

The pilot banked hard in the direction Rulon pointed. Following Rulon's instructions, he descended until he was on the same level as a nearby brush-covered hill.

"Is that a forest ranger?" asked Yohaba. "What's he doing here?"

Stanley Merrifield stood up out of the bushes and frantically waved his wide-brimmed ranger's hat and binoculars at the helicopter, telling it to go away.

"Can you get closer?" said Rulon. The pilot gave Rulon a strange look but angled the copter closer until it was whipping the bush around Stanley and filling the air with choking dust. Stanley's hat flew away.

Rulon pressed his face against the window and stared at the little man in the ranger's uniform. Stanley stopped waving. Both men exchanged hard looks. Stanley peered back intensely and while protecting his face with his arms, walked through the helicopter's swirling dust to get a better look. Rulon squinted back to get a better look at his Adam's apple. Recognition dawned in both men's eyes at roughly the same time.

"It's him," said Rulon. He sat back in his seat. "Get us out of here." As the helicopter veered away, Stanley was already talking into his cellphone.

They landed in the yard between the house and the barn. The pilot killed the engine. Everyone piled out of the helicopter. Rulon looked around and said, "I hereby declare an official end to Operation Redfish." Everybody except Yohaba looked at him weird.

"Folks," said Yohaba, "for the past week, you've all been on Operation Redfish. Rulon forgot to tell you."

Behind them somebody coughed. Everyone turned around, and there was Rulon's father sitting on the porch swing in the shadows. He said, "Son, if you've been looking for trouble, don't bother. It's been looking for you." Mr. Hurt stood up and walked to the edge of the stairs where he could get a better look at Rulon. "Well, looks like you're still using your face for a punching bag."

"Hi, Dad," said Rulon. "How come you're not milking the cows?"

"Don't try changing the subject. Hi, Yohaba. Hi, Brother-in-law. You've really done it this time, son," said the father. "They're ALL after you this time. You can't stay here."

"Who's after me?" asked Rulon. "Did you know there's a forest ranger out there with binoculars?"

"Of course I knew. He's the one that started it all. He's got the NSA, the FBI and the ATF after you. You stepped right into Ruby Ridge, son. They think you're some kinda international arms dealer with a side business in aphrodisiac animal parts."

"ATF?" asked Brother-in-law. "Did they search the place?"

"No, your illegal armory's still safe," said the father, "but it wasn't for lack of trying."

"Excuse me, Rulon," said Klendenin, "but we've got to go."

"Who is she?" asked Mr. Hurt, nodding at Batu.

"Klendenin's daughter and a friend," said Yohaba. "We'll explain later.

"Klendenin's right. They need to go," said Brother-in-law. He turned to Batu and said, "I'll call you." She moved towards him for a proper goodbye. He brushed her hair gently away from her ear and kissed her lightly on the lips. She hugged him and said something in his ear fiercely in Swahili that no one else could understand. Klendenin took her by the arm, and the father and daughter got back on the helicopter. The pilot fired up the engine again. Batu waved goodbye from the window as the chopper lifted off.

The helicopter headed south and the whup-whup of the blades grew distant. Everyone in the yard started moving again. Rulon said to his father, "I've been trying to call you. Why didn't you pick up?"

"With the NSA on your tail, I'm not answering any of your calls," said the father. "They could triangulate."

"My dad," said Rulon with pride. "Say, what's for dinner? I'm starved."

"Milk the cows first," said the father. Rulon laughed. He was okay with that. Yohaba gave her father-in-law a big hug. They left their luggage in the yard and sat down on the porch steps to talk. Except Brother-in-law. He went into the house with his mostly empty duffle bag, Tripod trailing along.

Rulon brought his father up to speed, at least as much as he could without making him an accomplice. "What are we going to do about the ranger?" asked Rulon finally.

Brother-in-law came back. "Yeah, what are we going to do about the ranger?" he repeated.

"He's here more than you. I'm thinking of offering him a job," said Mr. Hurt. He looked up. From the field, the cows were mooing, irritated that their schedule was broken and that a stranger was approaching. "In fact, you can ask him yourself."

Stanley Merryfield, in full uniform, and on a squeaking K-mart-special mountain bike, came rolling into the yard and stopped in front of the porch. As he got off his bike, his pants cuff caught the peddle, and he almost fell. He recovered his balance and some of his dignity, laid the bike on the ground, spread his legs, and put his fists on his hips. "At last we meet," he said.

Rulon, Yohaba, and Brother-in-law all looked at each other. Rulon's father nudged Rulon and said, "He's talking to you."

Rulon snapped out of his bewilderment and said, "I'm not your evil nemesis. I'm a defender of the weak and helpless."

"Save it for the judge," said Stanley.

"That's the way he talks," said Mr. Hurt. "Don't take offense. Now, Stanley, we've been through this before. My son's not an endangered species killing, gun-running, aphrodisiac snorting pervert."

"Thanks, Dad," said Rulon.

"There's a grizzly bear family out there somewhere that would disagree," said Stanley.

"I don't know what to say to that," said Rulon.

"Let me handle this," said Brother-in-law. He stood up and drew his Browning. "Dance, sucker." But equally quick, Rulon was on his feet and slowly easing Brother-in-law's hand with the gun back to the holster.

"Look," said Rulon. "Yes, I was stalking a grizzly bear when he charged at me and my wife. Yes, I emptied my gun into him. Yes, he died in the lake, and I had to chop up his body so it wouldn't rise to the surface and scare the tourists. Yes, I started a bonfire you could see from the moon, but there is a logical explanation for all of this."

A satisfied smile crossed Stanley's lips. He reached into his pocket, pulled out a small tape recorder, held it up for all to see, and clicked the off button. "Convicted by your own bravado, Mr. Hurt. The classic blunder of the narcissistic criminal mind. Thank you." Stanley looked at his watch. "As we speak SWAT teams from three different federal agencies are bearing down on this position. Your days are numbered, Mr. Rulon Hurt."

Brother-in-law started to get up again, but Yohaba laid a hand on his arm. "Better leave while you can, Dudley," she said menacingly to Stanley.

Stanley got on his bike and rode off, trailing an irritating squeak with each turn of the pedals.

Rulon looked in Stanley's direction. "Do we believe him?" he asked. Before anyone could answer, Rulon's cell phone rang. It was Klendenin.

"Listen, Rulon," said Klendenin, "We're about ten miles outside of Twin Falls, and there's a motorcade coming your way. There's a couple of M1151 armored Humvees with them. I should know, I consulted on that defense contract. Anyway, it's more like a military convoy."

"Dang it," said Rulon.

Yohaba asked, "Who is it?"

Before Rulon could answer, Brother-in-law appeared next to them with a very heavy duffle bag and his Henry double-barreled 500 Express over his shoulder. "What's up?" he asked.

"Hold on," said Rulon to Klendenin. To Brother-in-law, he said, "In about twenty minutes, we're gonna have company. Dang it all. Dad, where's the pickup?"

"It blew a piston yesterday," said Mr. Hurt. "I've got the engine mostly taken apart. Tractor's working though."

"Can't escape on that," said Yohaba. "What are we going to do, Cowboy?"

"Can we all fit in Brother-in-law's jalopy?" asked Rulon.

"The electric choke don't work, remember?" said Brother-in-law.

Rulon stood up and looked around. He took off his cowboy hat and scrunched it in his hands. "That ranger didn't ride his bike from Redfish. When he's watching the place where does he keep his truck, Dad?"

"Don't know," said Mr. Hurt. "He parks it off the property somewhere and rides the bike in."

Rulon gritted his teeth and made a decision. He spoke to Klendenin. "I have a favor to ask. Can you come back and pick us up?"

"I don't know," said Klendenin. Rulon heard Batu shout something unintelligible in the background. Klendenin said, "Hold on." Ten seconds later he was back on the phone. "My daughter insists. Okay, be there in ten." He clicked off.

Rulon turned to the others. "Klendenin's coming back for us."

"Then what?" asked Yohaba.

"I got a gig in South Africa," said Brother-in-law. "Wanna come?"

"You got a gig," repeated Rulon suspiciously. "In South Africa."

"Yeah," said Brother-in-law. "It's up near the Mozambique border. Seems they got a lot of folks trying to slip into South Africa by jumping the fence at Kruger Park. Problem is the lions know their routes and wait for 'em. An old friend wants me to go kill those lions. You should come. You too, Yohaba. If you don't wanna miss the fun."

"Is this like a paying job?" asked Yohaba.

"Yeah, some," said Brother-in-law. "Doesn't pay much, but we'd be sleeping in the field, saving lives. Sounds like a good salary to me."

"Hunting lions," said Rulon. "Always wanted to give that a shot. How many are we talking about?" They could hear the chopper approaching.

"About sixty man-eaters," said Brother-in-law. "You might know something about hunting if you survive that.

Only problem is South Africa has an extradition treaty with the U.S."

"Yeah," said Yohaba, "but Mozambique doesn't. We could easily slip over the border from there if we had to."

"Wait, wait," said Rulon. "What about your boys? You were going to go look for them?"

"They both got sick and died," said Brother-in-law. "Steenberg found out. C'mon. Make up your minds." Rulon and Yohaba paused with their mouths open as the shock creeped like molten lead through their ears and into their souls. Yohaba rushed to Brother-in-law and threw her arms around him. Rulon embraced them both, looked heavenward and fought off the tears. The three of them stood there. The only movement, Yohaba's shaking shoulders. The only sound her sobbing. The chopper began its descent. Tripod barked.

"Enough," said Brother-in-law, but Yohaba and Rulon held on. "Enough," he said again, and this time he wrenched away. "They're dead. We're alive. We have a decision to make, and this is exactly why I didn't tell you before."

"I'm so sorry," said Rulon. "So, very, very sorry." He held Yohaba close with his arm around her shoulders. He looked into her red, swollen eyes. "What do you think, Babe?"

"Now even the good guys want to do us in," said Yohaba, suddenly fierce and angry. "Let's do it, Cowboy." The helicopter landed and quickly lifted off again with the team aboard. Mr. Hurt waved goodbye and went off by himself to milk some irritated cows.

❧❦❧

Andropov and Gramanko watched from their position in the hills as the helicopter took off, banked to the east, and flew right over their position heading south towards Twin Falls. When the chopper was out of sight, Andropov began disassembling his monster VKS sniper rifle, almost four feet long and sixteen pounds. He first detached the 18-inch barrel and laid it in its case. "Well, this was a waste of time," he said as he worked.

"We had him," said Gromanko. "All we needed was the phone call. I'm as frustrated as you are, but we did the right thing."

"We have time. We could still pop the father," said Andropov. "That would send a message."

Gromanko had his back to Andropov. He watched the father walk to the north paddock and fiddle with the gate to let the cows out. "He killed two of my friends," said Gromanko, more to himself than to Andropov.

"What?"

"Rulon Hurt," said Gromanko. "He killed two of my friends in CERN. With a hammer."

"You already told me," said Andropov. "Not a nice way to go."

Gromanko watched the father and did a quick calculation. No one else was around, and the ranch rarely had visitors. They would be back in Russia before anyone even found the body.

"Reassemble your rifle," ordered Gromanko. He was already tearing the POSP rangefinder out of its leather case as he spoke. "Do it. Do it now. We're not done here."

"Well, about time," said Andropov. He smiled and worked quickly.

A minute later, Gromanko was on his stomach looking through the rangefinder and calling out the distance to his prone partner. Andropov was next to him with the crosshairs of his rifle's scope firmly planted on Mr. Hurt's head two hundred yards away. Andropov breathing deeply, sinking into his sniper's zone, Gromanko calling out numbers, their concentration was suddenly broken by the sound of the helicopter engine revving higher some distance away and the pitch changing. Both men turned their heads towards the sound. They scanned the sky. The whup-whup of the blades bounced around the hills making it hard to pinpoint. They exchanged puzzled looks.

Gromanko rolled over to see better. Suddenly, the engine roar engulfed them as the chopper rose from a deep arroyo on the other side of their hill. A bullet hit Gromanko in the shoulder and then a stream of them ran a diagonal across his chest. Next to him Andropov scrambled to his feet with the VKS in his arms just in time to suffer the same fate.

Brother-in-law kneeled in the open doorway of the helicopter with his M16 and looked back over the scene. "I don't want to hear any flack," he shouted over his shoulder. "They were definitely setting up for a shot."

"I know, I know," shouted Rulon over the roar of the chopper's engines.

"One more pass, just to be sure," shouted Brother-in-law.

In the cockpit, Rulon nudged the ashen-faced pilot with the barrel of his Colt. "You heard him," he said.

The End

About the Author

Jim Haberkorn was born in Brooklyn. From 1969 to 1975 he fired an M1 Rocket Launcher (bazooka) for the Marine Corp Reserves and had many interesting adventures. In 1975 he began serving a two-year mission for his church in North Carolina where he met the real-life "Brother-in-law," one of the heroes in his newest book, Redfish, his third novel."

In 1978 he began working for Hewlett Packard in Palo Alto, CA. He continued working for HP for the next 37 years until his retirement in 2016. His work took him around the United States as well to Johannesburg, South Africa and Zurich, Switzerland. During his many hours on airplanes, he began writing thrillers to relax. He published his first book in 2011. His second thriller was published in March 2013.

His hobbies are hiking, exploring Switzerland, watching episodes of NCIS, church work, and learning German. Currently he lives in Zurich, Switzerland with his wife Kim.